About the Authors

Ann McIntosh was born in the tropics, lived in the frozen north for a number of years, and now resides in sunny central Florida with her husband. She's a proud mama to three grown children, loves tea, crafting, animals (except reptiles!), bacon and the ocean. She believes in the power of romance to heal, inspire, and provide hope in our complex world.

Susan Carlisle's love affair with books began when she received a bad grade in maths. Not allowed to watch TV until the grade had improved, she filled her time with books. Turning her love of reading into a love for writing romance, she pens hot medicals. She loves castles, travelling, afternoon tea, reading voraciously, and hearing from her readers. Join her newsletter at SusanCarlisle.com

New Zealander **Alison Roberts** has written over eighty romance novels for Mills & Boon. She has also worked as a primary school teacher, a cardiology research technician and a paramedic. She is living her dream of living – and writing – in a gorgeous village in the south of France.

Christmas in the Highlands

ANN McINTOSH

SUSAN CARLISLE

ALISON ROBERTS

MILLS & BOON

First Published in Great Britain 2025
by Mills & Boon, an imprint of HarperCollins*Publishers* Ltd
1 London Bridge Street, London, SE1 9GF

www.harpercollins.co.uk

HarperCollins*Publishers*
Macken House, 39/40 Mayor Street Upper,
Dublin 1, D01 C9W8, Ireland

ISBN: 978-0-263-41920-7

FSC www.fsc.org
MIX
Paper | Supporting responsible forestry
FSC™ C007454

This book contains FSC™ certified paper and other controlled sources to ensure responsible forest management.

For more information visit: www.harpercollins.co.uk/green

Printed and Bound in the UK using 100% Renewable Electricity
at CPI Group (UK) Ltd, Croydon, CR0 4YY

THE NURSE'S CHRISTMAS TEMPTATION

ANN McINTOSH

For Tom, Vanessa and Patrick,
who've improved my life immeasurably.

You helped me grow up more than I helped you!

CHAPTER ONE

AT HER FIRST sight of Eilean Rurie, or Rurie Island, rising like a granite fist from an angry, frothing sea, Harmony Kinkaid gave a satisfied nod.

Rugged black cliffs fronted dismal light green hills wreathed in mist, and the overcast sky was giving everything a sad gray tone. Mizzly rain pattering down on the ferry deck in fits and starts elevated the entire scene to the epitome of dreary.

After the year she'd had, it was the perfect place for her.

Set in the sheltered curve of a sea loch, Eilean Rurie was just far enough from the west coast of Scotland to give Harmony the sense of leaving everything behind. Of course, she had no idea what she was facing once she got there. Being on a somewhat remote island and not knowing anyone would be out of her comfort zone, but she was determined to be up to the task.

The job had come up suddenly, but at just the right time. And when Caitlin, a friend from nursing school, had called out of the blue, Harmony hadn't been able to help thinking it was a sign.

"Hey, I'm in the hospital in Fort William, and I won't be able to go back to work on Eilean Rurie. Can you take over for me until Dr. MacRurie finds a permanent replacement?"

"What's wrong?"

"Preeclampsia. They've put me on bedrest for the duration, and the island's too remote to make it feasible for us to stay there. I know you're in between jobs, and I hoped you'd be willing to fill in for me."

Caitlin was expecting her first child, and Harmony had heard the stress in her usually placid friend's voice. But before she'd been able to reply, Caitlin had continued.

"It's very different from working in London but Cam—Dr. MacRurie—is easy to work for, and there are only about two hundred and fifty people to tend to overall. It would mean being away for Christmas, though…"

Harmony's fingers had tightened on the phone, and she'd hastily swallowed the lump in her throat and replied, "That's all right. Of course I'll do it. I could definitely use the money."

And, even more importantly, it would mean not having to spend the holidays alone in a bare house that had used to be Christmas central.

Before Gran had died, and Mum had decided to take off to Yorkshire with her new man, Fred.

Oh, she wasn't angry about Fred. He was a nice man, and Mum deserved to have a life after devoting hers to looking after Harmony and then Gran too. It had just felt horribly like a betrayal when Mum revealed her holiday plans.

"Fred's got some time off over Christmas, and he wants to spend it with his children and grandchildren. It would be a good time for me to meet everyone, so I've agreed to go."

Harmony had been so shocked and hurt she hadn't even been able to reply.

Mum must have seen her reaction on her face, because she'd quickly added, "You're welcome to come too."

The worry in Mum's tone had brought Harmony back

to her senses. "No, Mum. You go and have a great time. I have a few applications out there, and I'm going to want to be on hand if anyone calls me to come in for an interview."

Yet inside it had felt like the last straw in an awful year. First her two-year relationship with Logan had ended, and only a couple of months later Gran had passed away unexpectedly, leaving Mum and Harmony heartbroken. Her mother's mother had lived with them since her dad had died, when Harmony was only six, and had been an integral part of their little family.

Then, as if those things weren't enough, Harmony's boss of six years had decided to retire. Although the staff had been assured their jobs were secure, one of the first things the new GP had done was let them all go.

When Mum had dropped her bombshell Harmony had been totally set adrift. She didn't like change. Life had been fine the way it was, and now suddenly it was all upside down. The loss of their traditional mother/daughter Christmas in particular had left her in a tailspin.

She felt as though everyone and everything she cherished about the season was gone, and all she could anticipate was loneliness. Just thinking about it made her eyes watery.

But maybe saying to heck with Christmas and having the enforced alone time that was ahead was exactly what she needed. Getting away from the familiar to really think about where she wanted to go in life.

From all she'd heard and read about small communities like this one, she wouldn't be surprised if it took a lot longer than she would be around for people even to warm to her. That suited her just fine. Peace and quiet were what she was looking for. Although it would be lonely living by herself for the first time, and in a new environment to boot, it would also be the best opportunity to contemplate her next move.

"Your first trip to Eilean Rurie?"

The deckhand's voice pulled her out of her sour thoughts, and she blinked to chase away the silly tears before they fell.

"Yes," she said, as the ferry rounded the end of the island and headed to what she assumed was the port.

"Bit drab looking right now, but it'll be better in a few days."

"What happens in a few days?" she asked. But he had already hurried off—no doubt to prepare for docking.

Other than a magical transportation of the island to a tropical location, Harmony couldn't think of anything that would make it look better. The town and dock area continued the gray-on-gray theme, although she had to admit that had more to do with the overcast day than anything else. Most buildings were either whitewashed or cream-colored stone, and the overall effect was of a somewhat quaint, old-fashioned village.

The cry of sea birds and the sound of the wind along with the brisk, damp air was strangely invigorating, and Harmony felt a little surge of excitement. This peaceful place, far from the rush and noise of London, would surely be perfect for the quiet contemplation she needed to figure out her future.

The serene effect was shattered by a *whoosh* that was easily heard over the ferry engines, and the sight of a man rocketing up from the water. It took Harmony a couple of confused seconds to realize he was wearing a water jetpack, which had propelled him high into the air. As she watched he swooped down, then started twisting and turning close to the surface of the loch, doing stunts.

She couldn't decide whether or not riding the contraption was crazier than going into the no doubt freezing water but, however she cut it, he was clearly out of his gourd. Horrified and fascinated all at once, she stood watching his performance as the ferry moved closer to shore.

He shot high into the air again and then, in an instant, plummeted toward the water. Harmony wanted to close her eyes, so she wouldn't see him die, but couldn't look away, covering her mouth to curtail the shriek of fear rising in her throat. Somehow, seemingly inches from the water, he got the spluttering jetpack back under control and rose again.

She turned away, her hands shaking, pretending to fuss with her luggage so no one would realize how scared she'd been.

Why did people do these daredevil things? Didn't they realize how dangerous it was? That they could lose their lives doing that kind of nonsense?

Anger superseded her fear, and she mentally cursed the man who'd upset her just before she was supposed to meet her new boss. Her heart was pounding, her shoulders were up around her ears, and her stomach roiled. Taking a deep breath, she forced herself to relax as best she could.

Taking out her compact, she slicked on a little lipstick and, noticing the stress lines between her brows, forced herself to release as much tension as possible.

A little calmer as the ferry approached the dock, she glanced down at the shore, trying to see if she could pick out Dr. MacRurie. There was one elderly man there, but Harmony was sure he wasn't the doctor, who Caitlin had said was in his thirties. Hopefully he hadn't forgotten she was arriving today, although no doubt she could find her own way to the surgery and the apartment above it where she was staying. The village wasn't that big, after all.

Glancing at her watch, she realized the ferry was actually a few minutes early. The doctor was probably on his way—unless there'd been a medical emergency somewhere.

Without thought she let her gaze track back to where the man with the jetpack had been, and found him wading out onto the shingles alongside the loch. Even from a distance she could see he was in amazing shape, with the wetsuit clinging to muscular thighs, bum, and torso.

Suddenly, as though sensing her interest, he turned and looked back at the ferry. It would be impossible for him to make her out from that distance, but still she ducked away, embarrassed for no good reason. Nothing wrong or illegal about admiring a man's backside—especially when he couldn't see you doing it. And she did love a good backside…

Hopefully he was just a visitor to the island and she wouldn't have to interact with him. That way she wouldn't be tempted to tell him how crazy she thought he was, doing what he'd been doing. Besides, even if she hadn't been turned off by his daredevil stunt, good looking men were on her no-no list right now.

Her experience with Logan had been lesson enough. She'd thought him the perfect fit for her: a handsome yet staid and sensible Certified Public Accountant with a solid head on his shoulders. At least that was what she'd thought until he'd told her he was in love with an intern at his office and was giving up his job to move to Australia with her and start an Outback tour company.

She'd been totally gobsmacked, in equal parts desperately hurt and angry.

Her mum had seemed sympathetic, but unsurprised, while her gran had said, "He's too boring anyway."

But Logan's lack of excitement was one of the things she'd liked best about him. The last thing she wanted in her life was someone like Dad, whose recklessness and need for adventure had gotten him killed on a mountain that, because of his health concerns, he should never have been climbing. She wanted someone safe, reliable, who wouldn't break her heart or leave her to struggle on her own to raise their child the way her mum had had to.

Maybe she was better off on her own long term, anyway. Loving others just brought pain as far as she could tell.

As the ferry docked, Harmony put her baleful thoughts aside to heft her tote bag onto her shoulder, then pull up the handle of her wheeled suitcase. Taking another deep breath, she set off for the gangplank, ignoring the flutters of anxiety in her stomach.

Somewhere along the line she'd come to the conclusion that life went on, and that what happened was out of her hands. All she could control was how she faced it, and this new job, in this strange place, was to be met head-on, and with a certain amount of panache, to make up for her fear of the unknown.

Pausing to let an older lady go ahead of her, Harmony ran her hand over the faux fur collar of her favorite tweed trench coat, letting the softness of the fabric soothe her jangling nerves. She'd thought about wearing more casual clothes, but dismissed the impulse. Just because her new job was on an island it didn't mean she wanted to arrive looking as though she didn't take it seriously. Besides, she liked nice clothes; she felt more confident when she was well dressed.

With her head determinedly high, Harmony went down the gangplank to the dock. When no one stepped forward to meet her, she kept walking toward the building marked "Dock Master's Office" for all the world as though she knew where she was going.

Suddenly four older ladies, whom she'd thought were there to meet the woman she'd let go down the gangplank ahead of her, surrounded her, bringing her progress to a screeching halt.

"Nurse Kinkaid?" one of them asked with a smile. "You *are* Nurse Kinkaid, aren't you?"

"Yes."

"Oh, wonderful! Isn't it wonderful, girls?"

Unsure about what was so wonderful, Harmony made no comment, simply plastered a smile on her face as all the women seemed to be speaking at once.

"So lovely to have you!"

"Are you Scottish?"

"What a looker you are!"

"Do you craft?"

"How old are you?"

"I adore your coat!"

Stunned by the barrage, Harmony let go her suitcase and held up her hands, one of which had her umbrella in it. Three of the ladies fell silent and stepped back in unison. The fourth stood her ground, the smile on her face never faltering.

"Don't mind those chatterboxes, Nurse Kinkaid. A bunch of magpies, they are."

She held out her hand and Harmony instinctively took it, receiving a hearty handshake.

"I'm Eudora Moxley, but call me Dora. And these old bags are Ingrid, Sela and Kat."

"Katherine," the tallest of the others growled.

"Kat's a little touchy about her name, but don't let it worry you. It's the English coming out in her."

"For goodness' sake, Eudora." The other woman huffed. "I've lived here for nigh on thirty years. Don't I merit being Scottish by now?"

"You got here thirty years too late for that, Kat," one of the other women interjected, although whether it was Ingrid or Sela, Harmony had no idea. All the women except for Katherine tittered.

"That's enough of that," Katherine retorted. "The nurse is going to think we're loopy."

"Oh, but we are—and best she knows it from day one," Dora retorted, giving Harmony's fingers one last squeeze before finally releasing them. "We're the Crafty Islanders, in charge of—well...almost everything here on Eilean Rurie. We wanted to be on hand to greet you and welcome you to the island."

"Thank you," Harmony replied weakly, still somewhat shell-shocked by what they called a greeting but felt more like a mugging. "Do you have any idea where I might find Dr. MacRurie?"

"Oh, he'll be along any minute now. The Laird is always on time, and the ferry was early."

"Laird?" Wasn't that Scottish for some kind of a peer? Caitlin hadn't mentioned anything about him being a peer.

"That's just a nickname, dear," Katherine said. "Although he does own most of the island, Cam's not one to stand on ceremony. It's not like he's a duke or anything like that."

"There you go. That's why you're not Scottish yet, Kat." Dora smirked. "Laird is far better than Duke any day."

"Tosh" was the testy reply. "You've no idea what you're talking about."

And they started in on each other again, leaving Harmony's head swimming as insults and ripostes flew back and forth.

If these ladies really did run the place, how did they get anything done? Whether they would impact her ability to do her job was another question she really wanted answered too. As assisting nurse and office manager, she'd brook no interference in her work.

"Ladies," she said, loudly enough to cut through the arguing, and was relieved when they all stopped and looked at her. "It was lovely meeting you, but if you would just point me in the right direction…?"

"No need," Dora said, beaming at something behind her. "Here comes the Laird now."

Instinctively Harmony turned, looked, but all she saw was the guy in the wetsuit coming up along the sea wall. No one else.

Then it struck her—hard.

Her new boss was the handsome jetpack daredevil with the nice bum.

Oh, no.

CHAPTER TWO

CAM WAS STILL buzzing with adrenaline from the jetpack as he made his way up from the beach along the path on the seawall. It had been such a rush he'd ridden it for longer than he'd planned, and had missed his chance to change before meeting the ferry. Hopefully his new nurse would be the easygoing type, and wouldn't be fazed by meeting her new boss when he was wearing a wetsuit.

It was a shame he hadn't been able to give Sanjit permission to offer water jetpack rides to visitors, but he'd had to nix the idea even though Sanjit had put up a good argument.

"It could be a new draw for visitors in summer, when we have our slump. Another activity to add to the website, making a trip here more attractive at times other than Christmas."

"True, but the liability issue is one we can't get away from." He'd slapped the younger man on the shoulder, then reached for his towel. "It's a lot of fun, but one major accident and the entire island would suffer the consequences."

It was true. Because the MacRurie Trust owned most of Eilean Rurie, no matter what insurance Sanjit might purchase to cover operating a water jetpack rental, the trust—and Cam as its director—would still be considered liable should anything go wrong. One major lawsuit might break the bank, or at least severely deplete it. He considered the island to be entrusted to him for posterity, so protecting it and its inhabitants was his first order of business.

But, wow, it had been tempting to give Sanjit the go-ahead—if for no other reason than being able to ride the jetpack himself.

Approaching the dock, he saw the Crafty Islanders had beat him there, and had a well-dressed woman he assumed was his new nurse and administrator surrounded. She seemed to be fending them off with her umbrella—a sight which made Cam snort, as he tried to hold back laughter.

Not that he blamed Nurse Kinkaid in the slightest. The CIs *en masse* were a force to be reckoned with. There was no doubt in his mind they were peppering her with intrusive questions and firing off comments before she could even decide whether to answer or not. That was their usual *modus operandi*, and they could frighten the stoutest of souls.

"Please don't scare off my lifesaver," he muttered, picking up his pace, hoping to break up the interrogation before it got too bad.

Then the young woman looked over her shoulder, her thick, curly hair swinging away from her face as she did so. Her gaze tracked past Cam, then snapped back to him, and her eyes widened.

Cam, midstride, had to catch himself so he didn't falter under what he could only describe as the glare she sent him.

But even with lines between her eyebrows and her lips pursed into a disapproving rosette, she was gorgeous. He had only a moment to register her high cheekboned face and skin like golden syrup mixed with cinnamon before she turned back around, but the effect lingered.

Something about the curve of her cheek and chin, the long line of her throat, gave him a jolt of adrenaline on top of the residue already keeping his nerves jangling. It had been a very long time since the sight of a woman had brought him to total awareness, filling him with curiosity and inciting the kind of physical interest he least expected, or wanted.

Since leaving his job with a refugee agency four years before, and taking over the management of Eilean Rurie, he had made the island his base. The transition to being in one place after travelling the world had been difficult, but in a strange way it had afforded him the chance to do more of the adventurous activities he enjoyed.

He had time to travel now, to climb, cave, to do whatever else he wanted, and he was having the time of his life. There was no room in his life for the kind of visceral fascination he felt with just one glimpse of this young woman.

It would be okay, he reassured himself as he finally neared the group. She wouldn't be around for very long. He just had to get through the Christmas rush, and then he could find a permanent replacement. Ignoring this strange attraction wouldn't be too hard.

"There you are—finally," Dora said.

"You'll be late for your own funeral," Sela added.

"The later the better. But I'll have you know I'm exactly on time," Cam retorted, giving his watch a pointed glance before turning to the silent young woman and holding out his hand. "Nurse Kinkaid, I presume?"

"You presume correctly," she replied, seeming to hesitate for a moment before taking his outstretched hand and giving it a brief, firm shake. “And I understand you're Dr. MacRurie?”

Her eyes were gorgeous. Hazel, fringed with dark, tightly curled lashes, they matched her skin tone and gave her the look of a haughty lioness. Her watchful gaze, coupled with the low, husky voice made his toes curl.

Taken aback, especially by his reaction to her, all he could manage to say was “In the flesh.”

“You mean in the wetsuit, don't you?” Ingrid asked, making all the CIs snicker.

Suddenly aware of his state of undress—which hadn't bothered him in the slightest before—Cam frowned, making them all giggle harder. Nurse Kinkaid didn't join in, but the little lines between her brows quickly came and went.

“Yes, well… If you'll come with me to the Dock Master's Office, Nurse Kinkaid, I'll change and take you over to the surgery.”

“So, did you give Sanjit the approval to run his new business?” Katherine interjected, before he could make his escape.

“Unfortunately, no.”

“Liability?” asked Ingrid, who was a retired barrister, and Cam nodded.

“Got it in one.” Before any of them could get going again, he quickly added, “Let me take your suitcase, Nurse Kinkaid, and we'll be on our way.”

As he matched actions to words the CIs chorused their goodbyes, peppered with lovely-to-meet-yous and we'll-catch-up-soons, all aimed at the new nurse—who, wisely, exited their orbit with just a friendly wave and the slight upturning of her lips.

“Will we see you at the planning meeting this evening, Cam?” called Dora.

"Of course," he called back, making sure not to break stride in case they took it as an invitation.

"Wow," the nurse said, as soon as they were out of earshot. "They're something, aren't they?"

"That they are," Cam said, but was suddenly protective of the women who often drove him bonkers. "But, despite being a pain in my rear most of the time, they're invaluable to the island. With such a small population it's good to have people willing to get involved and organize things."

"I'm sure. However, I hope that doesn't apply to your practice? I find I work best with only one boss. Causes far less confusion."

"Good Lord, no." Cam actually laughed at the thought of the CIs butting into his real work.

He opened the door to the Dock Master's Office, and stood back for her to enter ahead of him.

"They're involved with practically all other aspects of life on the island, though, just so you know."

"I can see that being the case."

She'd stepped through the door ahead of him and Cam found himself admiring her figure, which was full and curvy. Lush hips swayed with a siren's rhythm as she walked, mesmerizing him until he caught himself and resolutely tore his gaze away.

Even more aware of the wetsuit, and feeling silly in the face of his new, rather formal nurse, Cam said, "If you'll wait here, Nurse Kinkaid, I'll get changed as quickly as possible and take you to your apartment."

"Please, call me Harmony," she said, while looking around the office. Seemingly without conscious thought, she straightened a pile of magazines on the table beside the door. "When I hear 'Nurse Kinkaid' like that, I instinctively look around for my mother."

"Sure," he said, seeing an opening to get to know her

better but unable to take advantage of it. She completely unsettled him, making him want to get away and catch his breath, not to mention get out of his wetsuit. "I'll remember that. Be right back."

But as he shimmied out of the wetsuit he found himself wondering what she'd look like if she truly smiled. Something told him that rather prim mouth would turn sumptuous and appealing.

Become eminently kissable.

Cam cursed to himself.

She's definitely going to be a problem.

He just had to make sure that, no matter what happened, the problem didn't involve him.

The interest she stirred in him wasn't something he'd ever consider acting on. Even if getting involved with an employee wasn't tacky—which it was—he liked his relationships short and with no strings attached. No matter how quickly her tenure on the island would be over he'd have to work with her, and the chances of it all going sideways were large.

Finally dressed in his street clothes, he grabbed his jacket and went back out into the main part of the office. Danny Smith, the Dock Master, wasn't there, so Harmony was still alone, standing in front of one of the myriad pictures on the wall. It was a painting of one of the rescue boats that used to be launched from the island in rough seas back in the early part of the twentieth century.

"That's my great-grandfather in the prow of that boat," he said, going to stand beside her. "They were probably going out to help with a sea rescue after a wreck—or at least that was what the artist was portraying."

She sent him a brief glance, and once more he felt a zing of electricity when he realized her eyes were more green than gold. Getting used to them was going to take some doing.

"Do you still have a lifeboat station here?" she asked.

"I wish," he said.

How many times had he stood staring at this painting, imagining himself on that boat, fighting the seas, on his way to save lives?

"Now the Coast Guard handles all the rescues. In the old days almost all the islands had manned boats, because it took the authorities much longer to get to the site of a wreck. Now, once someone radios the helicopters can be in the air in a matter of minutes. The private rescue units aren't needed anymore. I think the last one was disbanded here in the nineteen-seventies."

"Hmm."

It was a noncommittal sound, and he figured the conversation was over. "Shall we head over to the surgery?"

"Sure," she said, but she stared at the painting a little longer before turning away.

He led her out through the other side of the building, which took them onto the main street through the village. This time of the afternoon, there weren't many people around, but he knew many of the residents were peeping out from behind their curtains. Everyone knew the nurse was arriving today. Everyone was curious.

As they walked he pointed out the Post Office, the grocery store, the pub, and Sanjit's restaurant, thinking them the most important.

"The Ladies from Hades?" she said, obviously catching sight of the pub sign, with a kilted and armed Highlander painted on it.

"It's a play on the nickname for a famous Scottish regiment."

"The Black Watch," she said, surprising him. "Must

have been opened by an ex-military man. And you have a curry shop here too?"

He wanted to ask how she knew about the Black Watch and their World War I nickname, but left it for another time.

"We're actually very lucky," he explained, speaking a little louder than usual because of the sound of her suitcase bumping along behind him over the cobbles. He'd left the sliver of sidewalk to her and her high heels, since the last thing he needed was for her to twist her ankle before she even started working. "Eilean Rurie has attracted a variety of artists, farmers, and business people over the years, making our population rather more eclectic than some of the other islands."

"Like the owner of the curry shop?"

"Exactly. Sanjit Gopaul came here on vacation with his parents and, for whatever reason, fell in love with the island. He came back and asked if I'd be willing to let him open a restaurant, and I said sure. That was five years ago. He's been an amazing addition to the island and shows no signs of wanting to leave. In fact, he also runs a canoe rental and tour operation during the summer, and he's always looking for new businesses to start."

"Including that jet thing?"

There was no mistaking the disapproval in her voice, and his look at her profile found it echoed there in her pursed lips. It made Cam's hackles rise a bit.

"Yes, like the water jetpack. I was sad to have to tell him no. It was a lot of fun. Wouldn't you like to have a go?"

She gave him a bland look, all censure erased from her expression. "I should say not. I'm not into that kind of thing."

Striving for a light tone, he teased, "What kind of thing? Having fun?"

Looking into the window of the shop they were passing, she replied, “More like stuff that’ll get you killed or maimed.”

“Ha! It’s safe as houses if you’re careful and know what you’re doing.”

The skeptical look she gave him scorched him to his toes.

“No wonder you didn’t give him permission to offer it to visitors.” Then, as if tired of the discussion, she changed the subject completely. “Your village is beautiful—although I’ll admit when I first saw the island from the ferry I thought it looked like something out of a very scary story.”

That made Cam chuckle, even though he still felt the sting of her retort about the jetpack. He knew the exact vista she was talking about.

“Eigg Point, no doubt—before you round the headland and see the village. That sheer black cliff with the sea foaming around its base does look like it belongs in a horror movie on a misty, overcast day like today. On a sunny day, though, when the hills are so startlingly green they look like they were drawn with crayon and the water is smooth and clear, it’s very different. There’s the surgery,” he added, pointing across the grassy village green to the three-story building beyond.

“That’s your surgery? It looks more like a fancy hotel!”

Cam chuckled. “My great-grandfather built it to try and attract a decent doctor to take up residence. I used to tease my grandfather that he only took up medicine so he’d be able to work in the second nicest building on the island. He didn’t deny it.”

“I don’t blame him,” she said.

The appreciation in her voice was pleasing.

"Normally I'd cut across the green to get to the surgery, but it's pretty wet right now and your heels would sink in."

"Thank you."

She had a prim way of speaking he rather liked, and an intriguing way of pronouncing some words that gave unusual flavor to an otherwise very North London voice. Caitlin had mentioned that Harmony's mother's family had originally come from Jamaica, and he thought he could hear an echo of that migration in the nurse's voice. It was so nice, especially with its husky tone, he was tempted to keep her talking so he could go on hearing it.

"Patients come in through either the front door or the one closest to the car park on the north side," he told her as they approached the surgery. "But you have your own entrance on the other side."

Cam led her around the building, and as they got to the door heard her give a little gasp.

"Oh! What's that back there?"

She was looking up the hill through the trees, along the track he used every day.

"That's the nicest building on the island—Rurie Manor."

Big hazel eyes stared at him. "You live there?"

"Yeah," he said, opening the outer door and holding it for her, once more pleased at her awestruck reaction to his home. "But only in a small part of it. Most of the Manor is a hotel now."

Harmony turned back to stare at the Manor a moment more, before stepping through the door and into the entryway.

Cam glanced at his watch. Time to test his glucose levels.

Handing her the keys, he said, "There's another door at the top of the stairs, and the door behind me leads into the surgery, so I sometimes come in this way, but otherwise you'll be the only person using it. Go on up and check out your apartment, and I'll bring up your suitcase in a moment."

"Thank you."

Her slightly stiff reply made him want to break the ice a little more. He was used to a relaxed atmosphere in his practice and hoped to establish that type of working relationship with her too. Even with his niggling suspicion he should actually keep her as distant as he could. Just standing in the small entryway she seemed too close, with her citrusy perfume warming the air between them and those golden eyes surveying him with solemn intensity.

"Hopefully life on the island won't seem too tame and boring for you after living and working in London. At least Christmas should be exciting."

His words stumbled to a halt, arrested by the flash of pain crossing her face.

"I'm looking forward to the quiet," she said, turning toward the steps and hitching her tote bag higher. "And Christmas can pass me by and I won't complain."

Had he somehow put his foot in his mouth? He couldn't see how. Everyone loved Christmas, didn't they?

But even as he was trying to figure out what he'd said wrong he found himself staring once more at her delectable rear end, until it sashayed around the corner of the landing and disappeared.

CHAPTER THREE

HARMONY STOOD IN the middle of the apartment, not even taking in the space around her, annoyed at herself for being so curt with her new employer. Not to mention for the sarcastic comment she'd made to him earlier about the water jetpack.

It wasn't really like her to be that way, but hearing him make light of her innate dislike of risky behavior had irked her—so, like her mother always said, she'd run her mouth, speaking before thinking.

But there was something about him that had put her on edge from the first time she'd looked him in the eyes. He was, she had to admit, a fine specimen. Handsome, in a rugged, outdoorsy kind of way, with brown hair just shy of ginger and blue-gray eyes, his looks alone made him a standout. Couple his face with a body that looked amazing even in a wetsuit, and Harmony knew he must make women's heads turn faster than wheels on ice.

But it wasn't his looks that were making her snarky. There was an air about him—an aura of confidence and ease that, conversely, made her tense and jumpy. And when he'd mentioned Christmas, just as she'd promised herself a hiatus from the entire season, it had brought all her pain flooding back.

For almost as long as she could remember Christmas

had been a special time for Mum, Gran and Harmony. There was always a flurry of baking, both English treats and Jamaican. And a night specially planned to trim the tree while listening to a variety of holiday music or old movies.

They'd also watch *Greetings from Yaad*, an hour-long special filmed in Jamaica, in which people could wish their loved ones in England a Merry Christmas. Harmony had used to dislike the amateurishly filmed show, until Gran had said, "We may not know any of these people, but it makes me happy to hear the accents of my youth."

That had always led to conversations about old times in Jamaica, and even how things had been for Gran when she'd first moved to England. She'd been part of the Windrush generation, coming from the colonies to help with the rebuilding efforts in the UK after World War II. She'd had to leave all her family behind, including Mum, but once she'd gotten herself a job and somewhere to live she'd started saving so she could send for her husband and daughter.

Grandpa had decided he didn't want to live in England, so eventually Mum had travelled to the UK with her Uncle Shorty, Gran's brother. Uncle Shorty, a perennial bachelor, had settled in Birmingham, but had come to visit every Christmas until he died, adding to the family fun. Harmony could still remember his plaid driving cap, his booming laugh and the way the scent of smoke and cologne clung to his clothes.

On Christmas Eve they'd have neighbors and friends in and out of the house, each one of them bringing a little gift, receiving goodies in return.

Until they'd passed away her other grandparents had come too, on Christmas morning, even after Dad hadn't been there anymore, and all Harmony remembered was the joy and closeness. The laughter and sometimes a few shared tears too.

All that was gone now—and darn Dr. MacRurie for reminding her of what she'd lost this year.

But it wouldn't do to start their working relationship off on a bad footing, and she wondered if it would be politic to apologize to him for her behavior.

Harmony considered that option, then dismissed it. Unless he brought it up, she wouldn't either. Less said, soonest mended, right?

Suddenly realizing she was in danger of having the doctor come up and find her still standing there like a ninny, Harmony quickly took off her coat and shoes, stowing them in the entryway closet. Then she took a really good look around.

The apartment was a lot larger than she'd expected, with an L-shaped living and dining room and a kitchen almost as big as her mum's. There were also not two but three good-sized bedrooms, all tastefully decorated with a combination of new and more traditional furniture. And the bathroom, with its deep soaker tub and a separate shower, made her coo.

The entire space had obviously been modernized, but whoever had done it had been careful to keep a lot of the original Victorian elements. The living room fireplace, which was lit, had the most amazing carved mantel and pillars, along with a tile surround and hearth. There were medallions on the ceiling, and intricately carved jambs around the doors. Even the door knobs were decorative, and Harmony found herself smiling as she palmed one of the floral patterned porcelain ovoids.

She staked out the bedroom she wanted, which had a sleigh bed and large windows that were letting in the last of the afternoon light. Outside was a tiny balcony, just big enough for a miniscule wrought-iron table and matching chair, and in the distance was Rurie Manor, sitting in solitary splendor on the top of a gently sloping hill.

It looked gorgeous, and she wondered if she'd get a chance to see the inside. Although if it had been turned into a hotel, she might be disappointed.

Hearing Dr. MacRurie coming up the stairs, she went back into the living area just as he came through the front door.

"Here you go," he said, putting down her suitcase, seemingly not at all put out by her ill-mannered behavior. "Have you decided which room you want? I'll put your case on the luggage stand for you."

"Thank you. That one," she said, pointing to the still open door, determined to put her best foot forward.

He wheeled the suitcase across the living area, speaking as he went. "I hope you'll be comfortable here. Caitlin and her husband had a dog, so I gave them a cottage instead—for convenience. Knowing you'd have to be here over the holidays, I figured this place is big enough that if you have someone come for Christmas they can stay with you."

There he went with the whole Christmas thing again!

"I won't." It came instinctively, pain pushing the brusque words out. Drawing herself up, and not wanting to sound as churlish as she felt, she added, "But thank you."

"Oh." He'd put her bag in the room and was standing in the doorway, his gaze sharp. But all he said was "Well, if that changes you'll be all set. But if not at least you won't be bored. This time of year is nice and busy."

"This time of year? What's so special about it?"

Giving her a surprised glance, he said, "Caitlin didn't tell you?" Then he answered his own question. "Of course, she had other things on her mind. Eilean Rurie is famous for its Winter Festival. Well, it used to be called the Christmas Festival until the eighties, when my grandfather changed the name. We're called the North Pole of Scotland, and we attract hundreds of people every year."

Oh, come on.

"You're kidding, right?"

"Nope."

He gave her one of his killer smiles, and Harmony's stomach fluttered, making her look away in case her reaction showed.

"Did you know that celebrating Christmas—well, really it was Yule back then—was banned in Scotland in the sixteenth century? Christmas Day wasn't made a public holiday until 1958, and Boxing Day was only recognized in the seventies. My great-grandfather decided he wanted to make the holidays a big splash, and encouraged all the islanders to do it too, once the ban was officially lifted. It evolved into the Christmas Festival, and then the Winter Festival, and it's grown with each year."

Plunking herself down onto the squishy sofa, Harmony only just stopped herself from putting her head in her hands in disbelief. Hundreds of people, running around singing carols and doing who knew what else?

Just shoot me now!

Yet the smile on the doctor's face told her there was only one of them in the room who viewed the upcoming festivities with horror. The happy anticipation on his face spoke volumes, and it made Harmony pull herself together once more, even while wondering how many other times this man was going to throw her off-kilter.

"How on earth do you accommodate hundreds of people here? The village doesn't look big enough."

"Well, the manor has a lot of rooms, and most of the villagers offer bed and breakfast services, using their spare rooms, or even small apartments attached to their houses.

Most of the temporary staff are island kids coming back for winter break, but the others who don't have a place to stay have dormitories behind the church. A couple of really entrepreneurial souls have even put up a few tiny houses on their properties, and rent those out to visitors. We also get quite a few daytrippers, and the ferry runs more frequently to accommodate them. Most of the residents benefit in some way from the festival. If they didn't we wouldn't bother. It's a lot of work."

Harmony shook her head in disbelief, still not sure he was telling the truth. "But there's nothing going on. No one's putting up lights or decorating."

"It's too early," he said, somewhat cryptically, then added, "Poke around downstairs tomorrow, if you like, or just rest up from your trip. The surgery is closed on Saturday afternoon, and Sunday, although everyone on the island has my number and will call if they need me. I've made a list of numbers and left it on the hall table for you, in case you need anything, and the CIs have stocked the fridge—although, who knows what they put in there? Ingrid's a vegan, and Katherine's always on some kind of diet, Dora has a sweet tooth that won't quit, and Sela is crazy for cheese."

By the time he'd finished his recitation Harmony found herself chuckling. "I'm sure I'll be able to make a meal of whatever they've left, and I'll bless Dora forever if there's a chocolate something in amongst the rest."

Cam was grinning too. "I have no doubt there is, but if you feel up to it nip over to the pub too. They do a really great Scotch pie on Saturdays."

"Maybe I will," she said.

"Right, well… I have to go. Final planning meeting tonight, and it will no doubt be a fractious one. When we get to this time of year they usually are, because everyone is so frazzled and behind on everything. If you need anything give me a shout. I always have my phone on me."

He paused halfway out through the door.

"Oh, and there's an Armistice Day ceremony at the cenotaph on Monday, starting at ten. Come along, if you'd like."

Then he was gone, clattering down the stairs, leaving her to wonder why, when she had been so determined to stay away from Christmas, she'd landed in the North Pole of Scotland. And why, having decided to ignore men, she found her boss so damned handsome.

Cam had been right about the meeting being contentious, but he couldn't seem to keep his mind on the grumbles and arguments going on around him. Instead he found himself thinking about his new nurse. Her sometimes curt way of speaking, juxtaposed with her delightful throaty giggle as he listed the CIs eating habits, made her a fascinating enigma. And, yes, her delicious looks.

Even though he wasn't interested in relationships he was still all-male—able and willing to appreciate a beautiful face and a lovely curvy figure. As long as he remembered he could look but not touch, it was all good.

"Melanie, the theme was decided back in February. It's not our fault if you've not gotten on board with it."

At the sound of Dora's firm rebuttal Cam pulled his thoughts away from Harmony Kinkaid and back to the battle of wills going on in front of him.

"But it's silly. We did Love as a theme before. Why do it again?"

Melanie was as stubborn as ever, and as one of Scotland's best-known living potters always felt her word should be law. But Dora never fell in line with that concept.

"That was nigh on twenty years ago. And what better

theme could we have for the Winter Festival than that? No matter the religion, or the holiday, love is at the center of them all, isn't it?"

Cam intervened, before things got too heated.

"Melanie, you know full well it's too late to change the theme, so either you've gone with it or not. The choice was yours."

Then Hugh Jacobson had a complaint about the decision to extend the festival hours to ten at night. "The strain on the electricity grid will increase, along with the costs. I don't subscribe to this."

Cam doubted that was his real reason for complaining. Hugh was probably worried that the extra noise and lights would disturb his mother, but didn't want to come right out and say so.

"Hugh, the new wind turbine provides more than enough power to cover the additional load, and the generators were serviced last month. The increased revenue for us all will more than offset any additional costs, so I'm sure we'll be fine."

"But the noise…the lights on until so late. It's untenable."

"I'll buy you some blackout curtains when I go to the mainland next Wednesday," Sela interjected, and although Hugh still looked unhappy the meeting moved on.

Afterwards Cam realized he wasn't the only one thinking about Nurse Kinkaid—although, perhaps not in the same way.

"I thought your new nurse might have come to the meeting. She looks as though she'd be a good addition to the planning team" was Dora's opening sally.

The last thing Cam wanted was to spend more time with Harmony Kinkaid than necessary. His unsettling reaction to her made keeping her at arm's length a good thing. Besides, every time he'd mentioned Christmas she had withdrawn at the talk of the season.

But there was no way he was letting Dora and the rest of the nosy CIs know that. His nurse would get no peace until they'd ferreted out the reason for her aversion.

So, trying to protect her as best he could, he said, "First off, let her settle in a bit before you expect her to get into the middle of island life. And, secondly, she's only going to be here for a short time. Why would you think she'd be interested?"

"Oh, I don't know that she will be, but it's always nice to have a fresh face and a new viewpoint in the proceedings. I'm hoping she'll lend a hand once she finds her feet."

Thankfully, before he had to think up another round of excuses as to why Harmony probably wouldn't, Dora and the other ladies were departing with hugs and waves, according to their personal preference.

As he strode down Main Street Cam considered the unlikely friends, each so different and yet all completely devoted to the others. They were the soul and the backbone of the Winter Festival—a point Cam had to concede, despite being almost always annoyed with their attempts to interfere in his life too.

Their organizational skills alone were worth their collective weight in gold, but along with that they also contributed in so many other ways. Designing and sewing costumes, painting backdrops, deciding on the lighting for the public areas and the decoration of the green, making sure everyone who needed help got it… The list went on and on.

If they'd just accept the fact that Cam wasn't the type to be controlled or tied down, and nor would he be guilt-tripped into things, they'd all get along much better. He'd had enough of that growing up—from his mother. The last thing he needed now was to have four more women fussing over him, trying to get him to do what they thought was best.

When he'd been diagnosed as a type 1 diabetic at the age of four, his mother's reaction had been to coddle him, fearful of what might happen if he did any of the normal childhood activities. If it hadn't been for his grandfather, taking him in hand at the age of eleven and teaching Cam how to control his disease, encouraging him to be more adventurous, Cam had no idea how he might have turned out.

Nearing the cemetery, Cam instinctively turned in, walking the familiar path to the spot under a gnarled and now bare oak where a number of his ancestors were interred.

"Evening, Grand-Da," he said, reaching down to brush a couple of late-fallen leaves off his grandfather's headstone. "Just left the planning meeting. All the usual nonsense for this time of year. I wonder if there'll ever be a time where things run smoothly."

The bench was cold, yet dry, and the evening breeze brisk, but Cam settled in for a little visit. Stuffing his hands into the pockets of his jacket, he looked up at the sickle moon.

"Got a new temporary nurse in today and I'm hoping she'll work out okay."

He was hoping more than anything else that Harmony Kinkaid wouldn't turn the relatively stable island world upside down.

Wouldn't turn *his* world upside down.

As long as she did her job, he shouldn't care about anything else. He just needed to get through the winter rush with someone he could count on to keep the surgery going and his patients taken care of, along with aiding with any injuries. After that he'd have the time and head space to find a permanent employee.

All he could hope for was a certain level of professionalism and competence from Harmony Kinkaid. If she could produce that, all would be well.

CHAPTER FOUR

DAY THREE OF her island experience and Harmony looked at the clock again, giving a huff. Thank goodness this was a temporary position, because otherwise this place would drive her to drink. She'd been waiting for Dr. MacRurie's next patient to arrive for almost ten minutes and there was no sign of him. No call either.

She'd spent Sunday exploring the surgery, making lists of things she needed to get done. The lower floor held the waiting room, an X-ray room, the records room, two examination rooms and Dr. MacRurie's office, along with a reception/office area for Harmony and, in the back, a kitchenette.

Climbing the steps to the second floor, she'd found a larger office, now clearly used for old records and abandoned furniture, and five bedrooms, which seemed set up to house patients. This had been confirmed when she'd located a relatively modern elevator at the back of the building—big enough to accommodate a stretcher. Having not noticed any corresponding doors downstairs, she'd ridden it down and realized it came out into what she'd assumed to be a maintenance closet behind the kitchenette.

When she'd asked the doctor about the second floor the next morning he'd explained that occasionally they'd have a patient who needed overnight observation. Or, if the weather was forecast to be terrible and he was worried about outlying elderly folks, he'd bring them in and house them there.

While Caitlin had written her up a list of duties, with notations on where to find things, in just that first go-through Harmony had been able to see areas in need of improvement. Caitlin was a fine nurse, as Harmony knew, but her administrative skills left something to be desired. At least in Harmony's opinion.

She'd spent the first part of Monday morning trying to put the records into some semblance of order. The files weren't stored to her preferred specifications, and she had broken a sweat moving armfuls of records back and forth. Then, and only then, had she started on a pile of notes that hadn't been dealt with—probably from the time between when her friend had left and the present.

Luckily she was an expert in interpreting "doctor write," because Cameron MacRurie's penmanship was something to behold. She'd often thought that doctors wrote so poorly because their brains were going faster than their hands could follow. If that were the case, her new employer must be a genius!

They'd opened early, because of the Armistice Day ceremony, and she was down in her office before seven. But her frustration levels had risen as their eight o'clock patient had been a no-show, and the eight thirty had sauntered in almost fifteen minutes late. To add insult to injury, the woman had insisted there was no need for Harmony to do any kind of pre-examination tests.

Not that Harmony hadn't tried to get her job done.

"Dr. MacRurie will expect me to have weighed you, taken your blood pressure and temperature, plus asked you about the reason you're here so I can make notes."

"Och, no," Mrs. Campbell had rebutted, in the strongest Scottish accent Harmony had heard since arriving on Eilean Rurie. And from her steely glare Harmony had been able to tell she meant business too. “The Laird’ll do all that himself. I’ll show myself in.”

And before Harmony had been able to react the elderly lady had marched right past her and into Dr. MacRurie’s office without even a knock on the door.

Rushing after her, file in hand, Harmony had expected a reprimand from the doctor, but all he’d said was “Ah, here’s your file, Amelia. Thank you, Harmony.”

Taking it as a dismissal, and thankful not to have got a flea in her ear from him, she’d scuttled back to her desk. Yet, it had still burned when Mrs. Campbell had marched past her at five past nine without even a fare-thee-well.

She wasn’t used to patients totally dismissing her that way, and now, with their nine o’clock also a no-show, she was decidedly out of sorts.

She decided it would be best to ask how she was supposed to handle this type of situation, so she walked down to the doctor’s office and knocked.

“Come in,” he called, and Harmony pushed open the door, just in time to see him pulling up his shirt. “Is Mr. Gibson here?”

“Um…no,” she replied, surprised to realize he was injecting himself with an insulin pen. Taken off guard, she forgot why she was there and asked, “You’re a diabetic?”

“Yes. Have been since I was four.”

He said it casually, but Harmony was still taken aback. Caitlin hadn’t mentioned this, and all around the room there were pictures of him doing all kinds of dangerous stuff: mountain-climbing, caving, hang gliding, hiking through remote-looking terrain… Not that having diabetes should preclude him from doing any of those things, just as her father's heart condition hadn't stopped him from indulging his own daredevil spirit.

But look how that had ended.

Already in a bit of a snit because of the patients, now she found her mental comparison of Cam to her father was making her cross her arms, trying to hold in the spate of words hovering on her tongue.

Instead of letting them loose, she took a deep breath, then asked, "Did you plan to tell me?"

Cam glanced up, his eyebrows lifted. "Why would I tell you something so mundane when you'd no doubt find out about it sooner or later?"

Although his tone was even, there was an unusually cool expression in his eyes.

"Well, I'm your nurse. The only other medical practitioner on the island that I know of. What would happen if you went hypo or hyperglycemic and I wasn't aware of your condition?"

"I'm very well versed in the monitoring and treatment of my diabetes, and I haven't had an incident in ages. Don't fuss, Nurse Kinkaid."

She wanted to ask what he meant when he said, "ages," but there was no mistaking the steel in his voice. Not to mention his reversion from calling her Harmony to Nurse Kinkaid, so she kept her mouth shut, for a change.

"Was there something you wanted?"

He was putting away his diabetes kit, and although the chill might have gone from his voice, Harmony still felt the flick of his disapproval keenly.

She adopted a formal tone in return. "What is your official policy on missed appointments?"

"Reschedule the patient."

Really annoyed now, Harmony said, "No, I mean how

do I charge them for not showing up nor even calling to say they wouldn't be coming? Do I do it through the mail?"

Cam's eyebrows rose again, and he stared at her for a moment, before chuckling. "Ha! Only do that if you want to have a stream of highly upset people coming in to see you. Don't worry about it."

"But it's a waste of my time, and yours. Don't you charge them at *all*?"

Cam got up and stretched. "Most of the time everyone keeps their appointments, but this time of year things get a little crazy."

Distracted by the sight of his muscles rippling beneath his shirt, Harmony tried to look away, but she had a hard time forcing herself to meet his gaze.

"Since Mr. Gibson hasn't shown up I'm going to run back up to the Manor before the ceremony. After it's over I have a quick house call to make, and then I thought I'd take you around the island and show you where the patients you'll need to visit live. Interested?"

"Sure, that'll be really helpful." She'd been worried about losing her way on her rounds, so that was a relief.

"Actually, you can come with me to see Mrs. Jacobson too. She's just a few steps away from the surgery, and I'll be asking you to start looking in on her, as well. She's in the final stages of liver failure—cirrhosis caused by hemochromatosis, poor soul. She moved here to be close to her son, Hugh, once she'd decided not to undergo any further treatment. I've had her on a bi-weekly visit, but I think it's time to increase the frequency."

"Do you need me to pull her file?"

"No, I have it here," he replied, tapping the folder on his desk.

He spoke a little more about Mrs. Jacobson's prior treatment, and what he'd prescribed to battle the ascites and hepatic encephalopathy. It was, in effect, palliative care, and Harmony wasn't surprised he wanted to up the number of times she was seen.

"I told Hugh I'd be by at one, so maybe grab something to eat after the ceremony, and if you could be ready at a quarter to, that would be great. Oh, and do you have a pair of wellies?"

She'd been wondering why they needed fifteen minutes to go a few doors down when he asked the question and it distracted her. "I haven't worn Wellington boots since my days in the Guides. Do I need them?"

"Some of the farmyards will be a quagmire after the rain we've had, so they'd be a good idea for when you go to do your rounds."

Unimpressed with the thought of messing up her trainers, which were pretty new and had been a splurge buy, she asked, "Is there somewhere I can buy some?"

Cam shook his head. "You'd have to go to the mainland—or order online and have them delivered, which would take longer. We have a bunch of them up at the Manor. What size do you wear?"

"Seven and a half."

"Okay." He sent her one of his heart-stopping smiles. "I'll hunt out a pair for you."

Cam was already heading for the door and Harmony watched him go, still stinging from his earlier set-down, and annoyed at the way her heart leapt and fluttered whenever he grinned that way.

The thought of spending time with him as he showed her around the island flustered her. Hopefully it was just because he was her boss and she wasn't used to him yet, she mused, knowing it was more. She was attracted to him—which was another wrinkle in what was already a situation so far outside her comfort zone as to be in a different universe.

It would be a lot easier not to have a physical reaction to him if he were a little less handsome and didn't have a gazillion-kilowatt smile. Not even the knowledge that he was a risk-taking daredevil could stop those butterflies from invading her insides whenever he entered the room or smiled her way.

But it should, she reminded herself. The very last thing she needed was to be attracted to a man like her father. The type of man who put his need for adventure before everything else—even his health, or the people who loved him.

Cam made his escape, wondering how he was going to get through the next month and half.

Harmony Kinkaid, his fussy, big-city nurse administrator, was already making him crazy.

She'd rearranged all his files, so he couldn't find anything. She wanted to come down hard on patients who didn't turn up for their appointments. She'd silently showed her displeasure when he'd mentioned he'd be leaving on a hiking and rock-climbing trip to Peru just after Hogmanay, even when he'd said there'd be a locum to fill in for him.

But it had been her expression when she'd realized he had type 1 diabetes that had really aggravated him. She, of all people, should know it was no reason for him not to live fully.

Thank goodness for Grand-Da, who'd shown Cam that the disease wasn't an impediment to having a good, exciting life.

"It's something to be managed," Grand-Da had told him in his habitual no-nonsense way, that first summer he'd come to stay. "Once you learn how to do that anything is doable. You just have to accept you have it and be smart about it."

Learning how to control the effects of his diabetes had given him a freedom beyond his wildest imagining. Gone had been the days when he'd only watched other boys enjoying themselves, never being allowed to join in. And at the age of thirteen Cam had embraced his new-found independence with gusto. Pitting himself against nature, or against his own limitations or fears, had brought him fully alive.

He'd seen Harmony glance at the pictures on his wall, had almost been able to hear her internal dialog regarding the pastimes he chose. As she was a nurse he was surprised at her reaction. Hell, there were type 1 diabetics playing rough professional sports. It all came down to how you took care of yourself and managed the disease.

Maybe he wouldn't be so testy if it wasn't so close to the opening of the Winter Festival and everyone wasn't going bonkers. He'd had one or other of the CIs on the phone almost constantly, complaining about something or needing help with different situations. They kept trying to get him to recruit Harmony too, but so far he'd been able to still keep them at bay.

Settling into his vehicle, Cam ran his fingers through his hair and sighed.

The truth of it was, for all her annoying qualities, his attraction to Harmony hadn't abated one little bit. All morning, whenever they'd been in the same room, Cam had found himself watching her—not as a boss assessing a new hire's abilities, but as a man admiring a beautiful woman. He'd found himself liking the way she moved, liking the scent—something floral and sweet today—that wafted around her, and her expressions with those flashes of emotion she tried so hard to hide.

And those amazing eyes were golden again today. They had him constantly checking to see whether they'd changed to green again…

Despite her trying to boss him around and compulsively rearranging things, he couldn't get his mind off her.

"Don't be ridiculous," he muttered to himself, as he got True Blue started and, after her usual complaints, into gear. "You only just met her. It's just the draw of the unknown…"

But his words rang hollow in his own ears, and he was still obsessing over Harmony Kinkaid as he drove home, looking forward to spending the rest of the day with her.

And mentally kicking himself because he was.

CHAPTER FIVE

CAM STOOD WITH his head bowed as John Harris read out the list of islanders who'd served in World War I and World War II. The Armistice Day ceremony was being held at the cenotaph at the north end of the village green, and Cam was aware of Harmony standing next to him, all her attention on the elderly wheelchair-bound gentleman.

He was one of the patients she'd be checking on when she was on her rounds, and Cam had promised at least to point out those who were attending, even if he didn't get a chance to introduce her to them all.

As the "Last Post" was played by a cadet, Cam watched in his peripheral vision as Harmony fished a tissue out of her pocket and dabbed at her eyes. He was always moved by the "Last Post" too—the long first call, and the trill of the bugle running and then coming back to the mournful last notes.

John Harris, ninety-eight years old and a veteran of World War II, had tears streaming down his cheeks too, and Cam knew he was probably remembering his old friend Dougal, who'd died the year before. The two men had enlisted together, served together, and had been friends all through their lives.

After two minutes of silence the National Anthem was

sung, then the crowd began to disperse and Cam took Harmony over to meet John Harris and his son Martin.

From then on it was a round of introductions, which seemed to last forever, before they could break away and head back to the office.

"Oh, my…" Harmony said, almost as though she were apologizing. "Those ceremonies get to me. My father's family are almost all military, so they always strike home, but I think Grandie would have approved of this one. He liked a nice simple observance rather than a lot of pomp and circumstance."

"I'm glad to hear you think he'd have approved," Cam replied. "Was your father in the military too?"

Her lips pursed as she shook her head. "No. He had a congenital heart defect which made him ineligible. He tried to sign up, to follow in his father's, uncles' and cousins' footsteps, but the army turned him away."

"That must have been hard on him."

Cam wondered why the subject of her father had made those lines come and go between her brows. But they were at the side door of the surgery now, and he opened it so she could step through.

"I guess so," she replied, with a touch of frost in her voice. "But he made up for his disappointment."

Before he could figure out what to say to that, she turned toward the staircase leading to her apartment.

"I'll see you at a quarter to one," she continued. "I promised the CIs I'd meet up with them for lunch and I want to change before you and I go on our tour."

"Don't let them talk you into doing anything you don't want to. The Winter Festival gets crazy, and they've already been trying to get me to recruit you to help. I've been valiantly staving them off."

She paused, her hand on the railing, one foot on the

lower step, and looked back at him over her shoulder. "Why?"

Self-conscious under her golden perusal, he shrugged. "You just didn't seem too keen whenever I mentioned the festival or Christmas."

Her lips twisted briefly to the side, then softened into a rueful little frown. "Sorry," she muttered, and then cleared her throat. "It's not that I don't want to help, it's just… I'm a little low on Christmas spirit this year."

It shouldn't matter to him why. In fact, he should be glad of it, as it meant she'd be disinclined to get too involved, giving him time to get over this unwanted attraction. Yet his curiosity was stronger than any sense of self-preservation. Harmony didn't seem the type to open up very often, so her showing him even a little chink in that practical armor was enticing.

"How come? Just too far from home?"

"That doesn't bother me," she said, but he heard uncertainty in the stout declaration.

Then she sighed, and turned back to face him.

"The truth is my gran died earlier this year, and Christmas was always a special time for us to celebrate together. It just won't be the same without her and Mum."

"Well, you have space here. You could ask your mum to come up and spend the holidays with you."

The cheerful note he'd tried to infuse into his voice seemed to have the opposite effect to what he'd intended as she slowly shook her head.

"Mum's finally getting a life of her own. Her new gentleman friend has invited her to Yorkshire to meet his family, so that's a non-starter." Drawing herself up to her full height and tipping up her chin, she continued, "But it's fine."

That should have been the end of it, but he knew all

too well what she was going through—the loneliness that cloaked the soul after the loss of someone pivotal in your life. The feeling that nothing would ever be the same without them, and the unsure sensation of the world being off-kilter, perhaps never to right itself.

"I get it. Really I do," he found himself saying. "Those firsts are always the hardest. When my grand-da died I didn't feel like facing the holidays either."

Harmony's lips came together in what he'd previously thought of as her disapproving expression. But now he was left wondering what it really meant, considering the pain lingering in her eyes.

"You were close to your grandfather?" she asked.

"Oh, yes. Closer to him than to my parents. I lived with him for a couple of years, and I used to come here every holiday I could to be with him. Even when I got older, if it was reading week at university, you name it, I'd be on Eilean Rurie. It was only after I started working with the aid agency that I didn't get back as often as I'd have liked."

"My gran had lived with us since my dad died, when I was six," she replied. Then, as though suddenly aware of what she was saying, she added, "I'm sorry. I don't usually have a pity party in front of my boss. I think the ceremony this morning has made me a little emotional."

"Don't apologize, please. I don't mind."

Those big golden eyes, slightly misty with tears, drew him in…had him fighting not to step forward. She was all he could see. The world had shrunk to just the woman in front of him, so valiantly battling for complete composure.

Normally he shied away from too much emotion, never trusting it to be genuine. His mother had been a master of using feigned sadness or disappointment to manipulate—until she'd realized it no longer worked on him and had turned it off like a tap.

Harmony Kinkaid was just his temporary employee—a woman he'd known for a couple of days. Why, then, was the urge to comfort her so overwhelming?

His heart was suddenly hammering, and alarm bells were going off in his head, but he paid the warning no mind. Instead he stepped closer and rested his hand on her shoulder, rather than on her cheek the way he wanted to. Her lips were soft now, full and inviting.

Begging to be kissed.

Cam exerted a Herculean effort and dragged his gaze away from her mouth to focus once more on her face.

"I'm sorry you won't be with your family this year, and that you've lost someone so important to you that it doesn't even feel worthwhile celebrating, but it'll be okay. You just wait and see."

And his chest grew suddenly tight as tears gathered at the corners of her eyes again. When the first one slipped free, before he could give in to the urge to wipe it away, she turned and started up the stairs, leaving him staring after her, confusion his only companion.

Cam had been right about the CIs trying to corral Harmony into helping with the festival, but she'd told them she'd only just got to Eilean Rurie and really needed more time to find her feet. While they'd grumbled about it, by the time they'd left the pub Harmony thought they'd given up on the idea.

Crossing the green to the surgery, Harmony thought again about her earlier encounter with Cam. She'd been obsessively going over it, alternately ashamed of telling him anything and grateful for his sympathy. But what totally floored her was her visceral reaction to having him so close.

When he'd touched her shoulder she'd wanted to make

the tiny movement that would have been necessary to get close enough to hug him. The simmering attraction she'd felt from the first moment she'd seen him had threatened to boil over. For an instant she'd thought he was going to make the first move…kiss her. She was almost sure his gaze had dropped to her mouth. The anticipation that had fired through her had been like an electric jolt, and just remembering it brought another shock of desire.

"Get a grip, Harmony," she admonished herself out loud, letting herself into the building, her cheeks hot, her insides fluttering as if a wild bird had invaded her stomach. "He was just being kind."

Besides, she hardly knew him. *And* he was her boss. *And* she was off men, to boot.

It was imperative that she got herself together and got real. She was here to do a job and that was all. Not to play Santa Claus, nor to make a fool of herself because she was feeling like Scrooge. And certainly, *definitely*, not to lust after her gorgeous daredevil boss, who had "heartbreaker" written all over him.

The CIs had been quick to tell her that Cam was single, and she'd been thoroughly grilled on her own status. She'd had no problem telling them about her break-up earlier in the year, although not in detail, since it had got them off the subject of Christmas.

She determinedly pushed all thoughts of her conversation with Cam aside, focusing on work instead. A quick look at the time told her she had just a few minutes to run upstairs and comb her hair before he arrived—if he was on time.

His rather *laissez-faire* attitude toward the way his practice was run would have made her think him a little scatterbrained if he hadn't been so clearly intelligent. But he'd frowned when she'd rearranged the filing system, and given her a blank look when she'd asked why there were over four hundred records when there were less than two hundred and fifty people on the island.

And she was still wondering why they needed fifteen minutes to go just down the road.

He did turn up at the appointed time, and Harmony's heart-rate picked up as she watched him from her bedroom window. He got out of his vehicle to open the gate before driving around to the front of the building. She made herself walk slowly down to join him, neither giving in to nor showing any of the silly eagerness bubbling inside her.

Outside, she found him leaning on the hood of his car, as handsome and relaxed as a magazine model. Clearly he wasn't suffering from the same reaction she had, and she was determined to meet his cool with all the calm in the world.

Cam explained the extra fifteen minutes while they were walking over to the Jacobsons' cottage.

"Hugh is in denial about the terminal aspect of his mother's disease, and he has a tendency to want to speak for her, saying how well she's doing rather than letting her tell me the truth. He's also a bit of a fusspot when it comes to time. If I get there a little early he doesn't have the tea ready yet, so I get a few minutes to talk to Delores alone and find out exactly how she is, and if there are any new developments. I keep the more clinical aspects, like taking her temperature and blood pressure, for when he's in the room, so he feels as though he's in the thick of it."

It made sense, and she made a note of it for future reference. Hearing his logic also made her contemplate how different this job was going to be from her last. There everything had been regulated, and although they'd got the chance to get to know some of their patients quite well, the little personal touches like those Dr. MacRurie had just described had often been missed.

The visit went as predicted, with Hugh Jacobson greeting them at the door, rushing to the kitchen to make tea, and apologizing for it not being ready when they got there. The doctor winked conspiratorially at Harmony, making her silly stomach flutter, and he pushed open the door to the front room where his patient was.

Mrs. Jacobson was a quiet lady, who smiled when she saw Dr. MacRurie and Harmony and seemed to know the drill. Wasting no time on small-talk, she answered the doctor's questions while her son was out of the room. But then, with a quick glance toward the open door, she grasped Cam's wrist, stopping him midsentence.

"It won't be long now, Cameron," she said, in her soft brogue. "But I just want to make it through Hogmanay. I don't want Hugh to be sad every Christmas because I died around the holiday."

Tears stung the back of Harmony's eyes, but Dr. MacRurie just patted Mrs. Jacobson's shoulder and said, "We'll do our best to see you through till then, Delores."

"Good," she replied, seeming to relax slightly in her chair. "I want to see the lights this year, even if I can't get out to enjoy the festival."

Harmony couldn't tell this sweet lady that it wouldn't matter to her son whether she made it through to the New Year or not. Her passing would hurt him whenever it happened, and he'd miss her every holiday thereafter.

Later, after they'd drunk tea with mother and son and were walking back to the vehicle, Cam said, "She didn't know she had hemochromatosis until after the menopause, and it had already caused extensive liver damage. She's not the complaining type, as you could see, and attributed the symptoms to simply aging. Hopefully we can keep her going the way she wants."

No matter how unprofessional it was, Harmony didn't feel able to discuss it just then. Not when seeing Mrs. Jacobson had brought all the pain of losing her gran rushing to the fore.

She made an noncommittal sound. Then quickly said, "I guess you weren't putting me on when you said there's a Winter Festival, although it's hard to picture." All she saw was a tiny village—nicer today, with the sun out, than it had been the last couple of days, but nothing special.

Cam opened the passenger door of his aged utility vehicle and Harmony tried not to wince at the metallic creak.

As she climbed in, he replied, "Wait and see. I think you'll be pleasantly surprised."

But she was still skeptical. After all, how fancy a show could the inhabitants of a tiny place like this put on?

CHAPTER SIX

CAM WALKED AROUND the front of the vehicle, glancing in at Harmony through the windshield. She was fussing with the seatbelt which, like most things in True Blue didn't work as it should, and just a glimpse of her furrowed brow and pursed lips made him smile.

Cranking open the driver's door, he levered himself into the seat just as she got the belt wrestled into submission. She was casually dressed, but the jeans, white shirt and red anorak did nothing to camouflage her lovely figure. Cam rather wished it did, so he wouldn't find himself admiring it so much.

Firing up the engine, trying to ignore how good Harmony smelled, he dragged his thoughts back to business. "I forgot to ask, can you drive a manual?"

"Yes," she said.

But just as he was coaxing the vehicle into gear and, and it ground its way into first, he glanced across and saw her concerned expression.

"My grandfather taught me, but although he always said if I could drive a stick shift in Jamaica I could drive anywhere, I don't know if I can manage *this* beast."

Cam chuckled. "No, I have an estate car for you to use. I'm the only one who drives True Blue. She's very persnickety."

"True Blue?"

There was no mistaking the laughter in her voice, and it made Cam's grin widen. "She's held together with baling wire and tape, but she's never let me down anywhere I couldn't walk home."

The sound of her amusement filled the rattling, groaning vehicle and made Cam unaccountably happy. He realized he'd never heard her laugh that way before; not a giggle but full-on belly laughter.

What started as a quick glance at her had him staring, his gaze riveted on her face. Amusement had taken her from beautiful to stunningly gorgeous, and it was only the need to watch where he was driving that tore his attention away.

"You live on a very small island. I'm guessing you'd be able to walk home from just about anywhere—am I right?"

He cleared his throat, being careful not to look at her again. "Yes, but don't tempt fate. We're in this together now."

That exchange seemed to set a good tone for the rest of the time they spent together. Harmony even relaxed slightly, so Cam asked about her grandfather, and heard the story of her grandmother travelling to England alone.

"She explained it by saying that Granddad had 'small pond' syndrome. He wasn't happy with the thought of leaving a place where he was known and had a certain status to start over in a much larger pond, where he'd have to begin again at the bottom."

Cam couldn't really relate. As a child he'd lived in more countries than he had fingers, and before moving back to Eilean Rurie he had seen even more working for the aid agency, which had sent doctors to refugee camps and disaster zones all over the world.

Despite his desire for a stable home when he was young,

if given the chance to start over somewhere new and exciting now, he'd probably take it. With his past experience, being tied to the island sometimes chafed.

Still trying to get a handle on her family, he said, "Oh, I thought at first perhaps it was your father's father who taught you to drive?"

"No," she said. "My dad was half English, half Scottish. No Jamaican roots."

Something in her voice stopped him from asking anything more about her father, so he just said, "How often do you get to go to Jamaica to see your family?"

"I went most summers before I started nursing school. I haven't been back in a while, though, and I should go soon. Granddad isn't getting any younger, and now he's my last grandparent left."

"I hardly knew my mother's parents, and my father's mother died before I was born. I think it made the bond between Grand-Da and me all the stronger."

"Did your mother's parents live far away?"

Cam eased True Blue into neutral and brought her to a stop at a T-junction before he replied. "No. It was my parents who moved around all the time. My dad is an archeologist, my mother's his archivist, and he loves working in the field—the more obscure and distant the dig, the better. The Middle East and Southeast Asia are his specialties."

The peripatetic nature of his childhood was something he rarely, if ever, talked about, and he was glad to be able to divert Harmony.

"Okay, now, it might seem logical to think this road goes all the way around the island, but it doesn't. If you continue along here you get to the Harris farm, and then to a dead end where we have a wind turbine installed. So you need to remember to take the turn here, rather than go straight."

Fighting the wretched gearbox, he made it back into first and turned the corner to continue circling the island. Since he'd introduced her to most of the people she'd be seeing on her rounds, he decided to simply give her the tour and then take her back home.

The less time they spent together, the better.

They crested a slight rise in the rolling terrain and the sea came into sight in the distance.

"Oh! How lovely!" Harmony said suddenly. "Can we stop for a second? I promised Mum I'd take pictures, and I'd forgotten up until now."

It was a glorious day, although chilly, with a cloudless sky, and he found her reaction to the vista charming. For all his wanderlust, to Cam, Eilean Rurie was the most beautiful place in the world, and he loved to see others appreciate it, as well.

As he brought the vehicle to a halt she fished her phone from her bag and then hopped out. Cam followed, noticing the way the breeze caught her curls and made them bounce.

She started snapping pictures. "I told Mum about the ferry ride, and she asked then if I'd remembered to take any pictures. I felt pretty silly telling her I hadn't."

"Your mum's okay with you being so far away?"

Harmony shrugged lightly. "I don't think she was happy with the idea, but she knew I needed a job, so now she's taking it in her stride, I think. I've been keeping her updated all along the way, and I got a chance to talk to her this morning before her shift. She's sent my other suitcase already, or I'd have asked her to put in a pair of wellies."

"I have a pair for you. At the Manor."

Her lips twitched. They didn't purse, just twitched.

"Did you forget them?"

"No," he said, stuffing his hands in his pockets, not sure

whether to be annoyed at her implication. “I washed them off and left them out to dry. We’re going to drive right past the front entrance to the Manor anyway, so we’ll stop and you can get them.”

Her eyes were shining when she turned toward him, and heat radiated up his spine as she smiled.

“Oh! Can I take a look inside? I’m so curious about what it’s like.”

“Sure,” he said, then had to clear his tight throat and get a grip on himself. What was it about her smile that made his entire system go into overdrive? “But we don’t start opening up most of the bedrooms until later this week.”

Harmony blinked at him, her eyebrows dipping briefly before she turned back to take another picture. He played back his words in his head, trying to figure out her reaction, and then suppressed a groan.

Had he really just mentioned bedrooms, as though they were what she should see? And now that he’d realized the connotations he could picture her in bed—all smooth golden-syrup-and-cinnamon skin and luscious curves, those wild curls spread across his pillow. Somehow, though he didn’t know how or why, he knew her eyes would be greener then, inviting him close, and closer yet…

His reaction to the image was visceral: a shock of heat along his spine, lust turning his blood to lava.

She still had her back to him, had made no reply, and he dragged himself from his fantasy to rush into speech, trying to salvage the conversation and his sanity.

“We only keep part of the hotel open for most of the year, since we just get dribs and drabs of visitors. But next week the entire place will be opened up and aired, and the decorating started, so you’ll get a chance to see all of it.”

“Okay.”

That was all she said, leaving him wondering if he'd gotten himself out of the suggestive hole he'd unthinkingly dug.

Harmony took a deep, silent breath, pretending total concentration on her phone, all the while trying to shake her imagined visual of Cam in bed.

Naked.

Aroused.

Making love to her.

Those chiseled lips on hers…his large, capable hands all over her body.

She was blushing. The heat caused by an intense rush of arousal had traveled from her chest into her face. So she kept her back turned to him, trying to get herself under control.

What on earth was wrong with her? She'd met handsome men before, even dated a couple, but none had affected her the way Dr. Cam MacRurie did.

Finally she got herself centered, and although her cheeks still felt warm, she thought she'd dare to turn around.

"I've got enough pictures," she said, trying not to look at him. "Shall we…?"

They got back into the vehicle and he ground it into first.

"True Blue sounds like her gearbox and clutch need some help," she commented, just to break the silence, which was weighing on her and giving her too much time to think.

"We only have a few cars on the island, since a lot of people use bicycles or scooters, so our mechanic went off to look for greener pastures. I'd have to take her over to the mainland on the car ferry to get her looked at. She's sounded like this forever, so I'm not too worried."

They drove through a cut in the low hills—a twisty road, with rough autumn-colored moorland punctuated by the occasional gnarled tree or low copse on each side. In the distance the hills rose, dark stone stark against the heather and grass. It was, Harmony thought, beautiful in a stern, unflinching way.

"Do you get much snow here?"

"Not really—the occasional heavy fall but usually just a light coating. Our location is pretty sheltered, and because the hills aren't very high storms tend to pass over us quickly."

Just then they crested a hill and there below was a small settlement and the sea again beyond. The afternoon light was wonderful, and the sun, which would set about four o'clock, hung low in the sky, casting a golden glow over the whitewashed buildings.

"Our fishing village," Cam said as Harmony leaned forward to see better. "My great-grandfather moved it here after a storm destroyed the old fishing village a little way down the coast. The entire spit of land gave way, and over the years the sea has eaten most of it up. You can still see the old buildings and what remains of the rescue station when the tide is low."

She risked a glance at him, but when heat threatened to overtake her again, looked away.

"How long has your family lived here?" she asked.

"Almost two hundred years," he said, and she couldn't help smiling at his obvious pride. "In 1853 my three-times great-grandfather won the island in a game of whist."

"A game of what?"

"Whist. It's a card game. The story is that the island's owner at the time was a bit of a wastrel. He lost a lot of money to my ancestor, and paid with the land. Charles MacRurie took the island, which was sparsely populated at the time because it was only used as a summer retreat and hunting lodge, and turned it into his private fiefdom."

"Clearly he wasn't the humble type, since he named it after himself."

Cam chuckled. "From all accounts he was not. At all."

They continued around the coast, with Cam pausing every now and then for her to take pictures, and Harmony keeping the conversation away from the personal and on the island and work.

She was amazed to hear there was an alpaca farm, which produced hand-spun wool, an artists' collective, and a pottery with a world-famous potter. Somehow it had never occurred to her that so small a place would have such an interesting and diverse set of artisans.

When Cam pointed out her patients' homes, and the side roads she'd need to take to get to them, she was able to ask informed questions, since she'd already read all their files. Cam slanted her a raised-eyebrow glance, but didn't comment beyond answering her.

As the gates of Rurie Manor came into sight he said, "The road continues on past Eigg Point, and then goes back to town, but we'll take the back road when you're finished looking around the Manor."

Call it cowardice, or the effect of the heat she could already feel building in her belly and snaking out to fill her chest, but Harmony had changed her mind.

"Why don't I wait until everything is decorated?" she asked. "I'm due to check on Hillary Carstairs tomorrow, aren't I? So I'll take the car and drive myself back to the surgery. It'll give me a chance to read her file more thoroughly and do any research I need to."

"Sure, if you'd like," Cam replied, giving her a look which she avoided, quite sure her cheeks were red again. "But it wouldn't be a problem for you to come in now."

She firmly refused, even though close up the Manor was so beautiful she itched to get inside and see it for herself.

Instead she put deeds to words, collecting her borrowed Wellingtons and then hightailing it out of Cameron MacRurie's vicinity as fast as possible.

CHAPTER SEVEN

HARMONY WOKE UP to an almighty roar and clatter, which got louder and then seemed to be coming into the surgery itself. They were back to their usual nine o'clock opening schedule, and normally she would have been awake long before seven, but she'd hardly slept and had hit the snooze button a few times.

"What on earth…?"

The noise was coming around the corner of the building, and she could swear that everything in the place, including her teeth, was rattling.

Kneeling on the bed, she pulled back the curtain and saw, in the gray morning light, two large lorries and a caravan going past. As she watched someone jumped out of the first truck to open the gate leading to the Manor and the cavalcade drove through. It was only when the trucks were going up the path that she realized there were a couple of SUVs following behind, as well.

She watched until the last vehicle was through, and the gate was closed behind them, before letting the curtains swing shut again. Reaching over and turning on the bedside lamp, now wide awake, she wondered what was going on. More vehicles than she'd seen on the entire island had just passed her window.

Sliding out of bed, she reached for her bathrobe, resigned to getting an early start on the day, although she'd planned to spend another half an hour in bed. Mum was working afternoons, starting yesterday, so there was no early-morning prework call to look forward to, and no good reason to be up earlier than necessary.

Not that she could talk to her mother about the main thing on her mind—Dr. Cam MacRurie, who'd cost her sleep and had her mind and body in a tailspin. While her mother was no prude, Harmony knew the fact that her daughter seemed to be going ga-ga over a man she'd literally just met wouldn't sit well with Delilah Kinkaid.

Heck, it didn't sit well with Harmony either, but she couldn't get the darn man out of her head.

Tossing and turning half the night, thinking about Cam, had left her frustrated and testy, wishing she could stay in the apartment all day and not have to face him. However, there were tasks that needed to be done in the surgery, and despite Cam telling her there was no rush she preferred to be ahead of the game, rather than stressing when a deadline loomed and she was unprepared.

Having showered and had some oatmeal, she went downstairs to the surgery and was surprised to see, through the front window, a crowd of people on the village green.

Going closer, to look out through the glass, she realized there was more than just people. There were a couple of pieces of what appeared to be farm equipment, some open-back vans, and lots of ladders, loaded pallets, coils of rope and large wooden boxes.

Harmony blinked a few times, trying to figure out if she was seeing things. There were only two hundred and fifty people on the island, give or take, and it appeared that all of them, probably plus a few more, were milling about on the green.

"What are they…?"

She almost had her nose pressed to the glass, trying to see what was happening. In the midst of it all was a figure in a Santa hat she was almost sure was Dora, who was gesticulating this way and that like a conductor on a podium.

Another figure broke from the group and came toward the surgery, and Harmony hurriedly scooted back to her desk.

She'd met the man in the pub—Broderick Thompson—and wasn't sure she liked him very much. He was a smooth talker, a little too full of himself for her liking, and his light gray eyes had seemed to be undressing her rather than holding her gaze.

Hopefully he wasn't on his way to the surgery, but if he was she'd rather present an air of professionalism rather than be caught gawking out of the window.

Sure enough, the door to the entryway opened a few seconds later, and the man who was the gallery owner came in, sleek smile in place, sandy blond hair ruffled by the wind, exposing his scalp.

"Harmony, beautiful lady! I saw the lights come on and came over to ask if you'd be joining us."

"I'm afraid not, Mr. Thompson," she replied, not returning his smile. "I have work to do."

His eyes took a break away from crawling all over her chest to glance around the empty waiting room. When he looked back at her his eyebrows were raised in exaggerated surprise.

"I can see how busy you are. *So* busy that I guess you wouldn't have time for a coffee with me? But I know the surgery doesn't officially open until nine, and Lalli's has opened early for the workers, so I'm sure you can spare a few minutes."

"No, I actually don't have the time."

She made no effort to soften the refusal, and she thought

his eyes hardened, although his smile stayed in place. Unfortunately, instead of leaving, as she'd hoped, he actually had the temerity to come over and plunk his skinny bum on the corner of her desk.

"Come on, now. All work and no play makes for a less than *harmonious* life."

Harmony just barely stopped herself from rolling her eyes at his heavy-handed banter. "I really have to get on with my job, Mr. Thompson. Was there anything else you wanted?"

He leaned forward, almost in her space, but Harmony held her ground, clenching her teeth as his gaze dropped to the front of her shirt again.

"Well…"

He let the word trail off suggestively, and Harmony narrowed her eyes. If this twit thought she was going to put up with any of his nonsense let him try her! She was ready.

"Broderick. Not lending a hand outside?"

Cam had come in through the back so quietly neither of them heard him. Harmony jumped with surprise, and when a wave of embarrassed heat rose in her chest she berated herself for it.

She wasn't doing anything wrong.

Broderick Thompson got up and stretched. "Just came in for the First Aid kit. Dora sent me."

Lying creep, Harmony thought, furious enough to want to smack him over the head with the kit once she'd fetched it from the store room. Instead she placed it on the desk, doing her best not to glare.

He picked it up, and gave her another of his smarmy smiles.

"So, what time for coffee later?"

Behind her she heard Cam's office door open, but his footsteps stopped. She knew he was listening, and the thought of him believing she'd go out with Broderick Thompson made her more curt than perhaps she should be.

"I already told you no, Mr. Thompson, and I tried to be polite about it too. If you'd prefer I be rude, ask again."

Broderick's cheeks reddened, but to his credit he just shook his head as he picked up the kit and said, "Can't blame a chap for trying. See you both later."

She restrained the urge to make a rude noise as the door closed behind her, but it was hard not to kiss her teeth. Very aware of Cam, still standing by his door, she reached for the supply list on her desk, intent getting on with the audit she'd put at the top of her day's to-do list. He'd explained that he usually put in a big order for a number of medical necessities just before the festival, in case they were needed, but much of it lasted the rest of the year.

"Whoa," he said, and the amusement in his voice made her want to blush all over again. "Remind me not to rile you up."

With her nose in the air she swept past him, on her way to the medical stores.

"I think it's be almost inevitable that you will at some point," she retorted, before she could stop herself.

The sound of his laughter smoothed the last of her ruffled feathers and she found herself smiling too as she set to work.

Cam was still chuckling to himself as he sat at his desk to switch on his computer.

Originally he'd come down to see if the noise of the arriving equipment had woken Harmony, and to tell her to take part of the afternoon off since she'd started so early. He truly loved this time of year, despite the stress of putting on the festival, but his excitement had shriveled on finding Broderick Thompson leaning close to Harmony, as though about to kiss her.

Her guilty start when he'd spoken had made the rest of his good humor flee, but hearing her give the other man that set-down had restored it. Clearly she had the good sense to see through that Lothario.

Even though Broderick ran a profitable business at the gallery, somehow acquiring really good artwork and having successful yearly exhibitions, he was a bit of a menace otherwise. The women on the island who had known him longest had learned of his wandering eyes over time, but to him every new arrival was fair game.

Cam wasn't surprised he'd tried it on with Harmony, but her clear and cutting refusal had been a thing of beauty.

Would she do the same to him, should he try to kiss her?

He realized he wanted to—badly. Every movement of her lips, whether they were smiling, pursed, or speaking, made him want to taste them.

And he wanted to know what she'd feel like in his arms. Those amazing curves snuggled against him, her arms around his neck, his mouth on that long, lovely throat.

Or anywhere else on her body she'd let him get at.

Arousal hit him, heating his blood. Shifting in his seat, he tried to banish the vision of a naked Harmony from his mind, so as to not cause himself any more discomfort. For goodness' sakes—what was he? Fifteen? Getting turned on just daydreaming over a woman he hardly knew?

Mind you, Harmony would make any red-blooded man think dirty thoughts.

And she made him completely forget what he was supposed to be doing—like actually turning on his computer instead of starting blindly at the still blank screen.

Hitting the switch, he waited for the machine to boot up.

The physical attraction would be so much easier to quell

if he didn't actually like her so much. Yes, she was fussy, and bossy, and on a couple of occasions she had reminded him of why he preferred a single life by giving him one of those "oh, really?" glances that activated his stubborn independent streak. But none of that negated his very real desire to get to know her better.

Much better.

Intimately, even.

She was his employee, though. Temporary, but on his payroll nonetheless. Professionalism dictated that he not get involved with her, no matter how short a time she was supposed to be on the island. Besides, there was an innate danger in getting too close to a woman like Harmony, even for a little while. She had the kind of forever vibe he assiduously avoided.

He might be an adrenaline junkie, but forever was one heart-stopping trip he didn't want to go on. Not when it would mean changing the life he enjoyed so much, and having someone else to consider every time he wanted to make a decision.

His childhood, stunted by his mother's fear over his diabetes and his own need to allay her panic, had made him recognize his need to be free of those types of entanglements. Even now, when he was speaking to his mother on the phone, he omitted telling her too much, knowing she'd be frightened to hear about his adventures. That was about enough of an emotional burden as he could manage.

The computer beeped, the cursor flashed, waiting for him to put in his password. Doing so absently, Cam found himself remembering Harmony's sadness when she'd spoken about how much she missed her grandmother.

He understood, completely. The first Christmas after Grand-Da died had been the hardest of Cam's life. Only the fellowship of the islanders, who missed the old man as much as Cam did, had eased the pain. It was a shame Harmony and her mother wouldn't be together to remember the old lady and all the good times the three had shared.

Then he frowned as the first notification to pop up on his screen was an email from Dora entitled To-Do List.

"Really?" he muttered to himself. "Don't you think that after four years I know what needs to be done?"

Yet still he opened it, and sat running through the various points until the phone rang.

Since Harmony was in the back, he called out, "I've got it!" and picked up the receiver.

"Cam MacRurie speaking."

"Cam? Are you coming by today?"

"Hello, Hillary," he said, noting the strain in the woman's voice. "Is everything all right?"

"Oh, yes, of course. I just wondered..."

"My new nurse, Harmony, is scheduled to come out and see you, Hill," he said gently. "Will that be okay with you?"

"Oh, yes, of course," she replied, and the automatic answer told him more than her words. "It's just that I don't *know* her. How will I know it's her? And I haven't had a chance to tidy up..."

"Don't worry about it, Hill. I'll come out with her and introduce her properly. That way next time you'll know who it is. Will that suit?"

"I... I..."

She faltered, and Cam waited, guessing she was trying to gather her thoughts.

"So you'll come, then?"

"Yes, Hill. I will." He infused as much of a soothing tone into his voice as he could. "I'll see you in a little while."

"Thank you." The relief in her voice was patent. "Thank you, Cam."

After he'd hung up the phone, Harmony, who'd come to the door, asked, "Her anxiety getting the best of her?"

Cam nodded, pleased that she'd picked up on that from the file. Hillary Carstairs had been born with spina bifida, yet had lived life to the fullest, getting around with leg braces and a cane until her later years. She had two children, one of whom still lived at home and helped his father on the farm.

Now confined to a wheelchair, Hill had developed agoraphobia and an anxiety disorder, which made her increasingly isolated. He'd prescribed antianxiety medication, which she'd refused to take, and offered to refer her to a specialist, but again she'd refused—perhaps because of having to go to the mainland for appointments.

It was at times like this when Cam felt the restrictive nature of the island keenly, and chafed at not being able to provide what was necessary.

"I'll ride out with you," he said to Harmony. "It'll allay some of her stress, and hopefully she'll be okay with you coming alone the next time."

"Okay, but it seems a shame to interrupt your day that way. No doubt you have scads of stuff to do."

Cam happily closed the email from Dora and grinned. "It's not an issue. Hill's health is the most important."

Besides, Hillary and Gavin's farm was in one of his favorite parts of the island, and showing it to Harmony suddenly seemed like a great idea. In fact, there was nothing he'd like more—although why that was wasn't something he wanted to think about too deeply.

CHAPTER EIGHT

THE CARSTAIRS' FARMHOUSE was filled with the evidence of Hillary's weaving business, although Harmony had seen no sign of the alpacas when they drove up, which was disappointing.

Hillary Carstairs was stressed and apologetic, but Harmony was adept at handling patients with anxiety disorders, and had her calmed down in a fairly short time. Hillary even agreed to allow Harmony to do her examination and change her catheter.

"Everything looks good," Harmony told the older lady as she helped her back into her wheelchair. "But I see from your chart that you've refused treatment for your anxiety disorder and agoraphobia. May I ask why?"

Hillary's eyes shifted away and she knotted her fingers together. For a moment Harmony thought she didn't intend to answer. When she finally spoke there was an air of surrender in the words.

"I've been poked and prodded and I've taken medication my entire life. Why would I add even more? Besides, going anywhere in this contraption takes so much effort. It's not fair to Gav."

Harmony tweaked the ends of Hillary's skirt so it lay flat, thinking through her answer before saying, "You realize what an anomaly you are, right?"

Hillary frowned slightly. "What do you mean?"

"Well, you've lived to be in your sixties with spina bifida. Had two children and a full life. It's only in the last few decades that spina bifida has been considered something other than a childhood disorder, since people diagnosed with it weren't expected to live very long. Why give up now?"

Hillary shrugged, but she was obviously listening, her gaze steady on Harmony's face, so she continued speaking.

"You already have some limitations placed on you by your disorder. Why not deal with what you can, so you can continue enjoying your life to its fullest?"

There was no reply, but as Harmony packed up her kit she left it at that, hoping she'd given her patient some food for thought.

They left the bedroom and found Cam and Gavin, Hillary's husband, in the large farmhouse kitchen, leaning on the counter, sipping from teacups.

Gavin was a short, stocky redhead with an infectious grin, who asked, "All right, then, love?"

"Yes," Hillary said, smiling back at him. "Everything is fine."

But Harmony found herself the recipient of a piercing interrogatory glance from Gavin, who only visibly relaxed when Harmony nodded her agreement.

"Good, good… Want a cup of tea, ladies?"

At their affirmative responses he set about pouring cups for them from the pot, while a black-and-white collie came over to say hello to Harmony. She bent to pet it, getting a lovely cold nose in her neck and a couple of licks before the dog slunk off in typical collie style to flop down on a cushion in front of the fireplace.

Gavin said, "I was just telling Cam that I've moved the

flock up to the old croft, which is why they weren't hanging over the fence watching to see who was arriving."

"They're a nosy lot," Hillary said. "I miss seeing them when I look out the window."

"I was hoping to get a glimpse of them when we arrived," Harmony said, adding a murmur of thanks as she took the cup from Gavin.

"Cam can take you up to get a look," he replied, turning to Cam as he continued. "Take the four-wheeler."

"I will," said Cam.

"Oh, that's not necessary," Harmony said, at the same time.

Cam laughed. "I think it's a grand idea. And, if you don't mind, I'd like to show her Ada Tor."

"Go right ahead," Gavin replied, resting his hand on his wife's shoulder as he passed. "I don't need the UTV again until later this evening."

Everyone else looked pleased as punch at this idea, and Harmony realized she'd look churlish and ungrateful by refusing, so she plastered a smile on her face. But she wondered what kind of vehicle it was they'd be taking, what kind of terrain they'd be traversing, and if any of this was safe.

She got her answer after they'd finished their tea. While she stowed her bag in True Blue, Cam and Gavin went into the barn. After a short time there was the clatter of an engine, which sounded like a large lawn mower, and a small four-wheeled vehicle came stuttering out. It had two seats, a flatbed in the back, no doors, and it bumped across the farmyard as though it had a complete lack of shocks.

Filled with trepidation, she cautiously approached as Cam brought it to a halt nearby.

At least it probably couldn't go very fast, she thought as she got in.

But with the way Cam drove it over the rutted tracks it might as well have been a race car. Even terrified half out of her wits, and hanging on for dear life, Harmony had to admit he handled the little vehicle well, with the kind of casual capability she couldn't help but admire.

When they got to a gate she got out rather shakily to open it, and then closed it behind the UTV once he'd driven it through.

"All right, there?" he asked with a grin as she got back in, before setting off again after her curt nod.

The land undulated, but Harmony got the sense they were going more uphill than down—a supposition that was proved as they went around a rise and she looked back to see the farmhouse below them. Ahead in the distance was a stone building, and even farther away what looked like a jumble of boulders all piled up together.

At the sound of the UTV, the alpacas came moseying out, and Harmony couldn't stop her little squeak of pleasure on seeing their cute, curious faces. Cam brought the vehicle to a halt and Harmony got out for a closer look.

The alpacas kept their distance, with the one in the front eyeing her suspiciously. As she got closer to the fence it huffed, and she stopped.

Cam came up beside her and pointed. "That's Sandro—the male. He's pretty protective of his flock. Not much of a spitter, according to Gav, but I wouldn't chance going much closer when his ears are flat like that."

"I was hoping to pet one," Harmony replied. "They look so soft…"

"Got their winter coats on," he replied, and she saw him looking at her out of the corner of her eye. "You really like animals, don't you?"

"I do. Gran had a little scruffy dog for years, and he and I were best buds. She didn't want to get another after Hobo died, and I was so busy I didn't think I'd have enough time to care for an animal myself, but recently I've really been thinking about getting a pet soon." It was her turn to look at him, now, wanting to see what his expression told her as she asked, "Don't you like animals?"

"Love them," he said, which came as no surprise to her, really. He seemed the type.

"So how come you don't have a dog or three?"

Cam shook his head. "Maybe one day I will, but right now a pet would tie me down too much. Every time I want to go away I'd have to find someone to look after it."

Unable to decide whether that was a smart or a selfish way to be, Harmony made no comment. Instead she made soft, hopefully enticing sounds to the alpacas, trying to coax them closer, but they weren't interested and, after a short time, they turned and started back toward the building.

"That was where Gavin's parents lived," Cam said. "He and his four siblings were born and grew up in that crofter's cottage. Gav built the farmhouse for himself and Hillary when they married, and after his parents had passed away, and none of the children wanted to come back here to live, he converted it into a supplementary barn."

"Wow. Seven people in that little building? Must have been cramped," he said as they were heading back to the vehicle.

"I think they were used to it," he said, as they got back in. "And they spent enough time outdoors to make it doable. They all had to help on the farm when they weren't at school, and with sheep—which is all Gav's father had back then—there's always something needs doing."

Further conversation was curtailed by the racket of the motor starting up. Then they were off again, heading for the up-thrust of boulders, which she discovered was far larger and higher than she'd first thought.

Cam left the path and bumped across the field, straight for it. Harmony was hanging on, wanting to tell him to slow down but finding the words caught in her throat. He finally slowed, then stopped within a couple of yards of the rocks. When he turned off the vehicle the sudden silence rang in her ears.

There was a wild, stark beauty to the landscape: gray rocks interspersed with autumn-colored ground cover and a few bare-limbed trees. In the sky a raptor of some type circled, and the whisper of the wind was the only sound. When Cam spoke it was in a low tone, as though he didn't want to break the spell of quietude.

"Come on. Let me show you the best view in all Eilean Rurie."

They got out, and Harmony followed Cam to the boulders. But when he started to climb she hung back, shaking her head.

"I'm not going up there," she said, trying not to show her instinctive fear. "I don't know how to climb."

Looking back at her, he said, "This isn't climbing, really. Just a little scramble. It's perfectly safe, and if you're not feeling confident go ahead of me and I'll guide you."

Oh, how she regretted not wearing the Wellington boots, which would have given her a solid reason not even to attempt the climb. But she'd worn her trainers instead, and with Cam's eager expression and outstretched hand she was completely torn.

Anything to do with climbing—even what he called a scramble up some boulders—filled her with terror.

"Scared?" he asked, his eyebrows going up. "Are you afraid of heights?"

Was there a condescending note in his question?

Whether there was or wasn't, it got Harmony's dander up and she lifted her chin.

"No, I'm not," she said, gathering her courage and stepping up on the first rock. "Lead the way."

Cam climbed with the ease of familiarity, but made sure to look back often and make sure Harmony wasn't having any difficulties.

They didn't talk, except when he warned her of a longer step, or a spot where there was a crack to watch out for. She was obviously inexperienced, hesitating in places, searching for a good hand or foothold in areas where, to him, it was obvious. But he had to admit she was game, and she grew even higher in his estimation.

He'd been sure she'd refuse to go to the top of Ada Tor. In fact, he would swear she'd been petrified when he'd suggested it. Yet here she was, more than halfway to the top, soldiering on. Hard not to admire her grit.

When he got to the top he reached back to help her up the last little bit, but she ignored his hand and scrambled up by herself. As she stood beside him, dusting her hands off on her jeans, he watched her look around, and he saw the dawning pleasure on her face at the vista laid out before her.

The land fell away in dips and swirls, the contours and colors reminding him of a Van Gogh painting, and in the distance lay the sea, a smooth blue expanse so far away. Just visible to the southeast were the roofs of the town, and to the west the little crescent of buildings making up the fishing village. Sheep and a few horses dotted the fields, but it was the quality of the air and the perfect height of the sun that really brought out the island's splendor.

"How lovely…" she breathed, turning to look back toward where the mainland was just a smudge on the horizon above the trees along the northern coast.

"I told you it was the best view," he said, and found himself taking in the familiar sight and appreciating it even more than usual. Something in her awestruck expression made him see it through fresh eyes.

"Is this rock formation natural?" she asked, still turning slowly to see everything all over again.

"I think it is," he replied. "Although there isn't another like it on the island. Legend has it that there's a Celtic princess buried under it, but I don't think it's true."

"Hence the name Ada Tor?"

"Yes."

He sat down on a handy rock, still gazing out. After a moment she joined him, and he shuffled over to give her more room. Her fresh, sweet scent wafted over him and stirred something deep inside.

In the distance a truck rumbled along the road, and she pointed to it briefly. "I can't get used to seeing so many vehicles here all of a sudden. It's surprising after hardly seeing any at all."

"They're probably delivering Christmas trees to Angus's farm. He always gets his early because he has so much work to do. The rest will come later in the week."

Harmony sighed quietly, and he somehow knew she was thinking of her family and all she'd miss this year.

"Will you tell me what you used to do with your gran and your mum for Christmas? I'm curious to know about some of your customs."

She gave him a sideways glance, before staring out at where the truck had disappeared into a dip in the land.

"It wasn't much different from other English families, I guess," she said, but then proceeded to prove herself wrong.

It was as if a dam had broken, and Cam could only listen as she listed all the things she'd be missing this year. There were things he'd never heard of—what on earth was a gizzada, or jonkanoo?—but other things he completely understood. Lots of poinsettias, since they were such a popular tradition in the Caribbean. Watching favorite movies, listening to beloved songs. Decorating the tree together and inviting everyone they knew to come by to exchange gifts and have drinks.

It wasn't so different from what happened here, he thought as she fell silent. Some different cultural traditions, of course, but the picture she painted of family and friends, of a community sharing laughter and joy, labor and company, was the same.

Without thought he looped his arm around her shoulders and gave her a quick squeeze. When she stiffened he almost let his arm drop, but then she turned her face to look at him and he froze, captivated and enticed by her solemn eyes, her soft lips.

The wind had died, and their faces were so close together her breath rushed warm across his mouth. Cam inhaled, wanting to take it into his lungs, hold on to it just for a moment.

Want spiked through his veins, so strong it wrapped around his chest, making it tight. It was there in her eyes too, he thought, the same anticipation and curiosity that was heating him through.

Then she blinked, color flooding her cheeks with a rose-toned blush, and Cam finally heeded the danger signs flashing in his head as they pulled away simultaneously.

The sensation of having her warm, soft body against his side lingered, though, reminding him of what was so close and yet should be ignored.

He cleared his throat, searching for a memory of what

they'd been talking about so as to bring them back from the sensual ledge they'd stepped out on. "Christmas at your house sounds wonderful. I'm sorry you won't have that this year."

She turned her face away from his, but not before he saw that her eyes were misty.

"I just have to accept it'll never be that way again," she said quietly, a little quaver in her voice. Abruptly she rose and turned back toward where they'd climbed up. "Let's get down now. I have work to do."

He followed her lead without comment, but inside he was wondering what, if anything he could do to make the season ahead better for her.

Despite knowing it was ridiculous, his heart had ached on hearing her pour out her pain. And he certainly shouldn't want to hold her, comfort her, kiss her the way he was drawn to do.

Yet that was exactly how he felt.

CHAPTER NINE

I'VE HAD ENOUGH of this...

"This" was the Christmas music playing through the office, and Cameron MacRurie's occasional attempts to sing along.

He might be Laird of Eilean Rurie, and a good, well-respected doctor, but his singing left a lot to be desired!

Yet even as she had the sour thought Harmony found herself smiling and shaking her head. The song playing was an old one, sung by a crooner her grandmother had loved.

Harmony could almost hear Gran saying, *Lawd, tell the man to stop caterwauling.* But it would have been said through laughter, and the old lady would have gone and sung with him, trying desperately to get him in tune.

Not that it would have helped Cam, who was clearly tone deaf.

As the days had gone by she'd found herself shaking her head at Cam's behavior a lot—when she wasn't ready to murder him, that was.

On the day after they'd climbed Ada Tor, while still reeling from their near-kiss, she had been horrified to see him up on the half-built scaffolding being put up around one of the oaks on the green. Then, the next day, she'd come into the surgery to find not only that Cam had beaten her to work for a change, but that the reception area was packed to the rafters with boxes, as well.

"What on earth is all this?"

It had taken everything inside her to keep her voice below a shriek—especially when she'd spied the cobwebs liberally festooning the cartons.

"Decorations," he'd said, with just a hint of smugness in his voice. "I checked the calendar and, since we don't have any patients today, I figured it was the perfect time to bring them down. Don't look so annoyed."

Annoyed? She'd been livid.

But then he'd added, "It's a part of being Laird. I have to set a good example. And I hope, as my employee, you'll see fit to help me."

So she'd been stuck. How could she have refused without looking as truculent as she'd felt?

The kicker was she'd enjoyed it—once she'd gotten over her snit. Even being hyperaware of his movements, of every accidental touch of their fingers or his body brushing past hers, she'd found herself relaxing into the joy of bringing Christmas to the surgery.

The decorations were a mixed bag: some obviously old, some new, some elegant, others as chintzy as they came. But Cam had a story for almost all of them.

It had taken them most of the day to get most of them set up, with a break for lunch at Sanjit's restaurant. Cam's grandmother's porcelain Christmas village, dating from the fifties, delicately beautiful, had been placed on a shelf where it could be admired out of reach of little hands. His grand-da's collection of Christmas greetings cards from around the world had been strung on lengths of tinsel along one wall. An impressive nutcracker collection had ended up liberally covering almost every surface possible in the surgery, and paper festoons were hung all over the ceiling, with old-fashioned lanterns in between.

They'd argued over the placement of those, with Cam wanting to put them up willy-nilly and Harmony insisting on a more regulated design. She'd won, of course, and he'd been forced to admit that it looked better than he'd have ever imagined.

"The Christmas trees are coming in a couple of days by ferry," he'd told her, when she'd asked what he wanted to do with the tree ornaments. "We'll get that done up once I pick one out."

Spending that time with him had been so much fun, but in a strange way seeing him like that, being in close proximity with him again for an entire day, had also felt dangerous. Both the trip to the Carstairs' farm and their working together to decorate had taken him out of the "hunky doctor fantasy material" zone into something more intimate.

She kept replaying that moment she'd thought he would kiss her in her mind, telling herself she wouldn't have let it happen, but knowing she would have given in to her own desire. To her own chagrin she wanted to experience his kisses—and more.

That evening, curled up in front of the fireplace, Harmony had realized just how much she was starting to *like* Cam on top of being physically attracted to him. She liked his enthusiasm. The way he wasn't afraid to go head to head with her, but how he also backed down once he realized she just might be right. His tenderness as he'd brought out his grandparents' favorite decorations and told her their stories had touched something deep inside her.

Her ex, Logan, was the ultimate pragmatist. The kind of serious man who thought everything through and then announced the way things would go. He wasn't sentimental in the slightest, and he'd shied away from anything that even remotely resembled emotion even when they were alone. She'd thought him safe and steady, only to have him prove otherwise.

Somehow she was sure everything would be different with a man like Cameron MacRurie. It was there in his eyes. In the way he listened so intently when she was talking. In his smile...in his speech...even in the way he moved. The kind of man he was called out to the secret self she alone knew: the romantic, sensual side of her she rarely acknowledged.

And that secret part of herself wanted Cam—badly.

But, she reminded herself, Cam was a daredevil, a risk taker and, like her father, he appeared to turn a blind eye to a medical condition that could cause serious damage if not managed properly. Worse, it could be deadly.

As a nurse she knew she was being unreasonable about Cam's diabetes. With all the new ways of treating and managing type 1, people with the disease were living fuller lives than ever before.

However, as a woman, and one who knew what it was like to lose someone because they refused to accept their limitations, Cam was the last kind of man she needed in her life. Getting close to people just led to heartbreak, in her opinion.

Meeting him had had her thinking of her father more often than she usually did, drawing comparisons that made her both angry and sad. And no doubt having just lost Gran contributed to her general train of thought.

As the December first opening of the Winter Festival fast approached, the entire island was like a beehive, with everyone buzzing to get everything in place. Vendors were starting to arrive, and Harmony had been surprised at the number of people suddenly on the island, all pitching in.

Not even the rain, which came hard and fast one afternoon, deterred the workers for long.

"Come on, come on!"

The CIs took refuge in the surgery as the thunderstorm rolled overhead, and Dora was not pleased at the delay.

"Telling the storm to hurry won't make it pass any faster," Katherine commented helpfully, and then took a sip of her tea. "Besides, for once we're ahead of schedule. Relax for a moment."

"Hush!" Ingrid interjected, as herself, Dora, and Sela all gave the other woman dirty looks. "You'll jinx us."

Just then Cam came in, his hair soaked, his shirt damp enough to cling to his chest and arms. Harmony hurriedly looked away, his delectability quotient making her mouth water. Rising, she to the back and got him a towel, just as one of the CIs asked what on earth he'd been doing to get so wet.

"Got caught with just my windbreaker on," he said, taking the towel and giving Harmony a smile that almost melted her on the spot. "Gave my hooded anorak to one of the lads from the mainland who didn't have one. I have another at home."

Another reason to like him—although there were so many others screaming at her to keep her distance.

"I'm glad you're here, ladies. There's something I want to discuss with you."

Harmony wasn't sure whether he was including her or not, but Cam didn't tell her to come with the others when they trooped into his office, so she stayed where she was, feeling ridiculously put out.

It wasn't as though she was *involved* in the preparations for the festival. In fact, other than the surgery decor she'd done her level best to stay out of it. Although watching it all happen around her had made her realize what a

Scrooge she was being. Everyone else, from the oldest to the youngest, was lending a hand, and excited about it too.

Even her shut-ins wanted to hear every detail of what was happening in the village. Mr. Harris, in particular, had been talking her ear off about how things had been done "in the old Laird's time."

"All this hullabaloo about scaffolding around the trees to hang the lights? Not in our day! We'd shinny up those trees like squirrels and string the lights that way."

"Now, Da," his son Martin had said, sending Harmony a wry smile. "You have to admit the trees were smaller back then."

"Och, not so much smaller. And there was that big old oak that came down in the storm of seventy-two. She was a grand old tree—taller than any of them left there now!"

"Will you come to see all the lights, Mr. Harris?"

Harmony had just finished doing the older man's wellness check, noting that his oxygen saturation levels were fairly good and the edema in his feet was reduced. He'd been diagnosed with level two congestive heart failure just over a year ago, but had continued to work on the family farm until he'd fallen one day while out looking for lambs. After that, his son had put his foot down—although, he admitted, keeping his father in was like herding cats.

Cam had told her that Martin had gotten a gaggle of geese and put his father in charge of those, to make sure he had something to do that was close to the house.

"Of course." He'd sounded outraged that she'd suggested otherwise. "Wouldn't be Christmas without seeing the fair and all the lights and the gewgaws people put up, would it?"

Harmony was brought back to the present when she heard Dora clearly through the closed office door.

"It's not possible, Cam. Not at this late stage."

Then came a babble of voices, and a few shushing sounds, all of which left Harmony eaten up with curiosity. So much so that she was tempted to put her ear to the door—an impulse she was ashamed of immediately thereafter.

"'Eavesdroppers hear no good of themselves,'" she muttered, once more quoting her Gran, who'd been full of annoying sayings.

Oh, great, this place is turning me into my grandmother.

Thankfully, just then the door opened, giving her something else to concentrate on.

"Hello, miss," said a Christmas tree with legs, coming into the surgery. "Just dropping this off for the Laird. I'll leave it here, by the door, if that's okay with you?"

"Yes, that should be fine," she said, eyeing the huge fir as the man carrying it finally extricated himself from its grasp.

The ceilings in the surgery were high, but she wondered if it would fit or if, like in a Christmas comedy, they'd have to cut a hole up to the second floor to accommodate it. Trust Cam to choose the biggest tree of them all!

The CIs came out of Cam's office like a tornado, with Dora in the center. She was scowling, but Harmony thought the twinkle in her eyes looked rather dangerously amused.

"Good—the rain's stopped. Back at it, ladies. Especially since the Laird has added to our plate. Harmony, I'll see you over at the Manor this evening, right?"

Surprised, Harmony was about to say she didn't know what Dora was talking about when Cam quickly replied, "Yes, she'll be there."

Then the CIs were off, already bickering again.

"What's going on at the Manor tonight?"

"Progress meeting and the Manor's tree-decorating and lighting. I like for everyone to have a hand in it and see all the decorations before the craziness starts in earnest," he said, heading for the surgery Christmas tree. He whistled. "She's a beauty, isn't she? Not as magnificent as the Manor tree, of course, but perfect for in here."

"Don't you think it's a bit big? And when did you plan to tell me about tonight?"

Cam was rummaging in a box and emerged, triumphant, with the tree stand before he replied, "It's the perfect size—and I thought the CIs would have told you, so I didn't bother."

He shrugged apologetically.

Did he have to look so adorable doing that? she wondered, inexplicably annoyed.

They spent the rest of the afternoon putting up the tree—which was only just short enough for the star to fit at the top. It took both of them to wrestle the tree into the stand, and then Harmony went to get water to fill the receptacle while Cam cut away the netting holding the boughs against the trunk.

"Don't put the water in yet," he said, pulling the tree a little farther from the wall. "We're going to have to decorate the side that'll be seen through the window and then push it over. The water will make it heavier and harder to move."

They argued over the lights.

"If you wrap some close to the trunk, and then more at the edges, you'll get better depth of light," she said.

"*Depth of light?* What on earth does that mean?" he asked, his lips quirking.

"I can't believe you're the Laird of the North Pole of Scotland and don't understand that most basic of concepts."

He rolled his eyes, but gave in eventually. Of course then they argued about whether the white lights or the colored should go near the trunk, but she gave in on that one and they put the colored ones inside and white outside.

As they took out ornaments and placed them on the tree they looked specifically for those related to the Winter Festival theme of "love."

Finding a tattered but beautiful little heart made of felt, with an intricate design embroidered in the center, Harmony held it up. "This is perfect. A little stained, but right in line with the theme."

"Wow," Cam said, holding out his hand for her to give it to him. "I haven't seen this in years. The design is like a luckenbooth—a traditional Scottish betrothal gift. My grandmother made it, and Grand-Da used to put it on the tree in the Manor. I wonder how it got in with these?"

Instead of putting it on the tree, Cam slipped it into his pocket and Harmony's chest ached, just a little, when she noticed him touching the spot where he'd secreted it every now and again.

Later, after they'd finished decorating the tree and tidying up, he said he was going back to the Manor. When, a few minutes later, she saw him crossing the green, she knew he was going to the churchyard, as he so often did, to visit with his grandfather.

Why that should make her like him even more—*want* him even more—she didn't dare consider.

CHAPTER TEN

"WELL, GRAND-DA, EVERYTHING seems to be going smoothly, for a change. The trees are strung, the shops and roadways are decorated, and the firs all came in without incident. Remember that one year when they didn't get loaded onto the ferry?"

Cam had the churchyard to himself, as he usually did, but he was stooping at his grandfather's headstone since he'd forgotten to bring anything to wipe off the bench. It wasn't unusual for him to come by and give Grand-Da updates on his life, but today was different. He'd started with the mundane because the specific felt too hard.

"Tonight is Manor night. The place looks beautiful, as always. Got a really nice tree this year. I think you'd be pleased."

Despite his inviting her a few more times since his *faux pas*, Harmony still hadn't been up to the Manor. In a way he was glad, since she'd be seeing it at its best tonight. On the other hand he was nervous. He wanted her to like it, even love it, the way he always had.

Running his finger over his grandfather's name, Cam forced himself to get to the point.

Grand-Da had always hated prevarication.

Get to the point, son.

Cam could hear his grand-da's voice in his head, the

tone a mixture of annoyance and amusement. He'd always been able to talk to the old man about anything, although sometimes it had taken a while for it to come out, since Cam had been used to keeping his own counsel about a lot of things.

"I…" He cleared his throat and tried again. "Harmony found the heart. The one Gran made for you the first Christmas you were together. I don't know how it got into the boxes in the surgery, or why I never noticed it was missing."

It made him remember the story Grand-Da had told, about meeting Gran in London, knowing right away that he wanted to marry her. Gran hadn't been interested. She'd had other plans.

She was a city girl, your Gran. Had no interest in a Scottish country lad—doctor or no. Oh, she gave me a merry chase, and I had to seduce her around to my way of thinking, but I knew there would never be another like her in my life. If she hadn't eventually had me I'd be a lonely old man now. Instead I always have her love to keep me company.

It was as though he was sitting in front of the fire again with Grand-Da, chuckling to himself over the story. He'd been too young then to appreciate the strength and depths of true love. Yet the tale had always touched him, deep inside, and now to suddenly have it come back…

"Are you trying to tell me something, Grand-Da?" he asked aloud.

Cam was a man of science, but there were times like this when he had to wonder about greater forces and how they could manifest in life.

He didn't *want* to want Harmony. Didn't believe real love could blossom in the space of less than three weeks. Yet the draw she exerted, the mix of comfort and excitement he felt in her presence, was unprecedented in his experience. And when he'd seen that heart in her hand, that gorgeous, beaming smile, her eyes alight with pleasure, something had shifted inside him. A sea change of the soul.

"She's my employee, Grand-Da, and she's bossy. Plus, she's not at all into adventuring. I think it scares her."

The first was a sticking point, but the second he really didn't mind. In fact, he rather liked arguing with Harmony. She was logical, and forthright, and didn't hesitate to give as good as she got—which made it all fun.

The third point, however, was a bad one.

His friend Josh had sent him a video of a group BASE jumping with wingsuits. One of the men had been wearing a helmet cam and the footage as they arrowed along the side of the mountain was amazing. Josh had suggested they learn, and make it a part of their next adventure trip, and Cam had been researching equipment and locations when Harmony had come in to ask him a question.

She'd taken one look at the video playing on his computer and had frozen, her lips tightening, those lines between her brows suddenly appearing.

"Looks like fun, doesn't it?" he'd asked.

"No."

It had come out so forcefully, it had taken him aback.

"It looks like craziness. The type of stupidity that can get people killed."

Then she'd turned and walked out, apparently forgetting what it was she'd come for, or so disturbed she hadn't been able to bear to stay in the room.

"She's not for me, Grand-Da. I won't be hemmed in by anyone again. I need someone who'll want to go on adventures with me—not nag me to take care of myself, or get bent out of shape every time I want to do something fun."

It was just the wind rustling through the branches, but it sounded suspiciously like Grand-Da's laugh.

"Right—enough of this," Cam said, levering to his feet. "I'll just put it all out of my mind, get through the festival and send her on her way again."

It felt good to have made the decision, but he found he'd taken the heart out of his pocket, was holding it in the palm of his hand.

For a moment he thought about leaving the heart on Grand-Da's headstone, but instead he put it gently back into the pocket of his coat. He'd never known his grandmother, who'd died the year he was born, but suddenly he felt closer to her, handling something she'd made. A piece of her heart in the form of a heart.

Touching Grand-Da's stone one more time, he went over to Grandma's and touched it too.

And when he left the churchyard he felt both at peace and more confused than when he got there.

"First time at the Manor?" Dora asked Harmony as they stood to one side in the Manor's ballroom, each juggling a little plate of hors d'oeuvres and a drink.

"That obvious? I'm gawping, aren't I?"

And who could blame her? Everything about the house made her want to gasp. It might have been converted to a hotel, but it had lost none of its charm or its grandeur. For goodness' sakes, it had a real, live ballroom, complete with intricate parquet flooring, plaster swags on the walls and ceilings, and massive gold mirrors, which reflected the bank of windows on the other side of the room.

"I think we all did the first time we got a chance to see inside the manor," Katherine replied. "It's a thing of beauty."

Harmony couldn't argue with that assessment. She'd

had an Elizabeth-Bennett-sees-Pemberley moment the first time she'd glimpsed Rurie Manor, but she'd have never imagined how truly glorious the inside of the old house would be.

"When Cam told me most of it was a hotel I pictured them having gutted the place to modernize it and make it usable, but they've really kept all the lovely old features and atmosphere, haven't they?"

"Oh, yes," Sela agreed. "The Manor has been lucky in her custodians. The MacRurie family has kept it wonderfully. And in this day and age that's no small feat."

"The family has always been smart about it," Ingrid said, gesturing with a piece of celery for emphasis. "I think it was Cam's great-grandfather who turned it into a corporation and a trust, so they could avoid a lot of death duties and keep the place running. Not that they were lacking in funds. They all have that entrepreneurial and inventive streak in them, so they weren't dependent on inheritances alone."

"Really?" This was another facet of Cam's family coming to light for Harmony, and she couldn't hide her curiosity.

Dora nodded, swallowing a bite of cake before elaborating. "Cam's however many times great-grandfather—the first one to come here—was a train baron, who had a number of patents for various parts and equipment the railroads used. And the old Laird—Cam's grandfather—invented some kind of… What was it, girls?"

"A valve," Katherine supplied.

"Yes—a valve for a nebulizer machine to make it work better. And Cam's got a few patents himself…for safety equipment, I believe."

"He needs it," Harmony said, hearing the snap in her own voice and regretting it the moment she'd spoken.

Dora gave her a bump with her hip—Harmony assumed because she didn't have a hand free to swat her with.

"He's adventurous—but that's a good thing in a man, isn't it? Who wants an old fuddy-duddy?"

Harmony would have argued the point, except the topic of their conversation chose that moment to come over to where they were standing.

"Everyone having a good time?" he asked, with one of those smiles that never failed to make Harmony's knees weak. "Had enough to eat? Put an ornament or three on the tree?"

"I don't think that poor tree can take even one more bit of decorating, Cam. Especially the spot where the children were standing."

His smile turned to a grin. "Yeah, that side's looking a little heavy low down, but they had a grand time doing it."

"Have you taken Harmony on the tour yet?" Dora asked—a little too innocently to Harmony's ears.

"No, I thought I'd wait until things calm down a bit. I have to make my rounds and keep things flowing."

"You don't have to—"

What should have been a polite declining of the tour earned her another hip-bump from Dora and a poke in the back from Katherine to boot.

"What?" she asked, since what they'd done was obvious. "Cam's been running around like a chicken with its head cut off. He doesn't need to give me a tour if he doesn't want to."

Cam rolled his eyes. "Just keep her here until things quiet down and I'll be back to get her," he said to the CIs, adding, "Don't let her slip away. You know she'll probably try."

"Back at you," Sela muttered behind Harmony's back.

And before Harmony could ask the other woman what,

exactly, she meant by that, the CIs started arguing about the configuration of the vendors' caravans parked in the field behind the green and the moment was lost.

Every time she tried to give the CIs the slip and get out of there before the end of the party she was foiled. She didn't know why she was so resistant to getting a tour of the house from Cam. Okay, that was a lie. She didn't want to be alone with him right now. Not after seeing him so carefully putting that felt heart into his pocket, with a hint of deeply held emotion that had just melted her heart.

Gorgeous Cam in a wetsuit could be used as fantasy fodder. Dr. Cam could be treated strictly as an employer. Daredevil Cam could be firmly held at bay. But tender Cam? Sentimental Cam, who had immediately gone off to speak to his grand-da after she'd found that little ornament?

That Cam might well be irresistible, and Harmony knew her limitations.

But he wouldn't take no for an answer. As the staff were cleaning up, and the CIs were saying their goodbyes, he firmly guided her back into the hotel and took her through it completely. Even the kitchens, and upstairs to see the guest bedrooms.

Everywhere was beautifully decorated for the holidays, and lit in such a way as to enhance the best features of the house and its ornamentation.

"Rurie Manor is beautiful, Cam. Even the kitchens."

He laughed softly, taking her elbow to lead her back to the staircase. Just that small touch had heat pooling low in her belly. His obvious love of the house his ancestors had lived in and cared for all those years was patent, and she liked him even more for it. There was no hint of him taking it for granted, or being in any way anything but appreciative of being able to live there and oversee its upkeep.

"My ancestors loved Victorian splendor—even the later ones—so whenever there were renovations or updates to be done they naturally leaned in that direction. I'm not complaining, though. They really tried their hardest to keep the best features of the house."

"They did a wonderful job—and I can see you're carrying on the tradition."

At the foot of the grand staircase he hesitated. From farther down the hall she could hear staff talking softly, the clink of crockery and glassware, and the sound of a trolley being wheeled across the floor. There was the front door, just a matter of feet away, and Harmony knew she should make her departure. But she didn't.

The warmth of his hand on her arm, the fresh, warm scent of him, the way his gaze traced her face, all conspired to keep her there.

"Would you like to see my little corner of the Manor?"

No smile on his face. His voice low and serious.

Harmony's world tilted, leaving her unsteady, frightened, and she knew that a decision lay before her like the drop off a cliff.

Walk away and stay safe or step over?

Would she fly or plummet?

"I don't know that I should," she said, being honest, hearing the anxiety she was fighting echoing in her voice. Or was it the rush of desire through her veins making it quiver that way?

Cam's fingers shifted on her arm and he stepped a little closer. Without thought she moved to meet him, so they were only a hand span apart.

"It probably wouldn't be wise," he agreed, even as his head dipped toward her and her lips rose in invitation.

The kiss was light at first, an exploration, but it went to Harmony's head like a shot of one hundred percent proof rum. Firm lips searched hers, drawing her closer, setting her alight with a wild surge of arousal. Her arms went around his neck instinctively, and his encircled her waist, pulling her flush against his chest. The sound he made low in his throat washed through her—a benediction and a promise, all wrapped into one.

Deepening the kiss felt inevitable. Right and true to what was growing inside her. But the force of it almost knocked her off her feet. Clinging to him, she surrendered to the fire, taking his scent into her lungs with each rushed inhalation, her body tightening and softening all at once.

When he broke the kiss, lifted his head, she kept her eyes closed a little longer, savoring the untamable zing of passion discovered as it thrummed beneath her skin.

Finally forcing open lids that felt weighed down with need, she found herself trapped in his gaze, and the gleam of his desire, the rapt, stark lines of his face, let her know she wasn't alone in the wanting.

Then common sense crashed the party. And although she wished with all her heart she could just show it to the door, she knew she wouldn't.

Cam must have seen it on her face, because he sighed gently and brushed a finger over her cheek.

"Did you drive?" he asked.

"No," she replied, regretfully sliding her arms down from around his neck. Although her hands didn't seem to want to let him go, coming to rest on his broad chest. The feel of his racing heart beneath her fingertips almost made her change her mind about going.

"I'll walk you down," he said.

"Okay."

She couldn't help hoping he might kiss her goodnight. And he did better than that, kissing her silly in the apartment foyer, just inside the door.

Harmony lost herself in his arms. Every sipping kiss, each deeper exploration of her mouth, each brush of his hands, which had somehow found their way under her coat, dragging her under.

"You're delicious," he said into her neck, his voice muffled by the fur collar of her coat. "I should go before I can't."

"Yes, you should," she agreed, dragging his mouth back to hers, aware of the dichotomy of her words and actions.

She didn't want him to go. That much was obvious. But how much further was she willing to take this?

Letting him go, taking a step back, was the hardest thing she'd ever done, but somehow she achieved it.

"This is *so* not a good idea." She swallowed, trying to sound normal when every nerve in her body was tingling, her libido gone haywire. "You're my boss."

Cam's eyes were dark, his pupils so dilated they looked black, and when he scrubbed his fingers through his hair she saw his frustration.

Then one corner of his mouth kicked up. "Your temporary boss."

A huff of amusement escaped her throat, although there was nothing laughable about the situation. "True, but…"

She wanted to say she wasn't into casual sex, and that he wasn't the kind of man she'd ever get involved with otherwise. Wanted to list the complications their sleeping together might cause to a working relationship. Probably point out that there was no way they could sneak around without the entire island knowing what was happening.

Yet none of it crossed her lips. Mainly because it didn't seem terribly important just then.

"Look," he said, holding up both hands as though in surrender. "I know neither of us planned on this happening, but I'm not averse to us...*enjoying* each other while you're here."

Harmony thought about what he'd said. The temporary nature of it should be a turn-off, but strangely it wasn't.

Cam MacRurie wasn't the kind of man she'd ever get seriously involved with. He was too much like her father—a reckless adventure-seeker, who didn't take his medical condition seriously enough. She might have been young when her father died, but she remembered the turmoil, the pain both her mum and herself had gone through. It had shattered their world, left them devastated and emotionally scarred.

No, she realized. If she was going to be able to enjoy whatever this was sparking electricity between them, it would have to be with the inner understanding of the relationship's transient nature. Once she embraced that she'd be okay, because then she wouldn't get emotionally involved.

And, man, did she want to enjoy Cam. He was a temptation she hadn't expected and didn't want to resist. Her entire body reacted to the thought, and in that instant her mind was made up.

Slipping past him, she started up the stairs, and when he didn't follow she turned her head to look at him over her shoulder.

"Aren't you coming up?"

CHAPTER ELEVEN

HE KNEW HE shouldn't go up to her apartment. Despite what he'd said to her, Cam knew he was probably already in over his head. Making love to Harmony might just drown him. But in the back of his mind his grand-da's words rang.

Being afraid is never a good reason not to do something, son. It's a reason to consider whatever you're about to do carefully, but not a good reason to avoid trying.

Harmony frightened him badly. The way he felt when he was with her, worse when he held her in his arms, was beyond any sensation he'd ever known. It made him want to run, to avoid going deeper, and yet she was irresistible.

So he followed her gently swaying hips up the stairs, his arousal climbing with each step he took, anticipation sparking along his spine as he watched her slip off her coat.

Earlier that evening he'd noticed how her red sweater gave her skin a beautiful glow, had thought it was the perfect color for her. Now all he wanted was to get rid of it, so as to get to the golden skin beneath.

The lure of the unknown was heady.

What kind of lover would she be?

The need to know was like a fire in his soul, a kind of insanity he couldn't wait to embrace.

She was fitting the key into the door when he came up behind her on the landing. He couldn't keep his hands off her, and encircled her waist from the back, nuzzling her hair aside to set his lips on her neck.

Harmony shivered, a little moan breaking in her throat. Encouraged, he kissed and licked, scraping his teeth gently over the frantic pulse. When her head fell back against his shoulder, giving him better access, Cam took full advantage.

Then she had the door open and they shuffled into the hallway, his arms still around her, his mouth still on her skin.

"Cam..."

God, the breathiness in her voice almost undid him. He turned her in his arms, ravenous for her mouth again. The urgency he was fighting seemed matched by her own. Tugging and pulling, breaking away from each other's mouths only long enough to get her sweater off over her head, they were soon stripped to the waist.

He picked her up, and she wrapped her legs around his hips as he carried her through the darkness to her bed. They tumbled onto it, locked together, as though fused by passion.

Now—now he could explore that luscious body the way he'd wanted to the very first time he set eyes on her.

He took his time, despite his driving need, slowly removing the rest of her clothes, touching, kissing, caressing each inch of her body as he did so. She did the same to him, rolling him onto his back and straddling his thighs to get at his fly.

There was a moment of shared laughter as they realized he still had his boots on and, now they were trapped in his trousers, he couldn't reach them. She levered them off, then removed his socks. Tugging off his trousers, she began a slow rise up along his legs, teasing him the way he'd teased her.

After a very short time Cam sat up to yank her against his chest.

"Why'd you stop me?" she asked.

But he knew she knew why, because she was making him crazy, and he told her so, receiving another long, passionate kiss in response.

Lying side by side, they discovered each other's weak spots, the places and touches that made the breath catch, the body tremble, that had moans and soft cries of pleasure filling the room.

Their passion built, but Cam wouldn't be rushed, and when she tried to hurry him along he captured her roving, unrelenting hands and held them above her head.

"Behave."

It was a hoarse rumble, and the sound she made in response made his body tighten even more.

"I don't think that's really what you want, is it?" she replied, twisting her wrists between his fingers and arching her back so her breasts rubbed back and forth against his chest.

"No," he admitted. "But I want to take my time, to make it good for you, Harmony."

She froze, and in the dim light filtering through the curtain he saw her eyes close for a moment.

When they opened she'd quieted, and she said, "Kiss me again, Cam."

He'd never been happier to comply with a request in his life.

Sinking into the sensation of mouth on mouth, the sweet tangle of her tongue with his, was as natural as inhaling. When he released her wrists and her hands found his body again—gentler now, not as insistent—the sweep of them across his skin set his nerve endings afire.

Coming up for breath, he didn't know whether minutes or hours had passed—knew only that the desire he'd thought so intense before had grown exponentially, become impossible to contain.

Rolling to the side of the bed, he searched along the ground with his hands. Harmony snuggled up to his back, wrapping a leg over his, her lips weaving magic spells along his nape and across his shoulders.

She paused long enough to ask, "What are you doing?"

"Trying to find my trousers. I have a condom in my wallet."

"Mmm…" She was back at her sorcery, shifting behind him, her mouth following the line of his spine, her hand fluttering over his stomach and heading south.

With a harsh sound of triumph he found his clothes, dragged them toward him. Fumbling for his wallet, he had to pause to grab her hand, lest she make him lose control.

She giggled and he rolled over, trapping her beneath his body. "You're a bad, bad girl."

Harmony blinked up at him. "And you like it, don't you?"

No need to answer. She knew he more than liked it.

Keeping her still as best he could, he fished out the condom.

"Want me to put it on?" she asked.

"Oh, hell, no. That would finish me off."

She laughed softly again, and replied, "No finishing without me."

He couldn't help laughing with her as he rolled away to put on the condom—and she was waiting, arms outstretched, when he rolled back.

"Are you sure you're ready?" he asked. The need to make it perfect for her was paramount in his mind.

"Come here" was her only reply, and she suited actions to words, drawing him close, welcoming him into her body.

And of course he obeyed, finally where he'd dreamt of being since the day Harmony Kinkaid had landed on Eilean Rurie.

In her bed and in her arms.

Harmony awoke the morning after the Manor party alone. Cam had left before daylight, and although she hadn't wanted him to go, she knew her time on the island would be far more complicated if he didn't. People tended to look askance at women who slept with their bosses.

Not that it worried her overly much. December was a stone's throw away, the festival set to begin. By the end of January she'd be gone, and whatever gossip and ill feelings they might inspire with their affair would die down quickly once she left. She was more than willing to deal with the fallout for a couple of months if she could keep seeing Cam.

The night had been amazing. Magical, in a way. At least for her. Who knew that laughter could add such a new dimension to sex? Logan had been as businesslike in bed as he was in every other facet of life.

Funny to know that she'd felt closer to Cam, more connected, than she ever had with a man she'd spent two years with. It came from knowing Cam MacRurie cared—actually cared about her experience rather than just his own.

When Logan had dropped his bombshell she'd been more angry than hurt, which had made her question her motives for being with him to begin with. It had become comfortable, and his staid demeanor had seemed to make him the perfect partner. Yet, in the end his defection hadn't broken her heart as much as dented her pride.

Being with Cam seemed risky—way outside her comfort zone in a million ways—but since it was preordained to last only for a short time, she could simply enjoy his company without too much angst.

Checking the time, she hopped out of bed and into the shower, smiling to herself at a few unusually achy muscles, all an indication of how thoroughly loved she'd been the night before.

Her phone rang right on time, and Harmony hurried to pick it up.

"Hi, Mum. Everything all right?"

"Yes, yes," her mum replied, as she always did.

Sometimes Harmony wondered what her mother wasn't sharing, perhaps in an effort not to distress her daughter.

"You sound bright and cheerful this morning."

Harmony stifled the chuckle rising in her throat. "It's a beautiful day here, and last night there was a party up at the Manor. I had a good time."

"Hmm…" Her mother didn't sound convinced. "Are things still crazy there with the festival? No chance of you coming to Yorkshire over the holidays? Even for a couple of days?"

"No, Mum." Why did her mother keep trying to rope her into her Yorkshire trip? "I'll have to be here for the duration. There's supposed to be hundreds of people coming through, and although Cam says there'll be additional medical help on hand, he and I will still be the first line of defense."

"Okay, okay. It's just…"

There was a wistful tone to her mum's voice…a sorrow Harmony felt down to her toes.

"It's just what, Mum?"

"Oh, nothing important. Tell me more about what's going on there."

Lowering herself to the edge of the bed, Harmony said,

"No, Mum. Tell me what's making you sad. I'm not a baby anymore, who needs to be protected. I want to know."

There was a long silence, and when her mum spoke next Harmony knew she was near tears, if not already crying.

"It's just that I miss you…and the closer it gets to Christmas, the harder it gets."

"Oh, Mum. I miss you too. But you have your trip to look forward to, and Fred to keep you company…"

"But it's not the same. I was dreading Christmas, and I didn't feel up to any of the things we used to do, but now…"

How could she have been so blinded by her own grief and hurt as not to realize that her mum probably didn't know how to face the holidays without Gran? After all, she'd felt the same way when her mum had said she wouldn't be at home for Christmas, but she hadn't had the brains to make the connection then.

Harmony's heart hurt, and tears were filling her eyes to slip down her face. But she knew she had to be strong for her mother—just as her mum had been strong for her all these years.

"Listen, Mum. I know you miss Gran, but she wouldn't want you be wallowing in grief. I can almost hear her saying, *Lawks, who turned on de tap?* if she knew you were crying over her."

It made her mum laugh through her tears, the way Harmony had known it would, to hear Harmony impersonate her grandmother.

"I know nothing is the same this year," she continued gently. "But maybe it's time for you to think about *you*, to figure out what's best for you rather than anyone else. Start a new tradition…teach Fred how to bake a Christmas cake. I don't have the answers, and I'm so sorry I'm not there for you when you need me, but I love you and I want you to be okay."

"Thank you, love," her mum said, after a little pause and what sounded like a blowing of her nose. "You're right, you know. Even if you'd been here it still wouldn't have been the same, and we might have ended up moping around instead of enjoying any of it. And haven't I always been the one telling you to go off and live your own life? But here I am…crying because you've done just that."

"This job is only temporary, Mum." Why did this reminder to her mother make her suddenly feel even more depressed? "I'll be back before you can convert my room into whatever you've been planning all these years."

That earned her a heartier chuckle than her mum had been able to manage before, and they finished their conversation on a lighter note than when it had started.

But Harmony's heart was still heavy as she finished getting ready and headed off downstairs to open up the clinic. Although, the secretive intimate smile Cam gave her when he came in a few minutes later did a lot to lift her mood.

Though the smile on his face faded, concern darkening his eyes. "What's wrong?" he asked, his gaze searching hers.

She didn't know why, but it made her smile. "Don't worry, it's not remorse over a wild night."

He visibly relaxed, coming over to perch on the edge of her desk, lifting a gentle finger to touch her cheek. "Wild, huh? Not sure how to take that. But don't change the subject. You've been crying."

How on earth did he know that, when she'd been careful to use an extra touch of concealer under her eyes to camouflage the signs?

"I was talking to my mum and I realized what an insensitive beast I've been."

He was so easy to talk to, with his eyes never leaving

hers, all his concentration on what she was saying as it all poured out of her.

"How could I not realize how much harder it would be for *her*, this first Christmas without Gran?" she concluded, trying her best not to let the tears start up again.

"You're dealing with your own grief," he said, his hand on her shoulder providing more comfort than a simple touch should. "It's made it hard to see that her grief is what made her agree to go to Yorkshire with Fred. All you saw was her abandoning you, and the loss of all the things that meant Christmas to you."

"You're right," she agreed, miserable again.

"Harmony, come into my office and away from the windows. I think you need a hug, and if I give you one here then I may as well have slept all night in that wonderful bed of yours."

She chuckled, but got up, wanting that hug in the worst way.

"Wonderful, was it?" she teased, as she followed him into the office and watched him close the door behind them.

"Or wild, if you prefer," he retorted, enveloping her in his arms, taking her weight as she leaned against him.

At once she was more relaxed, and muscles she hadn't even realized were tight unraveled in the warmth of his embrace.

"Either one works for me," she mumbled, wishing they could go upstairs and do a hands-on assessment of which adjective worked better.

If she wasn't careful, she warned herself, Cam would turn her into a sex addict, and the withdrawal symptoms when she left would be horrendous.

CHAPTER TWELVE

"HARMONY, YOU HAVE to help me!"

Hearing Dora's near shout on the other end of the line made Harmony's heart-rate go into overdrive.

"What's wrong? Are you hurt? Where are you?"

"I'm at home. Come quickly."

"Do you need Cam?"

He was out, checking on a visitor who'd fallen off his scooter earlier in the afternoon, leaving Harmony to close up the clinic. She hoped she could deal with whatever it was happening to Dora.

"No, no. Just you. Hurry!"

Grabbing her jacket and a medical kit from the back, Harmony swiftly locked up the surgery. Normally in an emergency she'd drive, although Dora's house was only a short way away, but with the number of people on the roads, and walking all over the place, it would be a lot quicker to walk.

Or in this case trot—which was what she did, weaving her way through the throngs of visitors.

Hard to believe it was already midway through December, with the Winter Festival in full swing. Harder yet for Harmony to reconcile the sleepy little village she'd first seen on arrival with the wonderland it had become.

The lights, banners, decorations, and Christmas trees

in every window gave the village a truly festive air. And it wasn't just the village. A night drive around the island revealed light-encrusted fences, trees, and houses, a variety of seasonal lawn decor, and even a forest of firs in a field, all lit up and open to the public to walk through.

"Angus Stewart does that every year," Cam had told her. "He tried growing a grove of firs, but the soil was wrong, so instead he buys the trees and sets them up like a miniature forest. And right in the center he has baskets of rowan and a stack of Cailleach logs for anyone who wants burn them in his nightly bonfire."

"Cailleach logs?" she'd asked, bewildered. "What are those? And why burn the rowan?"

"Cailleach is also known as the Hag of Winter. It's an old tradition to carve her face on a log and then burn it to banish the cold, the darkness, and any coming hardship. The rowan is supposed to burn away any hard feelings between friends or family members."

Every day she learned something new. When she'd first heard about the festival she'd pictured something far less elaborate—although, to be fair, Cam *had* tried to warn her from the beginning.

On the other side of the green the fair grounds were a mass of people all day, and up until it closed at ten at night. She'd been twice already—once with the CIs and again with Cam—and she'd likened it to a cross between a Renaissance fair and a long, ongoing party. While she'd politely passed on the haggis, she'd enjoyed the Yule bread and the clootie pudding.

"It similar to a Jamaican Christmas pudding," she'd told the CIs. "But blander. Ours has rum, and a lot more fruit. My gran kept her fruit soaking in rum and wine all year long, so as to have it ready for Christmas."

The CIs had exchanged strange looks over that tidbit,

but Harmony hadn't been able to get them to say why. Maybe it sounded alien to them—just as things like the Cailleach and neeps and nips did to her. It was a whole different world, but she was loving it.

Especially since Cam, as the Laird, had lately taken to wearing a kilt.

It was easy now to see why women went bonkers over men in kilts. With his calves on full display, and the green, red and gold tartan swinging when he walked, he looked delicious!

Finally getting to Dora's cottage, she raced up the path to knock on the door. It was flung open, and a frazzled-looking Dora dragged her inside.

"Thank goodness you're here."

She hadn't released Harmony's arm, just continued to pull her through the living area toward the kitchen, her cat meowing and weaving between their legs. Meanwhile, Harmony was trying to assess whether Dora had an injury anywhere. With her strange behavior, maybe she'd fallen and hit her head?

"I need help."

"With what? Are you hurt?"

They got to the kitchen and Dora pointed inside, the picture of tragedy personified.

"Mince pies!"

"Can you imagine?" Harmony said later that night to Cam, when he arrived at her apartment. "There I am, thinking she's hurt, running like an idiot down the street to her place, only to find out she's baking mince pies and has fallen behind on production! I could have strangled her."

Her expression of outrage had Cam too busy laughing to reply, and Harmony flung a cushion at him in response, even though she was laughing too.

"She had me there until nine o'clock, cranking out twenty dozen pies. Thank goodness that's one of the things Mum makes, so I wasn't completely clueless. It could have been clootie pudding."

Cam didn't mention that twenty dozen was the number of pies Dora usually made every evening by herself during the festival.

"Did you have a good time, despite being used as unpaid labor?" he asked.

"Oh, I got paid," she replied, with a groan, flopping back onto the couch.

The royal blue terrycloth robe she was wearing gaped slightly at the throat, giving him a tantalizing glimpse of cleavage.

"I ate enough mince pies to give myself colic, but, yes, I enjoyed it thoroughly. Dora makes me laugh."

Her eyes glowed, amber tonight, and her smiling face warmed him quicker than the roaring fire. He went over and poked the logs, suddenly wishing she was up at the Manor with him.

They'd agreed for discretion's sake that he'd come down to see her at night when he could, since she'd either have to drive up to the Manor or he'd have to walk her home. Both of those scenarios would make it clear to anyone seeing them what was going on.

Each night since that first one he'd told himself it would be good to take a break, to sleep in his own bed and not get too used to having her in his arms. And each evening after dinner, when he was sure the island was settling down for the night, he'd found himself at the surgery side door, letting himself in.

She'd become his new obsession—and he was beginning to think she was far more dangerous than skydiving, caving and free-diving all rolled into one.

"I think the cat's out of the bag for us," he said, not wanting to spook her, but being honest. He didn't want anyone to make a comment she wasn't prepared for.

"I thought it might be," she replied, a cautious note in her voice. "You coming out of the surgery the other night instead of driving down from the Manor was probably more than enough to set tongues wagging."

Most visitors to the island came fully prepared to enjoy the sights and were a good-humored lot. There had only been one skirmish so far, when a pair of friends, having had too much beer, had got into a wrestling match outside the pub. It had been swiftly broken up, and the two friends had been sheepish after their nonsense, and apologetic.

But when the call had gone out for Cam to come and examine the patient, who was sitting on the curb outside The Ladies from Hades, he'd been with Harmony, and had had to leave from there right away to investigate.

He had to ask. "Do you mind? That people know we're seeing each other?"

What was he going to do if she said yes and decided they should stop?

"Do you?"

He still had his back to her, facing the fireplace, but he stuck the poker back into its stand and turned around.

"No." Not only didn't he mind, but he didn't care either. "It's really no one's business but ours."

"Okay."

"What does that mean, Harmony? That you do mind but you're okay with it?"

Her smile was beatific, a balm to his racing heart.

"No, I don't mind. We're adults having a good time with each other. Sure, the employer/employee aspect might make people a little upset, but I don't think they'll tar and feather me."

The muscles in Cam's neck relaxed.

But then she added, "Besides, I won't be here that much longer. It'll all blow over after I'm gone."

The words struck him like a claymore to the gut. It was the one thing he didn't want to think about—had assiduously avoided contemplating.

"Have you started looking at applicants yet?"

She sounded so cool, as though discussing the weather, while his insides rebelled at the notion of her leaving. Somehow, though, he had to match her calm. He, who more than everyone knew her leaving was both inevitable and right, wouldn't be the one to quibble.

"It'll have to be when things wind down, I'm afraid. There's just no time for it now."

"Fair enough," she said, rolling her shoulders against the arm of the couch, dropping her gaze for a second before meeting his again.

Her eyes had changed—gone from amber to green.

"Do you know your eyes change color?"

She tilted her head as though unsurprised. "I've been told that."

Cam stalked closer to the sofa, those amazing eyes following his every step. "Sometimes they're gold, sometimes hazel, and now they're green."

"It's the genetics wheel of fortune," she replied. "My dad's family mostly have green eyes, and my mum's father came from near a place called Seaford Town, where there's a settlement founded by Germans who immigrated to Jamaica. His eyes are light too, so I got the recessive genes."

Beside her now, Cam sank down onto the couch, and she moved over to give him space to fit right into the inward curve of her waist. He braced one hand on the back of the couch, the other on the arm, bracketing her, hemming her in.

She didn't move, just watched him.

"Doesn't explain why they change color like that."

"Does it matter?"

She touched his face, a butterfly brush of soft fingers, soothing and arousing all at once.

It did to him. Was it an emotional barometer he could use to interpret her mood? Or just a trick of the light? A reflection of the color she was wearing?

"You're beautiful," he heard himself say, the spur-of-the-moment words flowing off his tongue.

Harmony smiled—a seductive curve of her lips that drew him to them—and Cam had no intention of resisting. All this talk about her leaving made him mad, ravenous for her, as though putting his mark on that glorious body, making her cry out with pleasure, would somehow make her stay.

But he held back. Once he started kissing Harmony it was hard to stop. He wanted to make her a little crazy, and watch her while she came apart.

He snaked a hand under her robe, found the soft flesh of her thigh. "What do you have on under here?"

The touch of her tongue to the middle of her lower lip sent heat up his spine, had his body tightening with need.

"Why don't you look and see?"

Using his free hand, he tugged on the tie at her waist—just as his phone rang.

Cam dropped his chin to his chest and cursed.

Harmony laughed. "Such language, Dr. MacRurie. You should be ashamed."

He moved over to pick up the phone from the hall table, still muttering invectives under his breath. "Cam MacRurie."

"Cam, it's Gillian. Those guests I was telling you about

are at it again. The mother has tripped near the bonfire and got a nasty burn on her leg. Can you come take a look?"

Suppressing another curse, Cam replied, "I'm on my way," before hanging up.

"What's going on?" Harmony had sat up and tightened the belt on her robe again—damn it.

"The couple staying over at Gillian Strom's are up to their old tricks. Mother has got burned by the bonfire."

They'd already gotten drunk one night and had a nasty argument in front of all the other guests, and their kids—one eleven and the other thirteen—were menaces. Cam was just about ready to send them packing.

"Need me to go with you?"

Sighing, he pulled his coat off the rack and shook his head. "No, stay where it's warm. Depending on what I find when I get there I might have to head straight back to the Manor."

He'd have to walk up to get True Blue and, depending on how late he was, coming back down to the surgery might not be feasible.

"Just take the estate car and your emergency bag from the surgery. Then come back when you're finished." She shrugged, seeming unconcerned, but those lines came and went between her eyes. "We already agreed our secret is probably out. Would it matter terribly if we're completely out in the open about what's going on?"

"If I had time I'd come over there and kiss you for saying that." Cam was shrugging on his coat, bracing himself for the stiff breeze he knew was awaiting him outside. "Keys?"

"On the hook by the door," she replied, getting up. "And in case you were still wondering…"

When she opened her robe Cam froze, every sinew straining to go back to her. She was completely nude, her skin glowing with a natural golden-brown light that seemed to come from within. Her lush body, all soft curves and secret glorious places he loved to explore, was the epitome of everything he desired, all in plain sight.

"Just to maybe give you an incentive to come back," she said, a little smile coming and going across her face.

"I'll be as quick as I can," he choked out.

He forced himself to turn toward the door.

Wanting nothing more than to stay.

CHAPTER THIRTEEN

A STORM ROLLED through the following day, bringing a coating of snow that, to Harmony's mind, added the final touch to the Winter Festival scene. To her surprise, she was enjoying the season far more than she'd expected or even wanted to—probably because everyone seemed so determined to make her a part of things. On one hand, it was heartwarming. On the other, she sometimes viewed it as almost a betrayal of Mum and Gran, although she knew neither of them would want her feeling that way.

"Don't get attached," Katherine warned her as she stopped by the clinic in the early afternoon to drop off a package for Cam. "Snow never lasts long around here. Something to do with the sea currents and how fast the storms pass over."

Harmony was more intrigued by the package than the Eilean Rurie weather patterns.

"What's in here, Katherine? It smells divine."

The older woman shrugged and said, "I don't know. Just dropping it off for Dora. Probably something for up at the Manor."

Giving the package an appreciative sniff, Harmony got up to take it into Cam's office. "Darn it," she said. "I hope I can get him to share. It smells a lot like one of my gran's gizzadas."

"Your gran's what?"

"Gizzada. It's a little tart with coconut filling." Harmony paused in Cam's doorway to look back at Katherine. "I've been such a slug this year. If I'd thought of it I'd have ordered the ingredients and made some for you all."

"Well, too late now, I should think," Katherine said in her brisk way. "Unless you want desiccated coconut. There's always some of that around."

"No, that wouldn't work. You need real coconut—straight from the shell and grated."

"Good luck finding that anywhere around here," Katherine called. "I have to run. Make sure Cam gets that, please."

"Yes, ma'am," Harmony muttered to the sound of the closing door.

Katherine, of all the CIs, was the hardest to get to know. Both Sela and Ingrid had asked for her help during the Winter Festival, giving her an opportunity to get better acquainted with them. Katherine, however, seemed to be a mist-shrouded island of mystery in their midst.

Going back to her desk, she looked out at the little flakes still coming down, wondering how things were going with Cam. They'd had a guest with chest pains up at the Manor, and he hadn't checked in since he'd left to examine her. The good news was that she hadn't heard a rescue helicopter flying in, and nor had he called to tell her to prepare one of the beds upstairs.

Another bit of good news was that the backup medical team was on duty that night, so she and Cam could spend some uninterrupted time together. He'd suggested Angus Stewart's fir forest and she'd agreed, although staying in was appealing too. She was determined to spend as much quality time with Cam as possible, and they could talk freely when they were alone. Not to mention be intimate.

The burn he'd gone to look at the night before had turned out to be minor, but he'd still been annoyed when he got back.

"That family are the one problem this year," he'd complained. "We usually have at least one, but these people take the cake. I read them the riot act, as politely as I could, but if they don't shape up I'm asking them to leave. Gillian's so fed up she said she'd refund them their money just to be rid of them."

Harmony had commiserated, having seen the family in action at the fair. The two boys had relentlessly heckled one of the performers, while the parents had stood by, beers in hand, as though nothing was going on.

After that she'd taken Cam to bed, warming his chilled flesh with her own, loving him until he'd turned the tables on her, taking her to heights of pleasure she'd thought were only fantasies dreamt up by authors.

Cam MacRurie definitely knew his way around a woman's body—or at least around hers—but for her it wasn't all about the sex, and that was worrisome. Yes, it was definitely worth it—having a man who could give her intense, mind-blowing orgasms—but the flipside was the sense of closeness she felt with him, the comfort and emotional attachment that was beginning to grow. At least on her side.

In her head she knew he wasn't the man for her. In a short time the Winter Festival would be over and Cam would be going on his next adventure. Maybe even trying that insane winged suit freefall thing. Just the sight of it had made her blood run cold and then boil with anger. Knowing he endangered his life with those types of activities made her want to smack him silly.

She was totally convinced there was no place in her life for a man like that. All she had to do was keep reminding her heart of it and everything would work out fine.

Checking the time, she called her mum, who was probably about to get ready for work. Although Delilah Kinkaid had enough seniority to request one shift and stick to it, she still rotated with the rest of the nurses.

"Hello, love."

Her mother sounded bright, chipper in a way she hadn't in a while, and it made Harmony smile.

"Hi, Mum. It's snowing here."

"Ha! We've had rain, and they're saying that's probably all we'll get before Christmas."

"Yuck," Harmony replied, although up until today Eilean Rurie had been similar. "Are you looking forward to your vacation?"

"More so than ever," Mum answered.

She must be having a rough time at work to be so enthused.

"Day after tomorrow is my last shift, and then I'm off for two whole weeks."

"Good for you."

But, even understanding why her mum had chosen to go to Yorkshire, and not being in London herself, it still made Harmony sad to know they wouldn't be together at Christmas.

Snapping herself out of self-pity mode, she asked, "How's Fred?"

And then she got a good laugh, hearing about her mum making him take her to the ballet, after being given tickets by a friend who'd broken her leg and couldn't go. Her mum, like Gran before her, was a born storyteller, and the tale was all the funnier for her going back and forth between English and patois, interjecting Jamaican phrases into the conversation.

By the time they hung up Harmony was still chuckling, and over her brief lapse into the doldrums.

Cam came in just then, knocking the snow off his boots at the door, those amazing eyes trained on her the entire time.

"You were talking to your mum? How is she?"

Surprised, since he'd come in after she'd hung up, she asked, "She's fine—sounded much more cheerful. But how did you know I was talking to her?"

"You have a special glow after your calls with her." He went past her desk, his hands full with his medical bag and the portable EKG machine. "It's obvious how close the two of you are."

Harmony got up and followed Cam into the medical store room, talking as she went. "We *are* really close. It still feels weird to know we won't be together at Christmas, but I guess that's how life's supposed to go." Not wanting to fall back into depressing thoughts, she asked, "How's the patient?"

"No signs of myocardial infarction, and she's feeling a lot better, but I suggested she get her gall bladder function checked when she goes home, and in the meantime stick to foods she knows don't give her indigestion. Turns out she has a lot of food allergies."

He'd stored the EKG machine away while he spoke, and when he turned around and tugged Harmony into his arms she squeaked, surprised by the swift move. But as soon as she was in his arms she melted, her muscles going pliant, her heart-rate kicking up.

"Looking forward to tonight?" he asked, in between feathering kisses across her cheek.

"Mmm-hmm…" She sighed, tipping her head to the side so those talented lips could find her throat.

"Good," he murmured against her neck, making goosebumps fire up and down her back and arms, and her nipples tighten to ultra-sensitive peaks. "I thought we could have dinner at the Manor after, and you could stay over."

She stiffened, and he leaned back so he could see her face. When he lifted a finger to stroke between her brows she knew she'd been frowning.

His voice gentle, he said, "I thought we agreed it didn't make sense to hide our relationship? Have you changed your mind?"

She'd made a point not to go up to the Manor, and had never seen his part of it—all in an attempt to maintain at least a modicum of distance from the rest of his life. Yet she had agreed there was no need for the discretion they'd tried to maintain to this point, and refusing to go with him, to sleep in his bed for a change, seemed silly.

But she was still unsure. Did this signal a change in their relationship? A new facet that could add more complexity to the situation?

The expression on his face—so serious, almost hurt—had her pushing her reservations aside. And when she replied, "Knee-jerk reaction, I guess. Of course I'll go," his smile made her heart sing.

Cam forced himself to let Harmony go and guided her back to the main part of the office. He had a patient coming in at three o'clock, and she was due to go and do her wellness check on Delores Jacobson as soon as she'd checked that patient in.

He was tired. Run off his feet by the festival. But he was enjoying it more than ever before. Somehow having Harmony to share it with had brought back the joy of it, which had been lacking these last couple of years.

From the reception area he heard Harmony start singing along with the Christmas song playing on the audio system, and he leaned back, smiling.

How different she was from when he'd first started playing them, when her lips had pursed, her brows coming together in that frown of hers. He'd picked music she'd mentioned that her gran had liked—not because he wanted to remind her of her sorrows, but because he truly felt hearing those songs, remembering the good times, would help her heal. Maybe he'd got it right.

Suddenly noticing both the box on his desk and the mouthwatering scent coming from it, he called, "Harmony, what's this on my desk?"

The singing stopped and she came to stand in the doorway. "I don't know. Katherine dropped it off—said that Dora asked her to."

"Oh." He was itching to open it, but instead swiveled in his chair to put it on the shelf behind him. "I'll have to take it up to the Manor before we go out."

"What is it?" she asked.

"Just some baked goods for…"

Damn it. He'd been about to say they were for dinner that evening at the Manor but he'd invited her to eat there tonight, and he didn't want her to see what was in the package. Not yet.

Thinking quickly, he said, "For one of the guests. Dora promised to make something specific for him as a special commission."

"Okay." Her face fell. "I was hoping they were for you and I could share. That scent takes me back to my mum's kitchen."

"Sorry," he said. "Maybe we can ask Dora to make you some."

"What are they?"

"No clue," he answered, trying his best to look innocent, and not sure he'd achieved it when those little lines came and went between her brows.

Luckily, just then he heard the front door open, and Harmony went to greet his patient and check her in.

She left to see Delores while Carmen Henriques was still with him, and after seeing the young mother and her baby to the door he rushed back to open the box full of pastries.

The gizzadas looked just like the ones he'd seen online, but just to be sure he pulled up the page with the pictures and the recipe again.

Gizzada—also called Pinch-Me-Round, because of the way the shortcrust pastry is pinched to create the free-form tart base—is a Jamaican delicacy.

The filling of grated sweetened coconut, spiced with nutmeg, vanilla and a hint of ginger, has a soft consistency, in contrast to the firm yet flaky shell.

Okay, he'd have to see if Dora had managed to capture the taste, as well as the look.

"Oh, yes!" Cam mumbled through a mouthful of deliciousness. Even if Dora hadn't perfectly captured the Jamaican flavor, she'd definitely created something absolutely mouthwatering.

Hopefully Harmony would like the gizzadas, along with his other surprises, when Doris made them again on Christmas Eve.

Early on, he'd realized his main mission that year would be to make sure Harmony enjoyed Christmas and found again the joy the season could bring. But he'd had no idea how to go about it until inspiration had struck.

If they could incorporate some of the things she'd said she missed about the holidays into the Winter Festival, maybe it would not only soften her grief, but make her feel a part of everything.

Dora had been incensed, saying it was far too late to add anything more to the plethora of activities and tasks each of them had taken on. In the end he'd had to compromise, agreeing that they'd add some Jamaican treats and traditions into the Christmas Eve celebration, which would give them enough time to sort things out.

Since then Cam had been inundated with calls, mostly complaining about the difficulty in finding ingredients, but as always the CI's seemed to be coming through for him.

As he ate the last of the gizzadas, so as to leave no evidence for Harmony to find, he realized his obsession with Harmony was overtaking his life.

Part of him rebelled at the thought. Another wondered if it were so bad. Before long she'd be gone, and he'd be back to his happy, carefree life.

Somehow thinking that didn't make him feel any better.

CHAPTER FOURTEEN

ANGUS'S FARM WAS crowded when Cam and Harmony arrived, but with almost an acre of fields turned into a fantastical tree maze there was more than enough room for everyone. And because they'd waited, opting for a late dinner at the Manor, by the time they got there most of the families with little ones getting cranky and needing to be fed were getting ready to leave.

The temperature had fallen with the passing of the cloud cover, and snow still lay glistening on the branches, although it had been mostly trampled away underfoot. It gave the already beautiful scene a sublime sparkle, and Harmony felt her spirits soar just looking at it.

Angus waved them through the makeshift turnstile with a grin. "Good to see you, Laird and Lady. Enjoy your ramble."

Harmony blushed to hear herself described that way, but thankfully she was too bundled up for it to be noticeable. And when Cam took her gloved hand in his she was tempted to tug it away again, but restrained herself.

"Are you warm enough?" he asked.

"Yes, thank you," she replied, sounding rather prim even to her own ears.

But her stiffness evaporated under the spell of the tree maze.

It was like walking through a fairytale, and all the children seemed to feel it. Although some of them ran hither and yon, it was with the joyous abandon of puppies, and with a minimum of noise, as though they instinctively knew that too much clamor would spoil the experience. Others were content to wander with their parents, looking at the lights, trying to find their way to the center.

The scent of the firs was divine, and even with the lights she could see constellations of stars in the cold, dark sky. Some of the trees had ornaments on them, adding to their beauty.

Cam released her hand to loop his arm over her shoulder, and being tucked up against his side perfected the experience.

They didn't talk much, just the occasional, "Oops, back we go," or, "Look at that," when a particularly beautiful tree came into view, and she appreciated the lack of chatter. There were some things in life best experienced in reverent quiet.

Angus had followed the theme of Love, so most of the decorated trees had heart ornaments on them, and one in particular caught and held her attention. The ornaments on it were all rustic hearts, made from wood, or wire, in old-fashioned fabrics such as gingham, or of tin.

It brought to mind the little red felt heart Cam had slipped into his pocket and made her wonder what he'd eventually done with it. Had he hung it on the tree at the Manor, where it had had pride of place for years? She was tempted to ask him about it, but didn't.

These last few days she'd found herself weighing the intimacy of everything she did, said, or asked, holding back as best she could, not wanting to open up any more to him than she already had. Nor to have him do the same with her, knowing it wouldn't take much for her to fall completely in love with Cam.

In many respects he was perfect: thoughtful, kind, respectful of her opinions and her wishes. His lack of arrogance was refreshing, especially since Harmony felt there was much he could be arrogant about. Being nominal Laird of Eilean Rurie could have certainly gone to his head, but it hadn't. There weren't that many men she knew who'd handle the situation as calmly and democratically as Cam did.

Heck, she'd worked with doctors who'd thought because of their profession they should be worshiped. Cam was both Laird *and* doctor, but he didn't put on airs because of it.

The laughter they shared was the icing on a rich and delicious cake. Even when they were making love it felt joyous, free and right. It was a whole new experience for her, and one she knew she'd miss terribly when it was all over.

And it would be over all too soon—because in the end Cam MacRurie was too scary a proposition. His daredevil ways, his need for a stronger and stronger adrenaline rush, would one day end in disaster, and she was determined not to be around to witness it. She'd had enough tragedy and upheaval in her life that she would not put herself into that kind of situation.

So, even if Cam were inclined to want her to stay longer, she'd have to say no and go back to London—even though Eilean Rurie had sneakily, quietly, snuck its way into her heart. Much as its Laird seemed set to do.

"Here we are," he said softly, breaking her out of her reverie as they rounded a corner to the center of the maze.

Harmony gasped, enchanted all over again. "How lovely!"

There was a gazebo entwined with greenery and thousands of fairy lights, red bows and hearts artistically placed throughout. It was a place to sit and dream, to soak in the spirit of Christmas.

Cam guided her forward to it, bringing her to a halt just beneath the first crossbeam.

"Look up," he said softly.

She did, and realized he'd stopped her under a kissing ball made of mistletoe.

"Cameron…" It was a warning, even as her heart beat a suddenly frantic tattoo against her ribs.

But he just smiled, and said, "Tradition can't be denied, Harmony. It's bad luck if you do."

"I've never heard that before—"

He stopped her protest with his lips, and she'd never been happier to be silenced, melting into his embrace, his kiss.

Yet it wasn't a passionate one. Instead there was a tenderness to it she almost couldn't bear. His closed lips moved over hers so sweetly it made her want to cry. If a kiss could be a prayer, or a benediction, this was what it would feel like.

Wanting nothing more than to sink into it and never have it end, instead she gently pulled away—just as a family came around the corner and the children's exclamations broke the mood.

A little dazed, she asked, "Where are these Cailleach logs you were telling me about?"

Anything not to think about how that chaste, glorious kiss had shaken her previously solid foundations.

"Over there." He pointed to where a lean-to had been set up to keep the wood dry.

Easing out of his arms, she went to investigate them, Cam following slowly behind. They were strangely beautiful, the faces roughly hewn, but with a haunting quality Harmony appreciated. Cailleach was portrayed on some as old, careworn—winter personified—in others as younger, yet still mature, with wisdom and promise in her knowing gaze.

"Angus and his sons carve them all through the year, but this year I wonder if they'll have enough," Cam murmured, as though also somehow under the spell of all those wooden eyes looking up at them. "Our visitor count is up tremendously."

She wasn't surprised. Everything about the Winter Festival had surpassed her expectations, and the residents of Eilean Rurie put their all into making it amazing and fun.

"Pick one," Cam said, then reached out and took the very one she'd had her eye on.

Harmony didn't tell him that, though. It was the kind of moment best left to pass unremarked, showing as it did another albeit small similarity between them. Another intersecting point.

After she'd made her choice, and Cam had picked a couple of rowan branches, they went back through the maze to the bonfire. There Harmony contemplated the reds, yellows and blues of the flames for a moment, feeling a sense of destiny mixed with melancholy taking over her spirit. Funny how before she'd come to the island she'd considered herself supremely practical—all business. But here she was discovering new depths of emotion, a strange connectivity.

She smoothed her fingers over her Cailleach's face, and then tossed the small log into the flames. The knowing gaze seemed to glow for a moment, and then it was consumed.

Perhaps it was the beauty of the night, or the sense of having undergone a kind of spiritual shaking, but Harmony was left feeling on edge. As though the Cailleach had tried to warn her that not all efforts to banish the darkness actually worked.

There was a commotion near the refreshment tent, and they both turned to look just as Angus came barreling through the crowd toward them.

"You're needed, Cam," he said, looking shaken, his eyes wide. "We have a medical emergency."

Cam rushed off with Angus, and Harmony took off at a run to the car, to fetch their medical bags, her heart hammering as she wondered what she'd find when she got back.

And ruing, just a little, the interruption of their peaceful, lovely night together.

The patient was a young boy, perhaps two or three, who was lying unresponsive in his mother's arms.

When Cam tried to take him from her she hugged him tighter, turning away and shouting, "No, don't touch him. Don't touch him!"

"I'm Dr. MacRurie—"

But the woman wasn't listening, just screaming and crying, clutching her son to her chest. Even with all that Cam could see the little boy's chest heaving as he obviously labored to get air into his lungs.

A quick look around didn't find anyone who looked as though they were with the woman, and Cam was momentarily at a loss as to how to proceed.

According to Angus, the woman had suddenly cried out, saying her son had collapsed. When Angus had looked at him it had appeared the little boy's face was exceptionally red, but he hadn't seen any sign of seizing. Angus's youngest daughter had epilepsy, so he was familiar with what seizures looked like, but until Cam had a chance to examine the little boy he couldn't rule anything out.

Turning to Angus, who was hovering behind him, Cam

said, "Call out the medical team. Tell them we need the ambulance, stat. And get me some warm blankets."

"Take him into the house if you can," Angus said, before hurrying away.

Cam stooped down close to the mother, trying to get her attention. "Your son needs medical attention. I'm a doctor. Let me help him."

But it was clear she wasn't listening. All she did was moan and rock back and forth.

Suddenly Harmony was there. Putting down the medical bags, she knelt in front of the woman and took her face between her palms.

"Shh…" she said. "Hush, now. We're here to help your son."

Surprisingly, the woman quieted, although she didn't release her convulsive grip on her child.

"What's his name?" Harmony asked, holding the mother's gaze.

"C-C-Cameron," she stuttered, tears still flowing down her cheeks.

"Well, would you believe me if I told you that's Dr. MacRurie's name too? Let Cam take a look at your Cameron, okay?"

As she spoke Harmony released the woman's cheeks and slowly reached for the little boy. Cam held his breath, waiting to see if she'd succeed in getting the mother to surrender the child. In the back of his mind he knew the clock was ticking. Depending on what was going on with the little boy, time could very much be of the essence. The delay chafed.

There was a collective sigh of relief from the crowd that had gathered nearby when they saw Harmony ease the child from his mother's arms.

"Take him inside," Cam said. Then, to the mother, "Come with us."

He didn't wait to see if she complied, taking off after Harmony as she ran toward the nearby house.

Once inside, she lay the little boy on the kitchen table, swiftly beginning to unzip his little parka, undressing him so Cam could do a comprehensive examination.

"Appearance of urticaria on his face and neck," she said as she worked. "And angioedema of the lips. Some sign of urticarial spreading to the chest and arms."

Cam had out his stethoscope and was listening to the child's chest. "Dyspnea and wheezing present," he replied.

The mother had come in behind them, hoarse sobs breaking from her throat as she watched them.

"I'm going to check his tongue and throat," said Cam.

Harmony had already taken out a tongue depressor and silently handed it to him, before tilting young Cameron's head back so he could get a good view.

But there was little room in the poor little fellow's mouth. His tongue was swollen and Cam knew they had to act quickly.

"Epinephrine—point one mil," he said, and watched as Harmony found the auto-injector and dialed in the amount. When she handed it to him he quickly injected the little boy in his thigh. Then he balled up a blanket and elevated Cameron's legs.

"Do you want to give him a dose of diphenhydramine also?"

Cam shook his head. "Not yet."

He was watching little Cameron, listening once more with his stethoscope to see if the wheezing began to lessen. When it did, he took the stethoscope out of his ears and made another visual inspection, noting the rash was receding and that two bright brown eyes were now looking up at him in some dismay.

"Mum, come and reassure Cameron that everything is okay," he said, waving the mother over, hoping she wouldn't upset her son more than necessary—which no doubt would happen if she started wailing again.

He heard the sound of the ambulance coming and looked across at Harmony. She was stroking the little boy's hair, speaking to him and his mother in soft, soothing tones.

Cam touched the mother's arm lightly, and she turned tear-filled eyes his way. "Your son has suffered anaphylaxis," he explained. "A severe allergic reaction. Does he have any known allergies?"

"No. None," she said, her eyes widening.

"Do you remember him eating anything unusual just before he went down?"

She shook her head. "No… We went through the maze, and he was running around as usual. We'd just come back to the tent and I was about to buy him something to eat when he collapsed."

"I think I might have an idea," Harmony said quietly.

When Cam looked at her she was holding up a tiny piece of fir.

"I did a mouth-sweep, just in case. This is what I found."

"Oh, Cameron!" his mother said, before breaking down into tears again.

CHAPTER FIFTEEN

THE NEXT FEW days were a blur of activity. With less than a week before the Christmas Eve Gala Cam was kept hopping, while Harmony held down the fort at the clinic. The medical team from the mainland, who usually alternated with Cam for the evening shift, was now put on call all day, in case Cam was on the other side of the island when someone needed attention.

For the most part, however, there wasn't much Harmony couldn't manage. There were some headaches, a few minor lacerations and some wonky tummies—usually from an overconsumption of sweets. Nothing else, thank goodness, as heart-stopping as the emergency at Angus's farm.

The weather had held, with the storm the meteorologists had earlier predicted blowing away to the north, but another one was due the next day, with wind and snow, followed by colder temperatures. Cam and all the organizers were rushing around, trying to secure the tents many of the vendors used to ensure the wind gusts didn't cause too much havoc.

She missed having Cam around all the time in the clinic, singing off-key, being annoyed because she'd rearranged some cupboard or filing system. Mind you, he'd been a lot better about those things once he'd realized she'd actually improved efficiency. When she'd first arrived she'd seen his instinctive protective reaction, but had forged ahead anyway.

Her next suggestion would be for a really decent computer system, but she had a feeling he'd balk when faced with hiring a data entry firm to deal with all the older records. Although, in reality, there weren't that many people in residence. She could probably manage to input the information herself, in between patients.

Harmony drew herself up, shaking her head at the thought. She wasn't going to be here long enough for that and, depending on the reliability and precision of his new hire, he might not want him or her to take on the job.

The one constant in this busy time was sharing the nights with Cam. Whether he picked her up and she stayed at the Manor, or he came and crashed in her apartment, they were together. It worried her how often she awoke in the night and reached out to touch him, as though needing the reassurance of his presence before being able to go back to sleep. Or how waking up in the mornings and having his arm around her gave her a sense of comfort and joy.

Good grief, now she was even starting to think in Christmas lyrics. And, worse, realizing it had created an earworm, so "God Rest Ye Merry, Gentlemen" played in her head on repeat for the rest of the day.

She was going to meet Cam up at the Manor that evening, but he called to let her know he was running a little late and would pick her up. For an instant she thought about telling him she'd stay alone in the apartment that night instead, but she felt a sense of the clock ticking the moments she'd have with him away.

Surely she could plan and execute a slow, steady withdrawal in January, leading up to her departure instead? So she agreed. And that night, as he made slow, lingering love to her, Harmony let the thought of leaving drift away, so as not to allow it to taint the pleasure of being in his arms.

The next morning she was in the kitchen, mixing the ingredients for quick pancakes together, when Cam came out of the bedroom, his diabetes kit in hand.

"Is that bacon I smell?" he asked, coming around to kiss the side of her neck. "Yum!"

She'd been up for a while, but knowing how busy he'd been had let him sleep awhile more.

"And pancakes to go with it. Won't take me more than a few minutes," she replied, just as his phone rang.

"Sounds amazing." He was already heading for the phone, which he'd left on the coffee table, and spoke over his shoulder. Picking it up, he answered, "Yes, Angus, what can I do for you?"

Then Harmony saw his face change, grow stern and angry, and when he let out a curse she instinctively turned off the flames under the half-cooked bacon and pushed the pan off the burner.

"I'll be right there," he said, putting down his kit and heading for the utility room behind the kitchen.

"What's going on?"

"Two children apparently went out to the old fishing village last night when the tide was out."

She went to stand in the doorway, watching him pull out his wetsuit and a bunch of harnesses with ropes attached.

"They must have fallen asleep in the old rescue station and by the time they woke up the tide was coming in. The older one made it back, but the younger is still out there. Angus says he's sure they were drinking."

"Did anyone call for the Coast Guard?" she asked, hoping to hear they had and that they were on their way. That Cam wouldn't have to do what she was sure he was planning to do.

"Yes, but it'll take them a while to get here. If the boys have been out all night they could have hypothermia, and we need to get that youngest one off there before the tide comes all the way in. It's the pair from Gillian Strom's place and the mother says the youngster's not a strong swimmer."

He was coming out, laden with gear, and she stepped back to give him room to put them down by the door. Then he took off at a run for the bedroom.

Harmony stood there, frozen for a moment, panic making her insides churn, fogging her brain. All she could think of was Cam going into the rough water which, raging with the tide and incoming storm, would suck him away. Every bit of her turned cold, as icy as the sea he was planning on fighting.

Then common sense took hold, and she hurried into the kitchen to grab a couple of protein bars and a bag of dried apricots she'd spied in the cupboard. Dropping them into her bag, she rushed back to the front hall to pull on her boots and jacket.

When Cam came out of the bedroom, she called out, "Take your levels before you go."

He didn't even look at her, just snapped, "I'm fine. Don't fuss."

"But—"

The look he gave her as he tugged on a jacket, made her turn to ice again. "There's no time and I'm fine. I don't need you to tell me what to do, Harmony."

As soon as the words had left his mouth Cam regretted them. Not just because what she was suggesting was wise, and the right thing to do, nor because it was a reminder he actually needed. No, it was the way Harmony's face paled, and her eyes widened and gleamed green with hurt.

Before he could say anything her face tightened, and her brows drew together as she said, "Don't be an ass, Cameron. You can't save anyone if you're in distress yourself. So I'll drive. You can take your levels and at least eat something. I've got a couple of protein bars and some dried fruit ready to go."

"You can't drive True Blue," he said, trying to figure out how to do what he needed to and still get out to the fishing village as quickly as possible.

Harmony just made a rude noise and pushed past him to grab his diabetes kit. At the door she picked up his medical bag, her bag, and his car keys. Then, as she went out, she said, "You're the one who's in such a damned hurry, so let's go."

By the time he got the gear stowed in the back of the vehicle she had it running. He'd heard her cursing under her breath as she tried to adjust the seat, which hadn't been moved in God only knew how long, but when he got in she was belted in and seemed ready. The determined look on her face would have amused him at any other time—but not today, with so much on the line.

Cam watched Harmony struggle for a moment with the clutch, which was stiff, and the gear lever, which was misaligned.

"I'll drive," he said, impatience taking over.

The look she sent him should have incinerated him on the spot, and without a word she slammed the vehicle into gear.

As they took off along the Manor driveway, Harmony blew the horn to get the early risers ambling around out of her way, and Cam fought his very real inclination to ignore the snacks on the seat between them and the kit on his lap.

She was right. And he knew it.

Who would be helped by his being stubborn and stupid

about his disease the way he had been as a child, when he'd hide from his mother when he knew it was time to test his blood or eat a snack? She'd used to tell people he didn't like the needles, but that hadn't been true. What he had hated was the way her over-solicitous care had made him feel—as though he had no control, wasn't able to have a normal life.

He'd gotten past all that with his grandfather's help, but now he realized the residual effect of his early years clung to him like an old, foul coat. Yet in a flash he knew Harmony wasn't like that. She'd made no mention of his diabetes since the first day she'd found out—never asked about his levels, or whether it was time to take them. Instead she'd clearly taken his word that he knew how to manage the disease.

Grabbing one of the protein bars, he tore the wrapper open and stuffed half of it into his mouth. As he chewed, he debated the necessity of taking his levels, and decided getting some food into his system was more important. He rarely suffered the "dawn phenomena," when his blood sugar spiked on waking, and didn't see why it should happen today of all days.

He finished the rest of the bar before saying, "I'll test my levels before going into the water, okay?"

Cam wanted her to know he understood what she'd said, and that he agreed, but when she only grunted in reply he felt his heart sink. Exactly when her good graces had become so important to him Cam wasn't sure. Moreover, when she'd become such an integral and necessary part of his life was an unknown too—but she was just that.

He'd fallen for her—all the way. For her charm and kindness, her spunky spirit and practical nature. Even for the fear in her eyes when she'd realized what he was about to do, which showed her concern for him. All of it.

The knowledge stole his breath, making his already racing heart skip a beat. The urge to blurt it out to her almost overtook his common sense, and he stuffed part of another bar into his mouth to stop it coming out.

This wasn't the time or the place. Besides, right now the distraction of thinking about what he was going to do, and if there was any hope for a deeper relationship, could be fatal. Pushing it all aside was one of the hardest thing he'd ever do, but he tried anyway.

By the time they got to the shore near the old fishing village he'd managed to eat both protein bars and a handful of apricots, and he made an effort to check how he felt. Sometimes he could feel the subtle signals his body sent, telling him his levels were high or low, but right then all he could feel was the surge of adrenaline.

As they pulled up behind Angus's vehicle he heard Harmony gasp—no doubt at her first sight of what they faced to rescue the boy.

Although the derelict rescue station was still above the waterline, waves were breaking high upon it, spray flying to the seaward side, water swirling and frothing in strong eddies on the landward.

Cam, from experience, knew the path to get from the shore to where the boy lay, curled on his side on what was left of the station, wouldn't be easy. Debris and obstacles stuck up through the sand the entire way, but it was a place he'd explored many times over the years, and he felt no trepidation about the rescue.

Angus came over as soon as they'd got out of the vehicle, and followed as Cam went to the back to get his wetsuit.

"Annie Howell was going out to tend her sheep when she saw the older one crawling out of the water and heard the younger one crying for help. Lucky for them she had phone signal and called me."

Cam was already stripping down to his briefs. "Why didn't she call me right off?" he asked. Even a few minutes could make the difference between the tide engulfing the child or not.

"I'm closer—and she thought we could use the boat and get him. Once I got here and realized the tide was too low I immediately called you. I sent the older boy back to Gillian's, where I understand he's puking his guts out in between fits of shivering. From the smell of him, he got into some whisky. He's a fairly good swimmer, his mum said, but his brother isn't—which is probably why he didn't try to make for shore with the older one."

"Damn it," Cam said. It had become even more imperative to get to the younger child now, who not only could be suffering from hypothermia but alcohol poisoning, as well. "Does anyone know how long they were out there?"

Angus shook his head. "The tide turned at three thirty this morning, and wouldn't have started covering the sandbar until about five. I'm thinking they spent the night out there—or at least went out after their parents were sleeping."

Cam was in his wetsuit, reaching for his gloves, when he felt a touch on his arm.

Harmony held out a lancet to prick his finger, her expression stern, unyielding. Without comment he stuck out his hand, and she collected the sample on the test paper, turning away to where she'd placed the glucometer on the car bumper.

Cam pulled out the harnesses and Angus helped him to unwrap them, the two men discussing the best way to rescue the boy. Harmony walked away with his kit and Cam knew, with a sense of relief, that meant his blood sugar levels were good.

From then on it was all business. Angus and his son Colin secured the lines, while Cam got into a life vest and one of the harnesses, attaching another set to a ring on the vest with a carabiner.

Once he'd checked everything was in place to his satisfaction, Cam said to Angus, "Make sure the Coast Guard helicopter is coming. I'm sending this child to Skye for treatment once he's on shore."

Then, with a quick look for Harmony, who was nowhere to be seen, he went into the water, all his concentration on avoiding getting swept away or gored by debris.

CHAPTER SIXTEEN

HARMONY WAS BACK at True Blue, getting out the warming blankets and anything else she thought they might need when Cam came back with the child. She'd not been able to just stand there and watch him go into the water. She had wanted to tell him not to, to wait for the Coast Guard, but knew it would have been no use.

Cameron MacRurie was not only a doctor intent on saving a patient, but the kind of man who thrived on pitting himself against nature. It would have been impossible to stop him.

Yet even as she told herself she wouldn't look Harmony couldn't help it, constantly checking over her shoulder to follow Cam's progress as she tossed a couple of towels onto the back seat, hoping they'd be needed. That the sea wouldn't swallow Cam whole.

She'd allowed him to tempt her into an affair which had now become so much more. It was her fault that the fear she felt for him was so overpowering—a byproduct of the feelings she'd let grow inside. For all she'd told herself it would be a fun fling, she now had to accept that the emotions she felt as she watched him battle the frothing tide had little to do with sex.

No. She'd let herself fall for him, even knowing where that would lead. There was no one to blame but herself.

Annie Howell came over and offered Harmony a steaming cup of coffee, which she took with thanks.

"Don't worry about the Laird," she said, using her chin to gesture toward the water. "He knows these waters better than almost anyone else, and he's trained in water rescue too. He wouldn't go in if he didn't think he could get to the bairn and bring him back safely."

Yes, he would, Harmony thought sourly. Even if he thought it too dangerous, he'd die trying.

She was still hurt by his reaction earlier, when she'd tried to get him to take his levels before they left the Manor. His response had been completely out of character, and over the top too. Yet her fear overrode all of that, leaving her shaken and cold.

There was a shout from the crowd around the shore, and Harmony spun toward it in time to see Cam clinging with one hand to a piece of wood sticking out of the water, clearly fighting to keep from being swept away. When he grabbed it with his other hand and seemed to get his feet back under him she realized she could breathe again.

"Almost there now," Annie said in a calm voice, but Harmony heard the undercurrent of worry.

Cam was trailing a rope, which was secured to the shore, but even so, if the tide caught him and they had to drag him back, he could get injured.

He got to the platform and heaved himself up onto it. Harmony could see him examining the boy who, after a moment, struggled into a seated position. Cam put on the child's life jacket, attaching it to his own before swinging his feet over the side and pulling the child into his lap.

This was the dangerous part. Harmony could hear the child's screams of fear, saw his legs flailing as Cam pushed back into the water.

How he found the bottom was something Harmony

didn't understand. She realized she had her fist tight to her mouth, her teeth digging into her knuckles, but she couldn't help it as she watched Cam's torturous, inch-by-inch progress back to shore. Angus and Colin, and Martin Harris, who'd arrived to help, kept the rope taut, winching it in.

Cam and his burden were near shore when Harmony was snapped out of her horrid fascination by the sound of an approaching helicopter. Picking up the warming blankets, she trotted down to the shoreline, so as to be there when Cam and the boy were heaved back onto dry land.

In the background she heard a commotion, but didn't pay it any mind, too intent on watching Cam make the last few agonizing steps through the breakers, and Angus wading in to help him carry the child up onto the shore.

Feigning a calm she didn't at all feel, Harmony rushed forward with the blankets as Cam unhooked the carabiner that was keeping the boy lashed to him. Quickly wrapping the child in the blanket, she held out her arms for him, but Angus was already carrying him toward where the helicopter team was coming along the road from where they'd landed. They had a stretcher with them, and Angus surrendered the child to them as Cam sank down onto the rough grass at the edge of the loch, panting.

Harmony draped the other blanket around his shoulders and he looked up to nod, give her a little smile. But she didn't have it in her to return it, her insides still churning with the tension engendered by what she'd just witnessed. She reached out to grip his shoulder, as though needing touch to reassure herself that he was there, still alive, in front of her, and he turned his head to kiss her fingers.

"That was a workout," he said, between gasps of air.

Harmony watched the rescue team going back up the road, the child's father with them. "What condition was he in?" she asked.

"Freezing cold, but with enough fight left in him to almost drown me on the way back," Cam answered, but his humor fell flat.

Angus came back over and stooped down beside Cam. "The Coast Guard is flying him to Skye and his dad is going with him."

"I'm going to go too," Cam answered. "Just to make sure he's okay. I should make a report, too, since we had to call out the rescue copter. Do you have time to take me over, Angus? I can wait for the ferry if you can't."

"Get you home to warm up and let me know when you're ready. I'll have the boat waiting," Angus replied immediately.

That news seemed to give Cam back the energy he'd expended on the rescue, and he heaved himself to his feet to take off the harness and hand it to Martin, who was collecting up the equipment.

Harmony surreptitiously checked Cam out for injuries, dropping behind him a bit as he strode toward the car. Then she was beside him in a flash, her heart rushing as she grabbed his arm.

"You're hurt."

He sent her a sideways glance, the edge of his mouth kicking up in a slight grimace. "Yeah. Caught the edge of something when that rogue wave knocked me off my feet. Tore my wetsuit."

Harmony let go his arm, staring at him for a long moment before turning back toward the vehicle. Here she was, fretting because he'd cut open his calf, and he was worried about his damn wetsuit! She strode off, leaving him to follow.

Cam stood on the passenger side of the vehicle with Angus as Harmony got in and started True Blue, hoping that when she cranked up the heat the old girl wouldn't expire. Martin and Colin had brought the ropes and harnesses to stow in the back, and through the window Harmony saw Cam twist, as though looking at the laceration on his leg. She'd have offered to put a pad on it at least, until they got back to the Manor and she could examine it properly, but his reaction earlier made her reluctant.

He was the doctor, after all, she thought a little sourly. If he wanted a bandage on it he would do it himself.

Cam finally parted with Angus and got in, still in the wetsuit, and Harmony reached into the backseat for the towels she'd stowed there. Then she jammed the vehicle into gear and drove a little way down the road to turn around.

"Well, that went as well as could be expected," he said. "Although Angus believes the father may try to cause some problems. I'll have to see which way the wind is blowing when I get to Skye."

She was coming down off the frightening high, suddenly exhausted, hardly able to think properly. All she could do was concentrate on not crashing True Blue on the narrow island roads.

"What kind of trouble?"

"Oh, he was quick to deny that his kids had been drinking, and he said something about how dangerous the old station was."

"But it's fenced off—and clearly marked with 'No Trespassing' signs." Outrage superseded her exhaustion for a moment and her fingers tightened around the steering wheel. "And how ungrateful could he be? When you went out there after that child…got injured rescuing him."

"Don't get upset," he said quietly. "I'll deal with whatever happens. And it's just a scratch, Harmony. I've gotten worse injuries doing far less important things."

No doubt he meant all his crazy pastimes. She didn't

answer, knowing that to do so would probably precipitate a fight. One she had no business picking with him, since theirs wasn't that kind of relationship. Just because she'd realized she loved him it didn't mean she had the right to question his life choices—especially since she knew there was no happy ending for them.

Cam MacRurie was far too dangerous a proposition for her, and if she'd only thought that before, now, after watching him put himself in harm's way and get hurt doing it, she knew it for a fact.

"And," he added quietly, "I need to apologize for what happened earlier, when you told me to take my levels before we left. I was out of line, the way I reacted, and I'm sorry."

"There's no need—"

"There's every need, Harmony, especially as you were right and doing nothing more than looking out for me. I guess I'm just used to going my own way, doing my own thing, without anyone questioning me. And I saw how scared you were, knowing I was going to do a sea rescue."

"That's fine," she said, knowing she was being curt, but not knowing how else to react. The pain of loving him and knowing she could never trust him to keep himself safe was too much to deal with right now. The urge to rage at him was strong, but she had her pride, and that had her saying, "I never told you not to go after that boy, did I?"

"No, you didn't, and I appreciate it." He sighed, but the air stuttered out of his lungs, and her quick glance caught him shivering. "I've always been the adventurous type, even as a kid, but my mother had a hard time with the fact of my having diabetes, and did everything she could to curb anything she thought was too dangerous. My grandfather, by teaching me how to manage my disease, set me free, and once I was old enough I let rip at whatever caught my fancy. I love the exhilaration of pitting myself against nature, or even against my own limitations. It makes me feel alive."

She pulled up at his private entrance to the Manor and engaged the handbrake before switching off the ignition and turning to him. His teeth were chattering.

"Go inside, Cam. Let's get you warmed up."

He reached out from beneath the towel he'd draped over his shoulders to grip her wrist, arresting her as she was opening her door.

"I need to know that you understand why I snapped at you earlier and forgive me."

Knowing he wouldn't move until she answered, Harmony said, "Yes, I forgive you—but I can't promise not to say anything if a similar situation arises. It's the way I am, and I can't change that."

His look of relief was immediate, and he leaned over to press his chilled lips to hers.

"I'm not asking you to change, Harmony," he said, thankfully releasing her and reaching to let himself out of the vehicle. "I just need you to understand."

And she did understand—perhaps all too well.

After setting a lukewarm shower, and helping him out of the wetsuit so he could get in and warm up, she ruminated on his words. Everything he'd said echoed within her, bringing back conversations she'd had with her mother about her dad.

"I think he took risks to prove something to the army after they rejected him over his heart defect," her mum had said, and the sadness and anger in her voice was still fresh all these years later. "It were as though he was driven to go after that high of surviving when they told him he wasn't fit to do what they needed him to."

Her dad had driven race cars and motorcycles. Then

he'd done skydiving, trying for lower and lower jumps, or longer freefalls. Eventually it had been climbing. He'd been working toward free-climbing when he'd died.

The friends her mum was still in contact with all called him by his old nickname "Risky Ricky" when they spoke about him, telling stories about his daredevil ways. Mum laughed along with them, but Harmony had seen the lingering pain in her eyes.

It wasn't hard to see the correlation between her father's need to prove himself and Cam's drive for adventure. Had his mother's overprotective behavior done the opposite of what she'd wanted? Pushed Cam to prove that, despite his diabetes, he could do whatever anyone else did, no matter how dangerous?

The whole situation was overwhelming and, coupled with the fright she'd just had, made her teary-eyed.

She couldn't go through what her mum had—didn't want to put herself in a situation where she lost the man she loved because of his recklessness and need for another adrenaline rush. It cemented her determination to distance herself from Cam as soon as possible, before leaving him became harder than it already was.

Somehow seeing that deep laceration on Cam's leg just made it worse. She wanted to dress it, to tell him compulsively to keep an eye on it, but held her tongue. He didn't want her fussing—he'd made that clear. So she just kept a weather eye on him while he took care of it himself, aching inside with the worry of infection and the slow healing so dangerous to diabetics.

Once he'd left to go to Skye, promising to let her know when he'd be back, she pulled out her laptop and started looking through job search sites, trying to find her replacement. Knowing that the sooner Cam hired someone new, the sooner she could leave.

CHAPTER SEVENTEEN

CAM STAYED ON Skye overnight, making sure the young boy was recovering from his ordeal and doing everything necessary to report the incident properly. It kept him busy, and he didn't get back to Eilean Rurie until the evening of December twenty-third.

The preparations for the Christmas Eve Gala were in high gear, with everyone rushing about trying to put the finishing touches to the church hall, where it would be held, but when Harmony had offered her help it had been refused.

"Too many people barging about in there as it is," Katherine had told her the afternoon after Cam had left for Skye, when she'd stopped by the clinic.

Although it was a Sunday, Harmony had opened up the clinic in case of emergency. After all, she hadn't had anything better to do with Cam gone.

"You're better off staying out of it."

"Whatever happened to 'many hands make light work'?" Harmony had asked, amused by the other woman's sour tone.

"That went out the window about three days ago," had been the crisp response. "If you really want to help, come by my place later and help me make clootie pudding."

Knowing the other woman's reputation for efficiency,

Harmony hadn't bought it. "You don't really need my help, do you?"

"No, I don't—but I could use the company. I hate baking, but this year I ended up on the list to make the puddings and I don't want to. At least having company will make it less painful."

So she'd spent the evening at Katherine's, discovering much more about the other woman than she'd dreamed possible, considering how closemouthed Katherine usually was. She'd spoken about her childhood in Bristol, and how her father hadn't believed in education for women.

"I left home at sixteen, and put myself through university. He didn't understand my ability with numbers and thought I was wasting time and money becoming an accountant. Apparently, I should have been married and having children instead."

It was toward the end of the evening. They'd finished cleaning up the kitchen and the puddings had been boiling. Wine had been poured and they'd settled into comfortable chairs in the living room.

"How on earth did you end up here?" Harmony had asked.

The last part of the story had been about some of the fun times the older woman had had, living in Southampton in the nineteen-seventies.

"I came here originally as bookkeeper at the Manor." She'd smiled slightly—a rueful twist of her lips. "I saw the ad in a newspaper and on a whim applied. I was adventurous back then, and I thought it would look good on my résumé too. I had an idea that one day I'd go to Australia to live, and I knew the more work experience I had, the better."

Harmony had believed she knew what had happened next. "You fell in love with the island and never left?"

Katherine had given her a sharp glance, and then looked down at her wine glass for a moment. "No," she'd replied, lifting her gaze to meet Harmony's. "I fell in love with the Laird."

Surprise had arrested Harmony's hand, so her wine glass hovered halfway to her lips.

"Not *your* Laird, of course," Katherine had continued. "The old Laird—Cameron's grandfather. He was a wonderful man, as handsome as could be, and I fell head over heels. He'd been a widower for a few years by then, and although everyone knew he was still grieving I thought eventually he'd be ready to move on."

She'd fallen silent, her gaze going to the fireplace, her eyes getting a faraway look, as though she were revisiting the past in her mind. Not knowing what to say, Harmony had waited, wondering how the story had turned out.

"He never did get there," Katherine said. "And I wasn't the type to throw myself at him—to let him know how I felt. Instead I just stayed, became his friend, did whatever I could to protect him and look after him. Sometimes… Sometimes I wonder if things would have been different if I'd told him…"

Before Harmony had been able to comment Katherine had stirred, her gaze sharpening. "Some men only have room in their hearts for one woman, and the old Laird was just that type. I still believe I would have had to leave out of embarrassment or a sense of self-preservation if he'd realized how I felt, and I'd rather have had all those years of friendship with him than not. Life is full of hard choices, and I stand by mine."

Knowing Katherine wouldn't want sympathy, Harmony had just nodded. But inside she'd ached for the other woman, who'd perhaps missed her chance at love because she'd not had the courage to say how she felt.

"I was here when Cameron came to live with his grandfather. The old Laird was so worried about him… Cameron was an angry young man, sullen and withdrawn."

"Cam?" Impossible to reconcile the man she knew with a description like that.

"Oh, yes. His grandfather asked me, 'If I don't help him what kind of life will he have?'"

"Cam said his grandfather set him free." Harmony hadn't wanted to go into what he'd said about his mother, but knew Katherine would appreciate the knowledge that Cam understood what his grand-da had done.

The other woman had smiled and nodded. "It wasn't easy for Douglas. He of all people knew how dangerous Cameron's diabetes could be, but he was determined to help his grandson accept the disease and learn how to manage it. He fretted constantly as he watched Cameron gain confidence and become the rambunctious boy he was meant to be, but he knew he had to give the boy the independence he needed."

The conversation had stuck with Harmony, still running through her head later that night, as she'd lain in bed, unable to sleep.

Cam was independent because his grandfather, who'd loved him dearly, had helped to make him that way despite his own misgivings. Harmony wished she had that same strength of character, but she didn't, and knowing her own weakness made her cry.

She wished she could talk to her mum about it, but she wasn't in a place, mentally or emotionally, to do so. No doubt her mother would have a lot to say about the situation, and Harmony wasn't at all sure she wanted to hear her mother's input.

Everything in her strained both toward Cam and away from him, and she felt trapped in an internal tug of war.

He called her when he got off the ferry the next evening.

"I'm just heading home to shower and change. Come up in a while, okay?"

She thought it strange that he wouldn't just stop by so she could walk with him to the Manor, but agreed to go up in about an hour.

As she strolled up she found herself greeting people she'd come to know in the short time she'd been on the island. Although she'd lived in the same house in Stoke Newington most of her life, and had friends of long standing there, the sensation of belonging she felt on Eilean Rurie was different. Somehow knowing you depended on your neighbors the way everyone on the island had to made fitting in a bit easier.

Funny to think how she'd worried that she'd stick out like a sore thumb and have a miserable couple of months. The stereotype of small places being unfriendly and hard to assimilate into certainly didn't apply here. She'd been welcomed with open arms, and knew she'd miss it terribly when she left.

Slipping in through Cam's private entrance, she found the most delicious scent reaching her nostrils, and she inhaled deeply as she shrugged off her coat and toed off her boots.

"What are you making?" she asked, walking through from the entranceway into the kitchen.

"Sugar cookies," he replied, giving her a broad grin. "I promised to make some for the gala tomorrow, and I was worried I wouldn't get back in time to do it."

Harmony surveyed the unholy mess on the counter, the flour and sugar on the floor, and shook her head. "Not something you do often, I suspect."

He chuckled. "Never done it before, but I think I'm getting the hang of it. I was going to borrow cookie cutters from Dora, but ended up picking up some for myself on Skye. Are you going to just stand there, or are you going to help me?"

Harmony laughed, opening the cupboard and taking out his broom. "I'm going to sweep up that flour before one of us slips and falls—then I'll help."

He looked so adorable, with a gingham pinny tied around his waist and his hair still damp from his shower, her heart raced and her stomach fluttered. The whole concept of steeling herself against the love and attraction she felt toward him seemed laughable.

"How could anyone be this messy?" she teased as she swept up the flour and sugar.

Cam shrugged, stamping out another biscuit and dropping it on a baking sheet. "I'm a pretty decent cook, but this is my first foray into baking, so excuse me if I didn't realize the mixer would send half the ingredients flying if I cranked it up to the highest speed."

That made her giggle, and they teased back and forth as she helped him with the next batch.

"How're you planning to decorate them?" she asked, when the sheets were finally in the oven and Cam was rolling out the next block of dough.

His blank look had her laughing all over again.

"Decorate? I'm supposed to decorate them too?"

"Otherwise they'll be pretty boring," she replied, getting her amusement under control. "Do you have any food coloring? Oh, never mind—I'll just look."

"All the baking supplies are in the last cupboard," he said helpfully. "On the left-hand side."

She found some ancient food coloring and some plastic bags and, as Cam watched with interest, made some colored sugar to sprinkle on top of the biscuits.

When she'd finished it was time to take the first batch

out, and she showed him how to make designs on the cookies with the sugar. Once the baking sheets had cooled they put the next batch on, and into the oven they went.

Cam picked up one of the first set of cookies and bit into it.

"Mmm..." he said, his eyebrows going up. "Not bad at all, if I might say so myself. Try it."

He moved closer to her, holding out the biscuit for her to bite, and something in his eyes made her heart leap. Obediently she took a bite, and nodded in satisfaction.

"Delicious," she said, after swallowing.

"Yes..." Cam agreed, but she knew he wasn't talking about the cookie.

His gaze was on her lips, his expression intent, and when he leaned in to kiss her Harmony melted just like the sweet confection had melted in her mouth.

"I missed you so much last night." His lips were against her cheek, his arms warm and strong around her waist. "I couldn't wait to get home to you."

She didn't reply, just cupped his cheeks and pulled his lips back to hers. She couldn't admit how much she'd missed him too. To do so would be too revealing, even as she felt the bonds tying her to him tighten.

Picking her up, he carried her to the living room and laid her down on the couch, kissing her again and again. Time slowed, became irrelevant, as kisses turned to caresses and Cam slowly stripped her of her clothes and her defenses. Saying no to his lovemaking never entered her mind. Instead she reveled in it, crying out with pleasure as he took her flying.

"You're so beautiful," he whispered, his face harsh with need.

"So are you," she said, the words coming from her soul.

And when they were ready and she straddled his body,

taking him deep, the pleasure she derived wasn't just from the sensations of his body in hers, as amazing as those were. Her joy was deepened, widened, by seeing his ecstasy as she took him to the edge and they plunged over together.

They came back to earth with a bump as the smell of something burning permeated the room.

"The cookies!" Cam cried, levering her off him and setting her back down on the couch before taking off running for the kitchen.

Still on a high, Harmony found herself laughing so hard at the thumping and cursing coming from the other room she couldn't get up.

Cam stalked back into the living room and stood over her, glowering. "Funny, is it?"

"Hilarious," she replied, gasping for air, holding her aching sides.

He pounced, growling, and they wrestled back and forth, with Harmony still suffering fits of giggles and Cam trying hard not to join in but eventually succumbing.

Entwined, they let their laughter turn to gasps for air, and Harmony relaxed into his embrace, blissfully satiated. Unthinkingly happy.

When he went up on his elbows she opened sleepy eyes to look up at him. Cam's expression banished her lassitude—brought her to full and frightened awareness.

"Stay here with me, Harmony. I love you."

CHAPTER EIGHTEEN

He hadn't meant to blurt it out like that, but something in the moment, in having her in his arms right then, had made him say it.

Having accepted that his love for her was deep and true, he knew the yearning for her while he was on Skye had just cemented it in his heart. It wasn't just physical intimacy with Harmony. There was something between them that both soothed and excited his soul, that made his lonely heart whole.

Her look of shock didn't surprise him. After all, he'd surprised himself with his words, although they were heartfelt. What he wasn't prepared for was the strength and ferocity with which she pushed him away.

Rolling away almost had him falling off the couch, which would have added embarrassment to what was already beginning to feel like a very bad scene. Insult on top of injury, or the other way around.

"No, no, no..." She got up, turned her back on him, covered her face with her hands for a moment. "Oh, Cam. Why did you have to say that? Spoil everything."

"Because I mean it," he said, not sure whether to be angry or sad. "I love you. I want you to be with me always. What's so wrong about that?"

"I can't!" It was almost a moan, and when she turned

to face him her face was pale, her eyes green and tragic. "It wouldn't work. I *can't*."

Wanting to take her in his arms, but knowing she wouldn't want that, he stayed where he was, flattening his hands against the cushions beneath him to stop himself from reaching for her.

"Why wouldn't it work?" He had to ask—to make sense of what she was saying. Was he the only one who felt how right they were together? Was he alone in knowing that what they shared was deeper, truer than mere passion?

She lowered herself into an armchair, pulling a throw pillow from behind her to hug it, as though shielding her body from his view. Or using it as a barrier to separate them.

"I… I never told you about my dad, did I?"

What did that have to do with anything? he wondered, but just shook his head.

"Remember I said he had a heart defect and wasn't fit for the army? Well, after that it was as though he had to prove there was nothing wrong with him. He was a daredevil, Cam—like you. His friends called him 'Risky Ricky' because of how he behaved—never cautious, always going full tilt into whatever crazy thing he was doing. He was a man who'd try any ridiculous stunt or sport as long as it gave him an adrenaline rush. Car or motorcycle racing, skydiving, mountain-climbing—you name it, he did it."

Cam wanted to argue—to say he wasn't that way, didn't do any of the things he did in an effort to prove anything to anyone but because he loved the adventure. But she was crying, and he couldn't bear the sight. It clogged his throat, making it impossible for him to respond.

"Eventually it killed him, Cam. He wanted to free-climb, and he wasn't ready for it. Or maybe his heart finally gave out on him. No one knows for sure. All we know is he lost his grip on that cliff and fell to his death."

"Harmony. I'm so sorry."

She held up her hand, tears still falling, but her face had taken on an expression of determination, and the lines between her brows were more pronounced than he'd ever seen them.

"I don't need your sympathy, Cam. I just need you to understand. I was six when he died. My mother was left to raise me alone. It took her years—*years*—to get over his loss. The entire time I was growing up she wouldn't date, struggled on her own. Because of his selfish need to prove himself he deprived me of a father and Mum of a husband. I had to listen to my mother cry at nights, when she thought I was asleep—had to see my grandparents get old before their time because of the death of their son, whom they'd loved so much."

She took a deep, shuddering breath and wiped her hand over her face, trying to erase the tears.

"I can't risk going through that again, Cam. I know why you do what you do, and I know how addictive extreme sports can be, so I would never ask you to give them up. However, I can make the choice not to watch you do them. Not to put myself into a situation where one day you might leave and never come home. I'm not strong enough to handle that."

Her words struck him like a series of knife-blows, each lacerating his heart a bit more until it felt as though there was nothing left of it.

Yet even though the pain was extreme, made him nauseous, his first impulse was to tell her that she was right. He'd never give up doing what he wanted—no matter how dangerous. And that impulse told him more about himself than he wanted to know.

"I understand," he said; they were the only words he could find in the midst of the fog clouding his brain. "I truly do."

What else could he say as he watched the woman he loved get up and start putting on her clothes?

Suddenly keenly aware of his own nakedness, he got up to tug on his trousers, realizing his hands were shaking as he did so.

Harmony dressed without saying anything else, and he trailed her to the entranceway and watched her put on her boots and then her jacket. When she turned to face him her face was expressionless, but the green of her eyes told him everything he needed to know.

"I've written up a job advertisement for my position," she said, her voice flat. "With your permission I'll start sending it out to the agencies. Perhaps put an ad in the Glasgow newspapers, as well."

He nodded, and somehow found his voice, despite the ache spreading out from his chest, choking him. "Yes, of course. Thank you."

A little smile tipped the edges of her lips, but there was little amusement in it and the sight was another heart-blow.

"Polite to the last," she said softly. "You really are an amazing man, and one day a woman with a stouter heart than mine will be very, very lucky to have you."

But I only want you.

Before he could say it, beg or plead the way everything in him told him he should, she was gone, shutting the door quietly behind her.

Around her were the sparkle of lights, the beautiful melodies of Christmas songs, the laughter of children. All the sounds of joy and happiness. But Harmony wondered if she'd ever feel either again.

Everything in her wanted to go back, to say she didn't mean it, but she couldn't—just couldn't put herself through living with and loving Cam.

Not when she knew what that entailed. What the likely outcome would be.

Who would put themselves into a situation like that knowingly, willingly, as though tempting fate to destroy them by stealing the person they loved away?

Letting herself into the surgery, she trudged upstairs.

She'd never felt more alone.

The only person she could talk to, who she knew would understand, was her mother, and she was loath to disturb her on her vacation. They'd spoken a few times since she had gone to Yorkshire, and Harmony was happy to know she was enjoying herself and liked Fred's family. She'd sounded happier than she had in a long time, and Harmony didn't want to upset that.

Yet eventually she ended up calling, desperate to hear her mother's reassurance that she was doing the right thing. If anyone would agree with her stance it would be her mum.

She'd hardly said, "Hello," before her mother asked what was wrong.

Unable to hold it inside, she let the entire story go, telling her mum how she'd fallen for Cam, and how he wanted her to stay but she couldn't.

"He's just like Dad," she said, crying. "I can't bear the thought of going through what you did, Mum."

"If he's like your father, dear, you shouldn't be afraid."

Startled, considering all she'd told her mother about Cam's adventures, she asked, "What do you mean, Mum?"

"Well, the truth is that your father was a wonderful man—loving, caring, intelligent and, yes, adventurous. But it was that combination that drew me to him, and I knew what I was getting into when I married him."

Her mum took a deep breath—Harmony could hear it through the receiver.

"Your father might have felt he had something to prove, but I really think it was more a case that he knew he was on borrowed time and wanted to live his life to the fullest. However, he'd told me that climb would be his last. He wanted to be home more—for you and for me. He just never had the chance to make good on that promise."

Shocked by her mother's revelations, Harmony said, "You never told me that, Mum."

"It hurt too much to think of. I felt cheated and angry."

Sinking down onto the couch, Harmony tried to take in what her mother was saying, but she couldn't escape what was, for her, the bottom line.

"I don't think I can deal with it, Mum. The thought of him going off to do all those crazy things, perhaps never to return."

"That's something you have to decide—but don't let cowardice cheat you out of something beautiful," her mum said softly, and the sympathy in her voice was almost Harmony's undoing.

"I'm afraid, Mum. I love him so much, but I can't stand the thought of losing him because of some silly extreme sport."

"Harmony, think about this carefully. I loved your father, and I knew who and what he was when I married him. I went into it with my eyes open, although I never expected to lose him the way I did. I was young, and I thought we'd both live forever. But although it ended tragically I wouldn't change anything—not one moment of the time I spent with him. We were happy for the short time we were together, and that's what I clung to all those years when I mourned him, even through my anger. Plus, he'd given me you, and you and your Gran kept me going even on the days when I thought I couldn't put one foot in front of the other."

"Oh, Mum…" Harmony was crying again, but they weren't the wrenching, heartbroken tears she'd shed earlier. There was a softer quality to them—healing rather than hurting.

"Do what's right for you, darling. But don't let fear alone rule your life. Nothing is promised. No one knows what the next day will bring. You have to live fully, wholeheartedly, and hope and pray for the best. Don't trouble trouble, 'til trouble troubles you."

Hearing one of Gran's favorite sayings made Harmony chuckle, but coming as it did through her tears, it sounded more like a hiccup.

"I miss Gran so much," she said. "And I miss being with you right now."

"I miss her too. And you. I didn't think I could face Christmas if it wasn't for this trip with Fred to take my mind off how much we've lost this year, but without you here to celebrate with us it won't be complete."

They fell silent for a moment, with Harmony thinking how lucky she'd been to have her mum, and her gran, to raise her. Just like Cam with his grand-da, she wouldn't be the person she was today without them.

Then, ever practical, her mum said, "Do you want to leave the island? We'll be in Yorkshire for another week. You could join us and go back to London on the train when we leave."

Horrified at the thought of leaving Cam shorthanded during this busy time, she said, "No, of course not. I won't leave until I've found a replacement. I won't let my personal issues interfere with my work. Besides, God alone knows what mess the surgery would be in if I did."

Her mum laughed softly, and said, "That's my girl—full of vinegar and Scotch Bonnet peppers. Now, have a good think about what I've said. I know you're not the type to take chances, but some chances in life are worth taking."

"Okay, Mum. Love you."

After they'd hung up Harmony sat for a while thinking about everything. Talking to her mum had brought to mind her conversation with Katherine, and how she'd missed out on love perhaps out of fear of rejection and hurt. She contemplated it all until the headache pounding behind her tired eyes overtook her and she realized making any decisions was impossible.

After all, tomorrow is another day.

Another of Gran's sayings, culled from one of the old lady's favorite movies.

With the comforting words echoing in her brain, Harmony went to bed. And, although she hadn't thought it would happen, she fell into a deep and dreamless sleep.

CHAPTER NINETEEN

Cam was up before first light next morning, finally giving up on his attempts to sleep. He'd tossed and turned the entire night, getting only snatches of shallow slumber, his brain refusing to shut down.

Very different from last evening, when he'd stood staring at the closed door and through a fog of pain and despair had been unable to form a coherent thought except for the hope that Harmony would come back.

Stumbling back to the living room, it had soon occurred to him to go after her. In the end it hadn't happened.

He'd been at war with himself—unable to understand how she could be so completely determined not to stay. At the same time at the back of his mind was the thought that it was better this way. If she couldn't accept him as he was, what hope was there for them to make a life together?

Those were the two thoughts in his muddled head until he'd lain down in bed. Then his brain had gone into the type of whirring overdrive that was incompatible with rest.

What she'd told him about her father made so many things he'd noticed before come into sharp focus. How scathing she'd been about the water jetpack, her reaction to the sky suit video. And it also made him appreciate how frightened she must have been watching him get into the water to rescue the boy stuck out in the old fishing village.

Yet she hadn't tried to dissuade him from doing it—just done everything she could to make sure he was fit for the job, even in the face of his disagreeableness.

She was a woman worth giving up the world for and he knew it. What he *didn't* know—and this was the part that frightened him—was what kind of person he'd be if he gave up all the things he enjoyed for her. Would love turn to resentment as he watched his friends doing all the things he wished he could?

It seemed asinine to allow what were really just diversions to dictate his happiness, when true, lasting happiness was within reach. Especially as he wasn't planning to keep doing extreme sports forever. No matter how fit he kept himself, at some point he'd have to dial it back. And he'd always thought if he had children he'd definitely keep his activities to the less dangerous type.

Not that he considered what he did particularly dangerous. Walking across the street could be dangerous if you didn't pay attention to what you were doing, and he was meticulous in his preparations and research before doing anything.

But there was no getting around her fears, and he wasn't sure he could leave his adventures behind just yet.

He couldn't help wondering if it was even fair of him to ask her to see it from his point of view. In reality, they both had a point. Her fear was no less important than his drive to experience new things. To pit himself against his fears and test his abilities.

One thing was clear, however. The thought of losing her was haunting.

Would he ever get over her? He doubted it. He'd never been a big believer in love at first sight, or soul mates, but he remembered how he'd almost stumbled over his own feet the first time he saw her…how his heart had pounded. And every moment in her presence after that had just pulled him closer, made him fall harder.

If a friend had told him he'd proposed to a woman he'd only known for a few weeks Cam would have suggested slowing it down, making sure it wasn't just hormones. But here he was in love with Harmony, knowing in his heart that it was forever.

Cam sat on the edge of his bed, head in hands, wondering how to work it all out and finding no immediate answer.

He didn't want to face anyone, wished he could stay in with his thoughts, but tonight was the Christmas Eve Gala and he had so much to do. Hiding was impossible.

It was as he was leaving home to go to the church hall that a horrible thought struck him.

Suppose Harmony decided to leave today? The first ferry would be docking at eight. Did she plan to be on it when it left?

He pulled out his phone to call her, then realized it was still too early. Not that she was a late riser, but suddenly, after what had happened the day before, he wasn't comfortable calling her before office hours.

Of course, she might have taken off before office hours.

When he got down to the clinic he saw the apartment was dark and his heart sank—only for it to soar with relief when he looked back at the front of the building and realized she was already in the surgery.

So he called her, wanting to hear her voice, although he'd try to keep things businesslike.

"Hello?"

There was a cautious note to her voice and his heart ached to hear it. Even before they'd come to know each other well her confidence had shone through.

"Hey," he responded, wanting to ask if she was all right

but not doing so. "I just wanted to let you know I'm over at the church hall if you need me for anything."

"Okay," she said, still stilted. "If I need you I'll call. But I know it's a busy day for you. The temporary medical team will be around, so I'll only bother you if it's an emergency."

"Right. Thanks."

He wanted to keep her on the line, and found himself standing still on the street, no longer walking, his feet itching to turn and go to her, just to see her face.

But all he could say was "Talk to you later."

Forcing himself to continue on toward the church, he braced himself for the day. Time to put on a happy face, since he couldn't stand the thought of having to explain to anyone, especially the CIs, why he wasn't his usual self.

Dora was like a whirling dervish, dashing about and making sure everything was set up to her specifications. Cam soon made himself useful, and had to smile when he saw some of the decor. The CI's had taken his request to make Harmony feel included to heart. Hopefully she'd like it.

Cam left a couple of times, to deal with matters on other parts of the island, keeping himself as busy as possible. Yet his thoughts never strayed far from Harmony.

Back at the church hall that afternoon, Dora came over, finally looking pleased. "The caterers are set up and already at work, and we're finally finished with the decorations. How does it look?"

"Wonderful," Cam said honestly. "You've outdone yourselves this year."

"You like what we've done for Harmony?" Dora looked unsure. "Do you think *she'll* like it?"

"I'm sure she will," Cam replied, suddenly struck with the thought that if he wasn't careful Harmony might not even see it. She was just the type to withdraw into herself and not come to the gala at all. And that wouldn't do. "Can I put you in charge of making sure she gets here on time? I have to go down and greet the guests at the ferry."

To his disbelief, Dora didn't even look surprised. If anything, her smile widened. "I will. It's going to be our best Christmas Eve Gala ever."

Cam smiled with her, but inside he knew it wouldn't be for him. Nothing would be the best without Harmony.

All day, while treating a variety of minor medical issues, Harmony had wrestled with the question of whether she would go to the gala or not. She knew how busy the CIs had been preparing for it, and wanted to be supportive. But she wasn't sure she was ready to face Cam, and wondered if her being there would make him uncomfortable. It was clear he loved Christmas, and he had been so excited whenever he spoke about the gala she knew he was looking forward to it immensely.

She kept busy in between patients by going over the advertisement for her replacement compulsively, and yet never quite got around to hitting Send to the various job sites. And the entire time her mother's revelations about her father kept playing through her head.

No matter what she thought of Cam's adventurous nature, or the reasons he'd gotten involved with extreme and dangerous sports, he was a very responsible person. It was obvious in everything he did. There was nothing truly selfish about him, even considering his determination to do the things she was so afraid of. To him they were just activities he enjoyed. It might have started as a way to exert his independence, but it had become important to him for other reasons. She suspected it was a way to stretch himself, maybe blow off the stress of his career and keeping the island running and profitable.

No, the real problem was with her.

There didn't seem any way to get past her fear.

Every time she thought about the video he'd been watching, with those crazy people jumping off cliffs in just a flimsy suit, not even a parachute, her blood froze. She didn't think she could bear watching him go off, knowing that was what he was planning to do.

Yet the love she felt for him was so strong she wasn't sure how she would be able to walk away. Oh, she'd no doubt that she'd do it, if only for her own self-esteem. But what would life be like after that? She had no idea—knew only that it would be bleak.

The question of whether or not she'd go to the gala was answered with a call from Dora.

"Harmony, we'll be by to collect you at seven for the gala."

"Oh, I don't—"

"Seven," Dora interrupted, in her brook-no-nonsense tone, effectively cutting off any resistance Harmony might have tried to put up. "And don't be late."

She didn't even wait for Harmony to respond, simply hung up, the conversation over as far as she was concerned.

And despite her heavy heart, and her misgivings about spoiling Cam's night by being there, Harmony did as ordered and was ready when the CIs arrived to collect her.

Without an extensive choice of wardrobe, she'd put on a red knit wrap dress she'd packed into her suitcase on a whim, and was happy that she had. Pairing it with knee-high boots that had small pointed heels—what she'd always thought of as her "witchy boots"—she knew that at least her feet and legs would be warm. It had been windy during the afternoon, as another snow squall came east off the sea, and there was the promise of snow in the air again.

She was shrugging into her coat when the ladies arrived, and even though she was used to their habit of talking over each other, Harmony sensed a special excitement in their rapid-fire chatter. Not to mention the way they surrounded her and whisked her out the door, as though they were afraid she'd change her mind.

"Wow!" she said as they walked through the small parking area in front of the church hall and she saw the usually rather prosaic building for the first time. "This looks amazing."

There was a series of arches set up along the path leading into the hall, all decorated with white and gold ornaments that twisted in the breeze, refracting the light from hundreds of tiny bulbs.

Pausing on the path, she was just admiring their handiwork as the first bits of snow started to fall, adding to the ambience, when Katherine said, "For goodness' sakes, let's go inside."

"What's the rush?" Harmony asked.

But none of them answered, just hustled her forward under the arches and into the building. In the vestibule they took off their coats, and Harmony followed the older ladies inside.

And came to a halt, her mouth falling open.

The hall looked lovely, but what immediately caught her eye was a tree covered in poinsettias, strategically placed so it was the first thing anyone entering the hall would see. Interspersed between the silk blooms were golden hearts.

The CIs were all watching for her reaction and Harmony felt her eyes sting as she looked at their hopeful faces.

"Did you do this for me?" she asked, her voice hitching.

"Well, Cam said you told him you always had poinsettias at Christmas, but we couldn't get enough plants in time, so unfortunately silk will have to do," Ingrid replied.

"It's beautiful!" she exclaimed, giving them all a round of hugs. "How sweet of you."

"Look at the tree skirt," Dora said. "Sela made it special."

Harmony went closer, then stooped down to get a better look.

"Jonkanoo!" she cried, as she recognized various figures from the traditional Jamaican Christmas bands, who dressed up and danced in the streets. "Sela, it's gorgeous."

"It certainly caught *my* eye. It's so much like the prints we have at home."

The voice came from behind her. It was one she recognized but couldn't believe she was hearing.

She looked up and had to put a hand on the ground to stop herself falling over. Then she was on her feet, rushing for a hug.

"Mum! Oh, Mum..." She pulled back, tears filling her eyes. "What are you doing here?"

"We were invited," Mum said, brushing Harmony's cheek with her hand.

"The Laird arranged it all," Dora said, with a suspicious little crackle in her throat.

Harmony suspected there wasn't a dry eye in their little group as she hugged her mother again, swinging her from side to side. Then she was hugging Fred, who was beaming from ear to ear, and she was introduced to his daughter, his son-in-law, his son and three grandchildren.

Yet, through it all, even with joy coursing through her heart, she was aware of one thing.

Cam wasn't there.

She knew because she kept looking for him—even when the CIs took her to show her the special dessert table, with gizzadas, sweet potato pone and Jamaican Christmas cake, the latter baked by her mother.

"How did you manage all this?" she kept saying, but the CIs just laughed and patted her shoulder.

Eventually the family group made their way toward the table reserved for them, but Harmony still couldn't see Cam anywhere.

"Did you meet Cam?" she asked her mother quietly.

"He met us at the ferry and took us up to the Manor. I haven't seen him since just before you came in, though."

Her mum's hand on Harmony's arm kept her in place for a moment.

"I think he's wonderful, Harmony. When he contacted me and asked if we'd come for Christmas I knew he was someone special. Selfless. The rooms he's putting us in should be making him money, not being given away, but he wanted you to be happy."

Then, with one long, meaningful look at her daughter, she let go and went to sit with Fred, leaving Harmony to chew on what she'd said.

CHAPTER TWENTY

THE SNOW WAS starting to come down harder, and the small, glittery flakes that had first fallen were replaced with bigger, fluffier ones. Cam brushed off the bench with his gloved hand, then sat facing Grand-Da's grave, looking up into the cloudy sky at the snow drifting earthward.

Every moment spent putting together the perfect Christmas Eve for Harmony had been worth it just to see the astonishment and happiness light up her face. He'd stood at the back of the room, out of the way, where he could watch her unfolding surprise and see her reaction, and his heart had soared when she'd hugged her mother, happy tears on her cheeks.

"I wish you could have seen it, Grand-Da. It was one of the most beautiful moments I've ever witnessed."

It had taken a lot of finagling and some downright deception to put it all together. When he'd first got the idea he'd been wary of calling Mrs. Kinkaid out of the blue and asking her if she would come to the island. After all, she didn't know him from a hole in the wall. Yet Harmony's mother had been gracious, and almost embarrassingly grateful for the opportunity. Cam thought she might even have been crying a little when he'd spoken with her the first time.

But he knew what it was like to go through the first

Christmas after you'd lost someone seminal in your life, and both Harmony and her mother were facing that alone rather than together. The year he'd lost Grand-Da, Christmas hadn't held the same magic for him until his island family had rallied around. His parents and cousins had made the effort to come too, and having everyone together had rendered the season not just bearable, but a lovely tribute to the old man.

Shoving his hand into his pocket, he fingered the felt heart. He'd kept meaning to put it on the tree up at the Manor, but somehow had always ended up sticking it back into his coat pocket. It reminded him of Harmony—of the day he'd realized the attraction he felt was far stronger than he had ever imagined.

"That's what Christmas is supposed to be, right, Grand-Da?" he said into the cold, wintry night. "Family. Joy. Love."

"And you've done so much to make my Christmas perfect, Cam."

The snow had muffled her footsteps, so he hadn't heard her approach, and when he turned to look Harmony was standing just behind the bench.

"I thought I'd find you here," she continued, coming forward to sit beside him.

"Just a little visit with Grand-Da. Being out here helps me think."

He couldn't take his eyes off her beautiful, shining face. Her eyes sparkled brighter than any of the holiday lights, shining amber in the glow of the nearby streetlamp.

"Thank you." The words were simple, but behind them was a wealth of joy.

Cam shook his head. "I don't need your thanks, my love. Just to know you're happy is enough for me."

She reached out then, and took his hand. She wasn't

wearing gloves, and instinctively he covered her fingers with his to keep them warm.

Harmony looked down at their hands, and then back up at him. "I've never been happier, Cam. But it's not complete without you."

Something shifted inside him—a deep soul-shudder that brought with it the realization that he'd do anything—*anything*—to keep this woman in his life.

He took a deep breath, the cold air filling his lungs and seeming to blow all his previous doubts away. Reaching across, he took her other hand. When she placed it in his, his pounding heart felt a little lighter.

"I'll give it all up—the mountain-climbing, skydiving, caving, hang gliding, everything—if you love me. I never want to hurt you, or make you worry. If that's what it takes to have you with me forever, I'll do it. I don't want anyone but you."

Harmony shook her head, those darling little lines coming and going between her brows, and he felt his heart break once more, thinking she was rejecting him again.

"I don't need you to do that," she said quietly, her gaze intent on his. "It's part of who you are…your adventurous spirit. It might make me feel more secure if you stopped, but it wouldn't make you happy, and letting you live your best life is important to me."

"The very best life I could live is with you," he replied, meaning it more than he'd ever meant anything in his life before. "You're all that matters—all I really care about."

Her frown faded and she smiled then—a sweet curve of her lips that made his heart race a little faster.

"I'm not willing to let my fears keep me from being with you, no matter what you decide. Go dive off one of those mountains in that wing suit and enjoy yourself. I won't promise to be there to watch you, and I can't say I won't be scared until I have you back safe, but I know you're not reckless. I know how responsible you are, and that you'll be as careful as someone doing something like that can be. But I also know that if you gave it all up for me you might eventually resent me, and I couldn't bear that. So go off to Peru, or wherever else you want to, and I'll be here, waiting for you when you come home."

He knew then there was no way he was letting her go and he told her so.

"I want to settle down with you, have children with you, make new traditions and have the happiness only you can give me. All those sports and pastimes are fun, but they're nothing when compared to the thought of having you by my side for the rest of my life."

Her gaze searched his for a long moment, then she smiled, and he somehow knew it would all be okay.

"Are we always going to argue over who's right?" she asked, the mischief in her gaze lightening his mood. "Even when we're trying to give in to each other?"

"I suspect we will, love," he replied. "But I look forward to every spat."

The wind picked up, just for an instant, and the snow swirled as though dancing a jig across the ground. Cam thought for a moment that the creak of the trees was like Grand-Da's laugh.

"I have something for you," he said, not knowing where the thought came from, but feeling the rightness of it.

Letting go one of her hands, he reached into his pocket and pulled out the heart, holding it out to Harmony. She took it, releasing his other hand to trace the luckenbooth design. Then she pressed it over her own heart, and when she looked up there were tears in the corners of her eyes.

"Cameron MacRurie, are you giving me your heart,

having already stolen mine?" Despite the quip, her voice was a little wobbly. "I promise to take good care of it."

He held out his arms and she slid into them, wrapping hers around his waist.

"You already had my heart, Nurse Kinkaid."

The wind faded slightly and Cam noticed for the first time the sounds of chatter and laughter from the hall, the holiday music borne on the breeze. It seemed to typify the happiness filling him to overflowing as he held Harmony close, felt her snuggle into his embrace.

"This is perfect, Cam." She was whispering, as though loath to speak too loudly lest the aura of peace and love surrounding them be broken. "I'll always remember this Christmas, this night, as the happiest of my life."

"To date, maybe?" he teased, thinking about all the days and nights to come, knowing the future was suddenly brighter than he'd ever imagined it could be.

She raised her head, brought her lips close to his, and said, "Definitely."

The temperature was dropping, and her mother was waiting in the hall. If he kissed her he might never want to stop. But resisting her lips was the hardest thing he'd ever done.

"We should go back inside," he muttered, sublimely aware of her breath against his face, the sweet, lush sensation of her body resting so perfectly on his. "Everyone will wonder where we are."

"No, they won't," she said, getting a millimeter closer, so he wasn't sure how there was actually still empty space between their mouths. "They're all smarter than that. Now, shut up, Dr. Laird, and kiss me."

So he did.

* * * * *

HIGHLAND DOC'S CHRISTMAS RESCUE

SUSAN CARLISLE

To Dallas
I'm proud of the man you are, and your father would be also.

CHAPTER ONE

AS THE TAXI rolled up the rise Cass Bellow looked out the window at the snow-blanketed Heatherglen Castle Clinic in northern Scotland. Why had she been sent here?

More than once she'd questioned her doctor's wisdom in transferring her to this private clinic for physical therapy. Weren't there plenty of other places in warmer climates? Particularly in her native US. Or, better yet, couldn't she have just gone home and handled what needed doing on her own? But, no, her doctor insisted she should be at Heatherglen. Had stated that he sent all his patients with extensive orthopedic injuries there. He declared the place was her best hope for a full recovery. Finally, at her argument, he'd bluntly told her that if she wanted him to sign off on her release she must complete her physical therapy at Heatherglen.

As the car came to a stop at the front door she studied the Norman architecture of the building with its smooth stone walls and slate roof. The place was huge, and breathtaking. There were more chimneys than Cass had a chance to count. This place was nothing like what she'd expected. Though it was early November, festive Christmas wreaths made of greenery and red bows already hung on the outside of the lower floor windows. They further darkened her mood.

When she had been given the search and rescue assignment assisting the military after an explosion in Eastern Europe, she had never dreamed she'd end up in traction in an army hospital on a base in Germany. Her shattered arm and leg had finally mended, but she needed physical therapy to regain complete use of them. Now she'd been sent to this far-flung, snowy place to do just that. All she really wanted was to be left alone.

She opened the cab door and wind blasted her. Despite the heat coming from the still running car, she shuddered. As Cass stepped out, one of the large wooden castle doors, decked with a huge Christmas wreath full of red berries, opened. A tall man, perhaps in his mid-thirties, with the wide shoulders of an athlete stepped out. With rust-colored hair and wearing a heavy tan cable sweater and dark brown pants, he looked like the epitome of what she thought a Scottish man should be. As he came down the few steps toward her, he smiled.

"Hello, you must be Ms. Cassandra Bellow. I'm Dr. Lyle Sinclair, the medical director here at Heatherglen. You may call me Lyle."

His thick Scottish brogue confirmed her earlier thoughts. Yet she was surprised by the way the sunny cheerfulness of his voice curled around her name, nudging at her icy emotions. Irritated, she pushed that odd notion away. This doctor was far too happy and personable for her taste. Her goal was to do what must be done with as little interaction with others as possible. She planned on nursing her wounds in private.

"Yes, that's me." To her satisfaction her flat, dry tone dropped the brightness of his smile a notch. If she could just get to her room and collapse she'd be happy. Her right side was burning from the ache in her arm and the agony of putting her full weight on her right leg.

"Flora McNeith, the physiotherapist whose care you'll be under, couldn't be here to greet you and asked that I get you settled in." Concern filled his face. "Do you need a wheelchair? Crutches?"

"No, I can walk on my own. Run, that's another thing." She pulled at her jacket to stop the biting flow of air down her neck.

A light chuckle rolled out of his throat and over her nerve endings. "I understand. Then let's get inside out of this weather." He looked up at the sky. A snowflake landed on the dark red five o'clock shadow covering his cheek.

Cass averted her eyes and gave the cobblestone drive, cleared of snow, a searching look. It was farther than she wanted to walk, yet she wouldn't let on. The three steps up to the door looked even more daunting.

All she needed was fortitude to make the walk and climb those steps. She had plenty of that. Soft snowflakes continued to drift down as she took a deep breath and steeled herself to put one foot in front of the other. With another silent inhalation, she started toward the entrance. Dr. Sinclair walked beside her.

She managed the first two steps with no mishap but the toe of her short boot caught the edge of the last one. Grabbing at air, Cass finally found the fabric covering Dr. Sinclair's arm. She yelped with the effort to hold on. Being right-handed, she'd instinctively flailed out that arm and immediately regretted it. Pain shot through it, but not as sharp as it had been weeks earlier. She gritted her teeth, thrusting out her other arm to ease the fall.

Instead of tumbling onto the steps, her body was

brought against a hard wall of human torso. The doctor's arm circled her waist and held her steady. Her face smashed into thick yarn. A hint of pine and smoke filled her nose. For some reason it was reassuring.

"Steady on, I've got you." His deep burr was near her ear.

Cass quickly straightened, getting her feet under her even though pain rocked her. She refused to show it, having already embarrassed herself enough. Her lips tightened. "I'm fine. Thank you."

Glancing at him, she got the weirdest impression that the concern in his eyes had nothing to do with her physical injuries, as if he was able to see her true pain. That was a crazy idea. She shook that odd thought off and focused on where she was.

Taking a third fortifying breath, Cass stepped into the massive foyer.

No way was she going to let him see the effort it took to keep walking. She'd lived through much worse. She'd always been self-sufficient. Weakness wasn't in her vocabulary. As a young girl she had learned the power of being emotionally strong.

Still, that brief human contact had been nice.

There were two enormous cement urns filled with pine and berries on either side of the doors. Cass looked further to see the stone arched beams of the ceiling then on to a grand staircase. On the floor beside it lay a pile of pine wood. Here she was in this strange place for the holidays when all she wished for was home. She would get her arm and leg strong again as fast as she could, then return to America to grieve her loss in private.

"Are you sure you're okay?" The doctor stood too close as if he was afraid she might stumble again.

"I'm fine." The words sounded sharp and overly loud

in the cavernous entrance hall. If she could just get to her room, she could nurse the excruciating throbbing in her arm and leg. She would be limping by then as well.

"On our way to your room, let me tell you where a few things are. This is Admissions." He waved a hand to indicate a room off the hall. "Louise, my administrative assistant, and I have our offices there. She's out this afternoon as well. You two can sort out the paperwork in the morning. I'm sure you're tired."

Cass was beyond tired. The effort it had taken her to travel from Germany to Fort William then the drive north had worn her out. She hadn't recovered anywhere near as much as she wanted to believe.

"Over here is the dining room." He walked across the hall and stood in a wide doorway.

Cass joined him. Despite her physical distress, she loved his accent. It was soothing, for some reason.

The room he wanted her to see was long and wide with a dark barrel ceiling sculpted out of wood from which hung large, black iron chandeliers. A fireplace Cass could stand up in filled the wall on the far end with flags arranged overhead. The walls were partially covered in wainscoting. Above that were a few male portraits in impressive frames. A huge table, surrounded by imposing matching chairs, capable of seating at least twenty people, stood in the center of the room. An oriental rug in blue and red lay beneath it. The only thing out of place was a pile of greenery on the floor in one corner and a few boxes stacked beside it.

He must have noticed the direction of her gaze. "Pardon the mess. We're in the process of decorating for Christmas."

Cass pretended he hadn't spoken. Not even the holidays could heal her broken heart.

Dr. Sinclair was saying, "All meals are served here, unless there's a reason the resident is incapable of joining us. We dress for the evening meal. It's at seven."

"Dress? As in diamonds and tux?"

Chuckling, he shook his head. "No. More like no workout clothes allowed. The idea is for the residents to use their skills and have something positive to look forward to. We work on the principle that if you don't use it, you lose it."

She glanced at him. He really was quite handsome in a rugged way. "Like?"

"Fastening a button, passing a bowl or even manipulating a fork." He turned toward the central hall.

"I have no trouble with any of those so why must I attend?" She joined him.

"Because we want our residents to feel like they're part of our family, which they are," he said over his shoulder as he started down the hall.

She had zero interest in being sociable. All she wanted was time to herself to think about what she would do next, where she wanted her life to go. How she could get past the mass of emotions churning inside her. Could she continue working in search and rescue? Work with a new dog? Learn to trust another man?

Maybe she could just make sure she wasn't around when it was dinnertime. This place sounded more like a prison than a clinic. "Hey, do you mind telling me why I was sent here?"

That got his attention. "So you can regain your mobility."

"I know that. I mean why here in particular? Couldn't I have gone to a clinic in America? What makes this place so special?"

He shoved his hands into his pockets. "As I understand it, your orthopedic doctor believes this is the right clinic for you."

She stepped toward him, pinning him with a direct look. "What led him to believe this specific clinic was the right place for me to complete my physical therapy?"

Dr. Sinclair shifted his weight and raised his chin. "I'm not sure what you're looking for but our residents have an uncommonly high success rate of making as complete a recovery as possible, and by recovery I mean holistic recovery. Our state-of-the-art clinic features a peaceful atmosphere conducive to healing..." he waved a hand around, indicating the castle "...and our canine therapy has proved to be fundamental in facilitating that recovery as well. Does that reassure you?"

Canine therapy. Cass took a step back, her chest constricting. She couldn't deal with this right now. It was too soon after the loss of her dog and partner, Rufus. "I'm not interested in canine therapy."

Her German shepherd-wolfhound mix partner had been with her for four years. She'd had him since he was a puppy. She'd even gone to Germany to pick him up from the breeders. They had trained together at a search and rescue school in California. They'd understood each other, trusted one another.

Now he was gone. Despite him being an animal, the hurt of his loss was more acute than the pain of broken bones or her ex-boyfriend's assessment of her ability to maintain a relationship. She and Rufus had been all over the world together, crawling in and over disaster sites that others only saw on TV while drinking their morning coffee. As a team, they had been a part of tragedies that no one should ever see or experience. Gratitude and guilt filled her in equal measure.

She felt the doctor's keen observation and focused

on his mild expression. He turned and started down an adjacent hall to the left, saying, "This way to the lift."

Cass glanced at the staircase in relief then followed, taking careful steps to ensure there wasn't a repeat performance of what had almost happened outside.

He looked over his shoulder. "As our residents improve, they use the stairs whenever possible."

Cass once more eyed the daunting set of wide steps made of gray marble. "And that's mandatory?"

Dr. Sinclair gave her a grin. "'Mandatory' is such an unfriendly word. Why don't we go with 'greatly encouraged'? It's part of the graduation program to be able to walk up and down the stairs, but we don't require that until you're ready."

Did her relief show on her face? "What makes you think I'm not ready?"

"Maybe the tight line of your lips that indicates that little stumble outside hurt more than you wish to admit."

Cass grimaced inwardly. The man had an acute sense of awareness. Could he see that more than her body pained her? That her heart hurt? Cass hoped not. She was nowhere near ready to share her feelings. "I don't hurt."

"Liar." He gave her a flash of a smile. One she was sure made people want to confide in him, which she wasn't going to do. As if he knew what she was thinking, he said in a gentle manner, "You do know it isn't weakness to admit you're in pain or that you need help. That's what we're here for."

She'd had enough of this. All she wanted was to get to her room. "Who're you, the resident shrink?"

They walked out of the elevator and started down a wide hallway lined with portraits. A few decorations were already in place here and there. A red carpet runner muffled their steps.

"No, but as clinic administrator and emergency medical doctor I help develop the patients' therapy. All the doctors here work together to form patient plans. Recovery is as much mental as it is physical."

"So you think I have emotional issues?" Cass certainly did have them. She couldn't keep her job without a dog, and she wasn't sure she could handle having another one. To possibly lose another best friend would be too much, too painful. To get close enough that someone or something mattered was more than she wanted at this point.

Lyle's…wasn't that his name?…mouth quirked as he stopped to face her.

"Why, Ms. Bellow, in some ways I think everyone has issues. So don't go thinking you're special. Here we are." He pushed open a thick wooden door. "Your room belonged to the lady of the castle."

Cass couldn't deny it was a grand room. Its large canopy bed was hung with seafoam green curtains and covered with a matching spread. Beneath a bank of windows was a seating arrangement of a loveseat and two cushioned chairs. A chest, which she guessed held a TV, was nearby and on the opposite wall was a large fireplace with a fire already burning. The gleaming oak floor had a plush rug in the center of it. The festive fairy had been at work decorating in here as well. There was greenery along the mantle and groups of candles on tables. If she must be in this clinic, then she had won the lottery for the perfect room. She could hide out here in comfort.

"One of the staff should've put your luggage in here." He looked around. "There it is. Great." He pointed to the far side of the room where there was another door. "Through there is your bath. You'll find a hot tub, which I encourage you to use often. I'll leave you now to settle in. You don't have to be at dinner tonight. A tray of food will be sent up. Breakfast is between six and eight in the dining room. I'll let Flora know you've arrived. She may not have a chance to check in with you this evening, but you can expect to see her first thing in the morning. One of the staff will come and collect you at seven for breakfast. Is there anything you need before I go?"

Cass had slowly wandered around the room as he spoke. "I don't think so."

"If you have any questions, just pick up the phone. Somebody is on duty twenty-four hours a day. I hope your stay is a positive one."

Before he could say more a man appeared in the hallway behind him. "Lyle, you said to let you know when Andy Wallace arrived. The ambulance is at the back entrance. I'm on the way after the wheelchair now."

"Thanks Walter. I'll go down." Lyle turned to her. "See you around, Ms. Bellow."

Later that evening after dinner, Lyle bowed his head against the howling wind as he walked to his cottage. Seeing the once strong, always smiling Andy Wallace with sunken eyes and needing a wheelchair had made for a tough last few hours.

Andy was older than him. They had only been acquaintances growing up. Still, Lyle could remember Andy and Nick, Lyle's best friend Charles's older brother, laughing and always into something. Now Andy was a shell of that person. After an IED had exploded under his Humvee in Afghanistan he was a patient in a clinic started in honor of Nick. The irony was sickening.

Ms. Bellow wore the same sad expression as Andy. That look implied the weight of the world lay on her slender shoulders. His staff had their work cut out for them with those two. He and Charles, the Laird of Heatherglen and a doctor as well, had discussed both patients but Lyle suspected there was more to Cassandra Bellow than was on paper. She didn't even try to hide her desire to be elsewhere.

That resolute and dejected air about Cass indicated a serious psychological injury, but she carried her issues like a backpack they were so obvious. Maybe being at Heatherglen would help her with not only her physical problems but with what was bothering her heart and soul as well.

He recognized that look in both his residents because he'd seen it in his own eyes every time he'd shaved while serving in the Royal Army Medical Corps. All the men in his family had been expected to make a career in the armed forces and he hadn't disappointed. As one of his father's two sons, Lyle himself had been encouraged, then expected, to join the army. The importance of serving had been drummed into him his entire life. Yet medicine had pulled at him. To find a happy medium he'd combined the two.

Despite that compromise, he'd found the discipline and unwavering devotion of military life wasn't for him. He wanted to concentrate on caring for people in the way he loved best, personally. To his father's disappointment and ongoing puzzlement, Lyle had resigned his commission and returned home, remaining in the reserves.

His father still hadn't given up on the belief that Lyle

would return to active duty someday soon. Every time they were together the subject came up. Now that his father's health was declining, the pressure had grown. If Lyle resumed active service, he could make his father's last few years happier, make him proud. But the exchange would be that Lyle would be miserable.

Charles had been in the process of setting up the clinic when Lyle had returned home from overseas. He'd asked Lyle if he would consider being the administrator, as well as run the emergency centre for the surrounding villages. Lyle had accepted and never looked back. He had found where he belonged. Still, his father's disappointment weighed on him.

The decision to return to the military hung there. Then there was his obligation to the clinic…

While he'd been in the Middle East that hopeless look he recognized in Cass's and Andy's eyes had grown in his own after receiving his "Dear John" letter from Freya. He had been caught in a net with no way out. Freya had called a halt to their relationship while he had been thousands of miles away, unable to talk to her face to face. For months the pain had been like a gnawing animal in his chest. It wasn't until he had returned and started work at the clinic that he could at last breathe and see the relationship for what it was.

Lyle continued along the snowy, muddy path toward his cottage. He knew this walk by heart. The moon was large tonight and he didn't need his torch. From experience he was sure his housekeeper had left a fire laid. The thought of lighting it and a warm drink kept him moving. Thankfully he had a full belly from the meal he'd shared with the residents before leaving the clinic. He wasn't required to dine at the castle, but Mrs. Renwick was a much better cook than he was. Since he didn't much enjoy eating alone, he ate most of his meals at the clinic. And just as he'd expected, the two newest residents hadn't been in attendance.

Going through some paperwork in his office the next morning, he allowed his thoughts to wander to Ms. Bellow. He had gone to Andy Wallace's room to make sure he was comfortable and had spoken to the overnight nursing staff about him. Yet despite his curiosity about Cass, Lyle hadn't searched her out. Because she wasn't under his direct care, he couldn't think of a reason to do so. Flora would have her case well in hand. Still, he felt compelled to see Cass.

She'd whetted his curiosity for some reason. Something about her sharp, self-assured tone and unwillingness to show her obvious pain made him want to understand what was going on behind those gloomy eyes. He'd felt her fragility when she had leaned against him. All bones and skin, as if she had lost weight. Being injured would have caused some of that but she was *too* thin. He felt the odd need to protect her, reassure her. Not that he would let that show. Still, just before lunch he couldn't stop himself from walking to the physical therapy department.

Lyle found Flora, with her dark head down, working at her desk. He knocked lightly on the door.

She looked up and smiled. "Hello, Lyle. What can I do for you?"

"I just wanted to check in on Cass Bellow. I haven't seen her today." He put his hands in his pockets.

"She was here for therapy this morning." Flora put down her pen. "She was ready to start when I arrived."

He leaned against the doorframe. "Great. When we met yesterday, I was afraid she might be resistant."

Flora shook her head a little. "If there was a problem it was with her working too hard. She acted determined to be finished with her recovery well before the prescribed time. I had to remind her that she could hurt herself further if she pushed herself too hard."

"I'm sure that you'll see she takes it slowly and easily." Lyle took a step into the office. "By the way, did you tell her there's animal therapy as well? I got the impression it was a surprise to her when I mentioned it. I don't think she was told by her doctors in Germany that it's a central part of our program here."

Flora's eyes darkened with concern. "I did mention it but was called away before more was said."

"I'll speak to Esme. If Cass doesn't show up at the canine therapy center, then I'll talk to her."

Flora nodded. "Good."

"I told Cass the residents eat together, and she didn't look any happier about that."

Flora picked up the pen and tapped it on the desk once. "You and I have been at this long enough to know how to handle an uncooperative patient. We know physical issues often include adjusting to a new way of life." She lifted her shoulders and let them drop. "Why would Cass be any different?"

"Agreed. What about Andy Wallace? Have you had your session with him?"

"I'll see him this afternoon."

"Let me know how it goes. I don't think he's in any better frame of mind than Ms. Bellow."

Flora grinned. "We don't get all those great accolades for being the best therapy clinic for nothing."

"You have a point." He nodded his head at the door. "I'm on my way to get a sandwich for lunch. Care to join me?"

"Thanks, but I need to finish some paperwork for the boss."

Lyle chuckled. "And he appreciates your efforts. See you later." He left, walking to the dining room to pick up some food before returning to his office. Lyle planned to continue checking up on Cass and Andy for a few days until he was satisfied with their compliance, then he'd back away.

After lunch, Cass sat in her room by the fire, rubbing her thigh, glad therapy was over for the day. It had been grueling. Less from what she had been asked to do and more from her pushing herself. She had broken into a sweat and had clenched her teeth more than once not to cry out as pain had shot through her leg. Flora had warned her to slow down. It had been strenuous and stressful at best. Even her arm had resisted a couple of the exercises.

Making matters worse was the discovery Cass had made that she had stamina issues. The hospital stay in traction had taken a lot out of her. She'd always been fit, had worked out regularly with ease. Now she just felt frustrated. Regaining her strength wasn't going to happen fast enough.

That morning she'd been up and dressed by the time Melissa, a staff member, had knocked on her door. She had slept well the night before. Sleeping in the hospital hadn't been ideal. The peace and quiet of this country castle did have its appeal.

She had on some of the few clothes she habitually kept packed in her to-go bag. The knit sweatpants and T-shirt would have to do for workout clothes. When she and Rufus had caught the transport plane to Eastern Europe, nowhere in her plans had she thought to prepare for weeks of being in a hospital or being in a physical therapy clinic in Scotland in the winter.

Melissa had escorted Cass by elevator to the ground floor. There she had been led to the dining room.

"I'll return in a few minutes to show you to the physical therapy department," Melissa had said.

There hadn't been anyone else in the room. Cass had been thankful for that. She'd gone to the buffet and helped herself to a boiled egg and a slice of toast. She had just finished her second glass of orange juice when the woman returned.

"Flora's ready for you."

After placing her dishes on a tray, Cass followed Melissa down a long hall off the main one. They entered an area that looked like a gym where exercise equipment faced a bank of three large windows. In another corner of the spacious room were mats. Two high padded tables sat in the middle.

"You can have a seat on a table and I'll let Flora know you're here," she'd been told.

Cass scrambled up on the table with more effort than she liked.

A leggy, dark-haired woman wearing what looked like the latest fashion in exercise clothes soon joined her. Dressed in a hot pink jacket over a black top and leggings that came to mid-calf she made Cass feel extra-frumpy in her outfit. The woman even wore makeup.

She offered her hand, "Hi, I'm Flora McNeith. It's nice to meet you, Cass. I apologize that I wasn't here to meet you yesterday. I'm sure Lyle took good care of you."

"Who? Oh, yeah, the doctor."

She chuckled. "Most woman consider him more memorable than that. We should get started on your therapy."

Over the next hour Cass showed Flora the range of motion in her leg and arm. For the first thirty minutes they concentrated on her leg and the last half-hour on her arm. Flora applied a cold compress before working with either part of her body, then a warm one after.

When they were through Flora said, "I'm sending you to the whirlpool for half an hour. After lunch someone will show you to your afternoon therapy at the canine therapy center."

She didn't give Cass time to respond before she turned to another patient who had entered the room. Cass had no intention of going to the canine therapy center. She wasn't ready to be involved with a dog again, any dog. Wasn't sure she'd ever be ready. Why had her doctors in Germany insisted on sending her to this clinic when they knew her background? Maybe they had thought it would be what she needed since she had been a dog handler, but she wasn't emotionally ready. She would just make it clear, without explanation, that she wouldn't be going to the canine therapy center.

As she walked toward the door marked "Whirlpool" Cass groaned. She almost cried with pleasure as she slipped into the hot swirling water. Today she had taken the first step towards her complete discharge and regaining her life. The one that didn't include Rufus.

After her trip to PT she'd stopped by the dining room long enough to grab a sandwich, leaving the soup behind. With food eaten, a warm shower taken and clean clothes on, Cass now had a nap on her agenda. She would be perfectly happy spending the rest of the day in her room.

She woke with a start when there was a sharp knock on her door. "Coming." Cass opened it to find a staff member there. This time it was a young man.

"I'm here to show you the way to the canine therapy center."

"I'm sorry but I don't feel like going." What she really meant was she *wasn't* going.

The man studied her a moment as if he expected her to say more, then nodded. "I understand."

Cass settled back in the chair and looked into the fire. She knew her abilities and strengths. The wound of losing Rufus was too raw. Her emotions in general were stretched to snapping point. She couldn't cope with the thought of interacting with a dog even if it was supposed to speed up her recovery.

She loved her job, but could she ever return to it, ever get so involved with another animal that she risked reliving this almost unbearable suffering? What if it wasn't a dog? Could she ever open up enough to anyone again to take the chance of losing her heart?

CHAPTER TWO

LYLE STOOD OUTSIDE Cass's door. She had refused to go to her canine therapy appointment. From the information he'd received from Flora she'd been more than game to do the work in physical therapy. Why was she balking at the rest of the program?

It was important. He and his colleagues had been highly successful in using canine therapy in the recovery of their patients. Cass needed to participate. He had read in her paperwork that she'd worked as a dog handler for search and rescue. Certainly she wasn't afraid of dogs. If anything, he would have thought that she would be eager to meet her assigned dog.

Lyle rapped on the door twice.

He heard a voice call, "Just a minute." Then a few seconds later the door opened.

Cass was dressed in a T-shirt, a zip-up hoodie, jeans and socked feet. She only came as high as his shoulders. She pushed at her short blonde hair, her tone demanding as she said, "Yes?"

"I understand that you don't want to go to your canine therapy appointment." Frustration with her resistance made him sound sterner than he'd intended.

"You understand correctly." She stepped back into the room.

He moved to just inside the doorway. "It's part of the program here. Everyone's required to participate."

"Why?" She stood feet slightly apart as if preparing for a fight.

He lowered his voice. "Because we've found that people recover faster when part of their therapy involves a dog. It's almost crucial to full recuperation. Why don't you let me show you the way to the center?"

"No, thank you." She put her hand on the door.

His brow rose. Did she intend to close it on him? "Are you in pain? Do I need to speak to Flora?"

A look of something close to panic filled her eyes. "No, I'm just tired. I don't feel like it today."

He checked his watch. It was too late now for her to go anyway. She had already wasted half her time. "Okay, that's understandable. Rest is good. Take the remainder of the afternoon off. I'll see you at dinner."

She made no comment as she closed the door.

Lyle had to back out into the hall to avoid having the door shut in his face. When was the last time he'd been thrown out of a room? He couldn't even remember one. People didn't treat him like that, yet Cass had effectively done so. He shook his head. She would be a tough nut to crack.

It was almost dark when Lyle started for home. Cass hadn't been at dinner. Neither had she ordered a tray. He had left his meal long enough to go to her room, determined he'd be less understanding this time. If she couldn't follow the clinic protocols, she would be transferred elsewhere.

There was no answer when he knocked on her door. He tried three times before he called her name. Finally, he opened the door a crack and listened for the shower running. Nothing. He called again then stuck his head in to look. Cass wasn't there. First thing in the morning he was going to confront her when she showed up for her PT session with Flora.

A short time later Lyle turned to go through the gate leading to his cottage when he saw a dark shadow of a person down the way. They were sitting on the fence. Who was it? He was acquainted with most people around here but didn't recognize this person. The locals knew better than to sit outside at this time of year. His conscience wouldn't allow him to go home without first checking on the stranger.

He didn't wish to scare whoever it was, so he approached slowly. Still, there was no movement. Were they so deep in their thoughts they didn't hear him walking up? He stepped closer. He still couldn't tell if it was a man or a woman. The person didn't move. He went nearer, close enough he could touch them. Just as he was about to, they turned and looked at him. *Cass!* He had assumed she was safely in the castle somewhere, if not already back in her room. He would have never thought she might wander out into the night and cold. What had possessed her to come outside?

All she wore was a thin jacket. Her hands were shoved into her pockets. She wasn't dressed adequately for this weather. She should have on a woolly hat and scarf and a thicker jacket. "What're you doing here?"

She looked away, toward the last of the dying light.

"Are you okay? It's much too cold to be sitting here."

"I had to get out. I've been cooped up in a hospital for weeks. I needed some fresh air." Her words were so soft he leaned forward to hear them.

Lyle glanced in the direction she was looking and saw nothing that should hold her attention. He could only guess that her thoughts were so deep she had no idea what danger she was in. Could she even find her way back to the castle?

But first things first. "How long have you been out here?"

It took a moment before she answered, "I don't know."

Had frostbite started? He needed to get her out of the cold.

"Why're you here, Doctor?" Her voice sounded stronger.

That was encouraging. Much more like herself than her first few words. He pointed. "I live just down the lane there."

"Oh." Cass glanced over her shoulder then shrugged as if disinterested.

"I went to your room looking for you during dinner. I thought by now you would've come out of hiding and gone to your room for the night, prepared to ignore any knock on your door." He took a seat beside her.

This time she really looked at him. "What gave you that idea?"

"The expression on your face when I told you that you'd be expected for dinner in the dining room. I guessed you weren't planning to come. However, I didn't expect you to run outside to get away."

She pursed her lips and nodded. "Yeah, I don't think I'm gonna make those communal meals. And I'm not running away."

"We're not going to discuss that now. What we need to do is get you inside and warmed up." He stood.

Cass didn't move. Instead, her attention went to the sky once more. "Don't worry about me. I'm all right."

Lyle's brows drew together. He was sure she didn't

appreciate the full effect of his reaction because of the dim lighting. “So you’re knowledgeable enough about the area that you can get around without getting lost?”

Cass straightened and glared at him. “I work in search and rescue. I assure you I can manage to get myself back to the castle.”

There was spunk in her voice. “That remains to be seen. You’re obviously ignorant of the danger of being out in this weather without adequate clothing. I’m not taking any chances on losing one of our residents to exposure. Right now, you’re going to the closest warm place and that’s my cottage. When you’re defrosted and dry, I’ll walk you back to the castle.”

It wasn’t until that moment that Cass registered she was bone cold. How long had she been sitting here, staring off into space?

“Come with me. My cottage isn’t far.” He offered his large gloved hand, palm up.

She stared at it a moment. Was she acting crazy, like he already thought she was? Cass took his hand just long enough to slide off the wall. He turned and she trailed after him. They didn’t go far before they entered a small clearing with a two-story stone cottage sitting in the middle. Trees surrounded it. A light over the door was on and another burned brightly in the window. Someone was expecting him.

“Is your wife going to mind you bringing a wayward patient home?”

“If I had one, she wouldn’t mind.” He walked to the door and opened it, then turned and waited for her to enter.

Cass stepped in, giving him room to follow. They stood in a small hallway. He waved a hand toward a room off to one side as he closed the door and began removing his coat. "Go on in and take off your shoes. They must be wet. I'll have the fire burning in a minute."

She entered what must be his living area. There was a small couch and a large leather chair situated close to the fireplace. The seat of the chair had a dip in it. It was obviously the doctor's favorite spot. A lamp and a stack of books sat on the floor beside it. A desk with papers strewn across it was against the wall with a window that faced the front lawn. Behind the desk stood a wooden chair. On the other side were shelves full of haphazardly placed books and a few framed pastoral scenes on the wall. The room had a very masculine feel to it. The man certainly owned his space. Cass found that comforting and reassuring in some odd way.

Lyle soon joined her, minus his outer clothing and shoes. He was in his socked feet, which made him seem even more approachable. "You don't have your shoes off yet? You need to get that jacket off as well. It looks like it's soaked through."

Cass started to remove a boot. "I can tell you spend a lot of time telling people what to do."

"You can thank my father and time in the army for that." He pulled a box of matches off the mantel, knelt and lit the fire. It soon came to life. "You really don't have any idea how long you've been outside?"

Cass considered pretending she hadn't heard the question. She'd gotten lost in her thoughts, her disappointment and grief, but the last thing she wanted to do was confess why she'd been out there. "No, I'm not sure."

He stood. "You really are going to have to be more

careful around here. It's easy to wander somewhere you shouldn't. With or without snow."

Although she hadn't yet gotten her boot off, Cass removed her coat. It was heavier than usual. He was right. She hadn't noticed how wet she had become.

The doctor reached for it and she allowed him to take it. Going to the desk, he hung it over the back of the chair, which he then pulled closer to the fire.

"Do you regularly bring patients home to sit by the fire?" She dropped one boot to the floor.

He grinned. It was a nice one. The kind that made her want to return it. "No. I'd have to say you're the first. But then I only do it for people sitting on my fence who are obviously about to freeze to death."

Shivering, Cass removed the other boot and let it drop beside the first one.

He pulled a colorful knit throw of orange, browns and tan off the back of the leather chair and draped it over her shoulders. She pulled the edges around her. Warmth filled her immediately. After letting it seep in, she removed her wet socks and spread them on the hearth. With a sigh, she stretched her ice-cold feet out toward the flames. Rubbing her stiff damaged leg, she got comfortable on the small sofa.

"I'll go and brew a pot for tea." Lyle started out of the room.

"The English and their tea," Cass murmured.

"I heard that. And I'm Scottish. Not English," he said with a clipped note.

Cass winced. She'd just been chastised. Her mother would be displeased with Cass for being rude, no matter what the circumstances.

He looked over his shoulder. "I forget you're American. Would you prefer coffee? I think I have some in the back of the pantry." He waited, an expectant look on his face.

She mustered a slight smile. "No, tea is fine. You've already gone to a lot of trouble for me."

"No trouble." He left the room.

While listening to him moving around in another part of the house, Cass laid her head back against the cushion of the sofa and gazed into the flames. The feeling was returning to her feet. She wiggled them. This was nice. The most peaceful she had felt in weeks.

Lyle returned with a small tray. On it were two steaming mugs, a milk jug and a sugar bowl. "Do you take yours with sugar and milk?"

"I don't know. My coffee I like with both."

"Then let's try it that way." The doctor mixed the ingredients in and handed her a mug.

She wrapped her hands around it, letting the heat seep into her icy fingers.

He sank into his chair with his mug in his hand. The chair fit him perfectly. "How're you feeling now?"

"Much better. I had no idea how cold and wet I was."

Leaning forward, he rested his elbows on his knees with the mug between his palms. "You really need thicker socks and boots. There's a good shop in the village for those."

"My sturdy boots were cut off and discarded when I was taken to the medical tent. I went straight from the tent to the hospital and from the hospital to here. When I can, I'll buy another pair. And maybe replace my cellphone." She had said more than she had intended.

His brows went up. "Medical tent? I had no idea. Do you mind telling me what happened?"

"It wasn't in my file?"

He pursed his lips and gave a noncommittal shake

of his head. “Yes, but I’d like to hear it about it from you. I think you need to talk.”

“Being a shrink again, Doc?”

“It’s Lyle, and I was going more for being your friend.” He leaned back, looking completely comfortable. “If you don’t want to talk about it that’s fine.”

Now she was being put on the spot. If she didn’t tell him something he would think she was a head case. “There’s not much to tell. I was searching for a girl lost in the rubble of a building after a major explosion in Eastern Europe. It had been two days and there wasn’t much hope. I found her alive but in the process a wall fell on me. So now you have it.” Cass had been careful not to use the word *we*. She didn’t want to talk about Rufus. She refused to break down in front of this stranger, no matter how nice he was.

“Wow, that’s some story.”

And he hadn’t heard it all. Wouldn’t ever as far as she was concerned. “Yeah, makes for a great party story.”

He gave her a direct look. “I think it makes you a pretty impressive person. Your type of work can be both rewarding and very depressing.”

He was right about that. His piercing empathy made her conscious of her vulnerability. She wasn’t used to people seeing through what she said that clearly. The men she’d had relationships with certainly hadn’t—including Jim, her latest disaster. Now she had scars on her body. How would men react to them?

Lyle put the mug down. “How’re your hands and feet feeling now?”

Relieved he’d changed the subject, she answered, “Instead of being numb they feel like needles are being pushed into them.”

“That’s good. The feeling is returning.”

Giving him a wry smile, she brought the mug to her lips again. The warmth flowed through her, matching the heat in the room. "So how come the administrator of the prestigious Heatherglen Castle Clinic is living way out here in the woods?"

Looking over the edge of the mug, he gave her an indulgent look. "In the daylight it's not that far out. This was the gamekeeper's cottage. When I returned from serving in the Middle East I needed a place to live. Turned out this came with the administrator's job."

"I don't see you as the military type." He didn't strike her as a squared shoulders, stand-at-attention kind of man. His smile was too quick, his manner too easygoing to fit into that strait-laced world.

"Aye. I was born and bred to it."

The words were flat, suggesting that hadn't been a completely good thing. There was more there but she didn't ask. It wasn't her business and she didn't like him prying into hers, so she wouldn't.

"You were overseas?"

"Aye, two tours in the Middle East."

"That couldn't have been much fun." She was sure that was an understatement.

A dark look came over his face. "It wasn't."

He must have seen stuff similar to what she had in her work. She would never have guessed they'd have anything in common. Cass didn't want to talk about the similarities in their backgrounds. Instead she would rather lock it away and not think about the past. Or the pain. "So you were raised around here?"

"Yes. In the village of Cluchlochry. My parents don't live far from here. Where're you from?"

His tone led her to believe he loved the area. "Indiana, but I live in Montana now."

He raised his eyebrows and nodded approvingly. "I've been there. Beautiful scenery."

"It is. That's my favorite thing about it. But even with all the snow, it's pretty around here as well."

"In the spring it's like living inside an emerald it's so green." Reverence made his Scottish accent more pronounced.

Did it do the same when he whispered in a woman's ear when he desired her? Heaven help her! *That* wasn't a thought she should be having. Where had that idea come from? She swallowed hard and wiggled her toes. Surely it was the fire making her skin so hot.

"Let me have a look at those. I want to make sure you don't have the beginnings of frostbite." He went down on one knee in front of her.

"Look at what?" Her mind had been in a completely different place. "Oh, my feet. I don't think that's necessary."

He gave her an odd look then patted his thigh. "But I do. Put your foot up here."

With reluctance she did as he requested. Lyle's leg was firm beneath her bare sole, his corduroy pants soft.

He cradled her heel gently in the palm of his hand. All his touches were functional and professional, yet a streak of response zipped through her. She pulled back and sat straighter, watching the top of his head with its light, curly red hair. Were those coils as soft as they looked? She almost reached out a hand. Almost…

"Wiggle your toes for me."

Her head jerked up. It took her a long second to comply.

His fingers traveled over her toes. She pulled back but he held her foot securely. He raised his head, a slight grin on his lips. "Ticklish." It was more a statement than question.

"A little." It sounded childish to admit.

Cass groaned inside.

"There's no sign of frostbite here. That's good." He placed that foot on the floor. "Let me see the other one."

Cass didn't even try to resist this time. He gave that foot the same attention as the other, but without tickling her. For some reason that disappointed her.

"Wiggle," he commanded.

She did.

"Good." He rose from the floor and moved to pick up one of her socks. "These are still damp. You really are going to have to get some thicker ones when you buy those boots if you plan to take walks. When the snow melts it can get very muddy. I'll get you some dry ones to wear back to the castle." He left the room.

It was past time for her to get back to the clinic but his place was so cozy, so comfortable. Too much Lyle's space. She shouldn't be having such a reaction to him. This wasn't the time to add more conflicting emotions to those she already had.

He soon returned and handed her a pair of thick, very masculine navy socks. She had no doubt these would keep her feet dry. He took his chair while she pulled them on. Immediately her feet were warmer."

"These feel great. Thank you. I'll have them laundered and returned as soon as possible."

He poked at the fire, making sure the screen was secure around it. "No hurry. I know where to find them if I need them."

Cass reached for her shoes. "I think it's time for me to be going. I've taken up enough of your evening."

Lyle didn't disagree with her. Instead he rose and

went into the hallway. With her shoes now on, Cass reached for her damp coat.

"Wait. You need a dry coat as well." He had one in his hand, holding it open for her. She slipped her arms in and he settled the heavy jacket on her shoulders. There was that same smell she had caught when she'd first met him. The coat swallowed her whole but it was like being wrapped in his arms. Although that was an unsettling and unrealistic notion, it was nevertheless a reassuring one.

Lyle pulled on his own outdoor clothing while she waited. He studied her a moment. "You need a hat, scarf and some gloves as well." Disappearing upstairs, he returned with a handful of woolen items.

"I can't take these. Surely you need them." She offered them back to him.

He shook his head. "I have a drawer full. My mother knits these."

Cass ran her hand across them. The wool was so soft. "It feels wonderful."

"Try on the hat. It may not be tight enough, but it'll be better than nothing." He watched her expectantly.

Cass pulled the dark tan hat over her head, tucking in stray hair around her face. She still held the scarf. "I'll be all right without this."

"No, you won't." His stern look stopped her from further argument.

Cass wasn't used to having people tell her what to do. A bit irritated, she wrapped the scarf around her neck. It too smelled of pine and wood smoke, like him. Those scents would forever remind her of Lyle.

She forced that thought out of her head and focused on tucking the ends of the scarf inside her borrowed coat. "Your mother does a beautiful job."

"Thank you. What I can count on is that you'll stay warm in them. These gloves will be far too large but they will work for right now. You'll need to buy some of those as well. Now, come on, it's time we got you back to the castle."

She inhaled. There was that scent again. Yes, she needed to get out of here. Something about Lyle and his home made her wish for things better left alone.

CHAPTER THREE

LYLE OPENED THE door and the bitter cold embraced her. Cass pulled the scarf a little tighter around her neck, glad to have it. Lyle closed the door behind them, blocking out all but the porch light.

It was cold and darkness had taken over. As they walked further away from the house she could see the stars shining brightly. She paused in awe. It was beautiful.

Cass had been to many places in the world, but few compared to how amazing it was here with the moon and the stars…and the peace. In the distance there was a rise with what looked like the ruins of an old building on its crest. She pointed. "What's that place?"

"That's the old castle keep. The first laird of Heatherglen build it. It's a tumble of stones now but you can get a beautiful view of the valley, including the village, from up there. There's a path to it, but I don't recommend you go off on your own. The path can be a bit tricky in a number of places."

"Are you worried about me wandering away?"

He searched her face for a moment. "I'd like to hope not, but based on the facts I have so far, I feel like you might."

"I repeat, I was a member of a search and rescue

team." One that was broken now. She no longer had a partner.

He pulled a flashlight out of his pocket and turned it on now that they were way from the cottage. "I understand that, but surely you've always had help."

She'd always had Rufus. Had relied on him to return them back home safely. Now she had no one. At this particular moment Lyle was fulfilling the role Rufus had had in her life. Still, she wasn't sure she could ever let herself truly rely or care for anybody, whether dog or human, ever again.

"Search and rescue is an interesting vocation. How did you get started in that?"

"When I was ten my younger brother got lost in the woods while my family was on a camping trip. He was gone almost twenty-four hours. My parents and I were terrified we would never see him again. The search and rescue people saved the day. Later on in college I realized I wanted to help people like my family had been helped." She paused. Why was she telling this virtual stranger all of this? What about Lyle had her talking so much?

He matched his pace to her slower one. "You and your kind are special people. I worked with a few of you while I was in the army. Did you do your training there?"

"No. I didn't start that until after college. While I was in school I worked at the vet clinic at the university. I was there most weekends as a volunteer. Some of the dogs were retired search dogs. After working with them I had no doubt what I should be doing."

"It sounds like an exciting way to make a living." He sounded truly impressed.

Sometimes it could be too exciting. She had no interest in reliving the last few months of her life. "It can be, but it also has its downsides. It's awful to see people desperately searching for loved ones or learn that a family member can't be saved."

"I know what you mean. War can do devastating things to a body. Trying to piece it back together can be the stuff of nightmares." His sincerity convinced Cass he understood all too well.

In spite of her determined efforts to conceal her private hell, she was feeling uncomfortably vulnerable yet again. "I'd rather not compare notes on what we've seen." Her last assignment was at the top of the list.

"You're right. Some things are better left in the past."

Cass couldn't agree more. She'd had enough issues generated in the recent past to last her a lifetime. She wobbled when she stepped into a snow-covered dip in the ground.

His hand nestled in her elbow. "How's that leg feeling?"

"Like a building fell on it and it had more PT than it liked."

"I bet it does. You're doing too much. A walk outside might have been over the top." He moved the torch so that it illuminated the snow in front of her.

"I'm handling it." She was, just barely though.

"I spoke to Flora and she said you might have overdone things today."

She pulled her arm from his hold. "Are you going around checking up on me?"

"That's part of my job." Nothing in Lyle's voice was apologetic.

Cass stepped as far away from him as the path would allow. "Well, I'll have you know I don't need a babysitter."

"I'll keep that in mind. I also understand you're in a

big hurry to leave us. You know, you can hurt people's feelings with that attitude."

When was the last time she had been teased? Her personality didn't make people do that often. "I'm not as interested in people's feelings as I am in getting my leg and arm well again. You do know I could've made it back by myself. All I had to do was come out the gate and follow the fence back."

"That may have been so, but I couldn't take the chance of you getting lost. It looks bad in the press for the clinic to lose a patient."

No matter how she tried to push him away, or how close she came to rudeness, he seemed to take it in stride. She had to appreciate his sense of humor and self-assurance. He had an ability to make her smile even when she didn't want to or feel like it.

A whimper from somewhere up ahead caught Cass's attention. Her senses went on full alert. She searched the ground for who or what was making the noise. Her reaction came from years of being vigilant at her job. Unable to see clearly in the small amount of light, she angled her head to listen. There it was again.

Lyle turned his flashlight toward a hedge nearby. The sound came again. It was animal, not human. This time Lyle stepped in the direction of it.

"Do you hear that?"

"Yes." She didn't move from her spot. The noises brought back painful memories. Like the ones Rufus had made just before he'd died.

"It's an animal in trouble." Lyle took small steps toward the shrubbery, making the light arc back and forth. The whimper came again, and he focused the beam in that spot. "It's a dog."

Cass's chest tightened. She couldn't deal with a dog right now. Even a stray.

"Hey, buddy, do you need some help?" Lyle asked in a tender, soothing tone. His shoulder moved as if he were reaching out a hand.

There was a growl.

Cass still remained rooted where she was. She couldn't make herself step forward.

"We can't leave it out here in the cold. It looks like it's starving." Lyle reached out his hand again.

Another growl.

Lyle spoke over his shoulder. "If I can get it to come to me I'll take it to the canine therapy center. Esme will check it out and see about it."

Cass forced herself to take a step closer. She looked over Lyle's back to where the light was directed. He reached forward once more.

The dog snarled, showing its teeth.

"It doesn't look like it's going to let me take it. I can't just leave it here. I'm afraid it'll freeze before morning."

Cass was shocked back to reality. The animal was so obviously undernourished. It shook in the cold. Its big brown eyes had a pitiful, fearful look. Cass's heart lurched. She had to do something. Everything in her that made her vulnerable to getting hurt again reached out to this pathetic animal. She didn't want to care but couldn't help herself.

Lyle didn't understand Cass's standoffishness. After all, she had worked with a dog. He glanced back at her. She just stood there, staring at him and the dog. "I don't recognize it as anybody's around here. I know them as well as I know their owners."

Finally, Cass blinked and stepped forward, but there

was little enthusiasm on her face. "Let me see if I can help." She went down on her knees, paying no attention to the wetness that must be seeping into her jeans. Removing a glove, she reached out her hand, letting the small scruffy dog smell her.

The dog slowly extended its nose. It obviously liked Cass far better than him. It crawled out from under the hedge and came to Cass. Just a puppy, it was small with muddy matted hair. One of its ears stood up while the other flopped. It had an oddly patterned coat, making it look of mixed breed. Cass lifted the dog to her chest.

Lyle stood. "It figures. I've always been far better with people than animals. It likes you."

Cass gave him a dry smile. When she struggled to stand he helped her.

"The canine therapy center is right down this way. Not far. Just behind the castle. It used to be the stables. It's just through the woods." He led them back to the path. "We'll take it there. Esme will see to it."

Cass didn't say anything as she came to stand beside him. As they walked she held the dog close but not overly so. Was she afraid of the dog? Or was there more going on? Lyle would have thought she'd be the first in on a rescue.

Soon they reached the center. The lights were still on. "Esme must be keeping another late night. I'm glad I didn't have to call and get her out in the weather again. She's the veterinarian. This therapy center/veterinary center is Esme's brainchild." He hurried ahead and held the door for Cass.

She moved in past him.

"Esme, it's Lyle," he called as the door closed behind him.

“Hey, be there in a sec,” came Esme’s voice from another room.

She soon appeared with a broad smile on her face. Her short blonde hair was disheveled, as if she had been running her hands through it. “What’s going on?”

Lyle nodded toward Cass, who still held the dog. “We have a patient for you.”

Esme looked at the dog then gave Cass a questioning look.

“Esme, this is Cass Bellow, one of our new residents. She hasn’t made it down to meet the dogs yet, so you haven’t met her.”

“Welcome, Cass. So, who do you have there?” Esme reached for the dog.

It growled.

“Aw, I see you have that special touch,” Esme said, speaking to Cass. “Bring it back here and I’ll give it a look.” Esme led them down a short hall into an examination room. “Put it on the table.”

Cass did as she was told.

Esme went to touch the dog again and it rumbled a complaint deep in its chest.

“I’ll give him something to ease his anxiety.” Esme went to draw up a syringe of medicine.

“Apparently Cass has that special something with animals.” Lyle looked at her, expecting to see a positive expression, but instead she appeared distraught. What was wrong?

Esme quickly and efficiently gave the dog an injection. It soon rested easily in Cass’s arms. “You can put him on the table now. He shouldn’t be any trouble.”

Cass placed the dog on the metal table and backed away. “I think you have this now.” She looked at him. “I can find my way back to the castle from here.”

Cass was out the door before Lyle could stop her.

"She seemed in a hurry," Esme murmured as she started examining the dog.

Lyle agreed. That accompanied intense curiosity about the stricken look on Cass face as she'd fled.

The next evening Lyle entered the dining room. A number of the residents were already there and engrossed in conversation. Cass wasn't one of them. He hadn't seen her since the night before. The few times he had left his office during the day she hadn't been anywhere in sight. After her reaction to the dog he'd been very interested in how she was doing.

Everyone was seated at the table and the food was ready to serve when Cass entered the room. Relief washed through him. He had feared he was going to have to go and find her and he hadn't been looking forward to the conversation that would have taken place.

She was dressed in a simple white button-down shirt and jeans. On her feet were the same boots she'd worn the night before. Her hair was brushed back and it didn't look as if she had any makeup on. There was a fresh, simple air about Cass that appealed to him. Something he was completely unprepared for.

For too long he'd held onto Freya because she had been something safe and secure in a world he'd been unable to control. He had been too young, too unsure of life and couldn't see that before he'd gone overseas. Still, the way their relationship had ended had colored how he viewed potential partners. He was gun-shy, and he'd be the first to admit it. The next time he got involved with a woman he wanted it to be a mature, mutual lifelong commitment. That certainly couldn't be with a resident who would soon be gone and had her own life thousands of miles away. He needed to stop any kind of thoughts like the ones he was having now.

"We're glad to have you join us," he informed Cass as he stood and pulled out the chair next to him. Smiling, he added, "I was worried I might have to go out in the weather to hunt you down."

She gave the therapy dog belonging to the resident on the other side of her a long uncertain look before taking the offered seat. "It isn't because I didn't think about skipping out."

"I'm glad you changed your mind."

She gave him a direct look. "Hunger pangs changed it for me."

He nodded. "Whatever the reason, I'm glad you're here. Let me introduce you to everyone."

"You don't—" She didn't finish the sentence when those at the table turned to look at her.

"Everyone, this is Cass." Lyle then went round the table, giving each person's name. They either nodded or said hello to her as he went. She offered them all a tight smile.

The food was served family style out of large bowls and platters, passed around the table. Cass only took small amounts of a few items. At this rate she would never gain back the weight he suspected she had lost.

"I thought you might like to know that the puppy we found last night is doing well. Esme said he's fine except for being underweight. He should make a full recovery."

"That's good." She started picking at her meal.

Cass wasn't helping much with making conversation. Lyle made another effort. "She's going to ask around and see if anyone claims him."

"That's nice." Cass took a bite of food as if she loathed doing it.

Roger, the man sitting on the other side of her, asked her a question. Cass gave him a two-word answer. Apparently, she didn't want to carry on a conversation with anyone. But she needed to. If he had ever seen someone badly in need of interaction, it was Cass.

He tried another approach. "I see the residents and staff have been busy in here today. It looks festive."

Cass looked around as if she was seeing the room for the first time.

How could she not react to the greenery and red bows hanging from the chandeliers, along with the large matching centerpiece of green boughs, velvet bows, and crimson balls? Or the mantel filled with decorations? In his experience it was the kind of stuff women loved.

Other than her hesitant look at the dog beside her, she appeared unaware of everything and everyone. He'd forced Cass into noticing him, but only for an all-too-brief moment. For some reason he wanted her to initiate an interaction with him. He wanted her to like him.

Lyle transferred his attention to Alice, who sat on his other side. Maybe giving Cass space would help open her up a bit. He and Alice carried on a lively conversation about the upcoming village Christmas market beginning this weekend. They went on to discuss some of the other events planned for the festive season, like the annual Christmas festival at the castle, and the live nativity in the village.

"I was told there would be a tree lighting in the village and a parade in a few weeks." Alice's eyes lit up with excitement.

"There is and they even include some of the dogs from the center."

He glanced at Cass a few times during the discussion and caught her listening. When she saw him looking, she focused on her food again. He decided to try to draw her into conversation once more. "Cass, do you like craft markets?"

Her head jerked up. "I…uh… I do."

"Then you'll want to be sure and catch the minibus into Cluchlochry on Saturday morning. The village has a pretty impressive one. Great place to buy Christmas presents."

"I'll think about it." She pushed back her chair. "Right now I need to go for a walk before it gets dark."

"Hey, before you go could I speak to you for a moment in private?"

Her expression said no. Yet she answered, "Okay, but just for a minute. I really want to walk."

"I promise not to take up too much of your time." He rose when she did and followed her into the hall. "Why don't we go to the lounge?" With a hand he directed her down the hall. She headed that way and he joined her. They turned a corner and entered another hall. At the first doorway, Lyle opened the door to the large room with numerous sitting areas. A fire roared in the fireplace in the center of the main wall. Windows filled the opposite side.

"Why don't we have a seat?"

"I'm starting to feel like I'm being brought into the principal's office. You could have gotten on to me about not going to canine therapy again today in the hall outside the dining room." Cass sat on the edge of a cushion of the closest sofa.

"I could have, but I'm more interested in finding out why you're so resistant to the idea of canine therapy. Especially since I know your job entailed working closely with a dog. I assume you at least like animals a bit. I noticed you were slow to help with the dog we found and left the center as quickly as you could. I read in your file that you lost your partner." He didn't miss the stricken look that flickered in her eyes. "Is that what the problem is? I'd like to help. The staff here would like to help."

Cass shot to her feet. "I don't want your help or anyone else's. If you want me to go to canine therapy, fine. I'll be there tomorrow."

"There you are." Charles walking toward them stopped anything further Cass might have said.

Lyle came to his feet. "Hi, Charles. I'd like you to meet Cassandra Bellow. She's one of our newest residents. Cass, this is Dr. Charles Ross-Wylde. Also the Laird of Heatherglen and Esme's brother."

Charles smiled at Cass. "It's nice to meet you. Please call me Charles."

"Hello. You have a lovely home…castle." Cass's words were tight and formal. She glanced toward the door.

Charles chuckled. "Thank you. You're American, aren't you?"

"I am."

"You must be the woman who works in search and rescue?" He gave her an earnest look. "Interesting job."

"It can be." Cass looked toward the door again. "Why don't I let you two talk?" She slipped away.

Lyle watched her go. He had no doubt Cass would keep her word about going to therapy. How much she would get out of it was another question. He'd just have to trust that the dog she was paired with would do what was needed to help her heal.

"Lyle."

He looked at Charles, who was grinning at him with twinkling eyes. "What?"

"You like her, don't you?"

"Why would you say that?" Lyle didn't want to discuss his confused reactions to Cass Bellow. Not even with his best friend Charles.

He laughed. "Because I called your name three times before you answered!"

Lyle wanted to groan. Now Charles would ask questions every time he saw him. "Did you have something important you wanted to talk to me about?"

Charles looked at him with a knowing smile on his lips. "It isn't as interesting as Ms. Bellow but we need to talk about Andy and his progress."

"Ah. Why don't we go to my office to do that?"

Cass was still stomping and swinging her arms in exasperation when she reached the main road after the long walk down the castle drive. How dared Lyle treat her as if she were a disobedient child? She was doing her physical therapy. Aware of what she needed, it wasn't canine therapy. But he wasn't going to give up.

She'd gone to dinner like he wanted, wasn't that enough? She would go to the canine therapy center tomorrow all right, but her participation in the therapy would be minimal and uncooperative. That should keep him off her case.

"Be strong," she said to the trees, and shoved her hands into her jacket pockets. When her brother had been lost, her mother and father had hugged her too tightly and had constantly reminded her they all had to remain strong. Afterwards Cass had used the mantra "Be strong" whenever she'd felt helpless. Even now, years later, she was using it to defy that feeling.

"Be strong!" she yelled to the sky.

She'd been strong when Jim had broken her heart,

then soon after that when she'd learned that Rufus was gone. She'd been strong when the doctors had warned her she might never regain full use of her crushed arm and leg. She had been strong during the grueling hospital stay. During her agonizing physical therapy sessions here. Only it didn't matter how strong she was. Nothing changed. She was alone with no one to lean on.

The sound of a vehicle coming up the road drew her attention. The driver was going too fast for the icy conditions. As it came around the curve the back end went one way and then the other. The skid landed the front end of the car in the stone wall between Cass and the road.

She hurried out the castle gate and over to the car with her heart pounding, ignoring the ache in her leg. The engine was still running even though the hood was crumpled. The hot air of the radiator hitting the cold air created stream, making it difficult to see.

Cass reached out to touch the side of the car with a shaking hand. She'd not done any rescue work or even given anyone medical attention since her last assignment. Now here she was faced with an accident without the support of her partner. Could she do it? Would she break down and cry? She inhaled deeply, bracing herself. "Stay strong."

She ran her hand down the side of the car to keep her bearings as she worked her way to the driver's door. Cass pulled it open. She could, would, get through this.

The driver groaned, his palm pressed to his forehead.

"Are you okay?" Her instinct and training kicked in. "Don't move. You could have more injuries."

"I'm fine." His words were slurred.

She placed a hand on the man's shoulder. "I'm an

EMT. I know what I'm talking about. More help will be here soon."

The man pulled his hand away from his head. Blood covered it.

"Don't move," she said firmly. "Keep your head back. I'm going to reach in and turn the engine off." She found the ignition key and turned it. The steam dissipated.

There was a moan from the back seat. She had someone else to check on. If she only had a cellphone to call for help. Hers had been damaged in her accident and she hadn't had time to replace it yet. Surely the driver had one. "Sir, do you have a phone? Tell me where it is, don't try to find it yourself."

The man gave her a weak yes and told her it was in his jacket pocket. Cass carefully reached inside his pocket and retrieved it.

Cass quickly dialed 999. When a person answered, Cass gave the call handler all the necessary information. She then stepped to the rear passenger door. Pulling it open, she found crumpled in the footwell a lady of around sixty. "You're going to be fine. I know you're in an uncomfortable position but try not to move."

The woman groaned, but Cass knew from the sound she was barely conscious. Using her fingers, Cass searched for a pulse in the woman's neck. She located one but it wasn't strong.

A voice she recognized as Lyle's said from behind her, "Don't move her. She may have concussion."

Cass said over her shoulder, "I've already told her that. And I've already called for help."

"I know. I must have called right after you."

She needed to get the man's bleeding under control. "Do you have any supplies?"

"No. I was on my way home when I heard the crash."

Cass stood. "You see about this woman and I'll look for a first-aid kit."

She worked her way to the front passenger door. Opening it, she searched the glove compartment for anything they could use. All she found was a stack of napkins. Those would have to do.

"Cass, we need to lay this lady down on the seat so I can examine her properly," Lyle said.

"Okay, take these napkins and have the man hold them to his head. I'll crawl in the back and help lift the woman up."

Lyle accepted the napkins and applied them to the man's head. "I need to get him to the clinic to stitch him up, but first we need to take care of this woman. She's lost consciousness."

Cass had been busy climbing into the backseat on her knees while he talked. Her leg rebelled at the position but she continued. She reached under the woman's arms and locked her hands across her chest. To Lyle she said, "Ready?"

"On three. One, two, three."

Cass pulled the woman against her chest. As the woman's back came up on the seat, Lyle grabbed her ankles and lifted. Soon they had her lying across the seat. She moaned and her eyelids flickered.

"Will you check her pulse and heart rate while I see if she has any internal injuries?" Lyle asked, as he started pressing on the woman's midsection.

"Her heart rate is steady but not very strong," Cass reported.

"Okay. So far I can't find any additional injuries." He continued to examine the woman.

A minibus pulled out of the castle gate and drew up alongside them.

"We need to get them both up to the clinic where I can give them a thorough evaluation." Lyle continued searching for problems.

Cass looked at the top of his head as he worked. "Shouldn't we wait on an ambulance?"

"That'll take too long. It has to come from Fort William. We're the emergency care for this area."

"Really?"

Now he met her look. "Rural area. That's how it is."

That made sense.

He was an impressive man to assume the responsibility for so many lives.

The staff member who had been driving the minibus joined them.

"Ron," Lyle said, "we need to get these people to the clinic ASAP. The man should be able to sit up front. We'll need the stretcher for the woman."

Ron nodded and headed back to the minibus.

Lyle backed out of the car. "Cass, would you please continue to monitor her while I have a look at the man?"

"Okay." Cass picked up the woman's wrist and placed two fingers on the inside. It took a second but she located a pulse. Still shallow but steady.

"I'm going to get this man into the minibus," Lyle called. "You good there?"

"Yes." Cass remained focused on the woman, trying not to think about her own recovering leg and arm as she began to worry about the injured woman being exposed to the cold. "Bring a blanket if you've got one."

"Will do." A few minutes later Lyle returned, pushing a gurney with Ron's help. "It's going to take all of us to get her loaded."

The two men positioned the gurney right outside the door.

Lyle handed her the blanket. Cass spread it over the woman. He tucked it around her legs. "Cass, if you'll support her head and shoulders while Ron and I get on either side of her and lift her out, I think we can make it work."

Cass wasn't looking forward to the pain she was sure would rocket through her leg and arm from the exertion. That didn't matter. Caring for the hurt woman was more important. Cass worked her hands under the woman's shoulder blades and supported her head with her upper arms. "Ready."

"Okay Ron. One, two, lift!"

Slowly the two men maneuvered the woman over the seat onto the gurney. Keeping the woman's upper body and neck as straight and stable as possible, Cass crawled across the seat and out the other door. By then electrifying pain was coursing through every nerve of her leg. Her arms and back were convulsing under the strain. When she tried to stand, her traumatized leg gave way. She grabbed the gurney. Though it wobbled on its wheels, she managed to balance on her other leg.

"Damn," Lyle swore as he reached for her. "I can't believe I got so caught up in what was happening I forgot you were a recovering patient. Sit down." He guided her to a seat of the vehicle. Giving her a stern look, Lyle ordered, "Stay there while we get this lady loaded."

Cass hated to admit it but she was relieved to sit. Her eyes were watering from intense pain. As she took a moment, emotions swamped her. Her loss of direction, missing Rufus, the fog of her future all came down on her. Sorrow tightened her chest.

Lyle gave her a concerned look. For a second Cass

feared he would question her but instead he said, "Ron, let's get this woman strapped down and loaded." Mere moments later he returned to her. "It's your turn."

Clenching her jaw, she stood. No matter how sick and unsure she felt inside, Cass refused to let it show, even if she had to struggle to do it. She feared Lyle was too perceptive and had already guessed. Cass said with more confidence than she felt, "I can walk."

"Maybe so, but you aren't going down on my watch." He wrapped an arm around her waist and guided her to the back of the vehicle.

Hot awareness of his strong sturdy body zipped through Cass as Lyle held her tight. Unable to stop herself, she leaned against him. After hesitating a moment, she rested her arm around his middle back and hobbled to the minibus. She couldn't ignore the sensations simmering in her core any more than she could ignore her agonizing leg.

Lyle held her steady until she reached for the frame of the door. Cass was climbing into the minibus when she was lifted off her feet and placed gently on the floor. She looked over her shoulder. "Thanks."

"No problem. Have a seat and move down." Lyle wasted no words. He was all business.

She did as she was told, scooting down to the end of the small bench seat. Lyle joined her. Their bodies touched all the way along one side. Strangely she wanted to rest her head against his shoulder but she resisted the urge. She refused to show any more weakness. What would Lyle think of her if she had given in to that impulse?

Ron close the doors. They were soon moving. Lyle's attention remained on the woman on the gurney, which was locked to the floor with straps. She still hadn't regained consciousness. Lyle took her pulse as they rode. He gave Cass a nod.

From what Lyle had said, Cass assumed that they were headed to the castle. By the winding of the road she could tell she was right. After making a big circle, Ron backed the minibus to a stop. Seconds later he opened the door.

Lyle climbed out with one agile move. "You stay put," he told her. "I don't want you to fall. Someone will be out to get you." He didn't wait for her response before he and Ron unhooked the gurney and rolled the woman inside.

Cass forced herself not to shake. Memories of lying in the rubble of that building flooded back. The sound of her calling Rufus's name and him not answering. The waiting until someone could get to her. Panic rose when Lyle didn't come. Pain throbbed through her body. She needed to get out of here.

She searched the area she could see. It was a part of the castle she wasn't familiar with. The vehicle was backed up to a small loading dock with two double doors. Her impatience grew to be an almost living thing. She had to do something. What if Lyle needed her help? Just as she was about to rise, Ron came through the doors, leaving them swinging. He gave her a glance then hurried down the steps nearby. Her heart dipped. He must be going after the man up front.

With Ron and Lyle concentrating their energies on the injured people, it would be some time before someone would come to assist her. She decided she wasn't in so much pain that she couldn't get herself inside.

Giving her leg a rub, she pushed up off the bench, making sure she didn't use her right arm. It took effort. With a tight jaw she made it to her feet. She slowly moved out of the minibus, steadying herself by pressing her hand on the side of it. Just as she was stepping off, the doors swung open again and out came Melissa, pushing a wheelchair.

She positioned the wheelchair just outside the van doors and stepped inside. "Lyle sent me out for you. He said you wouldn't stay seated long. I guess he was right."

Cass didn't like Lyle thinking he knew her that well, but she couldn't deny he was right. She took a step forward, trying to keep as much weight as possible off the leg. Cass couldn't deny the wheelchair was welcome.

"Here, let me help." Melissa supported Cass to the chair and assisted her into it.

With Cass secure, she pushed her inside. They entered a large emergency examination room complete with all the most up-to-date equipment. Cass was fascinated. She'd had no idea this area of the clinic existed. There were many facets to Dr. Sinclair and his "clinic".

Lyle stood beside the older lady, who still lay on the gurney. Thankfully she was now conscious and talking to him. Ron was busy cleaning the driver's head wound at an exam table nearby.

"What can I do to help?" Cass asked, putting her hands on the arm of the wheelchair, preparing to stand.

Lyle gave her a piercing look of reprimand. "Nothing. You've done enough. You need to take care of yourself."

"Surely you need some help." Cass looked from him to the man Ron was seeing to and back.

Another member of the nursing staff rushed in. Behind her came another.

"We have plenty of help. Melissa, please see that Cass gets to her room. I'll let Flora know what's happened. She may want to examine you. Melissa, Cass actually might also benefit from some time in the hot tub." Lyle's attention returned to his patient.

Seconds later Cass was being wheeled out of the room. It didn't take Melissa long to get her up to her room and hot water running in the tub. Cass gratefully slipped into the whirling water, looking forward to the relief it would bring her leg and arm. She'd survived her first emergency without Rufus. It had been a sad moment but somehow an encouraging one. In a small way, Cass was moving forward.

Lyle was ready for some rest but he needed to check on Cass first. The ambulance from Fort William had arrived to take the injured woman to the hospital. Lyle had stitched the gash on the man's forehead and sent him home with family members. After a quick check on Cass he was headed for his cottage and bed. The adrenalin spike of handling an emergency had worn him out.

He knocked lightly on Cass's door in case she was already sleeping. After waiting a minute and getting no answer, he turned to leave. He would see her tomorrow.

The door opened a crack. "Yes?"

He could only see a sliver of her but it was enough to tell that her hair had been pushed back and her face was freshly scrubbed. She looked adorable and unsure at the same time.

What was it about her that captivated him? That pulled at him like no other woman he knew did. Was it her strength? Determination? Her vulnerability? He needed to solve the puzzle and move on. Cass wouldn't be here long and he wasn't going to waste his emotions on anyone he didn't intend to keep forever. He'd already gone down that road.

The dirty street behind him was graveled with disappointment and heartache. He had vowed the lane ahead would be paved with the love and loyalty of a woman who wanted him as much as he did her. A lifelong partner. The next time he fell in love, he would get it right.

He shoved that fantasy aside and concentrated on what he was there for. “How’re you doing?”

“Better after a hot bath.”

“Good. You were impressive out there, Cass. You stayed in control. I know you must have been in pain. You should have said something. More than that, I should’ve thought.” Guilt filled him. “I’m sorry.”

She opened the door wider. “Hey, I’m an EMT. I’m trained to help.”

“True, but you’re also a patient here. I should have remembered that.” She looked cute in her T-shirt with her pink-tipped toes.

“I’m fine.” For once her eyes weren’t clouded with hidden feelings. In fact, there was a hint of a smile in them.

“I’m glad. Then I’ll let you get some rest.” He needed to go. Right now. He started down the hall.

“Hey, Lyle.”

He almost kept going, but curiosity got the better of him.

“You were pretty impressive out there too.”

He smiled. It felt good to have someone praise him, especially Cass. He was confident in his abilities, but it didn’t hurt to have others notice. His father certainly hadn’t. “Thanks. Sleep well, Cass.”

CHAPTER FOUR

CASS'S HAND SHOOK as she wrapped it around the handle of the glass door of the canine therapy center the next afternoon. She had said she'd keep her appointment and she would. But she wasn't looking forward to it.

The thought of having anything to do with a dog made her want to break down and cry. The pain of losing Rufus was still too raw. It might be silly for a grown professional woman to feel this way, but she didn't care. Rufus was gone. Some part of her clung to the irrational hope he would be waiting with his tail wagging when she returned home. No other dog could replace him.

She would do what she had to, then hurry to her room for a good cry.

When she jerked the door open the young man sitting behind the desk started. This was the same high-ceilinged room with the rough board walls where she and Lyle had brought the puppy a couple of nights before. He'd said it used to be the stables and she could now see that. The other night all that'd filled her mind was that she had a dog in her arms.

"Can I help you?" the man at the desk asked.

"I'm Cass Bellow. I'm a resident at the clinic."

He looked down as if checking a list, then back at her. "Oh, yes, we've been expecting you." As he got to his feet he added, "Come with me. Margaret assists with the canine therapy program. She's back here."

Cass forced her feet to move and followed him down a hall. It wasn't the same one Lyle and Esme had led her down to the examination room the other night. The man pushed through a swing door. Cass entered a room furnished with easy chairs.

A dark-haired woman was down on her heels next to a woman seated in an easy chair holding a small black dog of no pedigree. Cass recognized the woman in the chair from the dinner table at the clinic. Lyle had introduced them, but Cass didn't remember her name. Shame pricked her. She hadn't even tried.

"Margaret, this is Cass Bellow," the man announced.

The dark-haired woman looked at them, stood and came toward Cass with one hand outstretched. She smiled. "It's great to finally meet you."

Was that her subtle way of reprimanding her for not showing up for her earlier appointments? The temptation to run grew.

"I help Esme with the canine therapy here at Heatherglen," Margaret continued.

The man quietly left the way they had come in.

Staring at the small dog that was enjoying the woman's gentle pats, Cass's chest tightened. She wasn't ready for this. She had no interest in doing *anything* with a dog.

Margaret was saying, "I thought you might like to meet Muffin. He's a sweet little dog. He'll be your companion during your stay. Let me get him and you can get acquainted." She stepped through a side door.

Cass stood, knees shaking, in the middle of the room, looking everywhere but at the other woman. She didn't want any responsibility for a dog for the next month.

Especially one named Muffin. Her breathing became shallow. Her mouth turned dry. She shifted from one foot to the other. The need to leave intensified. This was too much. A meltdown was building if she didn't get out of there. She wasn't ready, might not ever be. What if she became too attached to the ridiculous Muffin? She would be leaving soon. All this pain would be there again.

Without thought Cass bolted for the door and up the hall to the front room. She had to get out of there. Ignoring the man behind the desk calling her name, she shoved the door open and stumbled into the cold air. Sucking in a deep breath, she kept going, heading toward the castle. By way of a side door she'd found yesterday, she slipped inside unnoticed.

Instead of going to her room, where someone would surely look for her, she headed for the conservatory. While exploring she'd also found an alcove hidden behind some large palm plants and banana trees with only a small sofa. There she could lick her wounds in private.

Relief washed through her when she found the floral fabric-covered settee empty. She sat, pulling her legs up under her and wrapping the coat Lyle had loaned her tighter. When would the pain go away?

She had no idea how long she had been sitting there staring off into space when she heard, "Cass?"

Lyle.

She stiffened. How had he found her? It didn't matter. She had no intention of explaining herself. Why couldn't he just leave her alone? "Go away."

He just stood there.

Finally, she murmured, "How did you know where to find me?"

"I saw you come in here. When I had a call from the center I knew where to look."

Great. She'd believed she'd made her escape. Her focus remained on the green spots showing in the snow that was melting outside. "So now you're riding to the rescue."

Lyle came to sit beside her. "I'd just like to help. Be a friend. I was told you looked upset."

Maybe if she ignored him he would go away. Instead of him taking the hint to leave, he settled further back into the cushions, his big body almost touching hers. They remained like that for a while, neither saying anything.

"You're not leaving, are you?" Cass stared at the dust motes dancing in the sunbeam streaming through the glass.

"Not until I know you're okay." He stretched his legs out and crossed his ankles.

She huffed. "Let me assure you I'm not going to harm myself."

"I didn't think that but it's good to hear."

He settled back as though he was content to stay the rest of the day. As the silence between them grew so did her temper. She hissed, "What do I have to say to get you to leave?"

For a moment she thought he was ignoring her. When he did reply, concern laced his voice. "I'd like to understand why you're determined to have no part in our canine therapy program, especially since you work with a dog all the time."

Could she tell him? Would he understand? Was that the only way to get him to leave her alone? If he knew, maybe he would see to it she didn't have to go to canine therapy.

She opened her mouth to tell him about Rufus but the words stuck in her throat. If she said it out loud, then it would make it true. She didn't want that. Couldn't live with that. She closed her eyes tight. Maybe if she said it really fast she could get it out. "Rufus, my partner, died. Now I don't know if I can be around a dog all the time."

The moisture she had been banking for days seeped out of her closed eyelids. She took a deep breath in an effort to stop the sob welling in her throat but it didn't work. Instead she doubled over in agony. As she tried to catch her breath Lyle ran his large hand across her back in a comforting stroke.

Then he cupped her shoulder and pulled her against his chest. She buried her face in his shirt, her fingers clutching his sides. All the emotions she had held in check since the day that wall had collapsed flowed freely. The pain deep within her consumed her. Rufus was gone. Life as she'd known it had gone with him.

Lyle held her close, rubbing her shoulders and back. "Let it all out," he whispered.

Cass did. All the raw feelings she'd held in check for weeks flowed, leaving her nothing but a heaving shell. She couldn't stop the pain, fear and sorrow from escaping.

Lyle continued holding her and murmuring soft reassuring words while she clung to him.

She had no idea how much time had passed when she woke with a start. Disorientated, she still had a sense of safety. Slowly it dawned on her she was still in Lyle's arms.

Embarrassment flooded her. Placing her palms on his chest, she pushed into a sitting position. Yet one of his hands remained on her back.

"I'm so sorry for that ugly scene," she heard herself

saying. “I don’t know why I fell apart like that. It isn’t like me.”

“I’d imagine it was because you needed to. You’ve been under a tremendous strain.” He shifted, putting his hands on his thighs.

She missed the reassuring weight immediately. Lyle was right, there was a lot of stress and emotion involved in her profession. She should be able to handle it. But where Rufus was concerned she was lost. Cass wiped at his sweater. “I’ve made a mess of your clothes.”

“I don’t mind. I’m glad I was here to help.” He sounded as if he meant it.

“So part of your job description is to have patients cry all over you?” Cass managed a weak smile.

He looked at her tenderly. “Not all patients. I have to say you’re a special case.”

Warmth gradually replaced the coldness running through her. Lyle was a nice man saying all the right things. For an instant she wished he wasn’t a doctor speaking to a patient.

“I knew about you losing your dog, it was in your file. But I had no idea that going to canine therapy would be so difficult for you. You’ve had a tough time physically and…” he paused “…emotionally. Flora, Esme and I didn’t recognize that. I’m sorry. Would you like to talk about what happened? I’m a good listener.” His words were encouraging, not demanding.

Cass shook her head, both in response and to clear it.

He waited a few moments then asked, “When did you learn the details of what happened?”

“I realized the wall was falling but I had no idea…” She swallowed. Her throat was tight and dry. Inhaling, she fought through the final pang of denial. “I didn’t find out Rufus didn’t make it until I woke up in the hospital. When I asked about him, one of the nurses had to ask around for the information."

Lyle put his arm around her shoulders again and gave her a supportive squeeze. "I'm sorry. It shouldn't have happened like that."

Cass continued to look at the windowsill. It was such a large one. Almost big enough to use as a seat. "No matter when I was told, or how, it wouldn't have made… the terrible truth any easier to hear."

"Maybe not, but at the very least the news should have been given to you in a sensitive manner." He sounded irritated on her behalf. "Will you tell me about your dog?"

She didn't want to, but he deserved to know why she'd just sobbed herself into an exhausted sleep all over him. "Rufus was more than my dog. He was my partner and best friend."

And her longest relationship. He been there more than once when a relationship with a man had ended. Those guys had either been intimidated by a woman who handled such an emotionally demanding job, or they didn't like her leaving for weeks at a time on the spur of the moment. For a couple of them her relationship with Rufus had been a bone of contention. They'd wanted all her attention and hadn't understood the uncanny connection between her and her canine partner. Now she had physical scars that they might find offensive, too.

Jim, the latest and the man she'd believed was The One, had felt her job was too risky. It had been nice to have someone worry over her at first, but it had soon started to feel restrictive. Despite their breakup he'd been kind enough to call her while she'd been in the hospital, but it had soon turned into a conversation that was more about him telling her *I told you so* than about his real concern for her. There had been no sympathy on his part for Rufus. She'd thought at one time they might have a chance at a real life together. Sadly, she'd really cared for Jim but there was no hope of that after their conversation.

Lyle removed his arm. She wanted it back. It was comforting. "How long was this dog your partner?"

"Four years. He was two when I got him. We spent the first eight weeks in training. He was born in Germany. Most good rescue dogs are. The Germans are known for breeding them to be work dogs. In fact, most of his commands I gave in German." It felt better, and was easier, to talk about Rufus than she'd imagined.

"Interesting." Lyle waited.

She looked at him. His expectant expression suggested he was truly interested in what she was saying. Yet she couldn't imagine him actually caring.

"How did you train together?"

"Are you really interested?" What if he was just asking to keep her talking as part of her "therapy"? None of the men she had known before him had cared one way or another. Why would he be any different?

"Aye. I wouldn't have asked if I wasn't." His voice carried concern. It had been so long since she'd heard that in a man's voice, it struck a deep chord within her.

"I had to do a written test and have a physical. Then I had to have a home visit so the powers-that-be knew I could care for a working dog. An animal like Rufus can cost as much as ten thousand American dollars so handlers are vetted closely. That kind of money can't be wasted. Rufus had to have a physical as well, and learn obedience basics and detection, especially body odor recognition. It was pretty intense for both of us."

"A powerful bonding experience for you both."

Cass's chest tightened from the memories. They had indeed bonded. She had loved the dog, heart and soul. At least Lyle *seemed* to understand. "Though he was only four, he was getting old for a working dog. Rufus was going to have to retire soon. I had already put in the paperwork to take him after he was done."

"Going to canine therapy was almost like punishment for you. You should have said something." His distress was evident in his voice.

She looked away in horror. "And embarrass myself, like I did a few minutes ago?"

Lyle took hold of her hand. His was large, secure… comforting. "You haven't embarrassed yourself. It's okay to be human."

"Yeah, but blubbering all over you is a bit too human."

He leaned closer until his shoulder touched hers. "I didn't mind. I'm just sorry I kept pushing you into canine therapy."

"I figured you'd seen it in my file." She winced at how pitiful she sounded.

"Yeah, but that didn't mean I understood how close you were."

Great. He probably thought she had really gone off her rocker. "I don't know if I can handle being around a dog right now. I'll be leaving here in a few weeks and I, uh, just can't risk becoming attached to another one." What she wasn't telling him about was the heavy guilt she carried over the fact that Rufus had sacrificed himself to save her life. If he hadn't barked, she would have never looked up to see the wall starting to fall. Or that he'd jumped and pushed her out of the way. It had been a split second between her life and Rufus's death.

"I understand completely," Lyle said sincerely. "Would you consider an alternative kind of therapy, if we can come up with one? Maybe just helping out at the canine clinic. Not having a specific dog assigned to you."

She was doubtful it would work but she could try. At least he was trying to work with her. Somehow she had to get past this grief, rebuild her life emotionally and move on. Yet her heart protested with a fresh pang even as she said with caution, "That might work."

"If it doesn't, then we'll try something else." His sincere tone and expression convinced her he would at least listen if she complained. Lyle's comfort was the first she'd had since Rufus had died. She was going to hang onto it.

He let her hand go and shifted away. "Do you feel up to a bite to eat?"

"I don't want to go to the dining room."

"It's too late for that." He tilted his head toward the glass.

Cass was shocked to find it was dark. How long had they been sitting there? "I'm so sorry. I made you miss dinner."

"Not a problem. Mrs. Renwick will have left me something in the kitchen. Let's go see what we can find."

"I think I'll just go up to my room." She wanted to get away. Regain her composure.

"Nonsense. You must be hungry, and I could use the company while I eat."

She had kept Lyle from his hot meal. She owed him. "Okay, I can do that."

"Not the most excited acceptance I've been given to a dinner invitation, but I'll take it." He stood.

Cass liked his sense of humor. He seemed to take life as it came without too much angst. She lacked that ability. Her way of meeting life's challenges now consisted of worry, fear of failure and the guilty conviction she hadn't done enough to make a difference. She wanted to save everyone, give them what her family had received. The chances of achieving that desire were slim to none, but still it was her goal. Now she was just a mass of nerves, help to no one. Not even herself. Squaring her shoulders, she said, "I'll try to do better in the future."

He offered his hand. "That's what I like to hear. That old tough Cass. You had me worried there for a while."

Lyle still thought she was tough? She would have thought he would have seen her as the opposite after the last few hours. She took his hand just long enough to get to her feet. "How's that?"

He put his hands in his pockets and rocked back on his heels. "I don't handle crying females well."

"I'm sorry I made you uncomfortable." She couldn't meet his eyes.

"Hey, I'm glad I was here to help. Now, let's go and get some dinner." He started toward the hall and she joined him.

Lyle led the way to the kitchen. His heart went out to Cass. She was distraught over the loss of her dog. He knew well the empty hole loss could leave in your life. He had felt it intensely when Freya had left him. When he'd told Cass that he didn't handle women crying well, he hadn't been kidding. All he'd done was hold her.

The fact that he'd liked having her cry on his shoulder was a bit unnerving. What had begun as a professional obligation to check on a resident in crisis had ended in a very personal act of compassionate empathy.

Was he drawn to her because he could sense her private suffering? Whatever it was, Cass held some sort of spell over him. One he didn't mind being captivated by.

Cass followed him quietly to the kitchen, seeming fine with doing so. They walked through the now silent dining room to the swing door beside the fireplace. He held it open for her as they entered the large commercial-style kitchen.

"Have a seat at the table." There was a small wooden one next to two corner windows in the large room. "I'll see what I can find in the fridge."

Her chair scraped over the tile floor as she took a seat.

Opening one of the doors of the very large fridge, Lyle announced with deliberate cheer, "Ah, we have roast beef and vegetable soup. How does a sandwich and a bowl of hot soup sound?"

"That's fine."

He glanced over his shoulder. "Again, I was looking for a little more enthusiasm."

A fake smile contorted her lips as she swung a fist overhead. "Great!"

He grinned. "That's more like it."

"Can I help?"

"Sure." He started pulling bowls and a platter off the shelves. When Cass reached him he handed her a few of them. She carried them to the table. Lyle followed with the rest. "You unwrap the containers while I get plates and things together." He searched cabinets and drawers for what they needed, making a couple of trips to the table to put everything down. She was halfway through removing the plastic wrap from the bowls when he said, "Now I'll warm up the soup if you'll make the sandwiches."

"All right."

He pushed the uncut loaf towards her. "I'd like two thick slices."

"Noted." She picked up a bread knife and start cutting.

Lyle ladled soup from its storage container into a saucepan and turned on the stove. As he stirred, he watched Cass work.

Standing, she placed two slices of bread on a plate and buttered them. That done, she unwrapped the rest of the containers. Next she cut slices of roast beef, laying them on the bread. She finished with condiments and lettuce.

Cass's movements were concise and efficient. She had a no-nonsense way about her. Her blonde hair swung over her cheek and she pushed it back with impatience as if she had no time for things to get in her way. She cleaned up as she went. He got the distinct impression she took responsibility for herself and expected others to do the same for themselves. It must have been a rare event for her to let someone witness her raw emotions. Strangely, he was honored he had been the one there for her.

Lyle carried the steaming saucepan to the table and poured the soup into the bowls he'd found earlier, then returned the pan to the stove.

As he came to take his seat at the table Cass inhaled deeply. "That smells wonderful."

He grinned. "I can take credit for it being hot but not for how it smells."

She returned his smile and his heart made an extra thump. He filled the two tall glasses with milk. "Those sandwiches look good."

"I can take credit for how they look but not how they taste." Cass was trying to mimic his accent.

They both laughed as they settled onto their chairs.

She gave him a shy glance. "I don't do Scottish well, do I?"

"I'm going with it needs work." He looked at her over his sandwich just before he took a large bite. He appreciated the sparkle in her eyes that had replaced the earlier dull sadness.

They ate in silence for a few minutes before Cass let her spoon rest against the side of the bowl. "Do you know how the woman we helped is doing?"

He nodded. "I spoke to her doctor this morning. They kept her in overnight for observation, but she seems to be fine."

Cass lifted a spoonful of soup to her mouth. "I'm glad to hear it. How about the man?"

"He'll come in next week to have his stitches removed." Lyle took another bite of his sandwich.

"You really are a jack-of-all-trades, aren't you?" She appeared fascinated.

He rather liked that idea. In fact, he liked her. It had been too long since he'd let himself be drawn to a woman. It would be short-lived, of course, as Cass would be returning to the States soon, but why couldn't he enjoy her company while she was here? It would certainly make his Christmas more interesting. "I wouldn't exactly say that I'm Santa, spreading cheer, but I try to help out where I can."

They finished eating and Lyle started cleaning the table. "Even with my special powers I'd better do the washing-up if I don't want to get on the wrong side of Ms. Renwick."

"I'll help," Cass said in such a firm tone he didn't dare argue.

Together they covered the food and returned it to the refrigerator. His hand brushed hers as she handed him a bowl and he saw color bloom in her cheeks. Despite her tough exterior, her face couldn't conceal her attraction to him. Her gaze met his before she quickly returned to the table to pick up their plates.

Instead of joining him again, she went to the sink and turned on the water. Now she was trying to hide from him. With that in mind, he did his best as he finished clearing away to give Cass space while she washed up. He was aware enough of her to realize she was trying to avoid more contact between them. Was she attracted to him? Was she noticing his every move, as he did hers?

Cass turned toward him, her hip resting against the counter. "Didn't you say that Ms. Renwick leaves food for you?"

"She does, but that doesn't mean she isn't particular about how her kitchen is kept." Lyle stacked the bowls in the cabinet.

"So, if I'm not careful I'll end up on her wrong side?" Cass hung a dishcloth back just as it had been when they'd come into the kitchen.

"I wouldn't worry about it too much, she's really a softy at heart."

Despite his assurance, they stood at the door and gave the kitchen one last look before they exited the room.

"I don't think we've left anything out of place," Cass said as the door swung closed behind them. "My mother is just as particular about her kitchen."

"I'm sure Ms. Renwick will be pleased." That was the first time she'd revealed a personal detail without being asked. He was delighted she had begun to open up.

Cass led the way through the dining room and continued into the hall, where she stopped and turned. Her eyes flickered up to meet his gaze then down to the floor just as quickly. "Thanks for supper…and for, you know…" she glanced up at him in a self-conscious manner "…a while ago. My…uh, meltdown."

She looked so apologetic he crammed his hands into his pockets to keep himself from hugging her. "Not a problem."

"I'll give the canine therapy another try." There was determination in her words.

"And I'll speak to Flora and Margaret and see if they can work something out so you won't have to work with one particular dog."

Cass gave him an earnest look. "I'll do what I can to make that work. I really do appreciate you letting me cry on your shoulder."

To his complete astonishment, Cass placed a hand on his shoulder, came up on her toes and gave him a quick kiss on the cheek.

Pleasure zipped through him. When he saw Cass's shocked face seconds later with its charming pink cheeks he was mesmerized. This tough woman appeared flustered. Her eyes had gone wide in surprise before she blinked a couple of times and looked away. She shook slightly and he feared she might fall. Lyle reached for her.

Cass stood close enough that he could smell the fresh scent of her hair.

"I'm sorry," Cass murmured.

Lyle lowered his head to hear her words, bringing

his lips closer to hers. He watched them, the soft full pads that looked so delicious.

"That was inappropriate. I shouldn't have done that." Cass glanced at him then away.

"I'm not," he said quietly. "I rather liked it."

Her eyelids fluttered closed, then her gaze met his. They stood there watching each other for precious moments. The tip of her tongue made a flicker of an appearance. Lyle wanted a taste, just a small one, of that glossy moistness on her bottom lip. He lowered his head and placed his mouth over hers. Cass remained still in his hands. Lyle took the kiss deeper.

Cass returned it for a second before she slipped out of his hands and whispered, "Goodnight."

Lyle watched her walk away. Disappointment filled him. Everything in him wished he could stop her without frightening her. He wanted more than a chaste meeting of lips. It hadn't been nearly enough. He sought a full, no-holding-back kiss from Cass. There was an attraction between them he wanted to explore. It had been a long time since he'd experienced such a driving need to kiss a woman breathless.

CHAPTER FIVE

CASS WALKED TO the canine center the next afternoon still astounded she had foolishly kissed Lyle. Making her embarrassment worse and her pleasure more, Lyle had actually looked pleased she had kissed him.

But she didn't do that sort of impulsive thing. Ever. She thought through her actions first. Never had she fallen apart like that in front of anyone. To do something so rash only showed how open the wound was that made up her life. Then there had been her crying jag. Until last night she had held it together despite all she'd been through. Talking about Rufus had broken her.

Lyle had been incredibly kind when she'd really needed someone. Beneath his attention she'd opened up like never before. He'd listened without judgement instead of running away. Lyle acted as if he cared, understood her loss.

Cass shook off that admission.

She'd kissed Lyle. What had she been thinking? She hadn't been, instead she had just reacted. It had been a stupid, careless move. Being here at the castle was about therapy and making a full recovery, not romance. Her heart couldn't handle those emotions right now. Even if it could, what did she imagine would come of it? Nothing, that was all that could happen.

As she entered the canine therapy center, Margaret greeted her at the door as if she had been waiting for her. Instead of taking her into the room where she had been the day before, Margaret escorted Cass into another one where the dogs were housed in pens with fenced runs. Cass shoved her shaking hands down into her coat pockets. She didn't want anyone to see that her hands were trembling.

Margaret stopped in front of the first cage. "The dogs on this side of the building are the ones we call the 'reimagined' dogs. They're working dogs that we get from all over the world. When they're too old we take in the ones we can, retrain them and give them new purpose. Esme also has a breeding program for specialized therapy dogs for epilepsy and diabetes patients. We train from puppy age until they are just over a year old. Those dogs are Labrador retrievers, Labradoodles and golden retrievers."

Cass nodded.

"Now, this is Oscar. He's a sweet dog and has been paired with Mr. Ellis."

"I've seen them together some." Cass recognized the small black and white, wire-haired dog, along with a number of others. They'd all been paired with patients at the clinic.

"And you should remember this one. He's the dog I understand that you and Lyle brought in the other night. We're calling him Dougal."

Cass nodded. Dougal suited the little dog. Rufus had already been named when Cass had got him, but his name had suited him too.

They moved to the next pen. The dogs were getting larger as they went.

"This is Morrow. He used to be a guide dog."

He was being “reimagined,” much as Cass was working to do with her life. If she didn’t return to search and rescue, what was she going to do? Could she accept a new partner and try again? A sick feeling welled up in her, but she forced it down with a clenched jaw. She’d already made a spectacle of herself in front of Lyle. She *would not* do the same in Margaret’s presence.

Margaret kept moving down the aisle, introducing Cass to dogs as they went. Cass battled to remain calm rather than listening until Margaret said, “…and he was a search and rescue dog. A good one, I understand. But he went blind in one eye and that ended his career.”

Cass’s attention remained riveted to the light-gray-furred German shepherd lying quietly in the back corner of the cage.

“He hasn’t adjusted to being here as we would like. I think we’re rather dull to him after his exciting life.” Margaret’s voice was sympathetic.

Cass empathized with the dog’s pain. She, too, was out of her comfort zone for reasons beyond her control.

“Now, this is McDuff. Everyone’s favorite.” A big dog with shaggy fur and wide brown eyes came to greet them.

Cass reached out to him without thinking. He smelled her hand, fluffy tail wagging.

“Now that you’ve met everyone I’ll show you where the supplies are and tell you some of your duties. I have to admit you’re the first resident to offer to help us with dog care and I’m very glad to have you. We don’t have enough help.”

Margaret showed Cass the room where food was stored, the grooming area and where cleaning tools could be found. She explained what Cass needed to do and on which days of the week. “Also, we would like you to walk any dogs that don't currently have assignments. That's the list on the board over here." She walked to the wall where a clipboard hung. "Currently there are just three dogs. You're free to take them outside for a walk on the lead or a run in the outdoor pen."

Cass would turn them out in the pen. Leash walking was more than she was emotionally prepared for. Too personal, too risky. She might start caring.

"You think you'll be okay with the work?" Margaret checked her watch.

Cass nodded. This she could do. She would be active instead of sitting around with a dog in her lap or on the floor beside her. Surely she wouldn't get attached tending to all the dogs on a daily basis. Having one assigned to her was the danger. She could feed them, walk them, and clean their cages and meet her therapy requirements then move on. All she had to do was make up her mind to do what she had to do. For some people that type of work might be beneath them. But it was the perfect means for Cass to ease back into interacting with a dog without the temptation of completely committing.

Over the next hour she fed and watered the dogs. When it was time to enter the search and rescue dog's cage, she had to read his name on the sign because she'd missed it when Margaret had said it earlier. She hesitated. Hero didn't scare her, instead he reminded her too much of herself. He remained in that corner as if he wanted to shut the world out. Was that what she was doing?

"Hey, fellow, it's nice to meet you. I understand we've been in the same business. I'm sorry to hear about your eye. That's tough." She moved to fill his food bowl. He watched her closely as she worked. Cass filled his water bowl from a bucket. He came up on his haunches as if he might be thirsty. "Come and get it. I won't hurt you."

"He mostly speaks German."

Cass heart clinched. Just like Rufus.

"I should have told you that." Margaret stood outside the cage. "But I'm sure he appreciates your soothing voice. I've been watching. You're good with the dogs."

"I've been around them all my life." Cass unlocked the cage.

"It shows. It's time for you to go." Margaret held the gate to the cage open. "I don't want to wear you out on your first day. I'll see you tomorrow."

"Okay. I need to put some things away before I go." Cass walked back toward the storeroom.

"Can you see yourself out?" Margaret called, heading the other way.

Cass placed the bucket she carried on the floor. "I can."

"Good. You did well today, Cass." Margaret gave her a smile and left.

Hopefully each day would get easier.

Three days later Cass was on the minibus to the village with five other residents. She looked out the window at the beautiful and fascinating countryside. She'd seen much of the world and, even covered in patches of snow, this place appealed to her. Her doctors had been wise to send her here.

Going to the canine therapy center still didn't fill her with excitement but it wasn't as difficult as it had been on the first day. She'd managed to interact with the dogs while remaining emotionally removed from them. She was pleased to see that Dougal was growing stronger each day. His odd appearance with some weight on him was beginning to make him look cute. The only dog that did disturb her was Hero. He still remained standoffish. Cass was trying not to let it bother her, yet it did.

Today she wasn't going to think about dogs or therapy or even the past. Instead she was going to enjoy her trip to the village. She didn't know what to expect of Cluchlochry, but she was enchanted from the moment she stepped off the bus. It looked like a scene from a Victorian Christmas card. Wreaths of fresh greenery with bows were on every building door and window. The main road was just large enough for two small narrow vehicles to pass. Her large American SUV would never be able to make it.

The sun was shining this morning, promising a warmer day than usual, and she was glad she'd left Lyle's scarf and hat behind, not wanting to have to carry them.

In the center of the village just feet from where she'd stepped off the bus was the cobblestoned village square. She followed the crowd to a building she'd overheard was called the community center. There were a number of tents set up outside, but Cass found the majority of the stalls inside. The individual areas each had their own holiday decorations. It was like entering a winter wonderland. Excitement filled her at the thought of some retail therapy. She wasn't much of a "girly-girl" where most things were concerned, but she did love a shopping trip. The van had come in early enough that the crowd was still comfortably small. Visiting the stalls should be fun.

She planned to buy boots and socks today as Lyle had suggested that first night. However, she would wait until later to shop for them to avoid carrying them around any longer than necessary. After she was finished at the Christmas market she would ask someone where to do shoe shopping. For now, she was going to see what the market had to offer.

The first stall she came to held handmade wooden figurines. Behind the table sat an older, grizzled man with the air of an outdoorsman. He glanced up for a moment then went back to whittling.

Cass picked up an angel and admired the workmanship. The texture was smooth and there was attention to detail. The face had the kind of expression befitting an angel. It was old-world craftsmanship at its best. Her mother would love any of the items on display. She would return to buy something for her mother before she headed back to the castle. Hoping she would make it home before Christmas, she planned on being prepared to celebrate with her family.

When they'd heard she was injured they had wanted to come to her in Germany. She had convinced them not to, assuring them she was going to be fine. Once she'd been sent to therapy she had persuaded them she would be home sooner if she concentrated on getting better. What she hadn't said was that she needed time to recover emotionally so she wouldn't fall apart in front of them, as she had with Lyle.

Cass paused at every stall, fearing that if she didn't she might miss something. At this rate she wouldn't see all the market today and would still climb back on the bus with an armload of purchases. However, she needed to get some local money to buy things. She went outside to the street and searched for an ATM sign. Soon she had some pounds in her pocket. Conscious of smiling for the first time in a long while she went to the nearest stall.

This one offered handmade Christmas-tree ornaments. Cass was enthralled. Each one unique, they were made out of natural things like nuts, twigs, and pine cones. They would be perfect on a tree. Once again she resisted the impulse to buy and moved on to the next display.

There she found leather goods of quality craftsmanship. She continued walking, merely looking at some stalls and handling items at others. Coming to town had been a good decision, even though she had initially intended only to buy new walking boots and socks. Nevertheless she was having a nice day. Even the bustle of the growing crowd made her feel more alive. She had needed this kind of therapy.

Spying a sign with the words "Aileen's Knitting" on it, she made her way over. It was past time to return Lyle's hat and scarf but Cass wanted to get her own before she did so. And some gloves.

The stall had two tables and a number of hat racks filled with hats and scarfs of every color. Cass went to one of the tables and ran her hand over a few of the items of outerwear, even trying on a couple. She studied herself in a mirror hung on a stand to see how she looked. The pale pink and gray striped scarf and matching solid pink hat she especially liked.

A plump middle-aged woman sat behind the table next to a small heater. Her needles clicked as she spoke. "That looks lovely on you."

Her Scottish brogue was so thick Cass had to concentrate to understand her. "Thank you. Your work is beautiful. And so soft." Cass pulled the cap off and picked up another in the same color but with a rosette on the side. She studied it.

At that moment a familiar masculine shoulder pushed a door open just behind the woman. Lyle entered, carrying a box. He turned and the door closed. She must have caught his eye because he looked at her with surprise. A smile curved his lips that made her middle flutter. "Well, hi, there. I see you took my suggestion about coming to the market."

Her face warmed. This was their first encounter since they had kissed. Surely if she acted like it hadn't happened, he would as well. "Yeah, I'm doing some shopping therapy, like the doctor ordered."

Lyle looked over the box at her. "I wouldn't say I ordered it, but I'm glad you came."

She nodded toward the box. "I see you're moonlighting. You don't have enough jobs already?"

He chuckled as he rested the corner of the box on the edge of the table, continuing to hold it. "It's more like helping my mother out. Muscles and all that."

Cass knew those muscles well. She had felt those strong arms around her and the firmness of his chest when she'd pressed her face against it. She glanced at Lyle's mother, who watched them with pronounced interest, her knitting momentarily forgotten.

Lyle's head turned as if following Cass's line of sight. "Mum, this is Cass Bellow. She's one of our residents at the castle. Cass, my mother, Aileen Sinclair."

Cass was unsure how to respond. Lyle's mother was looking between the two of them as if she suspected something Cass was refusing to admit to herself. A second too late to sound natural, Cass finally managed to get out, "It's nice to meet you. Your work really is lovely. I wish I had your talent."

The door opened again and a tall man who was undoubtedly an older version of Lyle joined them with a box in his hands. "Aileen, where do you want this?

"Over in the corner will be fine." Lyle's mother pointed to the one opposite hers. "I don't want it near the heater."

The man put the box down as instructed and turned to Cass. Something about his bearing made Cass want to stand at attention and pass inspection yet he looked in poor health. His was gaunt, far too thin for his height. There wasn't a sparkle in his eyes like Lyle's. His skin had a grayish tint to it. Lyle's father was sick.

"Sir, this is Cass Bellow. My father, retired Colonel Gregor Sinclair."

Still resisting the urge to salute, she settled for, "Hello, sir."

"Hello, young lady." The older man offered his hand. Cass put hers inside his. He still had a firm grip, but his fingers felt fragile in hers.

She looked at Lyle's parents. "It's nice to meet you both."

"You're not from around here, I can tell," Lyle's father said.

Cass chortled. "Is it that obvious? No, I'm from America. Montana currently."

Lyle's father nodded. "I worked with many Americans while I was in the military. Good sorts. I expect that Lyle will be working with some as well when he returns to active duty."

Her look swung to Lyle. Was he going to join the army again? He seemed to love working at the clinic.

Before she could ask, he took the hat from her hand. "This will look nice on you."

She unwrapped the scarf from her neck. "I think so

too. I'd like to get both of them, and the gloves as well. They're too nice to pass up. Plus I need to return yours."

"You do?" Lyle's mother gave him a questioning look.

"Cass didn't have a chance to prepare for our Scottish weather before she was transferred here." Lyle turned to put his box on top of the other one as if discouraging more of his mother's questions.

Cass pulled out her cash, counted out the correct amount indicated on a sign next to the mirror, then handed it across the table.

"Thank you, Mrs. Sinclair. Maybe one day I'll learn to knit and make something half as lovely as your work."

"If you'd like to learn I could show you. Lyle could bring you to the house some day for lunch." Lyle's mother looked from Cass to her son, a small smile on her lips.

Was Aileen's maternal intuition working overtime? Cass shook her head. "Oh, no, I didn't mean to imply you should teach me."

"Nonsense. I'd love to give you a lesson. And at this time of the year knitting is about all I'm doing anyway, with the Christmas market going until the season is over." The clicking of the needles started again.

Cass didn't know what to think about Aileen's invitation but she said the polite thing. "Thank you."

"Would you like a bag for those?" Mrs. Sinclair asked, a nod of her head indicating the knitted items Cass held.

Cass glanced down. "No, I think I'll wear them." She stuffed the gloves in her pocket, looped the scarf around her neck again and pulled the hat snugly over her head. "It was nice to meet you Colonel and Mrs. Sinclair." Giving Lyle a swift look as she turned to leave, she added, "Bye." Hesitating a second, she turned to look at Lyle. "Would you mind giving me directions to where I can buy some boots?"

"Why don't I show you instead?" he offered.

"I don't want to put you out. I'm sure your mother needs your help." Cass didn't need him thinking she was using that as a ploy to spend more time with him.

"I'm good for now." Aileen waved a hand. "While you're gone, Lyle, why don't you stop by McKinney's Pub and get Cass one of their pies?" She looked directly at Cass. "Best meat pies you'll find anywhere."

Lyle stepped around the table and came to stand beside Cass. His hand touched her back briefly and was gone. He called over his shoulder to his mother, "I'll do it."

They worked their way around the people coming and going as they walked in the direction of the door. A couple of times Lyle put a gentle hand in the small of her back while guiding her through the crowd.

"That hat and scarf color is very flattering on you," he said. "Reminds me of when you blush. Your cheeks turn that shade." He grinned as their gazes met. "Like right now."

The compliment gave her a luscious warm throughout her body like a hot drink heating her from the inside out.

They exited the building and turned left down the street. As they continued walking toward the other end of the village green they approached a monument. It consisted of a tall narrow shaft encircled by steps. On top was a small statue.

"What's this?" Cass stopped and studied it.

"It's a Mercat Cross. They have been used in Scotland since the eleven-hundreds to distinguish the right by the monarch to hold a market or fair. They were symbols of authority. There're aren't many of them left now. We're rather proud of ours."

"That's interesting." She liked learning historical facts about places she went.

"They're not only places for merchants to meet but places where state and civic proclamations would be made. Even to this day in Edinburgh the town crier will still make proclamations on occasions."

She looked up to where the statue stood on top. "I would love to hear one sometime."

"Maybe you will one day."

Cass doubted that. She wouldn't be here long enough for that to happen.

They moved on in comfortable silence until they made their way through the crowd and out into the open again.

"So how have your last few days of working with the dogs gone?"

Cass glanced over at him. "Don't you already know? I figured you've been checking up on me."

Lyle chuckled. "I have, but I'd like to hear from you."

She appreciated his honestly. "It's going better than I expected. I admit it was tough to get started, but I'm getting used to the dogs and them to me."

"I'm glad to hear that." He did sound pleased, as if her happiness really mattered to him.

She couldn't say she was happy yet, but she'd moved the needle that direction. "You're not really surprised, are you?"

"Not really. Canine therapy has proved very effective. Even on those who are resistant." He gave her a knowing look.

"Is that your way of saying I told you so?" Somehow she didn't mind if he did. This was the best she had felt since before the accident. Her thoughts weren't so dark anymore.

Lyle stopped in front of a shop built of brown timber. The upper half of the door had four window panes. A Christmas wreath hung low beneath the glass. Attached above the door was a swag of greenery entwined with red ribbon. On either side of the door were display windows filled with boots, coats and other outdoor wear. All of it was arranged to create the impression of presents under a Christmas tree.

Lyle opened the door for her. "The shoes are at the back on the right."

Cass followed him down a narrow aisle lined with high shelves stuffed with items. The dim lighting added to the alluring atmosphere. The place smelled of wood oil and pine. Cass inhaled, taking it deep into her lungs. It reminded her of Lyle. She was enchanted with the shop. In fact, she was charmed by everything about the Heatherglen area, including Lyle. What was happening to her?

They arrived at the back of the shop. There in one corner was a small wooden bench along with boxes of boots piled on the floor.

Lyle stretched to his full height and looked over the shelves. "Apparently Mr. Stewart isn't around. We'll have a look at these and he should be back soon. He must have stepped out for lunch. I have experience with this so we'll just help ourselves."

Cass lowered her chin, eyeing him dubiously. "You've been a shoe salesman?"

He gave her an indignant look. "I worked here when I came home on school breaks."

"Oh. So you *are* a jack-of-all-trades."

He stepped toward the boxes. “I wouldn’t exactly say that, but I can handle reading shoeboxes. What’s your size?”

“Eight and a half, US.” She sat on the bench.

Lyle nodded and studied them a moment. Moving a couple, he pulled one out. “I hope I made the European to American conversion correctly. Give these a try and we’ll see.”

She took the box from him and opened it. Removing her shoes, Cass pulled the new boot on her right foot. She stood and wiggled her toes. “Nicely done. Feels good but I would really rather have them in black.”

“I aim to please. Let me see what I can find.” Lyle shifted around a few boxes. With a bright smile on his handsome face, he handed her a box.

Cass sat on the bench again and started trying on the second boot.

“What’s your favorite color?” Lyle asked, his back to her as he straightened boxes.

“Why?”

“You need some good socks.” He studied her with visible curiosity.

She continued trying on her new boots. “Blue.”

He moved down the wall and seconds later handed her a pair of thick socks. “These’ll keep your feet warm and wick the moisture away. I promise you’ll like them.”

Cass removed the boots and her socks then pulled on the new ones. “I can already tell the difference.” She flexed her foot then slipped her foot into the boot. Nice. Quickly she pulled on the other boot and laced them both up.

Standing, she walked back and forth a couple of times, testing the feel of the footwear. “You know, if you ever decide to give up medicine you could have a future as a personal shopper."

Lyle gave a regal bow. "Thank you. I have to say with complete confidence that's the first time anyone has suggested that to me."

They both laughed.

When was the last time she'd laughed like this? How had she not noticed it slipping away?

She liked Lyle's relaxed view of life. With his job and military background she marveled he wasn't uptight and domineering. Instead he seemed to accept life as it came and made the most of it whenever he could. Cass needed more of that in her world.

Lyle had a way of making her smile, and she also needed more of that right now. However, she must not start depending on him to make her feel better. She had to depend on herself. She had to regain her strength. Be strong.

If she opened up to him any further, leaving him would be a new trauma, one she knew she couldn't handle. Her job certainly didn't lend itself to an easygoing and emotional personality. Even when she was at home her focus had been on working with Rufus to keep them both sharp. Had the men in her life been right? Did she live too closed off? Had been concentrating on her job and Rufus more than she should have?

"You want to keep those on?" He picked up the box.

"I believe I will. Start breaking them in." Cass picked up her other shoes and placed them in the box while Lyle held it. She met his gaze. "By the way, what's your favorite color?"

"Green." His eyes didn't waver. "I'm particularly fond of the shade of green of your eyes."

Her breath caught. "Are you flirting with me?"

"What if I am?" He took the box and set it on the bench. "I've been thinking about that kiss."

A tingle ran through her. "You shouldn't."

"What? Think about it or think about doing it again?"

"Both, " she squeaked.

"Why?" His voice turned gravelly, went soft. Lyle stepped toward her.

Because she was damaged. Because she was scared. Because she couldn't handle caring about anything or anyone again. "Because I'm leaving soon."

"Cass, we can share an interest in each other without it becoming a lifelong commitment. I'd like to get to know you better. Couldn't we be friends? Enjoy each other's company while you're here?"

Put that way, it sounded reasonable. Lyle moved so close that his heat warmed her. Why was it so hard to breathe? She simmered with anticipation. His hands came to rest at her waist as his mouth lowered to hers.

She didn't want his kiss. That wasn't true. Until that moment she'd had no idea how desperately she did want Lyle's lips on hers. Her breath caught as his mouth made a light brush over hers. He pulled away. Cass ran her tongue over her bottom lip, tasting him.

Lyle groaned and pulled her tight against his chest. His lips firmly settled over hers. Cass grabbed his shoulders to steady herself. Slowly she went up on her toes, her desire drawing her nearer to him. Sweet heat curled and twisted through her center and seeped into her every cell. She'd found her cozy fire in a winter storm.

The sound of the door opening brought both their heads up. Their gazes locked with each other's.

"Hello? Is someone here?" a man called.

"It's Lyle, Mr. Stewart. I'm in the boot section."

"Please don't do that again," Cass whispered, and stepped as far away as the small space would allow. She couldn't deal with the feelings swarming in her. This wasn't what she needed or wanted. She needed to figure out her life, not complicate it.

Now that she'd really been kissed by Lyle, she wanted more. *No!* And she couldn't handle the feelings his kiss had kindled in her. This was too much at the wrong time. Panic welled in her. She shook her head. Letting something grow between them would only turn into disaster. She didn't want to hurt Lyle, and she couldn't endure another heartache.

He studied her for a moment, then picked up the box, placing it under his arm as if nothing earthshaking had happened. "Let's go and pay for these then get one of those pies."

That suited her just fine. She could pretend nothing had changed as well as he did. Head held high, she followed him two aisles over to a wooden counter. A middle-aged man with white tuffs of hair, rosy cheeks and a white beard stood behind it. He could pass for a Santa Claus.

"Well, hello. How're you, Lyle?" Mr. Stewart gave them both a wide smile.

The man's accent was just as thick as Lyle's mother's.

"Fine, thanks, Mr. Stewart. We've been helping ourselves to some boots. I was just going to write you a note and leave the money."

"Give me a second to set this down." The older man placed a brown bag on the counter. "I went to get a meat pie before they were all gone. I look forward to Mrs. McKinney's pies all year."

"I hope you left some for Cass and me. We're on our

way there next." Lyle leaned toward the bag and inhaled deeply. "Mrs. McKinney makes the best."

While the men were talking, Cass managed to get her purchase paid for. She and Lyle exited the shop. The sun was shining but clouds were gathering.

"It looks like it'll snow again tonight," Lyle commented. "We need to go this way." He indicated to the left. "McKinney's Pub is down this way."

Cass shook her head. "I'm not really hungry. I think I'll just look around some more then go back to the castle. I appreciate your help with my boots."

Lyle said nothing until she looked at him. "Cass, I didn't mean to make things uncomfortable between us."

"You didn't."

He searched her face for a long moment. "Then you won't mind joining me for lunch. You don't want me to have to eat alone."

She pursed her lips. "Somewhere in there I think there's a touch of emotional blackmail."

He quirked a brow, his grin devious. "Could be. Live dangerously and join me."

She was doing that by just being around him. Her body still hummed with awareness, but she did owe him. He'd been nothing but kind. More than once Lyle had gone far beyond what was necessary. Helping her with her new boots was just one of the small things. Still feeling unsteady after their kiss, she was afraid that remaining in Lyle's presence might further break her tightly strung nerves. It was risky to her well-being for her to say yes. "If you're going to insist."

A winning smile lit up his face. "I am. You know how I hate to eat alone. This way."

They didn't walk far before they came to a building

with an elaborate sign stating that it was McKinney's Pub above the door. "Here we are."

Cass turned the doorknob and pushed the door open, to find a room with a dark timber-beamed ceiling, stone-flagged floor and a handful of wooden tables and chairs unoccupied. Men were standing at the bar with drinks and talking. She glanced back at Lyle to see him duck to enter.

"Why don't you go see if you can find us a table near the fire while I place our order?"

"Okay."

"Before you go, would you prefer beef or pork?" Lyle asked.

"I don't know. You make the call." She didn't often let others decide anything for her. Being with Lyle was definitely having an odd effect on her. For some reason she trusted him not to let her down.

"Okay. One more thing, hot drink or something cold?"

"Hot, definitely hot." She shivered. "I can't even imagine drinking something cold." Cass reached into her pocket. "Here's money for mine."

Lyle looked offended. "Put that away. I'll get this."

"I don't expect you to buy my lunch." She couldn't continue being indebted to him. "You're always doing something for me."

"You can return the favor sometime. Now, go and find us a seat." He started toward the bar.

"You don't need my help carrying the food?"

He shook his head. "I can handle it. You find us a place to sit before they're all taken."

"All right." Cass made her way to an empty table to one side of the roaring fire in the fireplace. She turned a chair toward the flames and sat down, stretching out her hands to the warmth. A couple of minutes later she looked around to see where Lyle was.

She quickly found him among the people at the bar. With his height and broad shoulders he stood out among the others. His hair was mussed but it matched his easy-going personality. Lyle was every bit as appealing to look at as he was to talk to. She was getting in deeper and deeper the longer she was with him. As hard as she tried to push away, the greater the pull he had on her.

Soon, carrying two drinks with steam wafting from them, Lyle joined her. He placed them on the table. “You got us a perfect table. How did you manage that?”

Cass shrugged and picked up her mug. “Lucky, I guess.”

Lyle picked his mug up as well. “This is hot punch. I think you’ll like it.”

She took a sip. “Mmm…”

“I like it when you make that sound,” he said, just for her ears. “You did it a while ago when I kissed you.”

“I did not!”

Lyle gave her a wicked smile that said, Do *you want to bet?*

Heat that had nothing to do with the punch surged through her. “You shouldn’t say things like that to me.”

“What, the truth?”

Much to her relief, they were interrupted by a young woman placing two plates on the table.

Lyle said politely, “Thank you.” The woman gave him a shy look and hurried away.

It appeared Lyle sent most women into a tailspin by just being nice. Cass had imagined he only had that effect on her.

She watched as Lyle used a napkin to pick up the perfect brown half-moon pastry. He closed his eyes and took a bite. His eyelids dropped as an expression of pure bliss washed over his face. He slowly chewed. Something low within Cass tightened. She shook off the vision of Lyle naked in bed, wearing that same expression. How could just two kisses cause such an idea to pop into her head?

Instead of concentrating on her traitor of a mind, she followed Lyle's lead and picked up her pie. She took a small bite of the flaky pastry. It melted on her tongue as the taste of tangy beef hit her taste buds. She closed her eyes and enjoyed the moment. Did she have the same look on her face as Lyle? She opened hers to find him watching her closely, an intense flame of desire in his eyes. Oh, yeah, she had.

His voice turned husky as he said, "You should look like that all the time."

"How's that?" Cass dared to ask, unable to take her gaze off him.

"Angelic, as if you had found nirvana."

Emotion that had nothing to do eating meat pie and everything to do with the fire in Lyle's eyes flashed through her. This caring and comforting man wanted her. That knowledge was empowering.

"Hello, Lyle." a woman's soft voice said from behind Cass.

The pleasure lighting Lyle's face went out, leaving a blank look with a hint of surprise. The woman was important to Lyle. Cass turned to see her. She had vivid blue eyes and was heavily pregnant. A sick feeling filled her stomach. Who was the woman to Lyle?

The last person Lyle had expected to see was Freya. He hadn't seen her for some time. Through his mother and father, he'd learned that she had married and moved to

Fort William. He was truly glad for her, but that didn't make the surprise of seeing her again any less nerve rattling.

He laid his food down and stood. "Freya."

"It's nice to see you, Lyle." She sounded hesitant, as if she was afraid of his reaction. "How are you?"

"Well. And you?"

Her hand went to rest on her protruding middle. "I'm doing fine."

Lyle felt a sharp, piercing pain. They had talked about and planned on now many children they would have. There had been so many dreams they'd shared. He mentally shook his head. Those were long gone. Their relationship had been doomed the minute he'd boarded the train for training camp. He knew that now, but back then he'd been too caught up in pleasing his father by joining the army and the image of his fiancée waiting on his glorious return to see reality. Knowing his own mind and what he wanted out of life hadn't entered the equation. Much less fighting for it.

Freya glanced at Cass, who was observing them with interest. Was Cass thinking the child was his? "Freya." He nodded toward Cass. "This is Cass Bellow. Freya is an old friend."

"Hello," Freya said with a small smile as the two women studied each other.

A man not much taller than Freya but with huge shoulders joined them. He studied Lyle then Cass before giving Freya a questioning look, his brows making a V at his nose.

Freya cleared her throat. "This is Angus, my husband."

Lyle extend his hand. "Lyle Sinclair." It took a second before the man's eyes widened in recognition, then narrowed.

Angus shook Lyle's hand briefly, then put his arm across Freya's shoulders in a statement of ownership. To her he said, "Your parents are waiting."

Freya gave Lyle a sad, apologetic look. "It was nice to see you, Lyle."

"You too, Freya." He watched them walk away. That had certainly been interesting. Why had the meeting left him feeling so disconcerted? He'd got over Freya years ago, yet it still shook him to see her again. At one time they had been so close. Now there was a fence between them so high that they would never be able to climb it. Her husband's actions and facial expression made him question how controlling and overly jealous he might be. Was Freya truly happy?

"I think it's time for me to get back to the castle." Cass stood. "I promised Flora I would help with some of the decorations today instead of formal therapy."

Lyle blinked. How had he forgotten Cass was there? She must think him an idiot. "But we haven't finished our meal."

She gave him a curious look. "I have. Thank you for the pie. I should go."

"I'll walk you to the minibus." He needed to answer the questions hanging between them.

Cass waved for him to sit down. "No, you finish your lunch. I can find my way. I'll see you back at the castle."

Before he could order his thoughts, she was gone.

What was Cass thinking? Imagining? Had she seen what had once been between him and Freya?

CHAPTER SIX

BACK AT THE castle Cass debated whether or not to return Lyle's coat and other belongings that evening or wait until she saw him during work hours. Surely he needed his clothes. Yet her growing curiosity about the history between him and Freya made her cautious about seeking him out. It really wasn't her business, and yet she couldn't dismiss the distinct impression that something between them had caused Lyle great pain. Or was the baby the issue?

She knew Lyle well enough to know he would take responsibility for a child he'd fathered. Having a family of his own would be a serious matter to him. So was the baby his?

As hard as Cass had tried to maintain her emotional distance from Lyle, she cared about him. He had made it impossible for her to remain uninterested. Not only did she find him attractive, he had also proved he was a good man. So here she was, caring about him, concerned for him.

The feeling he needed someone to talk to also nagged at her. She owed him. Maybe she could help.

With her new socks and boots on and wearing her own jacket, which she'd found a few days ago laid out on her bed, she bundled Lyle's coat, socks, scarf and hat in her arms and made her way out of the castle. It would soon be dark, so she had tucked her flashlight safely in her pocket for the return trip.

At the gate leading into his yard she stopped. Was she being too forward by coming to his home like this? What would he think about her just showing up? Still, the need to see him, be there for him if he needed to talk, neutralized her apprehension. Her outlook on life had improved so much since he'd let her spill her problems to him. Maybe tonight he needed someone to listen to his troubles. She owed him and cared about him enough that she should at least be here for him. They were friends.

Pausing in the act of knocking on the door, she had the uneasy feeling her "honorable" thoughts about Lyle needing her were just an excuse to see him again. He had friends, colleagues, even his parents to confide in, so what had possessed her to think he required her?

As if of its own accord her fist hit the door. Breath held, she listened for movement inside, half wishing Lyle wasn't home, half hoping he was. All of this was so against her nature. She'd always known her own mind. Why was she doubting herself now? Why had she started acting like a silly schoolgirl around Lyle?

She had stepped off the porch to leave when the door opened. Her heart beat faster as she straightened her back.

"Cass?" He sounded both startled and pleased.

Did he think she was seeking his interest by showing up like this? Was she? "I, uh, wanted to return your things now I have my jacket back and a new scarf and hat." She thrust them into his hands before turning away.

"Would you like to come in for some coffee?" He asked, sounding hopeful.

She looked at him, even less sure about being there. But hadn't she been eager for Lyle to invite her in? "Could we make that tea?"

He chuckled. "Of course. Come in."

Inside, Lyle helped her off with her coat. As he did so, his hands rested on her shoulders for a moment. She missed the heaviness of them the second they were gone. She had the impression he wanted to keep an appropriate distance between them. Wasn't that what she'd all but told him she wanted? Especially after their kiss in the shop. Or did she want that?

"Come and join me in the kitchen," Lyle suggested as he moved through the door opposite the living room.

"Let me take my boots off first. They're pretty muddy." Cass sat on the small bench underneath the coat rack and removed them, then followed him.

Lyle was already at the stove with the kettle in his hand when she entered. He placed it on the element and leaned against the counter. "I see you're wearing your new socks again."

"Yes. They're the best I've ever worn. I plan to buy a few more pairs before I leave for home." Cass settled into one of the wooden chairs at the small round table in the middle of the room.

"Flora tells me that if you continue making the progress you have been, it'll be sooner rather than later." He opened a tin filled with biscuits and placed it on the table before returning to the cabinets.

She reached for a biscuit. "I'm pretty determined to get through this as quickly as possible."

Lyle glanced over his shoulder, studying her for a moment. What was he thinking? He returned to removing mugs from an upper cabinet and added tea bags to them. "I noticed that."

Did it bother him that she so was eager to leave the clinic? Cass looked around. "I like your kitchen."

"Thanks." He put a bowl of sugar and small pitcher of milk on the table. The kettle switched itself off as the water was boiling. Lyle poured the steaming water into the mugs before setting one in front of her and the other at the place beside her, rather than across from her. He took a seat.

She liked him being close enough to touch. Maybe she had imagined he was trying to keep distance between them.

Lyle pushed the tin in her direction. "Have another if you wish. It's interesting you like my kitchen. These old cottage kitchens have charm but they're often difficult to modernize. I've been led to believe women like to have the latest and greatest to work with."

Cass added sugar and milk to her tea. "That sounds like you're speaking from personal experience."

"Yeah. Freya always wanted one of those new brick houses with all the glass."

A zip ran along Cass's nerves. He had made it that easy for her to ask about Freya. Still, she hesitated to pry. Would he be upset if she did? Cass watched him. Lyle studied his tea. "Would that be the Freya I met today?"

"That's the one." A pensive look remained on his face. "I think I owe you an explanation."

"Why?"

"Because I was kissing you and then a pregnant woman who I'm sure you figured out shared a past with me shows up. It didn't make me look good."

“You didn’t—don’t—owe me an explanation.” No matter how much she wanted to hear one.

“Maybe not, but I’d like to give you one anyway. The baby isn’t mine. I haven’t seen Freya in over a year. She was my girlfriend when we were teenagers. I asked her to be my wife the night before I left for basic training.”

“Now I understand the look on her husband’s face.” It had been jealousy.

Lyle nodded. “Yeah, I’m not his favorite person, I imagine. But he has nothing to worry about. It’s been over for a long time.”

“What happened?” Cass hissed in dismay. “I shouldn’t have asked that. It’s not my business.”

He finally met her look. “It doesn’t matter. I don’t want to have any secrets from you.”

What was he saying? That sounded too much like he wanted a relationship more intimate than friendship. Their kisses had certainly been a step beyond mere friends.

“I received the classic ‘Dear John’ letter. By the time I was able to come home months later she was already married.”

Cass placed her hand over his hand resting on the table. She had been right. He did need to talk. “I’m sorry that happened to you. You deserved better.”

He turned over his hand and held hers. “It was a rotten feeling at the time but far better than marrying the wrong person.”

She couldn’t disagree with him, but it must have been a horribly painful experience. To feel so helpless. She knew that all feeling too well. In too many areas of her life.

“It took me some time, but I realized that we would never have made it. Ours was a young immature love and an engagement based on me leaving, not on something lasting. I promised myself that the next time I asked a woman to marry me, we would both be mature enough to know what we were doing, and that we understood what real love is." He let go of her hand.

"Enough of this serious talk. Here I am dragging up my long-gone past while your tea is getting cold."

Cass took a sip from her mug. "I knew something big had gone on between the two of you. I just wasn't sure what. Her husband made a point of making it clear where she belonged."

"I noticed that as well. I hope she's happy. My mother said this is her second child." He bit into a cookie.

"I must admit I was curious. In fact, half of the reason I came tonight was that I thought you might need to talk. You helped me by listening so I thought I could return the favor."

He gave her a thoughtful look then grinned. "I see. And here I was thinking you wanted to spend more time with me."

Just like that Lyle had changed the atmosphere. He knew how to ease a tense situation.

She returned his smile. "Please don't let anyone tell you that you lack an ego."

His grin turned suggestive, causing her middle to quiver. "I'm not sure that was a compliment, but I'm going to choose to take it that way."

Cass huffed in humor. "Does anything keep you down long?"

"I try to keep a positive outlook where I can. I learned long ago that life was easier that way. How do you see the glass? Half full or half empty?"

She winced in her mind. Most of her life she would

have said half full but right now she wasn't sure she could. "Can I get back to you on that?"

Lyle watched her far too closely for comfort. "Sure. I just want you to know that I'm here for you."

"Thanks. I know I showed up at the castle with a chip on my shoulder. I'm trying to do better."

"From all I've heard, you are."

Cass pushed away from the table. "I should be going."

"Do you have to? Stay awhile and I'll walk you back later." His face was hopeful.

She ought to leave. Hadn't she already stepped over the line by coming here? Yet she did want to remain longer. "I guess I could."

"Great. Would you like to watch TV, play chess or maybe do a puzzle?"

She blinked and laughed. "Wow, you know how to show a woman a wild time."

He carried their mugs to the sink. "What can I say? Most of my excitement comes from accidents. I'm not planning one to impress you."

"I'll be more than happy to settle for a puzzle. I haven't done one of those in a long time." That seemed like a safe enough activity.

"During the winter months I keep one going all the time. It's in the living room. Go on in and see what you can do. I'll be in after I finish here." He turned to the sink.

Cass did as he suggested. A fire was burning. She found the table with the puzzle laid out on it behind the sofa. It had to have been there the other night but she had been so out of it she hadn't noticed. The puzzle was a picture of a lioness and her cub. A difficult one at best. She sat in the chair, adjusting the lamp over the table to shine it where she wanted it.

Lyle entered to find Cass sitting in his chair at his puzzle table. Something about the sight seemed right. She looked like she belonged, fit in his world.

Her head remained lowered. The glow of the fire reflected off her hair. He longed to brush his hand across it. Test its softness. Pulling another chair close, he joined her.

"So this is how you spend your evenings?" She picked a piece up and tried it. It didn't fit. She put it down and went for another.

"Not every evening." He wished Cass would put as much energy into getting to know him as she was into working on the puzzle. Was he really that desperate for a woman? No, it was more about the sensations Cass stirred in him. Sensations that had lain dormant for a long time. The same ones he'd been afraid to show for so long.

"I would think a hot young doctor would be too busy with the ladies at the pub to spend time doing puzzles." She put a piece in and made a tiny sound of joy, and it sparked something in him.

What would it be like to kiss her again? That thought was all it took to set his blood humming. How would she react if he tried to kiss her right now? Would she push him away or tug him closer, like she had at the shop? He had to stop these runaway thoughts.

Focus on the puzzle, he told himself. Concentrate on finding that one missing piece. Maybe if he did that, he'd forget the sweet smell of Cass's hair moving just inches from him, or the breathiness of her voice when she spoke or the soft touch of her hand as it brushed his when they both tried to fit a piece into the same space.

Minutes ticked by, the longing in him growing, groaning with the seconds. To stop himself from reaching for Cass, Lyle stood and went to the fireplace, using the need to put another log on the fire as an excuse. With his back to the warmth, he watched her. She truly was striking. Every fiber of his being was on alert for the least hint of encouragement.

Cass looked up. "Hey, are you going to leave all of this to me? This is such a great picture."

"I like the one I'm seeing." His gaze met hers and held.

Cass's head dipped to the side as if she was making a decision. Moments ticked by as they watched each other.

Lyle cleared his throat. "Cass, I've been thinking of little else but kissing you again. If you don't want that to happen then it might be better if you go."

She blinked. "Go?"

Lyle chuckled softly as he stepped toward her. "Or stay? That's up to you." When Lyle reached her, he lifted a strand of her hair and let it drift through his fingers. He didn't miss the hitch in her breath.

Taking her by the shoulders, he brought her to her feet and against him. The chair turned over with a bang but neither of them gave it any notice. His lips found hers. They were as soft and pliable and welcoming as he remembered.

There was no uncertainty on Cass's part this time. Her arms circled his neck, pulling his head closer as he took the kiss deeper. She moaned low, wiggling against him and sending his desire into orbit. Her mouth opened without his request and her tongue eagerly met his in a sensual dance.

With his desire for her increasing by the second, he buried his fingers in her hair. Cass gripped his shoulders as his mouth left hers to leave kisses along her jaw and up to her ear. She did a super-sexy wriggle against his taut length when he planted a kiss behind her ear.

Cass cupped the side of his head and guided his mouth back to hers, then kissed him deeply. His body throbbed in appreciation. Cass ran her hand over his chest and down to his beltline. There she pulled his sweater up and his shirt out of his pants. Seconds later his skin rippled with the pleasure of her hand moving over it.

Lyle had to touch her, all of her. He lifted Cass to the back of the sofa and stepped between her legs. Finding the edge of her sweater, he stripped it from her and let it drop to the floor. He kissed her temple. "I've dreamed of doing this for so long."

"You have?" Her whispered words held a note of wonder.

He looked into her eyes. "I have."

The smile that lit her eyes and curved her mouth was suggestive and stimulating, promising delights to come. Excitement set his blood on fire.

Cass reached for his sweater and started to remove it. He stepped back just enough to whip it off. As she balanced on the sofa back, her hands went to the bottom button of his shirt. She unfastened each one with astonishing speed, pushing the material to either side, exposing his chest.

When she licked her lips, he was almost undone. Only with self-control that he wasn't aware he possessed did he manage not to flip her over on the cushions of the sofa and have his way. But Cass deserved better than that. She was someone who merited the best he could offer, and he vowed she would receive it. He cared too much about her for their joining to be anything less.

Lyle watched her face as her index finger traveled across his chest, around his nipples, then followed the line of hair disappearing beneath his pants. She let that naughty finger dip inside his waistband and tugged him to her. Her eyes were wide, questioning.

He found her lips again. When she pushed his shirt off his shoulders, he finished removing it without his mouth leaving hers. More than once he'd seen the fire in Cass. Her intensity for life was momentarily banked but he hadn't been prepared for this profound craving to explore her passion. He wanted, needed, to see more of her, touch more of her, to experience all of Cass.

Pulling her shirt up, he ran his hand over the smoothness of her back until he found the edge of her bra and followed it around to her breast. His hand covered it. She stilled. Her breathing had turned into panting. Satisfaction filled him when just the brush of his thumb made her nipple harden, pushing against the material of the bra. He quickly found the back clasp and released the barrier. Pushing it away, he caressed her skin until he found her breasts once more. Cupping one, he judged its weight. Perfect.

Cass leaned back slightly against his arm. Her eyelids were half-closed and her lips swollen from his kisses. She was gorgeous. Stunning. Her lips parted. Heat shot through him. He pushed her shirt out of the way and covered her nipple with his mouth. Cass moaned. Her fingers ran through his hair as she held him close.

He twirled his tongue, teasing her nipple until it stood high. Cass made a crooning sound. When it turned to a coo, Lyle's heart sored. Pleased with himself, he moved to the other breast. As he achieved the same results his desire matched hers. Holding her securely around the waist with one arm, he leaned her back to view the full landscape. Cass lying out before him was beautiful scenery to behold. Eyes satisfied, his mouth feasted on her full breasts until she forcibly pulled his lips to hers.

As her flesh meshed with his, the aching in his body became raw pain. He pulled away, helping her to sit up straight. He steadied her with his hands on her waist. "Cass, are you sure you want to do this? Do you want to go upstairs? You decide."

To his alarm and disappointment, she pulled her shirt down over the mesmerizing view. Just as he let go of her waist so she could move away she said in a soft sexy voice, "I've always wanted to see your bedroom."

Lyle grinned. "Always, is it? I like the idea of that." He offered his hand, palm up. "Then let me give you a tour."

Cass floated more than walked up the narrow stairs behind Lyle. His firm hand clasping hers reassured her of his desire. She didn't want that to ever wane.

Even so, this impulsive decision to share Lyle's bed was reckless and far out of character. Yet this newfound freedom was intensely exciting. Anticipation tingled along every nerve. Lyle's touch, his smell, the flames of desire in his eyes all drew her to him. Being with him made her feel wonderful. Made her forget her losses. Dream of the gains. She wanted these precious moments and as long as he was willing to create them, she would take all he offered.

Tomorrow she would worry about the repercussions.

Right now, she was going to enjoy feeling, being alive as never before and leave her fear and hurt outside in the cold.

Lyle's bare back was wide, solid and strong. He was

everything she needed in life right now. Was she using him? Maybe, but she would see to it he received as good as he gave. Because of him she had remembered how to give and felt whole for the first time in weeks.

At the top of the stairs he turned right down a small hallway and entered a dark room. Not letting go of her hand, he continued to lead her across the floor. Her socked feet sank into a plush rug seconds before a click heralded light. A lamp sat on a small wooden table beside a large impressive bed. The dark headboard almost reached the ceiling while the matching footboard rose a few feet above the mattress. A quilt in browns and tans covered it.

Lyle turned to her. "Are you still sure you want this?"

Cass cherished his thoughtfulness. She cupped one of his cheeks. "Oh, yes." Going up on her toes, she kissed him.

That was all the invitation he seemed to require. Pulling her tight against him, Lyle tumbled with her to the bed. She winced.

Lyle said a harsh word under his breath. Raising himself so that he could see her, he asked. "Did I hurt you? I'm so sorry." He made a move to leave her.

She pulled him back. "Just a little tender. But I'm all right. How about kissing me?"

Lyle smiled. "With pleasure." His lips found hers.

As he kissed her his hands explored and caressed her waist and hips before lightly trailing between her legs. By the time they pulled apart, her center beat like a drum keeping rhythm with their heavy breathing.

Lyle rolled to his side, supported his head in his hand, and studied her. His other hand went to the hem of her shirt and beneath it. She shivered when his fingers found skin and skimmed along it. His heated gaze met hers. "Shh… I want to see all of you."

She looked away. "I have scars from the accident…"

Lyle's lips found hers briefly. "Even those. They're part of who you are now. The amazing person you are."

Cass had never thought of them like that. Her fear had been that they would be one more turn-off for men. She tried to relax as Lyle pushed her shirt and bra up, exposing her breasts. When he wanted to remove her shirt, she lifted off the bed enough for him to do so.

"More beautiful than I imagined."

She studied him in wonder. He'd been thinking about her, imagining her without clothes? The revelation was like a balm to her battered emotions.

Lyle gave her a gentle kiss before moving to one breast, then the other. "So sweet." He rotated her so he could see the injury on her arm then gently kissed the area. "I'm so sorry you were hurt."

Moments later his hand moved to the button of her pants and undid it. It took him no time to find the aching need at her center and slide a finger inside. She squirmed. Instead of giving her the relief she yearned for, his caress heightened her burning need.

"Lyle…" she crooned. Her gaze met his.

He kissed her deeply and continued his ministrations. Stopping, he tugged at her pants. Cass lifted her hips, assisting him in the process before kicking them to the floor. Lyle ran his hand along her right thigh. He paused over the puckered skin, then leaned toward it.

She shifted away. "Don't. It's so ugly."

"Shh… Nothing about you is ugly."

Lyle lightly kissed the area then his mouth moved to hers as his nimble finger entered her again. As it teased, his tongue mimicked the erotic dance.

Cass forgot everything but the sensation Lyle was creating in her. Cass's body tightened as the longing built, pleading for release. When she reached the limits of her endurance her body took over as if leaving her behind. She closed her eyes, flexed her back and tightened her legs around his hand, slipping into the land of wonder and delight that Lyle had built just for her.

Lyle's kisses gentled. He gave her one quick peck before he left her. Cass opened her eyelids just enough to see him shuck his pants in one swift movement. He stood strong and proud. Her breath caught in her throat at the beauty before her. She had caused this reaction in him. With that knowledge came a sense of amazement and power. Lyle obviously wanted her as much as she did him. He opened the drawer on the bedside table and removed a package, tore it open and rolled the condom on. Stepping to the bed, he looked down at her.

Cass opened her arms. Lyle came to her and she pulled him close. Her legs opened and he entered her slowly. She accepted all of him, but just barely. He eased out of her snug core, then plunged in again. Taking his head in both hands, Cass brought his mouth to hers. She loved kissing him. Loved how he made her feel—happy and healthy once again. Lyle increased his pace. The friction grew, building on itself. That growling need she'd known before returned with a vengeance.

Her eyes widened as she broke off their kiss and stared into Lyle's blazing ones. "Oh."

There was a lift to the corners of his mouth as she went over the edge of pleasure again.

Returning to herself, she saw the tension in Lyle's face that made his cheekbones more pronounced. His eyes were still locked with hers, but his attention was elsewhere. He thrust into her, faster and stronger.

Throwing his head back, he let go a throaty groan as he found his release.

Cass's eyes slowly closed as Lyle shifted to her side, still breathing heavily. He intertwined his fingers with hers. Like their lives had become.

Could she let them remain so?

Lyle returned to bed to find Cass napping under the covers with her head on his pillow. Her scent would linger there when she was gone. Fulfillment filled his chest, made his heart light. Cass had come willingly and given without reservation.

He eased in next to her and pulled her close. She was warm and sleek along his side. After murmuring something unintelligible she settled like a kitten beside him. He brushed her hair from her face. Her lashes rested in a dark semi-circle long her cheek.

With Cass he'd found the most pleasure he'd ever experienced. He'd had relationships since Freya but only Cass had managed to capture his attention so fully that he thought of her more often than his job. No matter what he was doing, she slipped into his mind. Even after she'd left the pub this afternoon, he had been more concerned about her reaction than his own to seeing Freya.

Cass shifted against him. He looked down to find her watching him. "Hey."

A shadow of uncertainty filled her eyes. "Hi. I didn't mean to fall asleep on you."

"I'm not complaining." He hoped it would happen often. His body was already coming to life. Leaning down, he kissed her.

Cass stopped him from taking it deeper and further with a hand to his chest. "I'd better go. I don't want to miss the head count at the clinic."

Lyle wanted her to stay but he wouldn't make her. Still, he had to protest at her leaving. "They don't do a head count, do they?"

She smirked. "So asks the man running the show."

"I'm not a dictator."

Cass sat up, bringing the sheet along to cover her. To his disappointment. Was she still self-conscious about her scars? "I know that. In fact, next to my father you're the nicest man I know."

Lyle's chest tightened. Having felt his father's disappointment most of his adult life, to hear Cass say that touched him. He felt valued. He put his hand behind her neck and brought her lips to his. "Thank you. I think that might be one of the nicest compliments I've ever received."

"You're welcome. Now I'd better get going."

By slipping off the bed and snatching up her clothes, she gave him no time to argue. "Bathroom?"

Lyle gave a fleeting thought to outright asking her to stay. He didn't. Apparently she needed distance to think about what had just happened between them. Maybe he wanted that as well. He pointed. "Door in the hall."

When he heard the door close, he got up, dressed and went downstairs. Cass didn't even come into the living room where he was. Instead she went straight to her boots. It was as if she was running. Was she regretting what had happened?

She was in the process of pulling on her jacket when he placed his hands on her shoulders. "Cass."

"Yes?"

"What's going on inside that head of yours?"

She didn't look up.

Suppressing a sigh of frustration, he said, "I think we've come far enough in our relationship that we can trust each other. Why the speedy exit? At this rate you're starting to put a dent in my self-confidence."

That brought her head up. "Oh, no. It has nothing to do with you. It has everything to do with me. I don't want the staff gossiping about us. But let me assure you your ego is well deserved."

He wanted to thump his chest but he settled for a big smile. "That's good to hear. I'll walk you back to the castle." He helped her on with her jacket then pulled on his coat.

Outside the cottage Lyle took her hand. He was relieved Cass didn't try to pull free, half-afraid she would.

At the side door of the castle, she held him back when he would have gone in. "It might be a good idea for us to say goodnight here. Do you really want the staff to know the despicable things you've been doing to a resident?"

Lyle chuckled. "Despicable? What about the wicked things you did to me?"

"Wicked?" She sounded appalled.

"I like the wicked you. But I agree. We should keep this between us. There's no reason we should be the talk of the clinic, or the village for that matter." She already had enough troubling her. He didn't want her worrying about gossip.

Cass reached for the doorknob.

"You're forgetting something." Lyle brought her to him and kissed her soundly. They broke apart and he searched her face. "Sometime soon I plan to have you to myself all night."

Cass's eyes widened, as her mouth opened and closed before she shut the door between them.

Gratification filled him. She was not as unaffected by what had taken place between them as she acted.

CHAPTER SEVEN

TWO DAYS LATER Cass sat in the castle lounge in front of the roaring fire snuggled into one of the wing-backed chairs. She was attempting to read a book she'd found in the library about the history of Cluchlochry. What she was really doing was thinking about Lyle. She had only spoken to him briefly a couple of times since they had been together. He acted as if he was abiding by her implied suggestion they make their time in bed together a one-time occurrence. Even though she had intentionally given that impression, she missed kissing him or being held in his arms. It was driving her crazy not seeing him. But she would be leaving soon. Could her heart stand for her to take it further?

Was he waiting for her to come to him? Could she let herself do that? Would she be able not to? Indecision roiled in her.

It was a relief to have the distraction when Melissa pushed a young man in a wheelchair into the room and over beside her. At least now she had something to take her mind off Lyle.

The young man, dressed in a T-shirt and sweatpants, looked older than she guessed was the reality. He was gaunt. Dark rings beneath his eyes emphasized his lost look. One of his hands had a tremor.

"Hi, Cass. Have you met Andy Wallace?" Melissa asked as she parked the man near the fire. A small brown and white cocker spaniel jogged along beside him, coming to lie at his feet.

"No, I haven't. Hi, Andy." A week ago, could she have sounded that friendly? Being at the castle had changed her…or had it been Lyle? The thought both worried and thrilled her.

Andy nodded, then looked down at his clasped hands in his lap.

Wasn't he the patient who had been admitted the same day as she had been? In all the time she'd been there she hadn't seen him. "I've heard of you. Nice to meet you."

Melissa locked the brake on the wheelchair. She patted him on the shoulder. "I need to check on another patient then I'll be back to take you to therapy. I won't be long."

She gave Cass a quick smile and was gone.

Andy's eyes flickered to Cass with a look of uncertainty before they jerked away.

She leaned down and patted the dog. Not long ago she wouldn't have done that. "I do know Molasses. I work at the canine therapy center every afternoon so I get to take care of Molasses when she isn't with you. She's a good dog."

"Maybe when I start walking I can do that as well. The doctors keep telling me I'll walk again but I'm not sure that'll ever happen."

"Getting well takes time. I'm sure you'll get there." Who did she think she was to give encouragement when she'd been little more than a walking package of ugly emotions with a bad leg and arm a couple of weeks ago? This morning she'd even caught herself smiling when she thought of Lyle. Her leg was getting stronger and her arm was extending further. She smiled. Lyle had kissed her injuries. She had made more progress than she could have believed possible when she had arrived. For once she'd started thinking there was a future.

Andy said nothing more as he stared into the fire.

There wouldn't be much conversation unless she helped keep it going. She sensed he needed it. Wasn't that what Lyle had seen in her? The need to talk about the unseen trauma that physical therapy had no effect on? Could she help do for Andy what Lyle had done for her? Giving him an ear, just listen to him?

She raised the book in her hand. "I've been reading about the history of Cluchlochry. This is an amazing area."

He grunted.

A response. Somewhat.

"We don't have anything like this where I'm from." She waved a hand indicating the castle. "It's a special place."

"I used to spend a lot of time here," he muttered.

Cass had to lean forward to hear him. There was moisture pooling in his eyes.

"You've been to Heatherglen Castle before?"

"Yes. I grew up in Cluchlochry." His voice had grown stronger.

"It must have been a fun place for little boys. There are plenty of places to hide. Big spaces to run." The castle and grounds would be a wonderful place to spend a childhood. Would Lyle's kids one day do that? The thought of him having children with another woman caused a dull ache around her heart.

Andy's eyes took on a shadowed look. "Nick and I used to play hide and seek here all the time. I never could find him." He didn't say anything more, returning to staring at the fire. "He's gone now."

"Gone?" she prompted.

"Died in Afghanistan."

Cass sucked in a breath.

"Nick was my best friend," he mumbled.

She wasn't sure who he was talking about, but the name sounded familiar. Waiting, she hoped he'd answer her questions without her saying more.

"It should have been me who died. He should have got out of the army. Should have come home. Not gone back. I told him not to," he said, less to her and more to himself.

Cass's heart went out to him. She cringed, too well acquainted with loss. Of emotions so enormous and distressing they were difficult to live with. Hers had many fronts. Rufus being gone. What to do with her life now. Could she have a real lasting relationship with a man? Now to live with the scars. All of those were bundled into a massive ball of insecurity. She could understand the forlorn man beside her too well. That added to her discomfort. "Heatherglen was Nick's home?"

Andy gave her an odd look as if he was confused by her confusion. "Nick was Charles's older brother. Dr. Charles Ross-Wylde, the Laird."

"Yes, I've met the Laird. I know who you're talking about now. I'm sorry to hear about your friend. Losing someone you care about is hard."

"Have you lost someone?"

This was not the direction Cass had anticipated their conversation going. If she had she wouldn't have started it. Over the last few days thoughts of Lyle had managed to overtake all those ugly, sad feelings that had weighed heavy on her and she liked it that way. The pain had dulled. Maybe, just maybe, if she could share some of her pain with Andy, he wouldn't feel so alone, maybe believe that life could get better.

To her surprise, she had begun to believe that. It had slipped up on her but, yes, she did. "I have. It wasn't a person but the next thing to it. He was my partner and friend. Rufus, my dog."

Andy gave her a long searching look. "What happened?"

Cass wasn't sure she could go into the details but she'd opened the door so Andy deserved the truth. Her eyes clouded over. "We were a search and rescue team. We had just saved a child when there was a ground tremor and the wall of the building started to fall. Rufus barked, warning me. The wall fell on him. Hit me in the leg and arm." She could say this next part. Had to say it. "He saved my life and lost his."

Andy gave her a compassionate look. "I'm sorry about your dog."

Moisture filled Cass's eyes, making Andy a foggy blur. "I miss him every day. I'm not sure if I can or want to return to my job without him. It may be just too hard. But search and rescue is all I know."

Lyle walked to the lounge door when he heard Cass's voice. He halted inside the door, just in time to hear her confession about Rufus. He listened for more. She hadn't told him the entire story. No wonder she had been so devastated by what had happened to her. The loss of the dog was some of it but her fears and agony went deeper. Her world had been turned upside down. She was unsure what direction to take. The change in her life must be terrifying for her. She'd experienced a major loss of not only her dog but life as she had known it. He knew her well enough to know that, for her, losing her job was like losing her identity.

Yet she had shared her grief and feelings with another hurting person. That had to have been difficult for her. He should feel hurt that she had confided the deeper meaning of the loss of Rufus with Andy and not him, but what Lyle had just heard told him what a large heart Cass had for people.

Andy had refused to come out of his room for days. Lyle had finally convinced him to come down. On top of not wanting to interact with others, Andy refused to talk about his accident and about losing Nick. Lyle would be eternally grateful to Cass for getting him to open up, to take a metaphorical step forward.

Cass and Andy were so adsorbed in their conversation they didn't see or hear him. He shouldn't stand here eavesdropping but he couldn't move either. Thankfully that was taken out of his hands when Melissa brushed past him.

"Hi, Lyle. How're you today?" She kept going until she reached Andy.

Cass's head whipped around so that she looked directly at him. Surprise, concern and happiness ran over her features in rapid progression.

Lyle was glad to see her as well, but he was still disturbed by what he had heard and what it meant in her life. He had made less of it in his mind than he should have. He now understood why Cass acted the way she did about the dog they'd found, the sadness about her when she'd first arrived, even her not wanting to get too involved with him. Her emotions must be in turmoil. She had been and was suffering far more than he'd given her credit for.

He stepped forward as Melissa announced as she

took off the brake on the chair, "They're waiting for you in therapy, Andy. We must go."

Andy gave Cass a nod.

She offered him a wry smile. "See you soon, Andy."

Melissa rolled him back, turned him and they headed out the door.

Cass's eyes rose to meet Lyle's. "You heard?"

Lyle nodded. He didn't even try to question why she hadn't shared with him how losing Rufus had affected her. Now wasn't the time to analyze that. There might never be one. She didn't owe him anything. One hot evening together didn't mean they could or should bare their souls to one another. That was the way she seemed to want it. Didn't he as well?

Pushing herself to her feet, she said, "I'd better go."

He took a couple of steps forward, his voice going low. "I've missed you, Cass. I was coming to look for you when I heard your voice."

"Did you want something?"

"I'd like a kiss." He looked around, "But I won't do that here."

Cass rewarded him with a blush. She might be acting as if she was immune to him but she wasn't, not even a little bit.

"I'll wait until later. But I will kiss you." He stressed the last sentence.

She grinned at him. "Is that a promise, Doctor?"

Lyle's heart soared. He liked that much better than her sad look. "It is. I do have something to ask you, though. My mother rang and would like me to bring you around to Harlow House for dinner this evening. She wants to keep her promise to teach you to knit."

Cass looked away as if she was unsure. "That's not necessary."

He waited until she met his gaze again. "My mother will be disappointed if you don't come."

Cass looked down as if her shoes required her attention. "I'm just not sure that's a good idea."

"Why not? You have been invited." Lyle watched her closely. It shouldn't matter so much that she agree.

"I don't want to give her any ideas about us, with me leaving so soon."

"If that's now you feel…" He turned to go.

She reached out and grabbed his forearm. "Wait."

Lyle didn't realize until that second just how much he'd missed Cass's touch. He placed his hand over hers.

Cass's eyelids fluttered as she gave him a wary look. "I guess I could go. I'd never want to hurt your mother's feelings."

He made a *tsk*ing sound. "And here I was hoping you wanted to spend time with me. I'll meet you in the foyer at five."

She nodded.

Lyle ran his thumb across the top of her hand. "By the way, Cass, you're beautiful both inside and out. You really helped Andy out today. He needs someone to confide in, someone who understands where he's coming from. You're a special person, Cass Bellow."

Her eyes softened. Lyle had to leave before he kissed her right then and there.

A few hours later Lyle strolled into the foyer, expecting to see Cass waiting near the door. Instead he found her with a staff member and a couple of other residents, tying large red bows on the banister. The greenery had been draped the week before.

"It's really starting to look like Christmas in here." His attention was directly on Cass.

Everyone turned to him.

"Thank you," the staff member said. "I have some excellent help."

"I have one more bow to tie and I'll be ready," Cass called.

There was a happy note in her voice. That had been missing when she'd first arrived and he rather liked hearing it. Had he had anything to do with putting it there? He really hoped so. "We have time."

She moved up a step with only a slight hesitation. Soon she would be coming down those stairs as part of her graduation and be leaving him. The thought brought a wince deep within him. Did he want her to stay? Could he ask her to? He refused to do a long-distance relationship again. From experience he'd learned those didn't work. Cass's life was going all over the world, helping people, and his was staying here and doing the same. It would never work. It would be better for both of them to let go sooner than later.

Another few minutes went by before Cass came down the steps slowly, holding tightly to the rail, but she was doing it on her own. She approached him.

"You have made progress. It won't be long before you'll be going up and coming down the grand staircase instead of using the lift."

She smiled and his world brightened. "I have to admit that a few weeks ago I looked at it as if it was Mount Everest. I was halfway up before I knew it."

"You've worked hard. You should be proud of yourself." Lyle was.

"Thanks." Cass picked up her coat off a chair and slipped into it. Buttoning it, she quickly wrapped the scarf around her neck and pulled on her hat.

"Ready?"

"I am." She headed toward the front door.

Lyle followed. When they were out of hearing of the others he asked, "I thought you didn't want anyone to know about our…uh, friendship? You didn't seem to mind the others knowing you were going out with me."

Over her shoulder she said, "I told them you were testing my endurance by going for a walk with me."

"Ah, I see." He had a sour taste in his mouth. When she had suggested the other night that they keep their relationship between themselves it'd seemed the wise thing to do. Now he wanted people to know that Cass was his and he hers. Or was it really that way? "We do need to walk to my place and then take the car from there."

"Your parents live far?" She started around the castle toward the path to his cottage.

"No, but further than *you* would even wish to walk."

They were soon out of sight of the castle and Lyle took her hand. His heart thumped an extra beat when she didn't pull away. After they reached the seclusion of the large trees, he pulled her behind one and into his arms.

"I've waited too long to do this." His lips found hers.

Unsure what Cass's reaction would be, he was elated when she stepped into him and joined him in a kiss that should have melted the snow beneath their feet. They stayed like that until the wind blew and a pile of snow dropped off a branch, landing on their shoulders. They giggled like school kids then started toward his place again.

Once there, Lyle led her to the detached garage to where he kept his car. Inside it, he reached over and cupped her cheek. "I have missed you. I wished there was time to take you inside and have my way with you, but my mother is expecting us."

Cass smiled. "We all like to keep our parents happy."

He groaned. "That we do." He'd spent the better part of his life trying to do just that and was still managing to disappoint his father. If he returned to the army, he would be choosing his father's happiness over his own.

Cass looked over at Lyle as he backed out of the garage. It had been so long since she had been alone with him that she'd feared she might rush into his arms when she did have him to herself. The moment she had looked up from tying the bow to the spindle and her gaze had locked with his, her heart had galloped like a horse making the last quarter-mile.

What had he been thinking? Had he been as excited to see her? She'd left things between them as if their time together had been nothing but a nice evening. She'd been fooling herself. Being with Lyle had been more than that. She couldn't say that to him earlier in the lounge, so she was glad to have the invitation to his parents'. They would have a chance to talk. More than that, to touch.

She'd only agreed to help decorate the foyer because it gave her nervous energy an outlet. If she hadn't, she would have been pacing the floor when he arrived. It had to have been high school since she'd last been this wired up about seeing a guy. Her attraction to Lyle had tipped over into need in such a short time.

That horse had broken into an even faster gallop the second Lyle had pulled her out of sight of the castle and kissed her. She'd been back where she belonged. When the snow had fallen on them she had laughed like she hadn't laughed in far too long. Instead of having second thoughts about becoming involved with Lyle, she was running headlong into doing so. Especially by going to his parents' house.

After Lyle had driven onto the main road, he took her hand and held it as often as the narrow winding roads would allow. He drove through the village and out the other side. Soon he turned into a lane that led to a stately house that was a larger version of Lyle's cottage.

Lyle's mother greeted her by pulling her into a hug. Cass instantly missed her own mother, who she hoped to see soon. She glanced at Lyle. That would mean she would be leaving him. At that moment, she decided she would make the most of the time she had with him. She wanted this happiness to last as long as possible. The difference between misery and joy had been made clear over the last couple of weeks and she would take all the cheer in life she could grab for as long as she could have it. Right now, that meant being with Lyle.

When Mrs. Sinclair finished embracing Cass, she moved on to Lyle with the same vigor, as if she hadn't seen him in years. Done, she escorted them into a living area where the TV was on. Lyle's father didn't stand as they entered.

Mr. Sinclair did offer his hand. "Hello again, young lady."

Lyle would age well based on his father's looks, despite the older man's illness. Some other woman would get to watch that. Cass wasn't going to think of that now. "Hello. Thanks for having me."

"Glad to. Hello, son." He and Lyle shook hands.

Something about the action bothered Cass. Shouldn't they have hugged? A second of coolness seemed to surround them.

"Cass and I are going to the kitchen to have our knitting lesson," Mrs. Sinclair announced, and turned to Cass. "Unless you have changed your mind?"

"Oh, no, I would love to learn."

"Then come with me. Lyle, you watch the match with your dad while we have our lesson." Mrs. Sinclair waved a hand at him as she moved toward a door off the room.

Cass glanced at Lyle who was already settling into a chair. Maybe Cass had just been imagining things. Lyle acted as if spending time with his father wasn't a problem.

She found the more she was around Lyle's parents the more she liked them. His mother was what every mother should be—warm and open. His father was harder to get to know with his gruff voice and iron exterior, but Cass suspected he loved his wife and son deeply, and they him.

Cass followed Mrs. Sinclair into the kitchen. It, like the rest of the house, was in perfect order. The counter tops were spotless and the floor gleamed.

"Why don't we sit by the fire? We'll be warm there."

A large range sat against one wall with two rocking chairs in front of it. Beside one of the chairs was a basket full of yarn with large needles stuck in it.

Cass took the chair that didn't have the basket next to it, reasoning that it was Mrs. Sinclair's.

Lyle's mother settled into the other. "We're going to start with something simple. Just learn to knit. I think it will be all that you want to do in the first lesson. Now I'm going to show you how to start then I'm going to let you do it."

Cass eagerly sat on the edge of her seat, watching every move Mrs. Sinclair made. "That sounds fine. I know nothing about knitting."

Mrs. Sinclair's mouth formed a smile much like Lyle's. "Today you'll learn. Here are some needles and you pick out a skein of wool."

"They're all so lovely." Cass decided on a blue that reminded her of the color of Lyle's eyes. When she was gone at least she would have that to remember him by.

Lyle's mother picked up some needles and pulled out a length of wool. "The first thing you want to do is make a small loop and slide it onto one of the needles."

Mrs. Sinclair was already in her element. Cass watched intently.

"Now you bring this up around here, the tip of the needle through here and the wool around like this." The wool worked perfectly onto the needle. "Now I want you to try with your needles and wool."

Cass did as she had been shown until it was time to move the wool up and around the needle.

"Not quite, dear." Mrs. Sinclair's voice was patient. Did Lyle get that from her as well? "Let me show you." She brought the wool around and got Cass started correctly once again.

Cass had made ten rows and was proud of her accomplishment when Lyle's voice came from behind her. "It looks like you're making progress."

Cass held up what she had done. "Look, I'm actually knitting."

He smiled as if he was proud of her as well.

"She's a really good student," Mrs. Sinclair offered.

"Cass is good at anything she puts her mind to," Lyle said.

A warmth that had nothing to do with the fire spread through her. Looking over her shoulder again, Cass saw Lyle gazing at her with a twinkle in his eye. Was he thinking about their time together in bed? She gave him a shy smile then glanced at his mother to find her watching them closely. Did she see the attraction between them?

"I hate to break this up, but Dad and I were wondering how long it would be until dinner?"

Mrs. Sinclair put her work into her basket and stood. "Lyle Sinclair, you know as well as anyone that in this house we eat promptly at six. We have all your life. Gregor wouldn't have it any other way."

"Yes, once in the army always in the army." Lyle said it as fact, but there was a note of bitterness there as well.

She gave her son a direct look. "I'll have you know I don't worry about you starving when you eat Mrs. Renwick's food all the time."

Lyle's mood lightened. "I do have to be careful not to overdo it there."

Cass placed her work in the basket as well. "What can I do to help?"

"We're just having a chicken pie tonight. It's already in the oven so there's not much to do except set the table."

"Lyle and I can take care of that, can't we?" Cass looked at him.

An amazed look came to his face, but he nodded. "Yes, we can."

Over the next few minutes she and Lyle gathered what was needed. A couple of times he brushed past her, making her tingle all over. When she asked him for a fork he handed it across the table in a manner that let him trail his fingers over her palm, which started her center throbbing. She'd had no idea that setting the table could be such an erotic activity. Her eyes met his. She didn't see a flicker of desire there, but a fire burning.

His mother cleared her throat, bringing them back

to where they were. Cass dropped the fork with a clang onto a plate.

Lyle, the devil, grinned and picked it up. He put it in its place. "All done, Mum."

His mother smiled. "Thank you." She turned back to the counter to where a large bowl sat. "Oh, my goodness, we all need to give the pudding a stir. I don't want to forget it."

"Pudding a stir?" Cass gave the bowl a dubious look. "Exactly what're we doing?"

"Stirring the Christmas pudding," Mrs. Sinclair stated, as if it was a great occasion.

"I don't know what a Christmas pudding is." Cass looked into the bowl from which she had removed the cloth.

"I think they call it a fruit cake in America." Lyle moved up beside Cass.

"I have heard of them but never seen one or eaten one." Cass still studied the mixture.

"You'll have to join us for some in a few weeks." Lyle's mother pulled out a large wooden spoon from a drawer.

Cass felt more than saw Lyle tense beside her. Did it matter to him that she would be gone soon? It did her. She wanted as much time with him as possible before she left. "I'm not sure that I'll be here that long."

"Well, if you're here then you must come for a slice." Mrs. Sinclair didn't miss a beat. "You need to stir three times and then make a wish."

Lyle's mother handed her the spoon.

Wish? What should she wish for? To hurry home? For a new partner? She wasn't sure she was ready for that. She glanced at Lyle. To have him in her life always? What did she want most? Happiness. She glanced at Lyle. She felt that right now. But could it last?

It took more effort than she'd anticipated to stir the thick mixture but she managed to make the three turns. She made her wish.

"So what did you ask for?" Lyle took the spoon and started to stir.

"I can't tell you that. It won't come true." And she wanted it to come true no matter how improbable and unrealistic it was.

His mother stepped away. Lyle whispered, "Was it about me?"

Cass whispered back, "Such an ego."

"Lyle, if you'll carry the pie to the table and Cass brings the beans, I think we'll be ready." Mrs. Sinclair pulled a round golden-brown-crusted pie out of the oven. It smelled heavenly. She set it on the counter.

Lyle then picked it up and moved it to the table. His mother handed her the bowl with beans in it.

"Gregor," Mrs. Sinclair called. "Come to the table."

Lyle's father joined them, but it took him a while. He moved slowly.

Over the next hour they enjoyed good food and lively conversation. Cass looked around the cozy room. At Lyle. This was what she would like to have in her life. Lyle smiled at her. This was happiness.

"So what do you do in America?" Lyle's father asked her.

Her heart sank at the reminder. This wasn't her home. "I work in search and rescue." Did she still, though?

Gregor nodded. "Interesting work."

"It can be." She didn't really want to talk about it. "I understand you're retired military?"

He sat straighter, if that was possible. "I am. All the

men in my family have made a career in the armed forces." He gave Lyle, who had turned stony-faced, a pointed look. "I'm hoping Lyle will decide to go active again soon."

She looked at Lyle, who was pushing food around on his plate. Had she said something wrong?

"Dad, let's not get into that now."

For the first time since Cass had arrived Mrs. Sinclair had no smile on her face. An uncomfortable feeling settled around them, completely wiping out the ease of earlier.

She had said something wrong!

Lyle's request went unnoticed by Mr. Sinclair. "You need to do it soon or time will run out for promotions."

"Isn't Lyle needed here? You should have seen him in action the other night. He had two patients to see about and then me. I understand that he's the only emergency medical care around here. That's a big burden for anyone. I think there are different ways of fighting for people. You did it by being in the military and Lyle does it by caring for people when they are hurt. In my book you're both heroes."

The others looked at her, speechless. Not even Mr. Sinclair said a thing. Lyle gave her a tender look of wonderment and appreciation.

Mrs. Sinclair pushed back from the table. "I'll get those biscuits I bought at the market the other day for dessert."

An hour later Lyle was driving them back to his cottage.

"I hope I didn't say anything wrong at dinner," Cass said in a small voice. "I didn't mean to."

Lyle couldn't believe that Cass had even asked that. After her speech to his father Lyle's chest had puffed out like a bird preening for a new mate. Few managed to put his father in his place and Cass had done it effortlessly and had complimented his father at the same time. Lyle looked at her like she was a queen. "You were wonderful. The subject is an age-old sticky issue between my father and me."

"How's that?" Her attention was focused on him.

"You could tell that I'm a disappointment to him. He's sick. Dying, in fact."

Cass squeezed the hand he already held. "I'm sorry."

"I am, too. If I re-enlisted he'd be so happy. I could give him that before he died. Right now, I'm letting the family name down."

"You are not! He can't believe that. You help people. Look how much you have helped me."

Lyle raised a brow and gave her a suggestive look. "I don't help all the residents in the same way as I have you."

Her lips turned up in a smirk and she poked him in the shoulder with a finger. "And you had better not."

He was even feeling better about himself after that statement. It was the first time Cass had indicated that she felt any ownership of him, that he was important to her on a level outside bed. He liked the idea of her being jealous. She was definitely good for his ego.

Lyle pulled into his garage and turned off the engine. Twisting toward Cass he brought her to him. She looked at him expectantly. "I thought you were perfect tonight. Thank you for the vote of confidence. It means a lot. Especially coming from you."

Cass gave him a tender smile as his lips slowly lowered to hers. They were as soft as he remembered. A second later, her hands gripped his coat and pulled him closer. She returned his kiss. He lifted her onto his lap. It wasn't until she winced that he remembered her injuries.

He let go of her and she slid back into the passenger seat. "I'm sorry again. I keep forgetting you've been hurt. That hero certificate you said I deserved should be revoked."

"I'm fine. When I make certain moves my leg lets me know it doesn't like it."

"Necking in a two-seater car would be one of those times." What was wrong with him? He forgot everything but touching Cass when she was near. He climbed out of the car and hurried around to help her out. "I'm really sorry."

She wrapped her finger around his coat lapels and pulled him to her again. "Why don't you shut up and kiss me, then take me inside?"

He brought her into his arms with a smile on his lips. "I can do that."

CHAPTER EIGHT

FOUR MORNINGS LATER Cass was still in his bed when he woke up. Lyle liked it that way. Too much. She had stayed the night after they had gone to his parents'. They had agreed to eating dinner at his place the next evening.

As he'd held her in his arms after they had made love, he'd asked, "Will you stay the night?"

She'd leaned up to look at him. "I will if you understand that this can only be a short-term thing between us. As soon as I am given a clean bill of health, I'm going home. I can't handle anything serious in my life right now. I've just gotten to where I can get out of bed without dreading it."

Lyle had wiggled his brows. "That wouldn't be because you've been in bed with me, would it?"

She'd brushed a hand low over him and his body had twitched in reaction. "You might say that. I just need things to remain easy and fun between us. I've been on emotional overload for so long. I don't think I could handle more."

"I can do slow and easy. In fact, I'd like to practice now." He'd rolled Cass on her side and brushed a feather-light finger over her hip. Lyle had been rewarded with a shiver from Cass.

The next two nights they had eaten at the castle and then walked hand in hand to his place. Lyle had tried not to question Cass's decisions. Instead, he enjoyed having her in his life. No one at the castle had asked him where she was at night and he'd offered no explanation. All he knew was that life was better than it had ever been.

What they didn't do was talk about when she was leaving. Yet both knew it was coming. Too fast for him. Did Cass feel the same way? He didn't want to ruin what they had by asking.

On Saturday morning, they were lying in bed and Cass's hand was causally rubbing back and forth over his chest when she asked, "Hey, have you ever thought about making this place more festive? Everyone else is busy decorating for Christmas but you have nothing up."

"Are you thinking I should have a tree in my bedroom?"

Her hand gave him a light swat. Which he liked more than resented. "Of course not. I was thinking of you putting one up in your living room. It looks like Scrooge lives here."

"You can hurt my feelings, you know? I'd just planned to enjoy what's up at the castle. I've never really gone in for that sort of stuff, and I go to Mum and Dad's on Christmas Day." He pushed her hair back, letting his fingers run through it. "But maybe if I had somebody to help me, I could put a few things up. Would you be willing to help?"

Cass twisted around, looking him in the face while giving him a tantalizing view of the curve of her breast and hip. She seemed to give no thought to having scars anymore. "I thought you would never ask."

Lyle chuckled.

She grinned. "So do you have any ornaments or anything to put on a tree?"

"No. I hadn't had any need for them."

"Then we'll go to the Christmas market and get some. I saw some really pretty ones made out of natural stuff in one of the stalls."

Later Cass sat at the kitchen table, having a cup of coffee, while he scrambled eggs and prepared toast. She looked up and smiled. Lyle liked this Cass much better than the one who had first arrived at the castle. He would miss her when she was gone. "I really appreciate you talking to Andy. I've been worried about him."

"Unfortunately, I think we have a lot in common." There was a dejected note in her words.

"You might be right about that." He really couldn't break patient confidentiality. "I wish you hadn't kept all that happened to you from me, but I understand why you did. I'm so sorry."

She gave him a look of appreciation then went back to her coffee. Cass would talk more when she was ready. He finished the eggs, put the toast on a plate and carried it all to the table.

"I can help you." Cass reached for the plate.

"I told you that I wanted to cook for you. If we're going to get a tree and ornaments today you need to keep up your strength." He winked. "I might have other plans for you as well."

He was rewarded with an attractive blush. She never stopped amazing him. Cass was as tough as stone on the outside but could blush like a young woman after her first kiss. He loved the two sides of her. Love! Was he falling in love with Cass?

She spooned out scrambled eggs and took a piece

of toast. "So can we go to the market as soon as we're through eating?"

"Are we in that much of a hurry?"

Cass gave him an insistent look. "We have a lot to do if we're going to get this place looking festive today."

"We have to do it all today?" He gave a theatrical groan.

She put her fists on her hips and gave him a huffy look. "We do. I won't be here much longer, and I want to enjoy it for as long as I can."

That statement stabbed Lyle with reality, but he refused to let on that her leaving would upset him. She wanted casual and he would try to give her that. He chuckled. "Where did all this newfound Christmas spirit come from?"

Cass looked directly into his eyes. "From being around you. Thank you for bringing me back from that dark place."

His heart swelled. This was what it was like to be appreciated, valued for who he was as a person. He'd not felt that in some time. He needed it. Cass had given him a real gift. "You're welcome." He kissed her, keeping it tender, wanting her to sense his gratitude, then he pulled away, "You're right, I do need some cheer."

Soon after they'd finished breakfast, they left for the village. Few people were around. The sky was dark and it was starting to spit. It would snow again before the end of the day. Cass led the way to the stall with the ornaments she had seen. There, the owner greeted Lyle, whom he had known all his life.

Lyle told Cass, "Get whatever you think I need."

She grinned. "You shouldn't have said that." Cass went about picking out ornaments and putting them into a pile on the corner of the table.

Lyle paid the man, who was grinning from ear to ear as they walked off.

"Shouldn't we stop and say hi to your mother?" Cass looped her hand in the crook of his elbow.

"Yes. She would be hurt to know you came here and didn't say hello." Lyle led her down another aisle to his mother's stall.

His mother saw them and stopped knitting to greet them. "What're you two doing here?"

Cass gave this mother a self-satisfied smile and held up the bag she carried. "We came to get some ornaments for Lyle's tree."

His mother gave him a pointed look then asked with a sarcastic note, "Lyle's going to have a tree?"

He'd not had a tree or decorated his cottage since his return home. Freya had always made a big deal out of Christmas but he had never cared one way or the other. It wasn't worth the effort as far as he was concerned. But if Cass wanted him to have a tree, he would have a tree with all the trimmings.

"He is," Cass said proudly.

His mother looked from him to her and back again. Her smile had broadened.

"We're on our way to get one right now but we wanted to come by and say hi to you." The cheerful words seemed to bubble out of her.

"Gregor," his mother called.

Lyle turned to see his father shuffling toward them. He looked more tired than usual, older.

"Hello, son. I'm glad I got to see you. I spoke to Colonel McWright a minute ago. He said you haven't been by to talk to him about re-enlisting."

That was the last conversation Lyle wanted to have

with him. "I've been busy at the clinic. I'll try to get by sometime this week."

"You need to do so. He'll be retiring soon and won't have the influence he has now. If you want that position you need to be talking to him."

The smile on Cass's face faded to an expression of curiosity and concern. Lyle wanted that smile to return. His hand went to Cass's elbow. "I'll take care of it. It's good to see you. Cass and I are putting up a tree so we need to go and pick out one before they're all gone." He started them toward the door.

"Nice to see you, Colonel and Mrs. Sinclair." Cass waved.

"Bye, Mum. Dad," Lyle called as they walked away.

Cass pulled to a halt when they were out of sight of his parents. "Are you really returning to active duty?"

"No. Maybe. I don't know. Look, we have a fun day planned and I don't want to talk about that. Let's concentrate on putting up a tree."

Cass studied him a moment then smiled brightly. "Works for me."

He would miss that smile when she returned to America. A stab of pain shot through him. This wasn't supposed to happen. He didn't, wouldn't, do long distance. It didn't work. He'd learned that the hard way. Yet he couldn't stop himself from holding onto what time he had left with her.

Cass came to another sudden stop at a stall selling Christmas-tree skirts. She fingered a navy one with silver stars sewn closer to the trunk of the tree and sloping mounds of white depicting snowy mountains. Was she thinking of the night he had found her sitting on the rock wall? Lyle smiled. Even then he had been captivated by her.

"Get it, if you want it." He pulled out his wallet.

"I wasn't asking you to buy it." She gave him a concerned look.

He gave her an indulgent smile. "I know that, but every good tree needs a skirt."

A few minutes later they left. Cass carried their purchases with a happy look on her face.

On their way back to his cottage they stopped at a place on the outskirts of the village to buy a tree. He had to remind Cass that his ceilings weren't that high when she admired a ten-foot tree. With an exaggerated expression of disappointment, she located a six-foot tree that he still hoped would fit through his doors. Cass's happiness with her choice made him keep his concerns to himself.

They made one more stop at a shop and bought a tree stand and lights. They spent the remainder of the day putting up the Christmas tree and decorating it. Done, they switched off the main lights and sat by the fire with a hot cup of tea.

Cass laid her head on his shoulder. "What kinds of family Christmas traditions does your family have?"

"You already know about the Christmas pudding. One year when I was off on the other side of the world Mum posted one to me. I hate to admit I was pretty lonely that year."

Cass said softly, "It was the year you got the letter."

For once the mention of what had happened to him didn't include pain. "It was. I sliced the pudding and shared it with the patients in my unit and we had a right fine celebration."

Lyle looked at Cass. To his amazement she had tears in her eyes. "What's all this about?"

She took his hand and tenderly rubbed it. "I just hate to think of you away by yourself at Christmas."

"Aw, honey, I'm home now. My Christmases are happy. This one will be especially so with this tree." What he didn't say was that he wished she would be there as well. He wouldn't think about that; instead he would enjoy what he had at this moment. She would be leaving soon. They had an agreement. Still the need to keep her there pulled at him.

A heavy knock at the front door broke the moment. Lyle opened it to find one of the local police officers standing there.

"Lyle, a five-year-old girl has gone missing. She wandered off from the market. We need your help to search."

"Missing?" The low sound of Cass's voice held a looming note of fear.

He forced himself to concentrate on what the policeman was saying. Cass he would soothe later. "How long has she been gone?"

"Two and a half hours." The policeman was wasting no time in giving answers.

His next question made him sick to ask but it was necessary. "Do you believe someone has taken her?"

The man's lips thinned. "Right now, no, but we're ruling out no possibilities."

"What do I need to do?"

"We've made a grid of the area." He handed him a map. "We need you to look here." He pointed to a square.

Cass came to stand in front of Lyle. "Do you have a piece of the child's clothing?" she asked in a determined voice. "I can help."

"You are?"

"This is Cass Bellow. She's trained in search and rescue," Lyle offered.

Cass let him say no more. "Time's of the essence. Do you have something or not?"

The officer glanced at Lyle. He nodded. "I can get something."

"Then we'll meet you at the market cross in twenty minutes." She made that announcement, turned and started putting on her coat.

"We'll see you then," Lyle said.

The officer looked unsure, but nodded and left.

Lyle closed the door and asked Cass, "What're you thinking?"

"One of the dogs at the center has past search and rescue training. I've been working with him. He knows me. He might be able to help." She wrapped her scarf around her neck.

Lyle had to admire her. Working with a dog on a search had to take all her fortitude. For her to even volunteer said something about what kind of person she was. "You sure you can handle that?"

"Don't really have a choice. A child is missing." She jerked her hat down around her ears and opened the door.

"Hey, wait for me." Lyle snatched up his scarf and hat and hurried after her.

CHAPTER NINE

"Komm!" Cass commanded Hero out of his pen at the canine center. She had made friends with him over the past couple of weeks so she had no trouble encouraging him to come to her. As he exited the cage she clipped on the leash. "*Fuss.*" Hero walked beside her to Lyle's car.

He opened the door and Cass said, *"Komm,"* and Hero jumped into the backseat.

Less than a minute later they were on their way into Cluchlochry.

Cass clutched her hands in her lap. It hadn't been long since she'd had an assignment and worked with a dog, yet it seemed like years. She was a bundle of nerves. What if she broke down? What if they couldn't find the girl? What if…? All that fear and sadness that had held her heart in a vise had returned. If Rufus was here she'd have no doubts about locating the girl but she didn't know Hero well or his abilities. Still, she had to try.

Lyle drove faster than the speed limit, but every minute mattered. Hero sat calmly in the backseat of the car. Lyle pulled into a parking space close to the market cross. With the market over for the day, there were plenty available.

The policeman who had come to Lyle's cottage was

waiting. As soon as they joined him, he handed Lyle a small orange jacket. “I understand she was wearing this earlier today.”

“So she has no coat on?” Lyle asked, concern lacing his words.

Cass shivered as much from the cold as from her fear for the little girl.

The officer’s face was grim as he said, “From what her parents tell me, she’s wearing a jumper, jeans and boots. We don’t know if she still has gloves on or a hat, or anything like that.”

“Then we need to worry about exposure as well.” Cass’s words were flat and to the point.

“I’ll get a thermal blanket and my medical bag out of the car.” Lyle wasted no time in doing so.

“May I see the jacket?” Cass reached out her hand.

The policeman handed it to her and she knelt so that Hero could get a good sniff of the clothing.

Lyle returned with a satchel on his hip, the strap across his chest. He looked at her. “Ready?”

“Yes. You have a blanket?”

He patted the satchel and clicked on a large torch.

She gave the command to find. *“Voran.”*

Hero started off across the village square with his nose close to the ground. Cass followed and Lyle was close behind.

Hero led them down a side street and out into a lane. Cass remained encouraged because he acted as if he had located a scent.

Her hand stayed on the leash as they continued walking at a brisk pace. Well outside the village Hero headed off the road and onto a path.

“It looks like he’s taking us to the ruins,” Lyle said, walking close beside her.

Her leg began to burn as the gradient grew steeper. She would push through it; she had no choice. When she faltered, Lyle supported her with a hand on her forearm. "Let me take the lead. I know this path."

"Okay. I'll let Hero go off leash." She unclipped the dog and he moved ahead of them.

Lyle took her hand and they worked their way up the path. It became more difficult to maneuver the closer to the Heatherglen Keep ruins they climbed.

Occasionally Hero would stop and look back at them. He acted impatient for them to join him. He didn't have the same trouble with the steep terrain. Soon Cass's leg went from aching to really hurting but she wouldn't let on. She was the expert in this work. A little girl's life depended on her.

Now that the sun had gone down it was pitch black. There was no natural light from the moon. Making matters worse was the fact that clouds were rolling in. It would snow tonight.

When—if—they found the girl she could very well be hypothermic. She would need medical attention immediately. Could they find her soon enough?

Cass stumbled and Lyle caught her before she went down.

"Do you need to stop?" His concerned look touched her heart.

She shook her head. "No. We have to find her."

For a second he looked as if he were going to argue. "I don't need two patients."

"I'll keep that in mind." Cass trudged forward.

Lyle pursed his lips and nodded, then joined her.

Not soon enough for Cass they made it to the ruins. In the daylight she had no doubt the area was interesting but in the dark it had an eerie feel to it. Hero sniffed around, making a circle. Finally he stood beside a couple of huge stones and barked.

"Have you found something?" Cass said to the dog as she made her way toward him, with Lyle shining the flashlight that direction. *"Setzen."*

The dog sat.

She and Lyle were looking into a hole.

"This was the dungeon at one time," Lyle murmured.

"Looks about as much fun now. Do you see anything?" Cass searched while being careful not to lean over too far.

Lyle went down on this belly. He directed the light straight down.

"There she is," Cass cried. A small body lay curled on the ground, not moving.

She stepped closer and Lyle said, "Cass, careful! Don't fall in."

"How're we going to get her out?" Cass was already looking for things they could use.

"We'll call for help." Lyle pulled out his phone. "Damn, I don't have a signal. One of us will have to go for help. But right now we're going to have to see to her. Minutes could mean the difference between life and death."

"We're going to have to get down to her somehow." Cass paused, panic filling her. The girl just couldn't die.

"I'll climb down." Lyle was already in the process of removing his bag.

"It looks too slick to do that. You'll have to lower me. I'm the lighter of the two of us. We can use the strap on your bag. It might not be long enough, but it'll get me close enough to drop the rest of the way."

"What about your leg? It might not hold up under

that kind of pressure." Everything in Lyle's voice said that he wasn't going to agree to her plan.

Cass faced him. "That's just a chance I'll have to take. You know the path back better than me. The girl needs help now. I'm not going to argue about it anymore."

The determination in her voice must have got through to Lyle because he started unclipping the strap from his bag. With it removed, he pushed the extender so that the strap was as long as possible. "You ready?"

Cass took an end of the strap, wrapping it around her hand. "I am."

They both moved to the side of the hole. Lyle shined the light into the hole.

"There's still no movement." Cass's chest tightened. They had to get to her soon. Was she gone already?

Lyle dropped the flashlight into the hole giving them some light to work with. He then wrapped the strap around his hand just as Cass had done. She lay on her belly and crawled backward, going feet first into the hole. Lyle went to his knees, holding her under her arms as she slipped over the side.

"Feel for footholds." His voice was tight from the effort of holding her.

She did as Lyle instructed and located one. It was near the foot of her injured leg. She couldn't let the pain that shot through her slow her progress. She had to keep moving. When she was completely over the side she hung onto the strap as Lyle lowered her. She went further into the dark abyss. Thinking she had gone as far as possible, there was a sudden jerk and she was lowered further. Lyle must be on his stomach with his arms extended. She could only imagine the strain holding her was putting on his shoulder muscles. Guessing she was only a few feet from the ground, Cass let go.

She fell, hitting the ground. Pain that made her clench her jaw rocketed through her leg. She rolled onto her hip. “Huh.”

“Cass?” Lyle’s fear-filled voice came from above her.

“I’m fine. Harder landing than I anticipated.” Cass picked up the flashlight and crawled over to the girl. She still hadn’t moved. Worry leaped in Cass. Was she already gone? No, she wouldn’t believe that.

Placing two fingers to the girl’s neck, Cass found a pulse, but it was weak. The child’s skin was icy to the touch. Hypothermia had set in. Pulling off her jacket, she wrapped it around the girl. Cass removed her hat and scarf and put them on the girl as well.

“Cass, move far to one side so I can throw the bag down. I want vitals before I leave.”

“Ready.” A few seconds later Lyle’s bag landed with a flop a couple of feet from her.

“Check her temperature and let me know what it is. Also, can you tell if anything is broken?” Lyle was giving her more orders than she could carry out at once. He was in full doctor mode.

Cass pulled the bag to her. Searching through it, she found the thermometer. Cass positioned the flashlight so that it shone on the girl. Thankfully Lyle had a battery-powered tympanic thermometer that Cass could just push into the girl’s ear. Removing the girl’s clothing would only make things worse. At least she wasn’t wet.

Hero barked.

“Bleib!” Cass yelled and the dog stopped barking. *“Braver hund.”* She called up to Lyle’s shadow as she spread out the thermal blanket. “Temp is ninety degrees Fahrenheit—that’s 32 degrees Celsius. Pulse is weak.

Skin pale and cold to touch. Her breathing is shallow. I'm wrapping her in a blanket now."

"Can you do a BP?" There was an anxiousness to his voice.

"I'd rather not remove the warmth I've already given her."

"Aye. There's no question she has hypothermia."

Cass lay down on the thermal blanket and pulled the girl to her then wrapped the shiny, crinkly material around them. Maybe her body heat would help some.

Lyle's voice rang out again. "There are two heat packs in the bag. Squeeze them and put them under her arms. Don't put them against her skin."

She already knew that from her own training, but Lyle could only be frustrated by not being in the hole and the one taking care of the patient. He was a hands-on type of doctor.

"I'm leaving to call for help. Please don't take any chances. Stay put. I'll be back as soon as I can."

"Hurry."

"I will. Cass? I want your promise you won't do anything foolish." Lyle's worry laced every word.

Cass's heart swelled. He was such a good man. "Hero will be here. We'll be waiting for you."

"I'm counting on that."

Lyle hated to leave Cass but he had no choice. He had to go for help. They needed more than his to-go medical bag to save the girl's life. She needed hospital care. Right away.

Without his flashlight the walk down the rocky narrow path was slow, frustrating and dangerous. The fact that it had started sleeting only added to the difficulty.

Despite that he had to keep moving. Not just for the girl's sake but for Cass's as well.

Lyle stopped often to see if he had a cellphone signal. Everything in him pulled at him to return to Cass. As brave as she was, she still must be frightened in that black hole with a child close to death. Lyle worked his way down the hillside. He had no idea how far he would have to go before he found a signal but it couldn't be soon enough for him.

The weather was taking a turn for the worse. To complicate the conditions, the ground was slick, the path narrow and the rocks numerous. Could the situation get more dangerous?

His heart jumped when the phone connected and started ringing. Finally. The police officer answered. Lyle told him where they were and that they had found the girl. He then gave him instructions to call the hospital in Fort William and have the ambulance sent. Also, to call the clinic for the medical van. They would meet the ambulance. Every second counted. The girl might not make it if she didn't get to the hospital right away.

Lyle wasted no more words and started climbing up the hill once again. More than once he slipped as the sleet grew harder. Before he reached the ruins the sirens of help could be heard, filling the air. On flat land again at the top, he ran to the hole. Hero was still obediently sitting beside it.

"Cass!" There was no answer. "Cass?" Still nothing. Fear washed through him. What had happened to her? Had a rock fallen and hit her? All kinds of horrible scenarios played like a movie through his head. He couldn't lose Cass. He yelled louder. "Cass!"

"I'm here." Her voice wasn't strong, but it was there.

Relief flooded him as if a dam had broken.

She turned on the flashlight and pointed it toward him. "I hope help is on the way. I know now why the dungeon was the least favorite place in a castle."

Lyle chuckled. "Help is on the way. Has there been any movement out of the girl?"

"No. But let me take her temp."

He waited impatiently for her report.

"It's ninety-one Fahrenheit—a little under thirty-three Celsius."

"That's progress." He would take that. "How're you doing?"

"I'd rather be cuddled up next to you."

Lyle's heart melted. He wished that too. He was in love with Cass, he realized. "Honey, I promise you I'll make that happen just as soon as I can."

"Promise?"

"You have my word on it." When he got his arms around Cass again he might never let her go.

The sounds of people hurrying up behind him drew his attention. "Over here." A group of six people headed his way. "They're down here. In this hole."

"They?" one of the rescue men asked.

"Yes. A friend of mine, a woman who works in search and rescue. I lowered her down." Guilt pricked him. He should have gone. "We'll need a rope. I'll go down."

"You're staying put. We'll need your skills up here when we get them up." Les McArthur, the leader of the group and a man Lyle had known all his life, said, and pointed to a spot near the dog. "You stand there out of the way. What's the name of the woman in the hole?"

Lyle didn't like the idea of not being the one in charge but he did as he was told, knowing his friend was right. Still, that didn't calm his nerves. "Cass."

One of the men dropped a bag on the ground and unzipped it. He pulled a rope ladder out. Securing it to a large slab of stone, once part of the keep, he dropped it into the hole.

Les walked to the edge. “Cass, it’s Les McArthur. We’re coming down. Rope ladder first.”

“Okay.”

Lyle watched as Les went over the side. Behind him was a man with a foldup stretcher strapped to his back. Soon a bright light shone from the hole. Apparently Les had a portable light in the pack on his back.

“We’re going to need ropes down here,” someone called from inside the hole.

Another man pulled ropes out of a bag.

Lyle shifted from side to side, not just to keep warm but in his need to do something active. “Can I help?”

“No, this will go a lot faster if you let us do our part. Then you can do yours,” one of the men said. “They’re going to be fine.”

Cass had better be. The girl as well.

The men threw the ropes in. A few minutes later Les called up, “Ready.”

Everything in Lyle wanted to go down into that hole to Cass. Instead he stood watching all that was happening with his hands fisted at his sides and shoulders braced against the sleet-filled wind that was blowing harder by the minute.

Slowly the men started hauling the rope up. Soon the stretcher with the girl on it was being laid on the ground. At her feet was his medical bag. Cass had made sure he would have what he needed. She impressed him more every day.

“Let me check her pulse. I need to tell the hospital what to prepare for.” Lyle went down on his knees beside the stretcher. He wasn't going to stand on the sidelines any longer.

The child was wrapped up in the thermal blanket. On her head was Cass's hat and around her neck was her scarf. Lyle pulled a section of the blanket back. And there was her coat. Cass had nothing to protect her from the elements.

With two fingers, he checked the child's pulse. He found it, but it wasn't easy to locate. The girl needed to leave for the hospital now. As much as he hated it, he had to trust that Les would take care of Cass. His next call after the ambulance would be to Charles and Flora. They'd also see to Cass. But he wouldn't be satisfied until he had her in his arms again.

He quickly stood, putting his bag under his arm. Giving the hole that Cass hadn't emerged from a longing look he said, "Let's get her down the hill. There's no time to waste."

Cass's body shook violently. She was so cold. Where was she? In a damp, dark, freezing hole.

No, that wasn't right. She had been cold, down to her bones. Now she was in a soft place, huddled in warmth. Her eyes flickered open. It was dark outside and a fire burned in the fireplace. She could see the flames reflecting off the wall. That was the only light in the room. Her room at the castle.

She turned her head to find Lyle asleep in a chair too small for him next to her bed. He was close enough to reach out and touch. His hair was tousled, as if he had run his fingers through it more than once. He snored softly. He must be exhausted.

The last thing she had a clear memory of at the ruins was the men securing the girl to the stretcher. She'd been so cold that all she'd been able to think about was sleeping. One of the men had given her a blanket but that hadn't stopped the cold from seeping deeper. She vaguely remembered her teeth chattering as she'd stumbled down the hill with the help of one of the rescuers.

Lyle hadn't been there when she'd come out of the hole. She'd known he wouldn't be. He would be with the girl, as he should have been. Still, that didn't mean she hadn't missed having his arms around her or his heat. It would have been preferable to those of a stranger, no matter how nice they were.

At the bottom of the hill a police car had been waiting. She'd climbed into the rear seat and the officer had turned the heat up high. Despite that, she had been bitterly cold and in a daze when she'd arrived at the castle. Charles and Flora had been waiting for her in the foyer.

"Lyle called us. Gave us strict orders to give you a full examination," Charles had said, pushing a wheelchair over to her.

Cass had been glad to see it, despite saying, "I don't think all that's necessary."

"Lyle does. And based on what he told us, you earned our attention. Thanks for what you did," Flora had added.

"Hero?" Cass had mumbled as Charles had pushed her and Flora had walked beside her.

"Esme is seeing to him. One of the police officers took him to the center. I understand he's going to get an extra helping of food. Esme said she could use a person with your skills at the center."

Cass had gone in and out of awareness while Charles had been examining her. When he'd finished, Flora had taken her turn, flexing and contracting her arm and leg.

"We need to increase your therapy a bit for a few days, but I don't see why you can't be discharged on time."

Cass looked at Lyle. Discharged. At one time, all she'd wanted to do was to get home. That day would be here soon. Flora hadn't given her a specific date yet, but it was coming. Her leg and arm were much better. Despite all her efforts not to become involved, it had happened. It would be hard to leave Lyle. But she must.

She'd arrived with her emotions in a jumble and they weren't in any better shape now. In fact, her feelings for Lyle had only added to the issues. He deserved better than a woman who was so messed up. How did she even know the feelings she had for him were real? Maybe she was just reacting to her need to have someone care about her in a weak moment. That wasn't fair to him.

It didn't matter. After all, they had agreed only to a good time while she was here. Lyle hadn't said anything about wanting more. She'd made it clear she didn't. So what was she worrying about? She would leave as planned. He understood that. She would be home for Christmas.

But what if Lyle asked her to stay? Would she?

She couldn't. Heavens, she didn't know what she wanted. Taking a chance on them being together would be like jumping off a ledge. They didn't really know each other. What if it was just sexual attraction? It was best for Lyle to think of what they'd had as a nice friendship and let him move on.

It would be better for her as well. She'd learned last night that doing search and rescue was too emotionally hard for her. If that little girl had died, she would have as well. So what would she do now to make a living? Where would she end up living? There were too many unknowns.

Cass shifted. That was enough to wake Lyle. “Hey.”

He sat straighter in the chair. Wrinkles filled his forehead as he studied her. “How’re you feeling?”

“Better.” She looked toward the window. “It’s not morning?”

“No, it’s still early. Do you need anything?” He leaned toward her, studying her.

“A hot bath.”

“That I can handle.” Lyle got to his feet.

Cass was confident he could handle almost anything.

“Let’s get you into the bath. While you’re there I’ll go down and brew you some tea.”

She grinned. “There it is again. The cure-all, but it does sound wonderful.”

He started toward the bathroom. “I can tell your smart mouth isn’t frozen any longer.”

She giggled.

“You stay put and I’ll be back for you,” Lyle ordered.

“I can walk.”

“Maybe so, but I’d like to carry you.”

She would enjoy that. Seconds later water began running into the bath. The sounds of Lyle opening and closing cabinet doors soon followed. In a few minutes he returned to her.

“I know you’ve been sitting here thinking how you could walk in there by yourself but it’s not going to happen.” His accent became more pronounced when he was trying to make a point.

“You don’t know me well enough to know what I’m thinking.”

He put his palms on the bed and leaned in close enough that his nose almost touched hers. “Then deny it.”

She met his gaze with a smirk. “I do. I was actually thinking how much I’d enjoy being in your arms.”

Lyle's look turned to one of bewilderment as he continued to stare at her. It quickly changed to one of pleasure that included a smile spreading across his face. "Then we have a plan."

Cass pushed the covers back. Lyle placed an arm around her waist and under her legs then lifted her against his chest. The overlarge T-shirt she wore slipped up, exposing her thigh. Lyle's hand was warm and sure on her skin. She looped her arm around his shoulders and enjoyed the ride.

He sat her on the side of the tub. "Let me check the water temp before you get in."

Cass waited, watching him trail his fingers through the water. She like the tender attention from Lyle. It made her feel cherished. When had another man come close to giving her that feeling before? Never.

Jim had come the nearest, but he hadn't understood her, her job—and especially not her relationship with her dog. His idea of caring had been to tell her she should quit doing something so dangerous. He'd never appreciated what drove her. If it had been him there tonight instead of Lyle, Jim would have never trusted her enough to care for the patient while he was gone. Jim hadn't seen her as a partner, a strong person. Lyle did.

She respected him for that. Felt Lyle returned that respect. He had searched for a missing child without questioning her judgement of using a half-blind dog, then had lowered her into the hole on her directive, and cared for the girl when she'd been pulled out. Now he was looking after her. Was there anything he couldn't do?

"How's the girl doing?"

"She'll recover with a good story to tell. I understand her family went hiking up there last week. She'd lost her doll and was convinced that it was in the ruins. She went looking for it."

"I didn't see a doll." Surely she would have noticed one.

"I didn't either, so I had a new one sent to her." He said it as if it was no big deal.

"Lyle Sinclair, you're a really nice guy." She meant every word. Too nice for her to screw up his life.

"This is ready, if you are." He reached for the hem of her T-shirt and pulled it over her head.

Cass watched him but he didn't let his gaze drop below her face. He was being such a gentleman. Scooping up her feet, he placed them in the water. Cass slipped into the bath with a sigh of contentment. It rose to just below her breasts. She glanced at Lyle. His focus had fallen lower now.

"Hey." She took his hand. His gaze met hers. A flame of awareness burned in his eyes. "It feels really wonderful in here." She closed her eyes and lay back, giving him the full view.

Lyle groaned. "I'm going down for the tea. I'll be back in a few minutes."

Cass smiled, then said in her best seductive voice, "I'd much rather have you warm me up."

"I'm the administrator of this clinic. I can't be climbing into the bath with a patient." He didn't sound convinced.

"Lock the door, put out the *Do Not Disturb* sign. Live a little. Take a walk on the wild side. You know you want to." She tugged on his hand. "Mmm…it sure is nice." Cass opened her eyelids to slits. She could see the small upward curl of Lyle's lips. He was weakening. "At least kiss me."

Lyle leaned over her, his lips finding hers. She

wrapped her arms around his neck and gently pulled him into the tub. Water sloshed everywhere but she didn't care and apparently neither did Lyle. She continued to kiss him as he settled around her and brought her against him, taking the kiss deeper. When they broke apart Cass pulled at his long-sleeved shirt until her hands could wander freely over his back.

"Cass, you'll be my undoing. And the end of my job if I'm not careful." He kissed the sweet spot behind her ear.

She started working on the opening of his pants.

"How am I supposed to get out of your room without being seen in soaking wet clothes?" He sounded more perplexed than angry.

She wanted him that way. Her hand brushed across his hard manhood. "You have other things to worry about right now. I'll show you a secret passage out."

"Secret, uh?"

"First things first." She gave him an open-mouthed kiss while pushing his pants over his hips.

A few days later, Lyle sat on the couch in his cottage with his arm around Cass and her cuddled under his arm and her head on his shoulder. All the lights were off except for those on the tree. It was the prettiest Christmas tree he'd ever seen. Or maybe it was because he was sharing it with Cass. Yet he sensed something was bothering her.

She had walked home with him after work but had been more quiet than usual. Normally she told him about her day or something a dog had done during her therapy. Today had been different. They had prepared dinner of soup and sandwiches, working together like a long-married couple who knew the next move of the other. Still she'd said nothing.

Was it worry over her leaving? He'd certainly spent more time thinking about it than he found comfortable. Flora had said nothing specific about planning to discharge Cass, but he and Cass both knew the time was near. He would find out before they went to bed what was going on in that busy mind of hers.

Lyle smiled to himself. He had really come out of his respectable world with Cass's stunt of pulling him into the bath. She had added excitement to his life.

Cass had helped wring out his clothes with a grin on her face. They'd laid them to dry near the fire and climbed into her bed. Just before dawn he'd pulled the damp clothing on so he could go home and put on some dry ones. He'd shrugged into his coat, grateful it wasn't wet. Cass gave him a goodbye kiss that had been hot enough to make them both steam. He had slipped out of her room and down a back staircase, with the jubilant thought that he wouldn't be seen. The second he had put his hand on the doorknob, Charles had pulled the door open. Lyle could only imagine the dumbfounded look on his face at that moment. Charles often came in early, but Lyle hadn't realized he used the side door.

"Hey. Aren't you going the wrong way?" Charles looked beyond him as if searching for something going on.

"I was sitting up with Cass." And other things. Very nice things.

Charles's forehead wrinkled with concern. "I checked her out last night. She seemed fine. Was something wrong?"

"No, I just wanted to make sure she was okay." Lyle

made to step to past him. All he wanted was to get home and change his clothes.

A look of understanding came to Charles's face along with a grin. He gave Lyle a pointed look. "And is she?'

"She is."

Charles continued to block the opening. "Glad to hear it. Cass is a really special person. I heard what happened and how she jumped in to help."

Lyle couldn't agree more. Cass was very special. "She is special."

"Freya did you wrong. Not every girl will." Charles's words were said softly but matter-of-factly. "Maybe it's time to give someone else a chance."

Lyle had been thinking the same thing. "You're one to be talking."

"Just because I'm a bachelor it doesn't mean you should be one. Just think about it." Charles slapped Lyle on the shoulder as he went by. "Are you wet?"

Apparently his fingers had touched Lyle's shirt. "I fell in the bath."

He heard the roll of Charles's laughter as he hurried out the door.

Cass shifted beside him now. "What're you thinking about?"

He gave her shoulders a squeeze. "I was just thinking about Charles catching me leaving the other morning."

Cass smiled against him. "So he knows about us?"

"Yes. But he would anyway. The Laird knows everything that's going on in his domain."

"Do you mind?" She turned to look up at him.

"Mind? Why would I? You're wonderful, smart, beautiful, fun to be around. Why should I mind? I'm honored."

She shifted to face him and gave him a gentle kiss. "Thank you. That was a nice thing to say."

"I meant every word."

Lyle did. He wanted more moments like this with Cass. If the truth be known, he wanted her forever. Yet he wanted to do it right this time. Make no mistake. For him there could be no long-distance relationship. He didn't want to feel pressured to ask her to stay, because they would soon be separated. But could he let her go without letting her know he cared?

Cass moved away from Lyle, then turned to face him. They had to talk. She'd put it off while they'd walked to his place, through dinner, and now she had to tell him. It shouldn't be this hard—after all they had an agreement. She'd made it clear where she stood. So why was she having such a difficult time bringing up the subject?

"What's wrong, Cass? Tell me."

She clasped her hands in her lap. "I can't hide anything from you. You always read me so well. Flora said this afternoon she plans to discharge me in three days. I can start making travel arrangements. I'll be home for Christmas."

Lyle studied her a moment before he said, "I knew the time was coming. We both did."

"Yes, we did."

He had sounded resigned, while she was a ball of growing sadness. It should be easier than this.

There was a pause as if Lyle was considering what he was going to say. "If I asked you to stay, would you?"

Cass slowly shook her head. "It's a nice thought, but not realistic."

"What about it isn't realistic?"

Her chest tightened. "My life is a mess. I don't even know what I want to do for a job now. My emotions are everywhere. I fear I've used you because you were nice to me and I had no one else to turn to. I can't make a life-changing decision like staying here with you based on that. It might not end well and you deserve better."

"We can figure it all out together." His words were said softly, beseechingly.

"Lyle, I've enjoyed every minute. Well, almost every one of them." She made an attempt at humor, but his serious look didn't change. "But I have to figure out my life on my own, otherwise it would never work."

"It seems to me it's been working great up until now." He sounded mystified that she might not think the same.

"I'm just so confused. My feelings are so jumbled up right now. I have a poor history of keeping relationships alive. I'd never want to do to you what Freya did. You're a wonderful man who shouldn't be treated that way. I can't take the chance that you become like the other men in my life, and I disappoint you. I couldn't stand to see that look on your face."

Lyle watched her for a moment. There was grief in his eyes. "Do you really believe all that rubbish? After all we have shared?"

"We're good together in bed, but that was never supposed to last forever. We talked about this when we started out." She waved a hand between them. "We had an agreement. You can't change the rules now."

"The hell I can't. Why can't you call this what it is? A relationship. I care about you. I think you feel the same about me."

"And let's just say that I do, then what? I still live in America. I may return to a job that takes me all over the world. Anytime, day or night. Or what if I decide to do something else and it's still the States? Do you think we have a chance at a long-distance romance? How did that work out for you last time?"

He flinched. "There will be no long-distance relationship between us."

"So you plan to move to America to be with me?"

His face fell. "We can work something out."

She hated what she was doing to him. That she was pushing him away. "What I'm hearing is that you want me to give up everything and come here to you."

"Put that way, it sounds unfair. Still, I think we have something real here. Something that doesn't come along often in a lifetime. Come on, Cass, stop hiding behind your fear. It's easy to keep a wall up, it's harder to let go, start again. Stop being dishonest with yourself."

"Dishonest! Like you are with your father? Have you ever made it clear to him that you don't want to return to the army? Even tried to make it clear he can accept that or not, but it won't change things? That you want him to be happy, but not at the cost of your own happiness?"

Lyle looked at her as if she had slapped him. "It's complicated."

"And my issues aren't? I'm sorry. I shouldn't have said that. You and your father's issues are none of my business. But what I do know is that if you return to active duty for someone other than yourself you will be miserable. Do you really think that's what your father wants for you?"

Lyle stood. "You're right, my issue with my father isn't any of your business. It has nothing to do with us."

"I'm not sure that's true. Here you are, asking me to stay with you, yet you might be going off to who knows where with the army. What am I supposed to do? Sit here waiting for you? I thought that was the kind of relationship you didn't want. It seems to me that we both need to make some major decisions in our lives before we involve someone else in them."

The ferocity seemed to go out of him like air from an air-bag. "All I want to do is make his last days happy ones."

"I know. But is re-enlisting the right way to do that? Or would the truth be better? You deserve to be happy as well. If you make him happy, you won't be. I know for a fact you're valuable to the clinic and this area. That you're happy with the work you do now. You're thinking of making a decision, a life-altering one, based on emotion. That's not a good way to do things. I can't do that. My decisions have to be based on more than hot sex with a handsome doc. I need to think. Need to regroup." She hated to hurt him but one of them had to think rationally. "I think it's best we leave this as a nice interlude."

"Interlude," he growled with eyes blazing—and not in the way she would have liked. "An interlude. I see."

What did he see? Lyle made the word sound nasty, ugly. "That's what we said it would be."

"If that's the way you feel then I wish you the best. Since this *interlude* appears to be over, I should escort you back to the clinic." He walked into the hall and took her coat off the hook.

Cass didn't see Lyle again until three days later when she was getting into the taxi that would take her to Fort William to start her trip home. She'd cried into her pillow each night since their breakup as loneliness consumed her, then worked hard not to show her sorrow during the day. Still, she felt she had done the right thing, for both of them.

She looked longingly at Lyle. Her heart thumped in her chest. If he asked her to stay again, would she? She needn't have worried. He remained near the front door, watching her without a smile or raising a hand in farewell.

Cass closed the car door. As she rode away, she swiped at her cheek. Unable to resist one last look, she turned to see the steps empty. Lyle had gone back inside.

If the last three days had been awful, leaving Lyle was truly horrible. What would the next week or month, or her life be like when she was thousands of miles away from him? She couldn't count the number of times she'd told herself, "Stay strong."

What she had planned not to do she had done. She'd let herself take the chance of caring again. She had fallen for Lyle.

CHAPTER TEN

LYLE HAD LET Cass's words fester. He was hurt that she could so easily dismiss what he held as precious. He now understood the meaning of "It cuts like a knife." Cass's words that night had done just that. Over time he had examined them. She was right.

He had been unfair. She'd come to Heatherglen hurt and traumatized. Only a few weeks later he was making demands on her. Had he completely forgotten everything but his own needs? Cass *should* be upset with him. They both had issues to deal with before they could commit.

Lyle didn't plan to give up. He'd give her until January then he'd go after her. Surely they could find a compromise between their lives? He loved her, and he believed she loved him. There was no way he'd misread all those touches, looks and how they felt when they came together. He couldn't be that wrong.

The woman he wanted to share his life with would not only love him but support him. Cass had proved to know him better than he knew himself. She understood who he was. More than that, she complemented him. She had strength, confidence, and the largest heart of anyone he knew.

Cass was the one for him. Of that he had no doubt.

He needed to be worthy of her. Part of being that was breaking away from his father's expectations. He had only considered his father's wishes when he'd first joined the army. No matter how sick his father was now, it was time for Lyle to concentrate on his own desires. He'd lived under his father's demands for too long. Through the clinic Lyle was providing quality and necessary care for people who needed it. He was proud of that service. It didn't matter if his father felt the same way or not.

It was past time to have a frank discussion with his father. Really talk. Not dance around the issue but make it clear the direction he intended his life to go. It was with that intention Lyle drove to his parents' house that evening.

His mother opened the door. She looked surprised and pleased to see him. She glanced around him. "Is Cass with you?"

Lyle's chest tightened at the reality that she was actually thousands of miles away. He reminded himself that he would soon be going after her. "No, she was discharged and has gone home. She asked me to say goodbye to you." Cass had. Just before she'd told him the same at the castle door and had gone inside.

His mother placed a comforting hand on his arm. "I'm sorry. I could tell you really liked her."

Lyle did. More than that, he loved her. "I hope she'll come back."

"If she is as smart as I think she is, she will." His mother gave him a quick hug.

Lyle gave her a wry smile. "Is Dad home? I wanted to talk to him for a few minutes."

"He's inside, watching TV."

Lyle took a step and stopped. "How's he feeling today?"

Her look turned to one of slight concern. "He's having a good day."

"I'm glad." Lyle started toward the living room again.

"Would you like to stay for dinner?" his mother asked.

"I'll let you know in a few minutes after I've spoken to Dad." Lyle didn't look at his mother. He was sure her mouth was drawn with concern.

Lyle walked into the living room with his shoulders squared in determination. His father was watching TV. "Hi, Dad."

"Hello. This is an unexpected visit."

Lyle took a seat on the sofa instead of the closer chair so that the two of them faced each other. "Dad, I need to discuss something with you."

He turned off the TV. "Are you here to tell me you've signed up for active duty?" His delight showed clearly on his face.

"About that. Dad, I'm not going to go on active duty by choice ever again."

That joy on his father's face quickly turned to disappointment.

"I have a good job here. I'm needed and I believe I'm respected. Army life isn't for me. It never really was. I did it for you. That's not how I want to live my life. I need to do what I love and that's medicine here, at the clinic. I'm sorry if I'm disappointing you. I've known this for a long time and I've only led you to believe that I might one day go on active duty again to make you happy, and for that I apologize."

His father's look had darkened as Lyle spoke. He leaned forward and put his elbows on his knees and clasped his hands together. His expression didn't waver.

Lyle knew that one well from his childhood days when he was in trouble. "I can't say that I am pleased with your decision. It's in our family's blood to be career soldiers. I brought you up to think that way as well."

"You did. But I love private medicine more. I want to serve in another way."

His father settled back, looking both old and tired. "I see that now. I guess I didn't want to before. I grew up with my father stressing that our family fought for people by serving in the armed forces. I was given no choice, my father wasn't given one either. But we were both happy with our lots in life. It was our duty to protect. It was all I knew. All I knew to hand down to you. I never thought you would want to go another way, Lyle. I have to admit your young lady's impassioned speech did make me think, though."

Cass had done that. Lyle's ego still got a boost whenever he thought of her words.

"I heard the talk around the village about that girl going missing and what you and Cass did to save her," his father continued. "Since then others have stopped me and told me how much they appreciate you being here and the importance of the clinic. I'm proud when I hear it. I'm sorry that you're not going to return to the army but I do love you, son."

Lyle went across to his father and gave him a hug. Afterwards he called, "Mum, I'll be staying for dinner."

Cass had never known misery like the kind she'd endured on the way to the airport. Everything in her screamed to return to Lyle. But he hadn't even waved goodbye. Had she hurt him that much? She felt sick inside.

The tears had flowed the entire trip to Fort William

and then on to Aberdeen. More than once the taxi driver had looked in his rearview mirror with apprehension, but he'd said nothing.

She'd done everything she'd told herself not to. She'd let herself care. About him. The people at Heatherglen. Even Andy and that funny-looking dog, Dougal. Hero. Her emotions had been in a muddle when she had arrived at the clinic, and they weren't any better now that she'd left.

She'd known fear from when she'd almost lost her brother. She'd experienced deep loss from losing Rufus. And now Lyle was gone. This time was harder. She couldn't even breathe, the pain was so strong. Worse, she had chosen this. She wrung her hands.

She couldn't turn back. All she'd said to Lyle was true. She needed to have her act together before she made an emotional commitment to anyone, especially to him. Her parents were expecting her. It was Christmas, and they were worried about her. She had to see them first.

What her future would look like still needed to be decided. Search and rescue was no longer for her. So what would she do now? There was also her house to think about. When she had her life in order, she'd see if Lyle still felt the same. He deserved someone who knew what she wanted and had her head on straight. Only then would she return to Lyle and discuss any future they might have.

The flight home wasn't much better emotionally than her ride to the airport. She'd only found relief in the few hours she had slept. Her parents were there to meet her. They quickly enveloped her in tight hugs. She needed those more than anything at the moment. They insisted that she go to their house for dinner and stay the night.

Cass didn't resist. Right now she wanted their circle of security. With them she could just be, not think. She needed time to regroup.

Her parents' home was decorated for Christmas. Cass should have expected that. The minute she looked at their tree, her eyes filled with tears. It was all light, tinsel and glitter. It made her appreciate the simple, natural tree that stood in Lyle's living room. More than that, she wanted Lyle.

Her brother and his family came for supper the next day. With two young children, the meal was lively. Cass was glad to see them but she was so exhausted, both mentally and physically, that she excused herself early. Despite all the tears she'd shed during the day, she still wanted a good cry. She hurried to her childhood bedroom and closed the door. Minutes later she was in the shower, letting those banked tears flow.

By the time there was a knock on the door she was in bed. "It's Mom. Can I come in?"

"Yes."

Her mother entered, carrying a mug. "I brought you some tea. I thought it was too late for coffee."

That was enough to have Cass's eyes swimming once more. She'd never cried this much in her entire life. Never been this distraught. The idea she might never have a chance to share time with Lyle again had her emotionally splintered. She had to get control of herself. Showing her emotions like this wasn't her. But, then, much about her over the last few weeks was different. Like pulling Lyle into the tub. That had been so much fun, for a number of reasons.

Her mother set the tea on the bedside table then perched on the edge of Cass's bed. "I had no idea you hated tea so much, or is something else going on? What're you not telling us? Are you still in pain?"

Cass hated the fear she heard in her mother's voice. "I told you everything about my injury. I promise I'm much better. It's my heart that's broken. And I think I'm the one who broke it." She poured out her sorrow and what had happened while she'd been at Heatherglen.

Her mother held her while she cried. When she settled down her mother said, "So what're your plans now, honey?"

"I don't know. Tomorrow morning I'm going to call about my job. I'm going to resign from it. That work isn't for me anymore."

Her mother patted her leg. "Your dad will be pleased to hear that. We've worried about you being in all those far-flung places by yourself for too long."

Cass hadn't been by herself. Rufus had been with her. Now she had no one. "I've been thinking that I might enjoy training rescue dogs instead."

"That sounds like something you'd be good at. And what about that amazing doctor of yours?"

Hers? She hoped despite how she had left things between her and Lyle that he would at least speak to her when she saw him again. "Mom, he asked me to stay. I was afraid to make such a big decision when I was so messed up over being hurt, Rufus dying and not being closer to home. I didn't know what I wanted my future to look like then. I hurt him badly. I'm not sure he'll ever want me again."

"So, do you know how you feel now?" Her mother held her hand.

"I knew the minute I left the clinic. I wouldn't let myself turn around, though. I needed to come home.

To see you and Daddy." Cass looked directly at her mother. "I love him."

"Then I suggest you go back and tell him."

Cass murmured, "I don't know if he wants me anymore. He didn't even say goodbye."

"Honey, if all you've told me is true, I wouldn't worry about that. He wants you. I'd suggest you take care of business here as soon as possible then go tell him how you feel and see what happens."

"I don't know..."

She mother stood. "Our family knows better than most how easily something can be almost taken away. Grab every chance at happiness and have no regrets."

The one thing Cass had been with Lyle was happy—and at Heatherglen, too. "What about Christmas?"

Her mother shrugged. "We'll celebrate it early. Or late." Then she grinned. "Or come to Scotland."

"Oh, Mom." Cass wrapped her arms around her mother. "I love you."

Over the next few days Cass resigned from her job, packed her bags and closed up her house. She was on her way to find that happiness she wanted. And that started with Lyle.

Christmas had never really mattered to Lyle. Cass had managed to make it exciting for a while, but that had gone with her. He'd spent the last week going through the motions. To say he wasn't in a festive mood would be an understatement.

He was actually heading into the worst Christmas of his life. It was going to top the year Freya had left him, and the one when his father wouldn't speak to him because he'd said he was going inactive so he could take the job helping Charles get the clinic started.

Losing Cass was like losing an arm or a leg. He had to relearn how to function without her. Every day he forced himself to do what was necessary. People were starting to notice. The few times he had seen his parents his mother had watched him with worry and hugged him a little tighter than normal. Even Charles had made a smart remark about Lyle not looking as cheerful dry as he had wet. Lyle had snarled and stalked way.

No, Christmas couldn't go by fast enough for him. He was living for the new year. Surely he and Cass could sort something out? Find a way they could be together? If he had to leave Heatherglen and follow her all over the world, then so be it.

Now he was doing his duty as the doctor on call at the Christmas-tree lighting in the village square. He remained on the outside of the crowd around the huge tree. It was dark except for the interior lights of the businesses that surrounded the square.

As soon as he was no longer needed he would slip away to his cottage, even though he found no solace there. His home held too many memories of Cass. Their tree still stood in the living room. More than once he'd thought of taking it down but he couldn't bring himself to do it despite the fact it was a daily reminder of Cass.

Lyle stuffed his hands in his coat pockets and focused on Charles giving his Laird of Heatherglen annual Christmas speech. It was the only time Lyle smiled because he was well aware of how much Charles disliked being in the spotlight.

A movement in front of him and to the right caught Lyle's attention. *Cass?* He shook his head. For him she was like the ghost of Heatherglen. More than once he had walked around a corner and thought he'd glimpsed her. Or walked by the lounge and heard her voice. Each time he'd had to calm his rapid heartbeat as disappointment had set in. He had to remind himself she was in America.

He had laid out a plan, one he would adhere to. She would have the space and time she needed to think, and process what she wanted. Lyle was determined to give her that, even if it killed him. In January he would go after her. From there they would figure out what their future together would look like.

The person continued toward him. Lyle narrowed his eyes in the hope of seeing better. Despite his efforts not to let his heart race or hold his breath in anticipation, it didn't work. Still, in the dim light he couldn't make out any facial features.

It was a woman. She came nearer. Her walk was so much like Cass's. She held herself just as Cass did. Was his mind playing tricks on him?

Finally, she stepped close enough that he could see a scarf around her neck and a hat on her head like the one Cass had bought from his mother. Lyle remained still, sure she was a figment of his imagination.

It wasn't until she said, "Hello, Lyle," that he let himself believe and breathe. His heart raced as if he were running. It was Cass! She'd come back. Was really here. Unable to move, he stood there in disbelief.

She closed the distance between them. "Lyle?"

He put one foot in front of the other and grabbed her, pulling her against his chest. Lifting her off the ground, he was rewarded with a sigh from her as her arms tightly circled his neck. Sometime later, Lyle let her slide down his body and he stepped back. The last thing he want to do was scare her off. "Cass, is it really you?"

"Yes."

"Are you okay? Is your leg okay?" He gave her a searching look.

"I'm fine." There was a smile in her voice. "I just forgot something."

"Forgot something?" Now he sounded like an idiot. His hands shook in his eagerness to touch her. He shoved them in his pockets.

"Yes. You."

"Me?"

She watched him closely with a look of uncertainty. "Yeah, you. I was wondering if we could have that conversation about compromise you suggested."

"I'd like that. A *lot*." He pulled her to him again and kissed her with all the pent-up emotion he'd had to hold in check. It was a long and deep kiss.

The roar of the crowd broke them apart. They gave each other a startled look, then grinned. The cheer had been for the Christmas tree being lit.

Lyle looked at her beautiful, much-loved face. "I'm finished here. Where're you staying?"

"I was going to stay somewhere in the village, unless I had a better offer." Cass grinned.

"You have one now. Where are your bags?" Lyle looked around.

"At the airport, I hope. Long story that I don't want to talk about now."

Smiling, he took her hand and hurried her to where his car was parked. They needed to get away before people started talking to them. He held Cass's hand as much as the drive to his cottage would allow, afraid if he lost contact she would disappear.

As he helped her out of the car, he pulled her to him again, inhaling deeply and filling his head with her scent. "You have no idea how I've missed you."

* * *

A flutter like birds taking off filled Cass's middle. She looked at Lyle's handsome face. The one she had missed so much. "I'm glad."

"Glad?" Lyle sounded incredulous.

"Yes, I was afraid you wouldn't talk to me." She watched him for a reaction.

"Are you kidding? I'm in love with you, Cass. Nothing will ever change that."

"In love with me?" So this was what it felt like to have everything she'd ever dreamed of.

"What did you think I meant when I asked you to stay here with me?"

She lifted a shoulder in a shrug and let it fall. "I don't know. I had so much stuff going on in my head I wasn't sure what you meant."

His hands went to her shoulders. "Cass, I wouldn't have asked you to stay with me unless I meant forever."

"I should've known that. I should've heard you out. I was scared. Of myself and what you wanted."

"Come inside. We'll discuss this out of the cold. I want you to be warm and comfortable when I explain how much I love and want you." He gave her a quick kiss before he took her hand then pushed the car door closed.

Inside his cottage, Lyle helped her hang up her outer clothing. She took off her shoes, walked to the doorway of the living room and stopped. Their tree was still there.

"Is something wrong?" Lyle said from behind her.

She turned and smiled. "No, everything is perfect. I missed you and your cottage."

"I hope it was me more." There was still an unsure look in his eyes.

Cass went up on her toes and kissed him. "It was you. Almost all you."

When they separated, he called over his shoulder as he walked to the kitchen, "I'll make us some tea. We need to talk."

She liked the sound of that. They did. She needed to apologize and tell him how she felt. It was time to stop worrying about woulda, coulda, shoulda and try living. When she was around Lyle she wanted to live. She was happy. Blissfully so.

A few minutes later he offered her a mug of tea. Instead of sitting beside her, Lyle chose the chair. Cass couldn't help but pout. Maybe he was still mad at her.

"I'm sitting over here because I can't trust myself when I sit next to you. We need to talk."

Cass's heart jumped. "I know what you mean."

That brought a smile to his lips before he said, "I know I wasn't fair to you. I was so self-absorbed that I wasn't thinking about what was best for you. You were here to recover from a horrible experience, and I should've given you more room, not asked you for more than you could give. Before you left you said some things I needed to hear. I have to admit it made me angry but that didn't mean that I didn't need to hear them. Or that I didn't love you. I talked to my father. Told him in clear and concise language that I wouldn't be returning to active duty."

Cass hissed in a breath. "How did that go?"

"He didn't like it, but he accepted it. Even told me that he's proud of the work I'm doing at the clinic."

That had to have been a tough conversation for both men. She had to admire Lyle for doing it.

Lyle continued, "At least it's a positive start. I don't

think he'll ever get over it but, then, I can't live my life for him. I've got to live it for me."

"You're right. That's a hard lesson I've had to learn over the last few days as well. I knew the moment I looked out the rear window of the car for you as I was going down the drive that I was leaving behind the best thing in my life. That you held the key to my happiness. I was afraid that if I took what you offered, somewhere down the road it might be taken from me. I couldn't stand the thought of that happening. What I soon learned was that trying to live without you was far worse. I love you, Lyle."

That was all it took for Lyle to come to her. He wrapped his arms around her and gave her the sweetest kiss that held a promise that he loved her too.

After they broke apart, Lyle said, "If you don't want to live here, we can live in America, or anywhere else for that matter, as long as we are together. I can practice medicine anywhere."

"Oh, no, I would never take you away from Heatherglen. Cluchlochry. You belong here. Are needed here. I've been thinking about something Flora said. She mentioned Esme could use me at the canine therapy center. I think I would like to train dogs."

"That sounds like a wonderful idea." Lyle hugged her.

"You think you could stand to have me around all the time?" She studied his face.

He chuckled. "I can't think of anything better."

"I love you, Lyle."

"I love you, Cass."

Sometime later they were lying in Lyle's large bed in each other's arms. Cass had found the place where she belonged, where she was completely happy. "You know, there's something to the Christmas pudding thing."

"How's that?" Lyle's hand caressed her bare back over her shoulders.

"I asked to be happy." She cupped his cheek. "And I am. Blissfully so."

He gave her a quick kiss. "And I wished for you to stay longer."

"Why?"

"Because I need a date for the Christmas ball!"

* * * * *

A LITTLE CHRISTMAS MAGIC

ALISON ROBERTS

For Becky – who will always be with me for Christmas, no matter where she is.

With all my love.

CHAPTER ONE

WHAT EMMA SINCLAIR needed right now was a magic wand.

One that she could wave over the calendar on her wall and simply make the month of December vanish.

Turn it into January and the start of a new year. A new life.

Or not.

Maybe she could use the wand not to wish time away but to freeze it. To make it always early December, with her feeling so well she could imagine the last few years had been nothing more than a very bad dream.

It was getting a little stuffy in her tiny London apartment. Emma moved to crack open the window to let some fresh air in for a moment. Very fresh air. The sky was a dark slate and that cloud cover clearly swollen with moisture but it wasn't likely to start falling as pretty snowflakes. A bit of stinging sleet, maybe. Or freezing fog.

London could be so grey at this time of year.

So bleak. It was only mid-afternoon but already there were lights on everywhere. In the street below and in the windows of the apartment buildings she looked out onto. Not just ordinary lights either. Some people already had their Christmas trees up and the row of shops at street level had them in their front windows with multi-coloured lights flashing and twinkling. Somebody was dressed as Father Christmas on the street, too, handing out flyers to passers-by, probably offering a discount on some seasonal service or product.

There were lots of people hurrying about their business, wrapped up in coats and scarfs. Umbrellas were opening as the clouds decided to let go of some of the moisture. Mothers made sure their prams were well covered and tried to juggle parcels and small children to keep them sheltered.

So many people.

Families.

Funny how a crowd could make you feel so much more alone.

The phone ringing was a welcome distraction.

'Sharon... What's the weather like in sunny California?'

'Gorgeous. Doesn't feel right when it's December. And how did that happen? It feels like yesterday that I was having my summer wedding in good ol' Blighty. Is it all grey and freezing?'

'Sure is.' She would need to remember to close the window as soon as she'd finished talking to her closest friend. She stepped closer to the friendly glow of her small, gas fire.

'What are you doing?'

'Right at this minute? I'm looking at one of your wedding photos on my mantelpiece. You were the world's most beautiful bride. You look *so* happy.'

'Aww...I had the best bridesmaid. That helped.'

Emma laughed. 'You were marrying the love of your life—that's what helped. How's Andy?'

'Gorgeous. We were talking about you last night and

he told me to ring. We want you to come and have Christmas with us.'

'Ohhh...' The sound was a mix of frustration and regret. 'I can't. I have to be here for when they call me in. The three-month mark will be late December and they'll have to squeeze me in when they get a space. Jack told me I'd better not go too far away.'

'I feel awful I can't be with you for that. It's such a horrible procedure to have to go through on your own.'

'I'll cope.'

'I want to be with you. To drive you home afterwards and make sure you take your painkillers.'

'I know. It'll be okay, Sharn.'

'You could put it off until the new year...I'm sure that adorable Dr Jack of yours would be happy to oblige.'

Emma had closed her eyes as she took a deep breath. 'The waiting's hard enough without making it longer. I... don't think I could handle that.'

'I understand... It's rotten timing but the sooner it happens, the better. You'll let me know, won't you? The instant you have news?'

'Of course. You'll be the first to know.'

'It'll be good news. I'm totally sure of that.'

'No. It won't be good.' Emma had to swallow hard now. 'It'll either be the best news ever or the worst. No middle ground this time. If it hasn't worked it's the end of the road. Nothing more they can do. Just a matter of time...'

Her words went all wobbly and Emma kicked herself mentally for giving in to voicing her deepest fear. Maybe the uncharacteristic weakness had sneaked up on her because her gaze was resting on other photographs on her mantelpiece. The father she'd lost long ago. Her beloved mother who'd died just over a year ago now.

'You need distraction,' Sharon told her. 'Being cooped up all by yourself isn't helping.'

'You're right. I'm thinking of getting a job.'

'Really? Are you feeling that good?'

'I am. And there are plenty of temporary jobs that come up at this time of year. Do you remember the year that I was an elf?'

'One of Santa's helpers.' Sharon was laughing. 'I'm sure I've got a photo of you in that outfit somewhere. I'd better not show it to Andy or he might think he married the wrong girl.'

'Yeah, right…' But Emma was grinning. 'Or I could busk…' She shifted her gaze to a far corner of the room. 'My poor guitar's just gathering dust at the moment.'

'Sounds cold. Being an elf would be more fun.'

'Yeah…' It was getting cold in the apartment now. Definitely time to close the window. To get moving properly, even. 'You know what? I'm going to go down to the corner shop and get some papers. See what's being advertised under the situations vacant.'

'Go, you! Keep me posted.'

'I will.'

'Love you. Miss you heaps.'

'Same.'

When the call ended, all Emma could hear was the soft hiss of her fire and the patter of rain on the window. After the joy of conversation it was an unpleasant quietness.

A very lonely one.

Threatening. If she stayed in here it would pull her back into her pity party so allowing it to continue wasn't an option. Latching the window, Emma shrugged into her warmest coat and wrapped a scarf around her neck. She slung her bag over her shoulder and picked up her umbrella as she let herself out the door. She wouldn't get the papers at the corner store. She'd walk all the way to the high street and get the bonus of a decent bit of exercise on her mission.

'Ouch… That *hurts*, Daddy.'

'Sorry, pet.'

Adam McAllister suppressed a growl of frustration. Fine blonde hair was refusing to co-operate. How could his fingers be so deft when it came to removing a foreign object or stitching up a wound so that it barely left a scar but be seemingly incapable of braiding a small girl's hair?

'How about a wee ponytail instead?'

'No.' The headshake pulled the almost finished braid from his fingers and what had already been accomplished unravelled at the speed of light. 'Jeannie always has plaits and I want to look the *same*.'

'Dad? Where's my shoe?'

'Where you left it, I expect, Ollie.' Adam picked up the hairbrush again and the movement made him notice the face of his watch. 'It'll have to be a ponytail, Poppy, otherwise you're going to be late for school and I'll be in trouble with Mrs Stewart at the clinic. The waiting room will be full of cross people asking where their doctor's got to.'

Poppy burst into tears.

A crashing sound came from the living room, accompanied by a wail from her twin, Oliver. 'It wasn't my fault. It just falled over and now it's *broken…*'

The wind must have caught the front door to make it slam so loudly. 'I'm sorry I'm so late. The roads are so icy and old Jock was blocking the road with his tractor, helping someone whose wheels were in the ditch. I…' She stopped talking, taking in the scene of chaos in the kitchen.

'I take it she's gone, then?'

'Aye…' Gratefully, Adam pushed the hairbrush into his mother's hand. 'I've almost got the bags ready. I'd better go and see what Ollie's broken.'

'Little minx. I can't believe she's run off like that. With no notice.'

'She's nineteen. In love. Getting pregnant probably made the decision a wee bit urgent.'

'What's pregnant?' Poppy had stopped crying and was standing very still while her grandmother rapidly braided her hair.

'It means that you're going to have a baby.'

'Auntie Marion's going to have a baby.'

'Aye…she is. So's Kylie.'

'But Kylie looks after us. She's coming back, isn't she?'

'No. She's going to Australia—where her boyfriend comes from.'

'What's Australia?'

'It's a country a long way away.' Adam had gone as far as the door to see that the standard lamp had fallen in the living room, sweeping a photograph from the corner of the mantelpiece onto the hearth. Nothing life-threatening. He could sort it out later when he had a minute to spare. Stooping, he picked up an abandoned shoe.

'Ollie? Where are you? It's time for school.'

A small, tousled head with wide eyes appeared slowly from behind the sofa.

'Come and see your gran. You need your hair brushed too.'

'It's even further away than Canada.' By some miracle, his mother had found ribbons to tie on the ends of Poppy's plaits. 'Where Aunty Marion lives.'

She looked up as Adam came back with Oliver in tow

but then her gaze shifted to take in the pile of books and papers on one end of the kitchen table. A milky spoon from a bowl of cereal was sitting on top of a school book. Turning her head to look at the dishes piled up on the kitchen bench, she clicked her tongue.

'I can't do it,' Catherine McAllister said. 'I'm no' going to take off for Canada and leave you to cope with this lot alone.'

'You have to. Marion needs you. The bairn's due next week.'

'She'll understand.'

'This is my sister we're talking about.' Adam's smile was wry. 'She'd never talk to me again. She'd say I've had years of your help and she only needs you for a few weeks. It's not her fault my nanny's run off to Australia.'

Catherine raised her gaze to the old clock on the wall. 'You'd better go, son. Or you'll be getting the evil eye from Eileen Stewart. She's bad enough when an emergency comes in and puts out all the waiting times. I'll get these wee lambs off to school.'

'Thanks, Mum.' Adam pushed his arms into the sleeves of a coat that hadn't made it off the back of a kitchen chair last night. 'And you're not to even think of cancelling your trip. I've got ads in papers everywhere for a temporary nanny. I'll find help for while you're away at least, and then we can worry about something more permanent.'

'We'll see about that.' Catherine sounded unconvinced. 'My flight's not till Tuesday. If you haven't found help by then, I'm staying and that's an end to the matter.'

The train from London to Edinburgh arrived on time. The connecting train Emma needed to get out into the middle of a Scottish nowhere was clearly less reliable.

The wicked draught coming into the waiting room was chilling her to the bone and Emma huddled between the backpack full of clothes and her guitar case.

How crazy was this?

But that Dr McAllister had sounded so enthusiastic on the phone yesterday. Said he'd pay for her travel if she could come up for an interview and he was sure she'd be suitable so she might as well bring what she needed for the next few weeks and that way, if she was happy to take the position, she wouldn't need to go all the way back to London again.

And it all sounded so perfect. She already had the image of a pretty, old Scottish village with the stone buildings softened by a layer of fluffy snow and the sound of Christmas carols being sung by rosy-cheeked village children. What better place to spend these few weeks of the unbearable waiting? It wasn't as if she would have the responsibility of caring for a tiny baby or something. Looking after six-year-old twins—how hard could *that* be?

A piercing whistle and then a squeal of brakes announced the arrival of her new train. Emma picked up the straps of her backpack with one hand and the handle of the guitar case with the other. Then she put it down again to fish in her coat pocket. To make sure she had the appointment details for the meeting later this afternoon.

Yes. Four p.m. at the medical centre in the village of Braeburn. Only a short walk from the station, apparently. Across the square at the end of the high street and down the street. She couldn't miss it but if she got as far as the village hall she needed to turn around. She'd be able to meet not only the nice-sounding doctor but the children *and* their grandmother.

Gathering her courage, Emma got herself and her

belongings stowed into an eerily empty train carriage. Braeburn didn't appear to be a very popular destination. With no one to distract her with conversation, there was plenty of time to think about what lay ahead in her immediate future.

That last addition of the grandmother to the interview panel was the one that made her a little uneasy. Her imagination could conjure up a fierce, elderly Scot with no trouble at all. Short and wiry, with a hairnet keeping the corrugated-iron waves of her hair in place and a disapproving glare that would miss nothing remotely unsuitable about an applicant.

She'd be the one to convince.

Emma rested her head back on the faded seat and watched green hills and paddocks and the occasional river drift past. Beautiful country. A long, long way from London and big hospitals and fear of what the new year might bring.

She couldn't go back.

She *had* to get this job. It would be a reprieve from the fear. Time out. A family to spend Christmas with even, and wouldn't that be magic?

A touch to her hair reassured her that the unruly curls were suitably restrained. How good was it that her hair had grown back so enthusiastically after all the chemo? It would have been better to have had the time to buy some new clothes, though. She didn't have a skirt or dress to her name and, having lost so much weight, she was swimming in her jeans and pullover. Hardly the outfit to make much of an impression with but it was personality that mattered, wasn't it?

And this Dr McAllister sounded perfectly nice, with his deep voice and broad Scottish accent. A bit brusque maybe. Possibly a little terse after she'd replayed the conversation in her head a few times but he'd definitely sounded keen.

Almost…desperate?

Maybe the children were little monsters that ate nannies for breakfast and the granny would be glaring at her from a corner and constantly criticising her every move. And the doctor would take one look at her and ask what on earth she was thinking—that she could look after his precious children when it was obvious how sick she was herself?

No. Emma slammed a mental door shut on her unfortunately vivid imagination.

Fate was bringing her here. It had been the first advertisement she'd seen and, when she'd rung, the phone had been answered virtually on the first ring. She hadn't even had to queue for a train ticket. It felt like it was meant to happen.

She needed a bit of faith, that was all. Hardly surprising that that particular mental resource was somewhat depleted at the moment but it felt good to scrape a bit up and hang onto it.

Very good indeed.

It felt remarkably like hope.

The village was every bit as pretty as she had imagined with stone buildings and cobbled streets. Not that Emma had time to admire more than a passing impression because the train had been a bit late and now she had to hurry. That it was much darker for the time of day and probably a lot colder than London didn't seem to matter when the brightly lit shop windows revealed colourful decorations already in place.

She found herself smiling when she hurried past a pub called simply The Inn, which had sprigs of holly on the door framing a handwritten sign that said, 'There's plenty of room.' Maybe the innkeeper with the sense of humour was one of the group of people under the streetlamps, installing a massive Christmas tree in the village square that needed men with ropes and a lot of shouting in a brogue so thick it sounded like a foreign language.

Her heart sank, however, when she entered the medical centre and the grandmother of her imagination fixed her with a look that could probably strip paint.

'D'ye have an appointment? The doctor's no' got time for extras unless it's an emergency. Clinic hours are over.'

The bell on the door behind Emma clanged again before the grandmother had finished speaking and her attempt to decipher more than half the words she had just heard was interrupted by a woman's voice.

'I'll take care o' this, Eileen. We're expecting Emma.'

Her jaw dropping, Emma turned to face an elegantly dressed and very beautiful older woman, who was smiling warmly. 'I take it you *are* Emma?'

'Um…yes. And you're…?'

'Catherine McAllister. Adam's mother.' She looked past Emma's shoulder. 'Is Adam in, Eileen?'

'Aye. The wee bairns as well.' The sniff was disapproving. 'I've told the doctor it's no' a good idea, having bairns in there. They'll break something. Or—'

'Why don't you head off early, Eileen?' Catherine was still smiling. 'I know how busy you must be at the moment. Isn't there a choir practice this evening?'

'Aye…well, if you're sure, Mrs McAllister.'

'I'm just sorry I won't be here to hear all the Christmas carols.'

'It's tomorrow you leave, aye?'

'Mmm. I hope so.' She turned back to Emma. 'Adam's sister is having her first baby. In Canada.'

'Oh...how exciting.' Emma couldn't miss the play of emotion on the older woman's face. 'She'll be so happy to have you there. I...I lost my mum last year and I miss her all the time but *that's* when I'll miss her the most, I think.'

When she had a baby? *If* she ever had a baby would be more truthful. But she'd said too much already, hadn't she? Maybe revealed too much as well, judging by the searching look she was getting. Emma bit her lip but Catherine was smiling. Her eyes were full of sympathy and the touch on Emma's arm was more like a reassuring squeeze.

'Come with me, Emma. We'll go and find that son of mine.'

Could she leave her backpack and guitar in the waiting room? About to step away, Emma caught another glare from Eileen that was punctuated by another eloquent sniff. Hastily, she picked up her luggage and followed Catherine across the waiting room and through another door. She was still trying to readjust her mental image of the children's grandmother and, because she wasn't watching, the guitar was at enough of a sideways angle to catch on the door in front of her so she almost fell into what was obviously a consulting room.

The man, who had one hip perched on the edge of a large wooden desk, jerked his head in her direction. The two children, who were on the floor in the middle of a game that involved a stethoscope and bandages, looked up and froze.

There was an awkward silence and Emma could feel herself blushing furiously as she manoeuvred herself into the room. What had possessed her to bring such an unwieldy extra piece of luggage, anyway? Did she think she might go busking in Braeburn's village square if she didn't land this gig of being a nanny?

What made it so much worse was that the doctor who'd sounded nice but brusque on the phone was just as different from what she'd imagined as the grandmother had been. The fuzzy image of a plump and fatherly country GP had just been bombed. Adam McAllister was tall and fit. More than fit. With his jet-black hair, olive skin and sharply defined angles of his face, he was probably one of the best-looking men Emma had ever seen.

Except that he was scowling. While his mother had surprised her by being so unexpectedly nice, the pendulum had swung in the opposite direction now. Adam McAllister looked uncompromising. Fierce. Angry even?

At *her*?

'I'm sorry I'm late,' she said, the words rushing out. 'The train was…it was…' Oh, help. He was looking at her as if he *knew*. Had he somehow managed to access her medical records or something?

'The train's always late.' Catherine was pulling out a chair. She smiled down at the children. 'What's happened here? Has Poppy broken her leg *again*, Ollie?'

'Aye. I'm fixing her.' But the small boy's attention was diverted now. 'Who are *you*?' he asked Emma. 'And what's *that*?'

'I'm Emma. And this is my guitar case.'

'I want to see.'

'Maybe later.' Adam McAllister's offer did not sound promising. 'Your gran's going to take you to see the tree going up in a minute. And then you're going home for your supper.'

'After some proper introductions,' Catherine said firmly. 'Emma—this is Oliver and this is Poppy. Ollie and Poppy—this is Emma…Sinclair?'

'*Miss* Sinclair,' Adam corrected.

'Emma's fine,' said Emma. 'Hello, Poppy and Ollie. You're twins, aren't you?'

They stared at her. They had brown eyes like their father but their hair was much lighter. Poppy still had golden streaks in her long braids. She also had something clutched in her hand.

'Is that Barbie?'

Poppy nodded. 'She's got a pony,' she offered. 'At home.'

'Lucky Barbie. I love ponies.'

'I've got a pony, too.'

'Jemima's not a *pony*,' Oliver said. 'She's a *donkey*.'

Emma blinked. Catherine laughed. 'Adam probably didn't say much on the phone,' she said, 'but there are a few pets at home. Do you like animals?'

'Yes. I had a job in a pet shop once. We had lots of puppies and kittens and rabbits. Oh, and hamsters and mice and rats, too.'

Poppy's eyes were round. 'I *love* puppies. And kittens.'

'I love *rats*,' Oliver said. 'Can I have a rat, Daddy?'

'We've probably got some out in the barn.'

'I want one for a pet. Inside.'

'No.' The word was almost a sigh. 'You can't have a rat, Ollie.'

'But why *not*?' With a bandage unfurling in his hand to roll across the floor, Oliver scrambled to his feet. 'You said I could tell you what I wanted most for Christmas. And I want a *rat*.'

'They smell bad.' Emma had been the cause of what was becoming a family disagreement. She needed to do something. 'And they've got long tails that are all bald and pink and…icky.'

'Icky?' Adam was looking at her as if she was suddenly speaking Swahili.

'Icky,' Poppy repeated. She giggled. 'Icky, icky, icky.'

'*You're* icky,' Oliver told her.

'No. *You* are.'

'Time to go,' Catherine decreed. 'You've met Emma and she's met you. Now it's time for her to talk to Daddy.'

In the flurry of putting on coats and hats and gathering schoolbags, Catherine found time to squeeze Emma's hand.

'I do hope you'll still be here when I get back,' she said softly. 'I'd like the chance to get to know you better.'

She managed to say something to Adam as well, just before she ushered the children out of the room. Emma couldn't hear what she said but, as she sank into the chair as the door closed behind Catherine, he was still scowling at her.

Strength. That was what he needed.

This was his one shot at finding the help he needed so that his mother would not cancel her trip to Canada and this young woman was clearly… He closed his eyes for as long as it took to draw in a new breath. A complete flake?

She looked like a refugee from the sixties or something, carrying a guitar and a backpack. So pale he could almost count the freckles scattered over her nose and she was thin enough to have a waif-like air that probably made her look a lot younger than she was. And what was it with those oversized clothes? It reminded him of when Poppy clopped around the house with her feet in a pair of her grandmother's high-heeled shoes and a dress that was trailing around her ankles.

She was so obviously unsuitable that it was deeply disappointing. He'd have to go through the motions of an interview, though—if only to have ammunition for the argument he'd have to have with his mother later. Her whispered impression had been very succinct.

She's lovely. Give her the job, Adam.

How had this musically inclined waif managed to impress Catherine so much in such a short time?

'So…' He did his best to summon a smile. 'You're fond of animals, then?'

'Mmm.' She was smiling back at him. She had blue eyes, he noted. And brown curls that had a reddish glint where the light caught them. 'I am.'

'And children?'

She nodded enthusiastically. 'I like children, too.'

'Do you have any experience with them?'

'I've taught music classes. And…and I had a job working with children over a Christmas period a while back. I loved it.'

Because she'd never quite grown up herself? How many adults would use a word like 'icky' with such relish?

'But you've never been a nanny?'

'No.'

'Do you have any younger brothers or sisters? Friends who have small children?'

'N-no.' The smile was fading now.

'Do you have a full driver's licence?'

'Yes. I've got a motorbike licence, too.'

The image of this child-woman astride a powerful two-wheeled machine was disconcerting.

'I've even got a heavy-vehicle licence. I had a job driving a bus once.'

Maybe that image was even more of a worry. How had she had the strength to even turn such a large wheel? Or was it the overlarge sleeves on her pullover that made her arms look so frail?

'Can you cook?'

'Well…I did have a job in a restaurant once. I—'

But Adam was shaking his head. 'How old are you, Emma?'

'Twenty-eight.'

Really? Only a few years younger than he was? Hard to believe but the surprise wasn't enough to disturb his train of thought. 'Just how many jobs have you had?'

'I don't know,' Emma admitted. 'Quite a lot. I tend to like part-time or temporary work. That's why this job appealed so much. It's only for a few weeks, isn't it?'

'Aye.' But just because he only needed help on a temporary basis it didn't mean that he wanted to employ someone who was incapable of commitment or even reliability, did it?

Perhaps he should have tried to find something permanent instead of a stop-gap, but who went looking to move and start a new position in the weeks right before Christmas? How many people wanted to move to an isolated Scottish village anyway?

His mother was due to drive to Edinburgh tonight, ready for an early departure tomorrow. If he didn't take a chance on Emma, she would cancel her trip and she'd miss the birth of her new grandchild. She'd be miserable and Adam would feel guilty and the children would pick up on the tension and it could quite likely spoil Christmas for all of them. Not that Adam had found much joy in the season in recent years but the children were his priority now, weren't they?

And Emma had made Poppy giggle with that ridiculous word.

That delicious sound of his daughter's merriment echoed somewhere in the back of his head and it was enough to soften the disappointment that Emma was so unsuitable.

'It *is* only for a few weeks,' he heard himself saying aloud. 'But…ach…' The sound encompassed both defeat and frustration. How bad could it be? He really only needed a babysitter for the hours he had to be at work. 'Fine. The job's yours if you want it, Emma.'

'Oh…' Her eyes widened with surprise. 'Yes. Please. But…don't you have other people to interview?'

'You were the last.' She didn't need to know that she had also been the first, did she? 'I'll lock up here and then we'll head off.' He looked at the unusual luggage on the floor beside Emma's chair. 'Is that all you'll need?'

She nodded.

'And you don't mind being here over the Christmas period? You don't have family who will be missing you?'

'No.' She shook her head this time and dipped her chin so that her gaze was hidden, as if she didn't want him to see how she felt about that.

Maybe it stirred too many memories that were too painful—like it did for him? An emotional cocktail of grief and anger that the season of goodwill and family togetherness only served to exacerbate? The thought gave him an odd moment of feeling potentially connected to this pale stranger in her oversized clothes. Or maybe it was the poignant tilt of her head as she looked down.

He shook off the unwelcome sensation. He had more than enough people to worry about, without adding someone else. Emma's job was to make life easier for him for a little while, not to complicate it any further.

'Right, then.' His movements were brisk as he logged out of his computer and flicked off the desk lamp. 'It's getting late. I suppose I'd better take you home.'

CHAPTER TWO

THE DARKNESS OF a winter's night engulfed the vehicle as it left the outskirts of Braeburn village behind.

Emma eyed the dashboard radio controls longingly. Driving anywhere without music was an alien experience for her but Dr McAllister clearly wasn't going to allow distractions while he was driving. Fair enough. It was raining hard now and the lights were catching a mist of white speckles that suggested it was trying to turn into sleet.

Would conversation also be deemed a distraction? She risked a sideways glance and had to tilt her chin upwards. Even sitting down, Adam McAllister was tall. Well over six feet. Walking beside him into the clinic's car park had made Emma feel very small. He hadn't said anything then either, apart from an offer to carry her bag, which had sounded more like a command than an invitation.

Clearly she hadn't really made a good impression on her new employer but at least he was prepared to give her a chance. Any optimism that she could change his mind was fading now, however, as she took in a profile that was stern enough to suggest an inability to suffer fools gladly.

Imagine running the gauntlet of that snappy little terrier of a receptionist in order to see such an unapproachable GP? You'd have to be really sick, Emma decided. And I'll bet his patients never forget to take their pills.

'What?'

The terse query was enough to make Emma jump. Coupled with the effect of Adam taking his eyes off the road to glare at her for a second, it actually made her heart skip a beat, but the fear that she might have spoken aloud was forgotten as fast as it had appeared.

In the dim reflected light of the dashboard controls, Adam's eyes looked black under equally dark brows. His hair was long enough to be a little unruly and a single lock had detached itself from the rest to flop across his forehead. The crazy desire to reach out and put that curl back where it belonged was so inappropriate that Emma caught her breath in an audible gasp.

She must have sounded as if she'd suddenly decided she might be in the company of an axe murderer, given the way those dark brows lifted. With his gaze safely back on the road, Adam sounded vaguely uncomfortable with the effect he'd had.

'I thought I heard you say something,' he muttered. 'About the hills.'

'Oh…' Emma turned to stare ahead through the windscreen but her gaze caught Adam's hand on the steering-wheel as she did so. He had long fingers and neatly cut nails and…dear Lord…a wedding ring? Why hadn't he mentioned his wife? Why hadn't she been at the interview instead of his mother? Confused, Emma struggled to find a response to his comment. 'It *is* hilly, isn't it? Do you live far from the village?'

'Only another mile or so. Don't worry, you'll have a car to use.'

'Wow…that's great.' Personal transport was an unexpected bonus. 'Thank you.'

The soft snort sounded exasperated. 'You'll need it. There's a lot of driving involved in getting the children to where they need to be. Poppy has a Highland dance class once a week and Oliver is starting drumming lessons in addition to his bagpipes class. On top of that, the school does a nativity play and there'll be rehearsals almost every day after school. You'll also be responsible for grocery shopping and other chores, like going to the vet. One of the dogs is having treatment at the moment for a foot injury.'

Emma was trying to listen carefully to her job description but she was still thinking about the mysteriously absent wife. And then it was too easy to get distracted by the cadence of Adam's deep voice and the gorgeous accent. She only realised she was smiling when she caught the movement of his head as it turned in her direction again. Hastily, she rearranged her face.

'I'm so sorry to hear that. I hope it's nothing serious.'

'A torn pad, that's all. But I didn't notice in time and it got infected.'

Although it looked like they were in the middle of nowhere, Adam put the indicator on and slowed the vehicle, turning through a gap in a tall stone wall. The headlights shone on what looked like a scene from a gothic movie, with the bare branches of massive old trees twisting out to meet each other and create a tunnel—the smaller branches like claws reaching out towards Emma. She shivered.

'It'll be warm inside.'

Startled, Emma looked sideways but Adam was concentrating on driving around the biggest lumps the tree roots were making in the driveway. He couldn't possibly have seen her shiver unless he had exceptionally acute peripheral vision. She hadn't forgotten the way he'd looked at her in his clinic either…as if he knew something she'd rather he didn't know.

A prickle of sensation ran down her spine. She really needed to curb her overactive imagination. Any minute now and she'd have Mrs McAllister buried somewhere down that spooky driveway and she'd be going into the rather forbidding-looking two-storeyed stone farmhouse to find it devoid of a friendly grandmother or any children. There would just be a dark hallway and a ticking grandfather clock and Dr McAllister would shut the door behind her and turn the lock and say—

'So…here we are, then.'

She made an odd squeaking sound as Adam took on his role in her wild train of thought with such perfect timing but then the absurdity of it all surfaced and she had to stop herself laughing aloud.

And then—unexpectedly—she got a rush of pure relief. She'd come here in the hope of finding a distraction from the fear of waiting for news that would have her imagining only her own funeral. Well…she'd already succeeded, hadn't she? She hadn't given her upcoming tests a moment's thought since she'd arrived in Braeburn.

She found herself beaming at her new employer. 'I'm excited,' she confessed. 'I do love starting a new job.'

'So it would seem,' Adam said drily. 'Let's go inside, shall we?'

He led Emma in to the vaulted hallway of the house his family had owned for generations, making a mental note not to forget to wind the grandfather clock this week, heading straight for the door from which the most light was spilling, along with the sound of voices and laughter.

The kitchen. The heart of his home.

Halfway there they were mobbed by the dogs, who

gave their master only a perfunctory welcome before investigating the interesting new arrival. Adam paused to watch the effect, knowing that if Emma had been less than honest about liking animals, it would show up in a matter of seconds. And if she didn't like dogs, she probably didn't like children either and he'd know if he'd made a huge mistake in bringing her into his home.

Almost knocked off her feet by fluffy paws being planted on her stomach, Emma gave a startled exclamation but then her voice was stern.

'Paws on the floor, please,' she commanded. 'And then I can pat you.'

Amazingly, the dogs sat promptly, gazing adoringly up at the newcomer. Emma dropped to her haunches, abandoning her guitar case in favour of cuddling the animals. Getting her face washed enthusiastically, she was laughing as she looked up at Adam.

'They're gorgeous. And so...*hairy*.'

'That's Benji. He's a beardie. And Bob's the Border collie.' Part of him wanted to smile back at Emma but another part was fighting a sense of...disappointment? His new employee had passed this test with flying colours, hadn't she?

It looked like he was stuck with her for the foreseeable future.

The children weren't far behind the dogs.

'Emma—Emma! Gran says you're going to be looking after us now.' With practised ease, Poppy squeezed past the dogs to grab Emma's hand. 'Come with me. I want to show you Barbie's pony. And her caravan. And her swimming pool.'

Oliver eyed the guitar case and then his father. 'It's "later" now, isn't it, Dad?'

'Ach...' Catherine came out of the kitchen door, wiping her hands on her apron. 'Let's give Emma a wee bit o' time to get settled, shall we? Come on. All of you. Supper's almost ready.'

Adam left the backpack he'd been carrying beside the clock. Poppy kept hold of Emma's hand to show her where to go, with Benji following as closely as possible. Oliver picked up the guitar case, which was as big as he was, and struggled in their wake. Bob stayed sitting and held up a bandaged paw.

'I know.' Adam stooped to scratch the hopefully pricked ears. 'I need to take care of that paw but it'll have to be later. It's a bit of a circus for now.'

Like his life. A juggling act. One that entailed keeping far too many balls in the air without dropping them. There was no applause for keeping them going either—just the prospect of disaster if they got dropped.

After the spooky driveway and the austere outlines of the huge, old stone farmhouse, walking into the kitchen was so far towards the other end of a welcoming spectrum that it was almost overwhelming.

A crackling open fire at one end of the room made it so warm Emma knew she'd have to take her pullover off very soon. The lights gave the oak cabinetry a golden glow and there was an amazing smell of something hot and meaty that made her mouth water. Good grief…she couldn't remember the last time she'd actually felt *hungry*.

'Look…' Poppy pointed to a fridge that was covered with pieces of paper and photographs held in place by small magnets. 'I drawed that. It's my mummy. She's got wings because she's an angel.'

'Oh?' The statement had been completely matter-of-fact but Emma wasn't sure how to take it. Was Mummy exceptionally kind or was she dead? Catherine was busy putting oven gloves on and didn't seem to have overheard the comment and she didn't like to ask Poppy. No doubt she would find out in good time.

'I drawed this one, too. It's Daddy and Bob and Benji.'

'It's very good. They all look very happy.'

Not that Emma could imagine Adam actually having such a wide grin on his face. Glancing back, she saw him standing in the doorway, all but glowering at the scene in front of him. She also saw Oliver bumping the guitar case on the flagstone floor.

'That's a bit heavy for you.' Easing out of Poppy's firm grip on her hand, Emma went to rescue the guitar. 'I'll put it over here for now, yes?'

'No,' Oliver said. 'I want to see.' With his eyebrows fiercely frowning like that, he looked remarkably similar to his father.

'It's time to eat,' Catherine told him. 'Poor Emma's been travelling all day and she must be famished. And then I'm going to show her to her room and drive all the way to Edinburgh to the airport.'

Poppy's face fell dramatically. 'But I don't want you to go, Granny. You'll miss *Christmas*.'

'No, I won't.' Catherine was opening a door on the stove that was set into an old chimney lined with blue and white tiles. She took out a cast-iron pot that looked as old as the kitchen and carried it to the table. 'They have Christmas in Canada too, you know. I'll be calling you and telling you all about your new wee cousin.'

'We can video chat.' Adam moved to the table and picked up a bread knife. He began slicing the crusty loaf on a thick wooden board. 'You'll be able to see the bairn as well.'

Poppy sniffed loudly. Emma took hold of her hand

again and bent to whisper in her ear. 'Can you show me where to sit? It's such a *big* table.'

'You can sit beside me.'

In a short space of time Emma was installed on one of the old, oak chairs beside Poppy, with Oliver and Catherine on the other side of the table. Adam was at the top. Past him, she could see the dogs stretched out in front of the fire, with her guitar case propped against the wall nearby, looking as out of place as she was.

Except, oddly, she didn't *feel* out of place at all. She looked up at the whitewashed ceiling with its dramatic dark beams, across at the pretty tiles around the stove and the cluster of antique kettles and pots on the floor beside it. The room could have been part of a museum, except that it was so alive with the feeling of family.

It wasn't just the fridge that was covered with works of art and photographs. There was a huge corkboard on the wall and a bookshelf that had framed photographs amongst the books and a shelf clearly devoted to things the children had made, like an odd-looking robot constructed out of cardboard boxes and tubes and a chunky effort in clay that could possibly represent Benji. Or maybe Daddy.

'It's only stew, I'm sorry,' Catherine said, as she ladled an aromatic mix of meat and vegetables onto Emma's plate. 'I forgot that we might be welcoming a visitor today.'

A visitor? The feeling of family was so strong Emma had forgotten that that was what she was. How could anyone not feel completely at home in here? And the food was delicious.

'This is perfect,' Emma assured Catherine. A lot better than anything she'd be able to produce in the kitchen. Oh…help… Had she really made Adam believe she could cook in that interview? Her job in the restaurant had been limited to clearing tables and washing dishes. And had Catherine made that bread herself, too? Possibly even churned the butter, she thought as she accepted the blue and white dish being passed her way by Adam.

She didn't need to cross that bridge quite yet, though. And maybe it was Catherine that Adam had inherited that fey ability to see things from. She was smiling at Emma as they all tucked into their dinners.

'I've left lots of meals in the freezer and there's a modern oven as well as the big stove, if you need it. The children get a hot lunch at school so you'll only have to cope with breakfast for most of the time.'

'Did the turkey for Christmas arrive?' Adam asked.

'Aye. It's in the freezer as well. Don't forget to take it out at least a couple of days early. Leave it in the big tub out in the dairy to thaw.'

'I don't like stew,' Oliver announced a few minutes later. 'It's got carrots in it.'

'Carrots are good for you,' Emma offered. 'They help you see in the dark.'

'I don't need to see in the dark,' Oliver said with exaggerated patience. 'I'm *asleep*.'

'If you don't eat your carrots,' Adam said calmly, 'there'll be no ice cream.'

'I don't like ice cream.'

'I do,' Poppy sighed. 'I *love* ice cream.'

'Me, too,' Emma said. She beamed at Poppy. Impossible not to fall in love with a child who was so prepared to love everything life had to offer. Poppy beamed back. Shifting her gaze back to her plate, Emma caught Adam staring at her but he quickly shifted his attention back to his son.

'No television before bed, then,' he said. 'Vegetables are important.'

Catherine stood up to start clearing plates. 'Can I leave you to do the children's pudding?' she asked Adam. 'I'll need to head away soon and I'd like to give Emma a tour of the house and show her where her room is.'

'But Emma loves ice cream, too.' The horrified look on Poppy's face at the prospect of such an unwarranted punishment for someone stole another piece of Emma's heart. Oliver might prove to be more of a challenge but she knew that she was going to love her time with Poppy.

'I'll come back,' Emma promised. 'Save me some, okay?' She looked at Oliver, who was scowling down at his plate—the only one still on the table. He was pushing slices of carrot around with his fork. 'And by then,' she added casually, 'you'll have scoffed those carrots, Ollie, and I'll be able to show you my guitar.'

A lightning-fast glance back as she left the kitchen revealed a fork laden with carrot slices making its way towards Oliver's mouth and Emma hid a smile. Maybe the little boy wouldn't be too much of a challenge after all.

The tour of the house was a whirlwind and it wasn't just the speed of viewing the more formal rooms, like the lounge and library downstairs or the rapid climb to the upper level that had taken Emma's breath away.

'How old is the house?'

'The main part dates back to the seventeenth century but there's been a lot of additions and renovations, and thank goodness for that. I'd hate to be offering you a room that didn't have an en suite bathroom.' Down the end of a wide hallway that had dozens of framed photographs displayed, Catherine opened one of the dark oak doors. 'And here it is.'

'It's gorgeous.' Emma looked around the space that

would be hers for the next few weeks. The brass bed had a pretty patchwork quilt. The fireplace was tiled in blue and white, which seemed to be a theme throughout the house, and any draught from the windows was kept at bay by the thick velvet curtains that Catherine whisked shut.

'Poppy and Ollie's rooms are next door and they have their own bathroom between them. There's a playroom on this side and down the other hallway there are a couple of guest rooms and Adam's room is at the end. Have a good explore tomorrow, when you've got some daylight.' Catherine glanced at her watch. 'I'm so sorry, but I'm going to have to dash. I need to get home and collect my suitcase.'

'Home? Don't you live here?'

'Not any more. I moved out when Adam and Tania got married. It's been a family tradition for generations that the eldest son raises his family here. I have a cottage in the village.'

So it had been a family home for generations? That would explain the astonishingly homely feel of the house. And the enormous collection of photographs. Emma followed Catherine back into the hallway. She bit her lip but her curiosity refused to subside.

'Would it be awfully rude if I asked about…Tania?'

'Of course not, pet.' Catherine stopped in her tracks, turned her head to scrutinise the gallery of photographs and then pointed. 'That's her. I think that picture was taken on their honeymoon in the Maldives.'

A stunning beach scene. An even more stunning young woman with long, blonde hair and a model's body frolicking in the surf. Laughing. The joy was unmistakeable and Emma could imagine Adam standing there with the camera, capturing such a happy moment with his new wife.

'She's beautiful.'

'Aye…' The word was a sigh. 'Poppy has the look of her, I think. Ollie's more like his dad.'

There were more photographs, of course. Emma spotted a wedding portrait, with Adam gazing adoringly at his bride. A lovely black and white image of Tania and the newborn twins and more with the babies as toddlers.

'The bairns were only three when it happened,' Catherine said softly. 'They barely remember their mother so it's good to have so many pictures for them.'

Emma swallowed hard. 'What did happen?'

'A terrible tragedy. Tania liked to do her Christmas shopping in Edinburgh and she'd stay in a B&B so she could get it all done in a couple of days. There was a fire that year and she was trapped. She didn't get burned but they said she died of smoke inhalation.'

'Right before *Christmas*? That's so sad.'

'Aye.' Catherine caught her gaze for a long moment. There was a hint of warning in her gaze. And a plea. 'You might need to be patient with Adam. It's no' an easy time of year for him.'

'I can imagine.' No wonder he seemed so terse and grumpy, Emma thought. Or that she had yet to see him smile. How hard would it be to have the whole world joyously celebrating family and times of togetherness when it marked the anniversary of losing a beautiful and beloved young wife? The mother of his children?

'But Christmas is for the bairns, isn't it?' Catherine added. 'And they're old enough to see that their Christmas is no' like all the other bairns in the village and that's no' really fair, is it?'

Emma held the older woman's gaze. 'I'll do my best to make it a special Christmas for them,' she promised.

'Aye…' Catherine patted her arm. 'I've a feeling you

might do just that. Thank you.' Her smile was poignant. 'The bairns think their mother is an angel who's still looking after them. Maybe that was why you got sent to us.'

When his mother drove away from the house on the first leg of her journey to Canada, Adam was left standing on the front steps.

Stunned.

What had just happened here?

He'd been dreading this moment for months. Ever since he had learned of his sister's due date and realised that—for the first time since Tania's death—he might have to face this Christmas without the emotional support of the most important woman in his life. And worse, that the twins would be without their beloved grandmother, who was the one who insisted on making the day as special as possible for them.

He'd expected tears. Possibly tantrums, especially from Poppy, who simply adored her gran. Oliver was just as attached, of course, but he didn't wear his heart on his sleeve like Poppy. He was more like himself, in guarding his heart and not letting others see any private misery. His children were his life—both of them—but he did worry more about Ollie. Because he knew just how much misery it was possible to hide?

But the moment had come. They'd all been out there to say goodbye to Catherine. Even the unknown quantity that was the new arrival of the temporary nanny because his mother wouldn't let her hang back from the family farewell. She'd been standing there beside the children—looking remarkably like a wayward, teenage sister—getting one of those warm hugs that Catherine was so good at. And then she'd whispered something in Ollie's ear and his little boy had given a solemn nod and turned to lead the way back inside. Poppy had jumped up and down and tugged on Emma's hand and she was bursting with excitement as she dragged Emma back up the steps.

'We're going to see the *kit-ar*,' she informed Adam as they went past. 'I *love* kit-ars.'

Benji had bounded in their wake, of course. It was Bob who was sitting by Adam's feet and he saw the dog shiver. How long had he been standing here, wondering how on earth something he'd been dreading had turned out to be so easy?

Long enough for his dog to shiver noticeably.

'Come on, then, old boy.'

Back in the warmth of the house, he pushed the heavy door closed and then he heard it.

The sound of music coming from the kitchen.

Expertly plucked guitar strings. A song being sung in a clear, sweet voice that filled the air and made it somehow more of a pleasure to breathe.

A childish song, he realised as he stepped closer to the bright glow of the kitchen door. A nonsense song with tongue-twister words about a copper coffee-pot.

And it wasn't just Emma singing. Poppy was getting the words wrong and giggling but Oliver must have learned the song at school because he was joining in part of the chorus.

Not very loudly but he knew his son's voice.

He stopped again. Puzzled.

What *was* it about this girl?

His mother had seen it instantly. Poppy was prepared to love everybody. But Ollie…?

How on earth had she put her hands on a key to that little heart so quickly?

Adam shook his head and Bob lay down and put his nose on his paws to wait.

He knew when something big was changing. And he knew that it took longer for his master to recognise any joyful possibilities that something new could offer. His job was simply to keep him company while he had a little think about it all.

CHAPTER THREE

'So Mrs McAllister's likin' Canada, then?'

'Aye.' Adam glanced over his shoulder, reaching for the file on the end of Eileen's desk, as his next patient joined him for the short walk to his consulting room. The waiting area was still full, and while the women amongst the group seemed busy with their knitting or magazines, he knew perfectly well that they'd all been discussing his business while he'd been taking Shona Legg's blood tests.

Or, to be more accurate, they'd been comparing notes on the new arrival in the village. Emma had been here for a few days now and there was nothing like a bit of new blood to stimulate opinions.

Eileen had overheard the comment by way of greeting from the elderly woman who was moving slowly beside him. She sniffed audibly.

'Don't hold wi' havin' Christmas in foreign parts,' he heard her mutter. 'It's no' natural to be away from your home.'

Adam suppressed a sigh as Miss McClintock's progress slowed even more as she turned her head. 'Canada's no' so foreign,' she informed Eileen. 'And Christmas is about people, no' places. Dr McAllister's sister's there and she's having a bairn. It's where the first Mrs McAllister *should* be.'

'Come in, Joan.' Adam closed the door firmly behind them. 'And tell me what's brought you here today.'

'I'm a bit peaky is all.'

'Oh?' Adam smiled encouragingly but his heart was sinking. It had been, ever since that reference to the first Mrs McAllister. The title had come from the need to distinguish Catherine from the new woman with the same name—Tania. This was really what that overfull waiting room was about, wasn't it? It had happened all those years ago, too, when he'd brought his new wife home from the bright lights of Edinburgh. Who knew what interesting piece of information he might let slip when faced with the relentless curiosity of people who'd known him all his life?

They loved him. He knew that. They'd been prepared to accept and admire Tania, too, despite her being a foreigner from the bright lights of Edinburgh, and the excitement that her pregnancy and the birth of the twins had generated had kept the older biddies happy for months. So had the tragedy of her death. They'd closed ranks around him now and anyone who might pose even the smallest threat was going to be regarded with deep suspicion.

How on earth was Emma coping with that side of village life?

'What sort of peaky?'

Joan McClintock removed her hat. Adam obediently took it and placed it on his desk as she began unwinding her hand-knitted scarf from around her neck.

'I don't feel quite right,' his patient said vaguely. 'A wee bit giddy in my head when I stand up sometimes.'

Adam's nod was brisk. Blood pressure first, then. Possibly an ECG to check for an arrhythmia. At the very least a review of the medications Joan was taking. It was unlikely he'd be finished within the fifteen-minute slot that Eileen would have allocated in her appointment schedule but he would have to try.

'I saw the bairns in the square yesterday,' Joan told him as he helped her off with her thick coat. 'Watching the decorations go up on the tree. It's such a blessing they don't remember, isn't it?'

'Aye.' The agreement was as terse as Adam could make it without causing offence. A warning that discussing his private life was not an option. 'No, you don't need to take off your cardigan, Joan. We can just roll up your sleeve for me to do your blood pressure.'

It *was* a blessing that his children couldn't remember the dreadful Christmas of three years ago. Had Emma been given the story in lurid detail, as she'd done her chores in the village over the last few days? December wasn't just about a season of goodwill in Braeburn. It marked the season of remembrance for Tania McAllister.

His mother was lucky she was in Canada. She was getting a reprieve from being the unspoken centre of attention when family was being celebrated. Away from a village where Christmas had a distinct flavour of being a shrine to someone who had been elevated to the status of a saint.

Dear Lord…if they only *knew* the truth…

But he hadn't known so why should they? Oh, they'd all seen how she'd escaped the village more and more often but, while eyebrows had been raised about her time away from the children, it had been accepted as part of a glamorous woman's life and it had been forgiven and forgotten after her tragic death.

What none of them knew was that she probably hadn't been alone on any of those trips away.

He'd only found out because fate had stepped in and

provided the evidence and Adam had made sure that the scandalous information had gone no further.

Maybe that was the real blessing here. That the village—and therefore his children—would never know.

It was his burden and that was only fair, wasn't it? If he'd been a better husband, Tania wouldn't have needed anyone else. And it was a burden he was getting used to carrying. In many ways it was getting easier and he could hope that some time in the future he'd be able to cope with this particular time of year. Enjoying it was too much to ever hope for but another few weeks and things could get back to normal. A normality he would never have chosen, of course, but he could live with it.

He had no choice.

'That English lassie was wi' them.' Joan only just managed to wait until Adam was removing the stethoscope from his ears. 'I hear she's made friends with Caitlin McMurray at the school?'

His grunt was intended to express a lack of interest in his temporary nanny's social life. Why did some people assume that a monosyllabic response simply needed more effort on their part?

'I hear she's been *singing*.'

'Aye.' Adam was still having difficulty getting used to the sound of Emma singing. She did it *all* the time. When she was busy with some mundane task, like doing the dishes or sorting laundry, and a session of songs with the children was already a favourite part of their evening routine. She probably thought the nursery wing was far enough away from the rest of the house for him not to notice but she was wrong. He'd heard her late last night, too, well after the children were sound asleep. Alone in her room, playing her guitar and singing softly.

It wasn't that he didn't *like* the sound. It was just… different. Nothing like normal.

'She's no' a teacher.' Joan clicked her tongue. 'What's she doing at the school *every* day?'

It was the tone that did it. Adam was jolted out of his automatic defence mechanisms by the unexpected urge to defend his new employee. 'She *has* been a music teacher and she plays the guitar. The school's piano is apparently broken and the children want to learn carols. Now…stand up, please, Joan. I'm going to take your blood pressure again to see if position makes any difference.'

Joan levered her ample frame out of the chair. 'We knew about the piano. The committee's talking about whether to use the hall fund to replace it, but if we don't fix the hall it's going to get condemned and what would we do without the village hall? Where would the children put on their Christmas play?'

Adam resorted to his customary grunt and put the earpieces of his stethoscope into place to signal an end to the conversation. As he held the disc over Joan's elbow and pumped up the cuff, he took a quick glance at the clock on his wall and remembered the number of people in the waiting room.

It was going to be a long day.

The conversation stopped as soon as Emma entered the general store that was between the greengrocer and the bakery. She lifted her chin and put on her brightest smile.

'Good morning. I'm looking for some coloured paper. Do you have the kind that's sticky on the back?'

The blank stare made Emma reconsider her decision to shop in the village instead of driving for half an hour to get to the nearest larger town. It wasn't easy to keep the smile on her face.

'I want to make paper chains,' she explained. 'For Christmas decorations.'

The women exchanged heavily significant glances.

'*Christmas* decorations?' one of them murmured. 'In Dr McAllister's hoose?'

The subtext was in capital letters. You couldn't really celebrate Christmas in the McAllister house. Not without being duly reluctant anyway. Even the children were all too aware of that and it wasn't fair. She'd taken them to watch the big tree in the square being decorated yesterday and Poppy's eyes had been huge.

'I *love* Christmas trees,' she'd whispered. 'They're so *pretty*.'

'We'll make your Christmas tree just as pretty at home, you'll see.'

'We don't have a tree at home,' Oliver had said. 'Gran says it's because it makes Dad sad.'

'It makes me sad,' Poppy had said, '*not* having a tree.'

Emma had lain awake last night, mulling this over. She was here for the children, wasn't she? And she was here for Christmas.

And Christmas was for children.

It was a no-brainer, really. Surely she could find a way to persuade the taciturn Dr McAllister to put up with a few decorations? When Catherine had called from Canada early that morning to talk to the children before they went off to school, Emma had gathered her courage and asked quietly if it would be such a terrible thing to do.

'It would be the best thing to do,' Catherine had assured her. 'It's no guid for anyone, being stuck in the past. I've tried but…' The sigh said it all. 'Maybe *you'll* succeed, pet. He can't afford to chase you away, can he? Not before Christmas, anyway.'

The tone that suggested it wouldn't be an easy task

was being heavily underlined by the shocked look these women were now sharing.

'It's for Poppy and Oliver,' Emma said firmly. 'They've been making decorations at school and they want to make some at home, too. Paper chains are what I always made when I was their age.'

The mention of the children made one of the women nod. 'Aye,' she sighed. 'It should be all about the bairns, shouldn't it?'

'The paper's over yon,' the shopkeeper told Emma. 'Beside the magazines.'

The conversation didn't stop this time as she returned to the counter.

'Poor man,' one was saying. 'To lose the love of his life so young.'

'Like a princess, she was,' another agreed. 'Always so well dressed.'

Emma felt the collective scrutiny of her jeans and oversized jumper beneath her puffy anorak and she was perversely delighted that she was wearing her Tibetan knitted hat with its rainbow stripes and ear covers that trailed into long tails she hadn't bothered tying. That would really give them something to disapprove of at length as soon as she went out the door.

Her bravado faded as she picked up the guitar case she'd left by the umbrella stand at the shop door and went out into the chilly, grey afternoon, however. If making a paper chain or two was such a big deal, maybe she was only going to make things worse? How happy would the children be if their father was even more upset by someone who wasn't prepared to spend Christmas in a kind of muted mourning?

The Christmas tree in the square had taken days to decorate but it was looking magnificent now, with big, coloured lights and enormous red and silver baubles. Despite the cold, Emma perched on a bench near the church. She had half an hour before she was due at school. Checking her watch, she made a quick calculation. They were about eight hours behind Californian time and that meant that Sharon was probably at home. She hit the speed dial.

'Emma…I was just thinking about you. Is it snowing in Scotland?'

'Feels like it could be any second. I'm in the village square and it's absolutely *freezing*.'

'Ohh…I'm homesick. It's too warm to be Christmastime here. It's just *wrong*. But…you shouldn't be sitting out in the cold. Go and find somewhere warm, for heaven's sake. You have to take care of yourself.'

'I'm fine. It's too cold for bugs to survive here and my immune system is pretty much back to full power. I'm just killing some time before I go to the school for carol practice.'

Sharon laughed. 'I got your email. I can't believe you've got involved with village life that fast. No…on second thoughts, it doesn't surprise me at all. You'll be starring in the Christmas pantomime by next week.'

'No. That's Ollie and Poppy. They've been chosen to be Joseph and Mary for the school nativity play. They're so excited. I'm going to have to make costumes for them.'

'Uh-oh… Do they know you can't sew?'

Emma laughed. 'No. They don't even know I can't cook yet. Their gran left so much food in the freezer I've been able to keep my lack of talent well hidden.'

'Imagine if you gave the only doctor in town food poisoning?'

'Hey…that only happened once. I give chicken a wide berth now.'

'Good thinking. He wouldn't be happy.'

'He's not happy anyway. Do you know I haven't seen him smile once yet?'

'He's Scottish. He's supposed to be dour.'

'He still wears his wedding ring and it's three years since his wife died.'

'Hmm. He must have loved her.'

'Who wouldn't? From what I've heard, she was either a princess, an angel or some kind of saint.'

'Nobody's that perfect. People just forget the bad stuff when they're dead.'

Emma smiled but couldn't help wondering if Sharon would forget about the food poisoning incident if…

'Oh, my God…what *is* that horrendous noise?'

Laughter chased away the dark thought. 'There's an old guy in a kilt near the Christmas tree. He's warming up his bagpipes.'

'What? Sounds like a tribe of donkeys braying.'

'No. That's even worse. You should hear Jemima waking us all up in the mornings. She's very cute but remind me that I never want a donkey as a pet in the future, will you?'

'What was that? I can hardly hear you.'

'I'd better go, Sharon. I'm due at school. Talk soon. Love you.'

The piper was playing a real tune by the time Emma tucked her phone into her pocket and, instead of the brisk walk she had intended to get her circulation moving again, she sat there and listened for a minute.

It was such an evocative sound with a haunting edge that was a song of what…courage? Loneliness?

Maybe it was just the quintessential Scottishness of it but it made her think of Adam McAllister.

Did he ever wear a kilt?

The notion gave her an odd curl somewhere deep in her belly.

What *was* it about men in kilts that could be such a sexy image?

Or was it the image of Adam in the attire that was making her feel a little odd?

It was easy to dismiss such a ridiculous idea because something else was happening in her head.

Or maybe her heart.

Perhaps it was the Christmas tree she was looking at in combination with the haunting music. Or maybe it had something to do with that moment in her phone call to Sharon when she'd wondered if her friend would only remember the good things.

Whatever it was, Emma was facing the realisation that this could possibly be the last Christmas she would ever have.

And she was going to be sharing it with children who had no memory of what a happy, family Christmas should be all about.

With a man who couldn't see how precious life was and how you had to catch joy—not shut it out or allow it to be dimmed by shadows.

The fey notion that fate had sent her here for a reason suddenly made sense. If this was going to be her last Christmas, how lucky was she that she could share it with Poppy and Oliver?

She was going to make this the *best* Christmas ever.

Starting with paper chains.

CHAPTER FOUR

FLIGHTS OF FANCY first thing in the morning were a bit much but Emma seemed to have no control over this one.

Here she was, standing by the kitchen bench, breaking eggs, and a single glance over her shoulder to where the man of the house was having his breakfast had been enough to trigger it.

She could see Adam McAllister wearing a kilt. With his hair even longer than the current shaggy style so that dark, tangled waves kissed his shoulders. Standing in solitary splendour on the top of a hill, with a set of bagpipes tucked under his arm, offering a mournful lament to the universe. It was almost enough to bring a tear to her eyes. She certainly had to stifle a sigh.

In fact, Adam was wearing a dark jumper over his shirt and tie, buttering his toast and adding marmalade, just like any normal mortal. There was no excuse for the words that popped out of Emma's mouth.

'Is there a McAllister tartan?'

'What?' Adam's hand stopped halfway towards his mug of tea. He sounded both impatient and bewildered.

Emma made herself walk to the fridge to get some milk for the eggs but she couldn't look at Adam. She'd woken up a little nervous that this was the start of the weekend and she'd be seeing a lot more of the children's father. She'd been hoping to impress him by how well she'd settled into this new job but she'd obviously annoyed him by asking a stupid question.

'It's just that I saw a man playing the bagpipes in the village yesterday and he was wearing a kilt. I know that the colours and patterns vary according to clan and I just wondered...' Oh, help. Now she was prattling on. 'If, you know, you had one for your family.'

'Of course we do.'

'Oh...' Emma waited but that seemed to be the end to the conversation. 'That's nice.' She poured milk into the bowl of eggs and started whisking them. The silence stretched on.

'We're a branch of Clan Donald,' Adam said, with an air of having realised he might have been rude in giving such a terse response. 'The tartan's red and green with white stripes and a little bit of royal blue.'

'Sounds lovely.' Emma pressed her lips together but the question refused to stay unspoken. 'Do you ever wear a kilt?'

'Only for weddings.' She could feel Adam glaring at her back. 'And funerals.'

Oh...*man*. She took a deep breath. This was going to be a long weekend. 'Would you like some scrambled eggs? I'm making them for Poppy and Ollie.'

'No.' Adam's chair scraped as he pushed it back. 'I'm due at the medical centre. We have a Saturday morning clinic until eleven and then I've got my house calls to make.' Reaching for the crust of toast he'd left on his plate, Adam divided it and gave a piece to each of the dogs, who were flanking his chair. The action was as automatic as picking up his napkin to wipe his mouth and it made Emma feel better.

There *was* kindness lurking under that gruff exterior, wasn't there?

She almost changed her mind as he went to the kitchen door and raised his voice.

'Poppy—are you out of those pyjamas yet? Oliver—hurry up and find your chanter and don't forget your music book this time.'

He turned back to pick up the coat draped over the arm of the old couch near the fire. 'Do you know where you're taking them?'

'Yes.' Emma's nod was confident. 'I drop Ollie at Mr McTavish's house at nine o'clock, take Poppy to her dance class at the hall for nine-thirty, go back to get Ollie at ten and we pick up Poppy at ten-thirty.'

Adam gave a single nod. 'Good.'

'I thought we'd go into the village after that. We can see if they've finished decorating the big tree and get some fresh bread to go with our soup for lunch. Will you be back by then?'

'I don't know.' In his coat now, Adam reached for the leather doctor's bag that had probably been his father's before him. 'If I am, you can have the afternoon off. And tomorrow, of course, being Sunday.'

'But what would you do with the children if you got a call?'

'They come in the car with me. They're used to it.'

'I don't need a day off,' Emma told him. 'I'm loving being with the children.'

Adam paused en route to the door and the look Emma received was one of surprise. Had she sounded too enthusiastic perhaps?

Needy even?

Or maybe he thought it was some sort of rebuke directed at how little time he seemed to spend with his children.

Whatever was going on behind that dark, unreadable gaze, the eye contact made Emma's heart skip a beat. How could just a look feel like a physical touch?

It went on for long enough to make her start feeling a little peculiar and maybe he would have held her gaze even longer because Emma found herself unable to look away, but then the children burst into the room. Ollie had an instrument that looked like a recorder in one hand and a very dog-eared book in the other.

'I found them, Dad. They were under my bed.'

Poppy was right behind him. 'And I'm all dressed now. I just need Emma to do my hair.' Her face fell when she saw the bag in her father's hand. 'Are you going out now?'

'You know I have to work on Saturday mornings, love.'

Emma's gaze had been drawn straight back to Adam's face so she could see the softening as he looked down at his children. There was even a curl to his mouth that most would probably label as a smile but it wasn't a *real* smile. Had his children ever seen his eyes crinkle with happiness or basked in the joy of hearing him laugh aloud?

'I'll be back this afternoon,' he said. 'We can take the dogs for a walk if it stops raining and see if there's enough ice on the pond to go skating.'

His son's hair got ruffled and Poppy got a kiss on the top of her head and then he was gone. The children—and the dogs—were left staring forlornly after him.

'Who wants eggs?' Emma asked brightly.

'Me. I *love* eggs.' Poppy climbed up onto a chair.

'I don't.' Oliver kicked his chair leg before sitting down. 'I think they're *icky*.'

'Icky eggs.' Poppy giggled but then cast a doubtful look towards the pan Emma was stirring.

'That's only because you haven't tried my special scrambled eggs,' Emma said firmly. 'They're from your very own hens and they look yummy. I'm going to have some too and then we're going to get our skates on and get you to your classes on time.'

Poppy frowned. 'I don't think I can dance with my skates on.'

Emma laughed. 'It means that we need to be quick.' She put a plate of scrambled eggs in front of Poppy. 'To go fast, like we're pretending to be on skates.'

'I love skating.' Poppy picked up her fork. 'I hope the pond is all freezed up. Will you come and have a look on our walk, too, Emma?'

The wide-eyed, hopeful look that accompanied the invitation was irresistible but Emma rapidly replayed Adam's words in her head. He'd offered to take the children for a walk. He'd told her she could have the afternoon off. That added up to him wanting time alone with his children, didn't it?

'I might have some things I need to do,' she told Poppy. 'But you can tell me all about it later.'

Adam wasn't home by the time the soup was hot and the crusty loaf of bread had been sliced and buttered.

'I don't think we'll wait,' Emma decided. 'I can leave some soup on the stove to stay hot for Daddy and we'll save him lots of bread.'

'And a chocolate?'

'Does Daddy like chocolate?'

'Mmm.' Poppy nodded her head enthusiastically but then frowned. 'Not as much as me.'

Emma eyed the small bowl on the table. 'You didn't open too many doors on your calendar, did you?'

Poppy shook her head. 'That's Ollie's chocolates too. Is there really one behind every door until it gets to Christmas?'

'Sure is. Have you guys never had an Advent calendar before?'

Poppy shook her head again. 'Jeannie told me about them at school but I didn't believe her.'

A momentary doubt surfaced as Emma looked at the two Advent calendars now pinned to the bottom of the big corkboard, within easy reach of the children. Surely Adam wouldn't object to them having the excitement of opening the doors to find the treat and the tiny Christmassy picture every morning?

'Ollie? You can stop practising now. Come and have lunch.'

'I'm going to wait for Dad.'

'But we don't know how long he'll be. You must be hungry.'

Sitting on the sofa, Oliver shook his head and kept blowing on his chanter, laboriously changing his finger positions over the holes. The noise was terrible. No wonder the dogs were looking unhappy.

'Tell you what…' Emma had to raise her voice to be heard over the shrill notes. 'Why don't you have a little bit now and then some more when Dad gets home?'

Oliver appeared not to have heard the suggestion but when the telephone rang he dropped his chanter and ran to answer it. He came back scowling. 'Dad says Mrs Jessop is having her baby and it's coming too early so he has to stay and look after her until the ambulance comes and he might have to go into the hospital with her, too. He might not be home till teatime.'

'Oh...' Emma's heart gave a squeeze at the small boy's obvious disappointment. 'We'll just have to find something fun to do until then, won't we?'

Oliver's scowl deepened.

Emma tried hard to keep the children amused and cheer Oliver up. They all put wellies and coats on and took some carrots out for Jemima the donkey, who was very happy to have visitors. Emma scratched her woolly head and stroked the extraordinary ears.

'She has beautiful eyes.'

'She's really clever,' Oliver said. 'She can undo knots. Dad says it's no use ever tying her up.'

Poppy was being nuzzled gently.

'She's kissing me, Emma. See? She loves me. She 'specially loves it when I ride her.'

'Really? Does she have a saddle?'

'You don't need one,' Oliver told her. 'There's lots of fluff to hang onto and she never goes fast.'

'How does she know where to go?'

'She follows *me*,' Oliver said. He stood a little taller. 'That's why she's so good at undoing knots. She doesn't like being tied up because she wants to follow me. Jemima loves me, too.'

'She's quiet now,' Emma observed. 'She's pretty loud in the mornings, isn't she?'

'That's because she's lonely,' Poppy said sadly. 'Donkeys need to have a friend.'

'Can we go and look at the pond now?'

'Do you know where it is, Ollie?'

'Up there.' His arm waved vaguely towards the wooded hill behind the house that separated the garden from surrounding farmland. 'Somewhere.'

'Hmm.' It was tempting to take the children and dogs off for a walk but Emma had a sudden vision of them all getting lost in the Scottish highlands. She could imagine the activation of the local search and rescue team as the snow started falling thickly and what Adam's face would be like if she put his children into such danger.

Maybe it was fortunate that the leaden sky overhead decided to release the first fat raindrops on top of them.

'Let's get Jemima tucked up into her nice warm stable. I've got something special we can do inside.'

'What?'

'It's a surprise.'

It was certainly Oliver that the donkey was willing to follow. He didn't even need to hang onto her halter as he led her into the straw-covered stable. They closed the bottom half of the door so she could see out but the mournful braying started even before they got back to the house.

'She's lonely again,' Poppy said. Her bottom lip quivered.

'Oh…look.' Emma wanted to distract Poppy. 'That's a holly hedge. Let's pick some.'

'Why?'

'Because it's what you do at Christmas. We need branches that have lots of lovely red berries. Let's see how quickly we can find some and get inside before it really starts raining.'

The rain was pouring down by the time they reached the warmth of the kitchen again. The dogs left muddy paw prints over the flagstone floor and curled up close to the fire that Emma stoked. She cleared the table and produced the packets of coloured paper she had purchased in the village the day before and showed them how to cut strips and make interlocking loops by sticking the ends together.

'Do lots of different colours,' she said. 'And make them really long. I'll find something to stick them up with and we'll make the kitchen so pretty it will be a lovely surprise for when Daddy gets home.'

The task was a novelty that the children loved. The strips were a bit wobbly and the loops a variety of sizes but it didn't detract from the overall effect as the simple decorations grew. Emma cleaned up the lunch dishes and found a big bowl to arrange the holly branches in. She sang the Christmas carol the children had never heard about the little donkey and Poppy made her sing it again and again as she tried to learn the words.

Then she searched cluttered drawers until she found some drawing pins and tape that she could use to hang the paper chains. This required some effort, moving the table and then standing on a chair on top of it but by the time daylight had faded completely they were able to stand back and admire the team effort.

Rainbow chains linked all four corners of the room, dipping between the beams to give graceful curves to the lines. The whitewashed ceiling made the colours seem even brighter and the transformation from ordinary to festive was very gratifying. Who wouldn't love it?

The sound of singing was the last thing Adam needed when he stepped into his home after a long and difficult afternoon. The happy sound was totally inappropriate when he'd just left people who were suffering—like poor Aimee Jessop, who looked like she might lose yet another bairn.

The clock had stopped, he noted. Because he'd forgotten to wind it.

At least Bob wasn't limping as much but it had been Emma who had decided to take him to the vet to have his dressing changed and receive instructions on how to care for the dog. Had Jim, the vet, made some comment about how it was just as well it wasn't going to be left entirely in Adam's hands?

And it had been Emma who'd made him feel like he wasn't doing enough for his children, too. The way she'd said how much she loved being with them this morning. He loved being with them, too, but how many others would realise that?

He'd promised to spend the afternoon with them today and look what had happened.

A premature labour at only twenty-seven weeks for poor Aimee. Four weeks longer than the previous two pregnancies and she'd really begun to hope that this time she would get to take her baby home. He'd tried to keep her calm until the ambulance arrived and he couldn't have let her go to the hospital alone. Not when her husband was out on the oil rig for another two weeks.

Not even noticing the muddy streak Benji's paw left on his trousers, Adam kept moving. Maybe a wee dram of whisky before his tea would help. And some time with the children. He could read them a story before bed.

The words of the song were audible now. '"Little donkey, little donkey, on the dusty road..."'

Maybe the children would prefer to hear songs than a story.

Adam stepped into the kitchen. He was expecting warmth and the smell of hot food. The loving greeting his children always gave him and the prospect of winding down in the comfort of his favourite part of his house. He wasn't expecting to be hit in the face with a blinding kaleidoscope of colours.

'What in heaven's name is *going on* in here?'

'Daddy...' Poppy flung her arms around his legs. 'We've made decorations. Aren't they bee-*yoot*-i-ful?'

Adam took another upward glance at the desecration of the ancient, oak beams.

'And we've learned a song all about Jemima.'

'It's not about Jemima.' Oliver was right beside his sister now. 'It's about another donkey. The one that Mary was riding to get to Bethlehem.'

Christmas again. How did it manage to accentuate the worst of life in so many ways? Impossible not to think about a donkey carrying the pregnant Mary. With a full-term pregnancy that everybody knew ended up with a healthy baby, despite less than adequate birthing facilities. Unlike poor Aimee who had access to the best of modern care but now had a scrap of a bairn who was on life support in a neonatal intensive care unit in Edinburgh.

Adam tried to push the concern away. To focus on his own healthy children. Tried to centre himself by a glance around the room below ceiling level. At least that looked relatively normal. Or did it?

'*What…*' he actually had to swallow before he could find any more words '…are *those*?'

The children had fallen strangely silent. Even Poppy, who could never be called a quiet child. It was Emma who answered.

'They're Advent calendars. You get to open a little door every day until Christmas Eve and there's a new picture and a little chocolate. Very little and the children haven't eaten them all from the doors that already needed to be opened. They saved them. For *you*.'

She sounded nervous, Adam realised. He looked over the twins' heads and looked at her properly for the first time since he'd come into the room. He still hadn't got used to the way she looked, with that air of being a stray gypsy waif, but he was certainly letting go of the idea that she could be unreliable or unable to commit to anything. She'd thrown herself into being his children's nanny with her heart and soul, hadn't she? They loved her.

And she loved them. The way she'd said how much she loved being with them this morning had touched his heart in the way that only total honesty could.

And now she was looking at him with eyes that looked too large for her thin face. With a glow that was telling him that she was doing this to make his children happy.

Because she already loved them.

And because it was Christmastime.

There was a hopeful expression in those eyes, too, that was a plea that he wouldn't spoil it all by being cross.

He found himself unable to look away. Adam got a sudden vision of what it would be like to be seeing himself through her eyes and he didn't like what he saw. He forced a smile to his lips as he managed to break the eye contact with Emma.

'As long as you don't eat too much chocolate before dinner.' He looked up again. 'I don't think I've ever seen such long paper chains. You must have been busy all day.'

'I did my practice, too. D'you want to hear what I learned today, Dad?'

'Aye. Let me get my coat off, son. And I need a wee something to drink.'

He glanced across at Emma, feeling like he should apologise, although he wasn't quite sure why. 'D'you drink whisky, Emma?'

She shook her head but smiled. 'Let me find one for you while you listen to Ollie's new tune. You've had a long day. Dinner will ready in no time.'

There was no recrimination in her tone that she'd been left with the children all afternoon and that they'd been left without their promised walk or time with their father. No… Both the tone and the way she was looking at him gave him the odd feeling that she knew exactly how hard his day had been. He didn't have to say anything about what had happened but she was still willing to try and make it better.

Even more oddly, it *was* starting to feel better. He could almost dismiss the edge of panic at seeing how Christmas was invading his house again. Maybe that was because the decorations were so obviously made by children with their wobbly shapes and sizes. Tania might have gone overboard with decorations but she would never have tolerated something so far less than perfect. Even the bunch of holly on the table was real instead of a perfect, plastic replica.

This was different. This was Emma, not Tania. Couldn't be more different, in fact. Maybe it would even be okay.

'Thank you.' It felt like the first time Adam had ever smiled at Emma but surely that wasn't the case?

Maybe it was because he'd never seen *her* smile quite like that. A slow, delighted curl to her mouth that lit up her face and gave her a faint flush of colour on those pale cheeks.

She was pretty, he realised. Not flaky looking at all. Too young for her years, still, and too thin, but…yes… pretty.

Beautiful even.

CHAPTER FIVE

EMMA HAD A lot of time to herself on Sunday because Adam didn't get called out, although he seemed to spend a lot of time on the phone and she overheard a snatch of conversation about a sick baby who was in Intensive Care. The children—and the dogs—got their long walk to see whether the pond was frozen and Emma was glad of the time on her own.

She sat in her room, with her laptop and her guitar, working on her Christmas gift for Sharon. She was writing a song about friendship and the strength it could give someone to get through hard times, and she intended to record it as a background to a slide show of all the best photos she and Sharon had taken over the last few years. She might even use the very private ones—like the one in her hospital bed where she'd been so swollen by the steroids she'd been taking and completely bald from the chemo. Sharon had insisted she needed a photo so that Emma would be able to look back and see how far she'd come and then she'd said something about eggheads and made Emma laugh, and that was the moment she'd captured.

She'd been so right. It was hard to believe how far she'd come. And maybe—Emma squeezed her eyes tightly shut for a heartbeat—she would be able to look back from the distance of many more years. But if she couldn't, Sharon would have this gift from her heart for ever.

Back in the routine of the school week again, Emma was delighted to feel so at home with the routine of her new job. She was loving her time at the school, helping with the music classes, and the new friendship with the junior-school teacher, Caitlin, promised to be something special.

It was a bonus that Oliver took so long to find everything he needed to take home after school because it gave the young women a few minutes extra to chat.

'I was telling Moira Findlay that you have one of the most amazing voices I've ever heard,' Caitlin confessed on Monday afternoon. 'She said they might consider offering you an invitation to join the village choir.'

Emma grinned. 'I take it that's a huge honour?'

'You'd better believe it. Normally you have to be second-generation Braeburn, at the very least.'

'Did you tell her I'm only here till Adam's mother gets back?'

'No.' Caitlin's face fell. 'I'm kind of hoping you'll fall in love with the place and decide to stay. He's still going to need a nanny, isn't he, and the last few have been disasters—especially that Kylie, who was far more interested in her boyfriend than the children.'

Emma backed away from the conversation fast. 'My plans are totally up in the air for next year. I couldn't commit to anything and Adam hasn't mentioned the possibility, either. I…'

The urge to say something more was strong but this wasn't the time or place. Caitlin must have sensed something big but her curious glance lasted only a moment. Poppy was tugging on Emma's hand.

'Sing Miss McMurray the new song, Emma. The Christmas one.'

'We've got lots of carols we're learning already, Poppy,' Caitlin said.

'But this is Jemima's song. About Mary.'

'"Little Donkey",' Emma supplied.

'Oh...' Caitlin's eyes shone. 'That's one of my all-time *favourite* Christmas songs. How could I have forgotten it?' She began to hum but then stopped. 'That's the chorus. How does it start again?'

Emma could see that Oliver had been totally distracted from finding his reading book by watching the goldfish in their bowl on the science table so she sang the first few lines about the little donkey on the dusty road, plodding on with its precious load.

Poppy beamed and Caitlin sighed happily. 'Imagine our play with our Mary coming in on a donkey with Joseph leading her, and all the children singing that.'

'I'm Mary,' Poppy reminded her.

'I know, pet.' Caitlin patted her head.

'And I've *got* a donkey.'

'I know that, too. But Jemima's a *real* donkey. We can't use her in our play.'

'Why not?' Emma was caught by the image. Adam would be there in the audience, wouldn't he? How amazing would that be, to see his two children and their pet creating Christmas magic for the whole village? She could take photos and give them a new memory that would always remind them of a joyous moment.

Caitlin was staring at her as if she had lost her mind.

'She's a very good donkey,' Emma continued. 'And Poppy's used to riding her.' From the corner of her eye she noted that Oliver had stopped watching the fish and was now watching them. 'Would she still follow you in a strange place, Ollie? Would you be able to lead her?'

Oliver scowled at her. ''Course I would.'

'They could just come down the centre aisle and then the children could take their place on the stage and someone could take Jemima out the side door.'

'Ohh...' Caitlin was clearly completely captured. 'How would we get her to the hall, though?'

That was a problem. 'It *is* too far to walk,' Emma agreed.

'My brother's girlfriend's aunt runs a donkey sanctuary not far from here,' Caitlin said thoughtfully. 'I wonder if we could borrow a float?'

Poppy was bouncing up and down on her toes. 'Hooray...Jemima's going to be in our play.'

'Hang on,' her teacher warned. 'Don't get too excited. And don't tell anybody else about it. We'll have to get all sorts of permission, like from the hall committee and from your daddy.'

The bright glow of the idea dimmed for Emma. Neither authority was likely to be too enthusiastic about this inspiration but she suspected Adam would be the hardest to convince.

But he was okay with the paper chains now, wasn't he? And the Advent calendars and the holly? Maybe another small push forward would help get him into feeling the goodwill of the season more. When they passed a man selling Christmas trees off the back of a lorry on their way home, Emma stamped on the brakes.

'I think we need a tree,' she said aloud. 'What do you think, kidlets?'

The twins were silent.

'We could put it in the big living room,' Emma suggested. 'And we could make decorations for it. And then your presents can go underneath it on Christmas Eve. Is that what you usually do?'

'We don't have a tree.' Poppy's voice was very small. 'We only go and see the tree by the church and the one in Gran's house.'

A glance in the rear-view mirror revealed an expression on Oliver's face rather like the one that had been on Caitlin's when Emma had suggested adding Jemima to the junior school's play. As if she was completely crazy.

'Maybe that's because Daddy gets too busy at Christmastime. Would you like to have a tree, Poppy?'

Poppy thought about this for a long moment. 'Jeannie has her very own tree.'

'So does Jamie,' Oliver said. 'And Ben and…and *everybody.*'

Emma channelled Catherine McAllister. It was up to her to make Christmas happen for these children, even if the thought of the repercussions of this step were more than a little scary.

'Right, then.' She reached for her wallet. 'Come on. You can help me choose the *best* one.'

'No.'

'But, Daddy…I *want* Jemima to be in our play. *Please…*'

'*No.*' Adam's fork clattered against his plate in the silence that followed the resoundingly negative response.

It was just as well that Emma had waited until dinner was almost finished before broaching the subject of including the largest family pet in the nativity play. Her appetite evaporated in the face of the atmosphere that instantly filled the McAllister kitchen—her favourite room in this grand old house. That single word had somehow created an impenetrable barrier and Adam was clearly angry. Was he even tasting the casserole he was forking into his mouth?

The last of the wonderful meals Catherine had left in the freezer, Emma had noted with some alarm. She would have to cook the evening meals herself from now on.

The children began simply pushing pieces of food around their plates with as little enthusiasm as Emma.

'Eat your dinner,' Adam ordered, 'or there'll be no ice cream.'

'I don't *want* ice cream.' Poppy's voice wobbled. 'I *want…*'

No, Emma begged silently. Don't say it.

'I want Jemima to be in our play.'

Adam dropped his cutlery and his chair scraped back with a screech that made Emma flinch.

'It's the most ridiculous idea I've ever heard,' he snapped. 'And it's *not* going to happen. I don't want to hear another word about it.' The stern glare Poppy was being subjected to was transferred to Oliver. 'From *either* of you.'

Then it was Emma's turn to get the look. 'I expect this was *your* idea in the first place?'

For a heartbeat she felt frightened. It wasn't just about potentially getting fired from a job she was coming to love far more than she'd expected. It was more about the glimpse into what Adam McAllister would be like if he lost control. She was sensing the depth of emotion hidden away in this man for the first time and who knew what might happen if it broke through those rigid, self-imposed constraints?

But then Emma was aware of something she rarely felt.

Anger.

She could see that the children really *were* frightened.

Sitting there, like small statues, with pale faces and probably holding their breath. Scared that their daddy didn't love them any more because they'd done something bad.

Was it so bad to dream of doing something a bit out of the ordinary? Okay…a lot out of the ordinary, but this was about *Christmas*, wasn't it? About making a little bit of magic?

So she held Adam's angry glare and lifted her chin.

'Yes,' she said clearly. 'It *was* my idea. And Caitlin McMurray loved it. She said she'd talk to the hall committee about getting permission and that she could probably arrange transport to get Jemima into the village for the evening.'

Adam was on his feet now. He crumpled his serviette into a ball and threw it down beside his unfinished plate of food.

'Have you seen the state of the village hall? It's crumbling inside. The floorboards all need replacing. Quite apart from the public-health issues of an animal needing to relieve itself indoors, there would be the danger of the floor giving way. Imagine the panic that would create? Not only could Jemima get injured but so could anybody who was unfortunate enough to be sitting anywhere nearby. Like my *children*. You're suggesting that I allow you to put them in danger for the sake of a school *play*?'

'It's a *Christmas* play.' Emma was not going to let her voice wobble like Poppy's had but it was a close call. 'It's special.'

'*Ach…*' Adam turned and strode towards the door. 'I'm going to find somewhere I can get away from this nonsense. And I don't want to hear anything more about it. From *any* of you.'

Bob followed his master from the kitchen but his head

was hanging low. Benji started to follow Bob but then stopped and slowly slunk back beneath the kitchen table.

Emma swallowed a gulp. She reached out with one hand to squeeze Poppy's hand. She would have squeezed Oliver's too, but he promptly put both his hands in his lap to avoid her touch.

'It's okay,' she told them with as much confidence as she could muster. 'Daddy just needs time to get used to the idea. He's a little bit cross but he'll get over it, you'll see.' She found a smile. 'Why don't we all have some ice cream?'

'We're not allowed,' Oliver informed her. 'We haven't eaten all our vegetables.'

'I'll bet Benji would eat them if we put them in *his* dish.'

The children looked astonished. Was an adult actually suggesting something naughty?

It wasn't the first time that Emma had been struck by how like his father Oliver was. He was deep, this little boy, and there was a sadness in him that shouldn't be there. It made her heart ache.

'Sometimes,' she said softly, 'we all need a cuddle. And having a treat like ice cream—it kind of gives us a cuddle from the inside and makes us feel better. A tummy cuddle.'

Poppy climbed off her chair and onto Emma's lap. She wound her skinny arms around Emma's neck and buried her face on her shoulder. Emma happily gathered the little girl closer and rocked her a little as she cuddled her. She held out her other arm in an invitation for Oliver to join them but he stayed where he was with his head bent as if he was staring at his hands.

They heard the roar from Adam all the way from the living room. Oh…dear Lord…Emma had forgotten the tree they'd installed in there as soon as they'd got home, thanks to the clever stand the Christmas-tree man had sold her along with the spruce the children had declared the best.

They could hear the furious footfalls as he came storming back into the kitchen.

'Whose idea was *that*, as if I couldn't guess?'

It was Emma receiving the full force of the glare this time.

'It has to stop, do you hear me? I won't have it.' Adam didn't have to reach far above his head to grab hold of one of the paper chains. And it didn't take much of a tug to have it break and drift down in pieces.

'We don't do Christmas.' He wasn't shouting but the quiet words were chillingly final. 'Not in this house.'

Poppy burst into tears. Oliver was staring at the falling paper chains and Emma just knew she was going to see this staunch little boy cry for the first time, too. But the sound that came out of his mouth was more like a cry of fear.

'*Daddy…*' His pointing was urgent and Emma turned her head automatically, in time to see the flames from the paper chain that had landed on top of the stove.

With a vehement curse Adam flung himself towards that side of the kitchen. He grabbed a tea towel, put it under the cold tap and then covered the pile of burning paper. It was all over in seconds.

Except that it wasn't over. Both the children were sobbing and this time Oliver had no objection when Emma gathered him under her free arm and took both children out of the kitchen and away from their father.

They were still sobbing by the time she'd got them bathed and into bed. Poppy fell asleep almost instantly, totally worn out by her misery. When Emma went back to check on Oliver again, she found he was also asleep—a tight ball of child entirely covered by bedding, with only his nose poking out. She bent and kissed the cold little nose.

'It'll be okay,' she whispered, just in case he wasn't really asleep. 'I promise.'

She would just have to make it okay, she decided as she forced herself to go back downstairs instead of going to hide in her room, which was what she would have preferred.

Somehow she would have to put things right.

Adam didn't hear Emma coming down the stairs but he knew she was on her way by the subtle change in the dogs. The way they pricked their ears and Benji's tail made an almost apologetic sweep of the tiles that he couldn't suppress.

He didn't look up, however, so he was still sitting there at the table with his forehead resting on one hand and a whisky glass encircled by the other as she came into the kitchen. He hadn't cleaned up the mess of charred paper yet and all he'd done with the plates of half-eaten food had been to push them to one side to make room for the whisky decanter and two glasses.

Two glasses?

Well…he had to start somewhere, didn't he?

'I'm sorry.' It was harder than he'd expected to get the words out. A shame it made it sound like he didn't really mean it but he did. He was absolutely appalled at how he'd behaved. And in front of the *children*…

He shoved the empty glass towards the closest chair at his end of the table. 'Help yourself.'

She probably didn't even drink whisky, he thought, as he remembered her refusal the other night. The night when he'd had the impression that she understood exactly how he was feeling.

Could he make her understand *this*?

The fact that she sat down in the chair and then reached to pull the stopper out of the decanter gave him a glimmer of hope. At least she was prepared to listen. He waited until he'd heard her pour herself a dram and then the clink of the stopper going back. He still couldn't look up to meet her gaze, however.

'It was the tree,' he said. 'It was in the same place. *Exactly the* same place.'

There. He'd said it. Only maybe it wasn't enough because all he got back was an expectant silence. He risked a glance up from the amber liquid he was swirling in the bottom of his glass.

Blue eyes, she had. With a hint of grey, like the sea when there was a storm on the horizon. Right now they looked as big as oceans, too. She looked as though she could already see all she needed to know but she wanted to hear the words as well.

Adam took a sip of the warmed whisky and felt the fire trickle down his gullet.

'The tree was right there beside the fire,' he said finally. 'When I got back home on Christmas Eve. It was covered with all its decorations and the lights were still flashing as though nothing had happened. All the presents were underneath, waiting for the bairns in the morning.'

Still Emma said nothing.

'I'd had to go all the way to Edinburgh,' Adam continued. 'To identify Tania's body. I'd been thinking all the way that she would be terribly burned and it would be the worst thing I'd ever seen but there wasn't a mark on her, apart from the soot in her hair and around her nose and mouth.'

It had still been the worst thing he'd ever had to deal with, though. The shock of seeing his dead wife had been terrible enough. To be told she hadn't been alone in her bed had been an additional blow he hadn't been able to handle.

The police had been so understanding. Apologetic, really, at having to deliver the extra blow. Sympathetic. It could be kept quiet, if that's what he would prefer.

Of course he would. Nobody would ever know. Emma certainly didn't need to know, even though it was tempting to tell her, thanks to the look of appalled empathy in her eyes. Did he want her to really understand? To feel… sorry for him?

No.

He cleared his throat. 'She'd died from the smoke inhalation, not the flames.'

Flames. How shocking had it been to see that paper chain erupt? The children must have been terrified and it was all because he hadn't known what to do with that dreadful surge of feelings that had been unbearable.

'It was very late by the time I got back. My mother was asleep upstairs with the children and it was the early hours of Christmas Day. The day I would have to tell my bairns that their mummy wasn't coming home.'

'I'm so sorry, Adam.' The words were a whisper and when he looked up again there were tears rolling down the side of Emma's nose.

'It's not your fault.' He wanted to reach out and catch one of those tears with his thumb and wipe it away. He wanted to go upstairs and kiss his children and tell them he was sorry and that they would never see him like that again. He would do that. Soon. Even if they were asleep. And then he'd do it again tomorrow.

'None of this is your fault,' he told Emma. 'It's me.'

'It's me who's tried to force you to bring Christmas into the house. I'm so sorry. For your loss and for the hurt I've caused. I was thinking about the children and *their* Christmas and I lost sight of how much it might hurt you.'

Emma was clearly not a practised whisky drinker. She took a gulp that made her cough and splutter and Adam had to resist the urge to pat her on the back.

To smile even.

'I'll get rid of everything,' she offered. 'I'll explain to the children that you're not ready to celebrate Christmas yet. That we can go and see the tree in the village and we don't need to have one in the house. We can take the paper chains to school and I'm sure Caitlin will let us put them up in the classroom. And I'll—'

Adam reached out and put his hand over hers. Only because she wasn't looking at him and he wanted her to stop talking.

It worked. Emma went very still but Adam didn't take his hand away from hers. It felt tiny and soft and warm under his and he liked it.

'No,' he said softly. 'What you can do is show me how to make a paper chain. I want to fix this one so it's right for when the children come down in the morning. And tomorrow I'll go up into the attic and find the box of decorations for the tree.'

'Oh…' There was a sparkle in those blue-grey eyes that looked like more than the remnants of tears. And her hand moved under his. Turned and twisted so that her fingers were grasping his palm. *Squeezing* it. 'Really? You'll let us have a real Christmas? In the *house*?'

'Aye.' It was impossible not to catch a little bit of that childlike enthusiasm. The sheer joy that was breaking through. 'Three years of grief is enough, I'm thinking. We'll do this for the children.'

'Oh…' Emma jumped to her feet and Adam found himself standing up, too. Had he guessed that she would stand on tiptoe and throw her arms around him?

'*Thank* you, Adam. Thank you *so* much…'

'I'll talk to the hall committee too, about Jemima being in the play. I still think it's a bit daft but if they know it's for the children—for the first real Christmas they're going to celebrate since their mother died—they might just come on board.'

She was beaming up at him. Impossible not to smile back. She was so loving, this gypsy waif of a woman. So full of joy.

It was he who should be thanking her. He knew that but somehow the words wouldn't form themselves. Instead, he felt his arms go around her. How long had it been since he'd felt the soft curves of a woman like this?

Three years—that's how long. He'd actually forgotten how *good* it could feel.

He smiled back at her and she stretched up even more and kissed him on the cheek. Except that he moved his head somehow and it was the corner of his mouth that her lips brushed.

And, heaven help him, for a heartbeat he wanted her to do it again. To kiss him.

And not on his cheek.

Maybe Emma had sensed the longing. She sprang away from him. 'I'll get the sticky paper,' she said. 'There's plenty left.'

Oh…*help…*

She hadn't intended to kiss Adam at all and she *certainly* hadn't been aiming anywhere near his mouth, but he'd moved somehow and her lips had been aware of exactly where they'd landed, albeit so briefly.

She'd dismissed the tingle that had run right through her body as embarrassment but it wasn't going away as they sat cutting strips of coloured paper. It was more than embarrassment at being so inappropriate, wasn't it? And hadn't the lines between employer and employee been blurred beyond recognition by Adam talking about something so personal?

So incredibly *sad*…

Emma could understand completely how Adam felt about celebrating Christmas now and yet he was prepared to put his own feelings aside for the sake of the children.

How brave was that?

She stole a glance at the man sitting at the table with her. Such a serious face. And skilful hands that could probably do all sorts of incredibly intricate medical procedures but were currently being used with intense concentration to manipulate strips of rainbow-coloured paper. It was ridiculous but she actually felt…*proud* of Adam? For putting his children first. For being staunch.

And that seemed to intensify the lingering tingle. Emma needed to distract herself before she said or did something else that might overstep a boundary that was becoming more difficult to identify. She looked at what Adam was doing. He had made two loops. Separate loops.

'Once you've made one loop, you need to thread the next strip through before you stick it into a loop. That's how they join up. Like this…see?'

'Oh…aye…' Adam made a face. 'I was distracted by the taste. I might need another wee dram to wash it away soon.'

He looked happier when he had three and then four loops joined together. 'I can see why the children enjoyed doing this. It's quite satisfying, isn't it?'

Emma nodded, smiling as she remembered how much

the twins had loved the activity. 'Poppy and Ollie are easy to entertain,' she told him. 'They're gorgeous children.'

'You manage them very well. For someone who's never been a nanny, you're doing a good job, Emma.'

It felt like high praise. Especially when it came with a smile and a softening of those dark eyes. Yes…the lines of those boundaries had definitely been blurred. Where exactly did they stop now?

Inexplicably, that silent query kicked the tingle up by several notches. In a kind of backwards trickle that went through her limbs and pooled somewhere deep inside.

'How do you know how to get on so well with kids? You said you didn't have any younger brothers or sisters, didn't you?'

She nodded again. 'I did have a kind of older brother, though. Jack.'

'A kind of brother?'

'He was the son of my parents' best friends. A lot older than me but we got on really well. Still do. He's…important in my life.'

That was an understatement but Adam had obviously picked up on the vibe.

'Your boyfriend?'

'Heavens, no…' Emma almost smiled at the question but there was something in Adam's tone that she couldn't place. Did he *want* her to have a boyfriend? So that those boundaries were clearly flagged? What would happen when he knew the truth?

'I love Jack dearly,' she said quietly, 'but definitely in the brother category. And he's happily married now with his first baby on the way. No…he's even more special now because he became a doctor and then a specialist in oncology. He kept Mum going for a lot longer than she might have had otherwise and she had a good quality of life until…the end.'

And he'd been her primary physician ever since her own diagnosis. How many people were lucky enough to get a doctor who cared so much? Who was so determined to succeed?

'How long ago did you lose your mother?'

'Just last year.' Emma met his sympathetic gaze. The boundary lines were totally invisible now. It felt like she was sitting here talking to a friend, not her employer. 'And I miss her terribly. You're very lucky to have your mum as part of your life.'

'I know. But she does too much. It's not fair…' For a heartbeat, as Adam held her gaze, it seemed like he was going to say something else. About his mother? About *her*?

Something that might reveal he was feeling the extraordinary connection that had Emma slightly stunned?

No. Emma couldn't tell if it was relief or disappointment that coursed through her as Adam frowned and looked away. Normal service was being resumed. Maybe a breathing space was a good idea. For both of them. Or maybe she'd just been imagining that connection.

He held up his paper chain.

'Will this be long enough, do you think? When it's joined to yours?'

By the time breakfast was ready the next day, the paper chains were back in place as though nothing had happened last night.

Poppy and Oliver had bounced back to normal in the delightful way children could. Not only was Adam apparently forgiven for his outburst, the twins were impressed that he had fixed the paper chain himself.

'All by yourself?' Poppy asked.

'Emma showed me what to do.'

Emma looked up from where she was spooning porridge into bowls and grinned at him. 'I expect you could have worked it out all by yourself,' she said generously. 'Coffee?'

'Please.' It made him feel good to remember their time together last night. Talking about things he would never normally share. Feeling as if he was in the company of someone he could talk to about anything at all. Adam began to smile back at her but he was aware of the intense scrutiny of the children so he smiled at them instead.

'It makes your mouth taste funny after a while, doesn't it? Licking the sticky paper?'

'Aye…' Oliver nodded solemnly as he climbed onto his chair. 'It does at that.'

Adam's mouth twitched into a wider smile at the adult turn of phrase from his small son but then it faded as he caught the glance slanted in his direction as Oliver reached for his glass of milk. There was a hint of wariness in those brown eyes that were so like his own. Ollie was on his best behaviour, wasn't he? Just in case…

And that hurt. How often had his children tiptoed around him? he wondered. To stop him being cross.

Or sad.

The resolution to put the years of mourning behind this family and move forward had seemed more of a mountain to climb when he'd woken this morning after a somewhat disturbing dream that had included the new nanny but Adam had gathered it back and shored it up.

Things *were* going to change around here.

And Christmas was the perfect time to start.

'Tonight,' he told his children, 'when I get home from work, we're going to have an expedition.'

'What's an exposition?' Poppy looked at the bowl Emma put in front of her. 'I don't like porridge.' She frowned. 'It's *icky*.'

'Not when you put a little bit of cream and some brown sugar on it. Here, I'll help you.'

'An expedition is an adventure,' Adam told his daughter. 'And when I get home, we'll get the ladder out and go up into the attic.'

Oliver stopped making roads through his porridge with his spoon. 'The *attic*? Where the ghost is?'

'There's no such thing as ghosts,' Adam said firmly. 'It's where the box of Christmas decorations is. We're going to find it and then decorate your tree.'

Poppy's gasp was one of pure excitement. She had to climb off her chair, onto her father's lap, throw her arms around his neck and plant a kiss—sticky with brown sugar—in the middle of his cheek.

The dogs caught the excitement. Benji barked and chased his tail over by the fire and staid old Bob's tail was waving like a flag. Even studious little Oliver was grinning widely.

Adam could almost taste the sweetness of the sugary kiss Poppy had bestowed but when she returned to her own chair he looked across to where Emma was sitting with her own bowl of porridge. He might have expected to see her beaming at him with that infectious joy she had but, instead, her smile was poignant and there was a sparkle in her eyes that reminded him of when they had been full of tears.

She knew how much of an effort he was making here. That things were going to change and that this was going to be the best Christmas he could manage for the twins.

The memory of that butterfly's-wing touch of Emma's lips on the corner of his mouth came flooding back. And that peculiar moment when he'd caught her gaze after she talked about her mother and he'd had the disconcerting notion that he was actually falling into those blue pools. And that merged into a remnant of his dream that he couldn't quite catch and probably didn't want to anyway, but *something* was hanging in the air between him and Emma.

Yes. Things were changing. Had he thrown a pebble into a still pond and the ripples were only just beginning?

That was disturbing. Adam fed his crust to the dogs and drained the last of his coffee.

'Time for me to go to work,' he announced gruffly, careful to avoid any more eye contact with Emma that might add to the alarming impression that he might have started something that could get completely out of control.

'You won't forget, will you, Dad?'

'What's that, Ollie?'

'About the adventure. In the attic.'

'No, son.' He ruffled Oliver's hair. 'I won't forget. I promise.'

He kissed Poppy and nodded farewell to Emma. And it only took that microsecond of a look to realise that there were other things he wasn't about to forget either.

However much he wished he could.

CHAPTER SIX

HE'D BEEN WRONG about the ghost in the attic.

Adam realised that the instant he stepped through the hole in the ceiling, even before he turned to help first Oliver and then Poppy to climb off the steep set of stairs cleverly concealed behind a door that had been locked for years.

The light switch he flicked made several bulbs glow but the light was inadequate for the huge space. Despite the shadows, however, his gaze went straight towards that long rack of dresses in the far corner where the roofline sloped sharply towards the small latticed windows. And the stacks of boxes beside it, full of other clothing and shoes and handbags. He could even make out the jewellery case sitting on top.

They represented what had attracted him to Tania in the first place. The beauty. The glamour. In retrospect he was ashamed of how shallow it was to judge people on their outward appearance like that. Look at how he'd judged Emma in her oversized clothes with her musical accessory as a refugee from the sixties. If fate hadn't stepped in and made it imperative that he give her a chance, he might never have discovered what an astonishing person lay beneath that appearance.

And fate had been responsible for discovering the real

reason for more and more of those 'shopping' trips that Tania had needed to keep her happy. Had she even worn half those clothes or had they only ever been a mask for her infidelity?

The presence of Tania's ghost was all he was aware of by the time Emma's head appeared through the hole.

'Oof… I feel like I'm climbing a mountain.'

The steps were certainly steep but shouldn't have been enough to make a young woman like Emma seem out of breath. Adam could feel his frown deepening as he automatically held out his hand to assist her. For a moment he thought she might refuse the offer but then he felt his hand grasped firmly as she climbed the last of the steps.

Like the children, Emma's eyes widened as she looked around. 'Oh, *wow*… This is a *real* attic. Full of *treasure*.'

She was grinning at Adam now and she still hadn't let go of his hand. He could feel the connection and it was warm and as alive as the sparkle in her eyes.

She'd never be able to cover up a lie, would she? Not with the way her emotions played over her face like this. The idea that she might need to lie felt ridiculous. The conviction that Emma would never be unfaithful to a man she loved came from nowhere.

So did the unexpected pang of something that felt like envy. Letting go of her hand didn't entirely dispel the disturbing sensation. Whoever it was, he would be a very lucky man.

'Ohh…' The gasp from Poppy was full of wonder. 'Look, Emma… It's a *pram*.'

She ran towards the part of the attic on the opposite side from where Tania's effects had been stored. Alongside an antique pram that had probably carried his grandmother and the double model that had been for the twins much more recently, was a smaller cane one. The one that had caught Poppy's eye had been made for small girls to carry dolls in. Adam had completely forgotten it was up here.

'Can I play with it, Daddy? *Please*?'

'Of course you can, chicken. We'll take it downstairs and clean all the dust off. I think it might have been Gran's when she was a little girl like you.'

Maybe it was the delight on Poppy's face or the warmth he could still feel from Emma's hand but the presence of Tania's ghost was receding. Being pushed into the past where it belonged by not only being in the present but thinking about the immediate future when they would all be safely downstairs and he could lock the old door again.

Poppy was squeaking with pleasure as she manoeuvred the cane pram out from behind the bigger wheels of the others. Oliver was not far away from her, peering into a tin trunk in front of a pile of old leather suitcases. His quietness wasn't unusual but the intent body language was unmistakeable.

'What have you found, Ollie?'

'I think it's a…*train*.'

It had been some time since he'd let go of Emma's hand. Odd that he still could feel the absence of it so strongly. Maybe moving further away from her would help. Adam walked towards his son.

'It *is* a train. An old wind-up one.' He lifted the heavy, metal engine from the trunk to hand to Oliver and then reached to pick up something else. 'These are the tracks that you can clip together. I used to play with it when I was your age, Ollie. And my father played with it when *he* was a little boy. I'm pretty sure he got it for a Christmas present one year.'

Oliver's face was solemn. 'That's what I'd like for *my* Christmas present.'

'You can't buy these now.' Emma had come over to look as well. 'They're very old and very special. Antiques. Adam, this is extraordinary. Is that a *harp* over there?'

'Aye.' There was a dusty, old cello keeping it company. Music had been in his family for generations. When had it stopped so completely? When his desire to make it had died along with the trauma of Tania's death?

Oliver was crouching beside the tin trunk with the train engine cradled in his arms.

Adam crouched down beside him. 'You don't have to wait till Christmas, Ollie. We'll take this downstairs, too, and you can play with it whenever you want.'

Oliver looked as though he couldn't believe his luck. As if something truly magic had just happened, and something squeezed inside Adam's chest. How easy it was to make children happy but he had never given a thought to the abandoned toys up here. He would never have thought of even unlocking that door if he hadn't remembered the Christmas decorations.

And he wouldn't have considered retrieving those if it hadn't been for Emma pushing him towards celebrating Christmas again.

Right now Emma was plucking the strings of the old harp, sending dust motes flying into the dim light in the attic. And she was singing...just softly. More of a hum really—as though she was in her own world and making music came as naturally as breathing.

Poppy had left the cane pram. She had a sad old teddy bear with an almost severed arm dangling from one hand and she was skipping through the gaps towards *that* corner.

Adam got to his feet hurriedly. 'Let's find those decorations,' he said. 'And get downstairs. I can hear Benji crying in the kitchen.'

But it was too late. Poppy had found the rack of dresses and her cry of delight made Emma stop playing with the harp and look up. Adam tried to distract them. He'd had an idea of where the boxes of decorations were and he flipped one open and held up a handful of tinsel and then a huge silver star.

'Here we are. Look at this star. Shall we put it on top of our tree?'

'Daddy…are these *Mummy's* dresses?'

The shocked look on Emma's face said it all. The ghost was here again. The tug of nostalgia and the pleasure in finding unexpected gifts for his children vanished. Now he could feel the pain of loss yet again. The *guilt*. The burden of the lie that kept the mother of his children as a perfect memory.

'It's a *blue* dress. Emma, look. You're going to make me a blue dress for when I'm Mary in the play, aren't you?'

'Um…yeah…' Emma had started to go towards Poppy but she'd stopped right beside Adam and she gave him an uncertain glance. 'Come on, sweetheart. We need to go downstairs. It's nearly teatime.'

But Poppy wouldn't let go of the folds of the shimmery, blue dress. 'Why are Mummy's clothes here, Daddy?'

Adam had to clear his throat. 'I…' What could he say? He'd had to get them out of sight and this had seemed the quickest and easiest solution? 'Maybe I thought you'd want them one day, Poppy.'

He hoped she wouldn't, he realised suddenly. He didn't want his daughter growing up to be consumed with keeping up appearances. Better that she didn't care.

That she was happy to wear baggy jumpers and peculiar, bright hats and could shine with an inner joy instead. Like Emma.

'I want this one *now*, Daddy. For the play.'

'It wouldn't fit you.'

'Emma could make it fit.'

'Could you?' Adam caught Emma's gaze again.

She still looked uncertain but nodded. 'I guess so… but…'

'That's settled, then.' Adam wanted to get out of there. As quickly as possible. 'You and Ollie go downstairs with Emma and I'll bring the dress down with the other things.'

Emma helped the children down the steps but then her head appeared again.

'You don't have to do this,' she said quietly. 'I can explain to Poppy. We can find some fabric to make her dress.'

'They're only clothes,' Adam growled. He shoved the rolled-up dress towards her. 'This one was never even worn—it's still got its label on it. They're only *clothes*,' he repeated, turning away to pick up a box. 'I should never have kept them.'

But Emma was still there when he went to put the box down close to the steps. 'You can still change your mind later.'

'I won't.'

'You might.' There was a curve to Emma's lips that suggested sympathy but she wasn't looking at his face. She was staring at the hand he had curled around the corner of the box of decorations. His left hand.

The one that still carried his wedding ring.

And then Emma was gone and he heard Poppy's excited voice fading as she went along the hallway, telling

Emma that she wanted the dress to be really long so that it floated on the ground.

It took time to get the treasures down the steps, especially when he had to unpack half the tin trunk because it was so heavy. Even in the inadequate light every movement seemed to create a glint on that gold band around his finger—an accessory he never normally noticed at all.

Why *was* he still wearing his wedding ring? Because everybody assumed that he kept it on as a tribute to a perfect marriage and they would have noticed the moment he'd removed it? A perfect marriage? Good grief… In the short time Emma had been here, it felt like she'd been more of a mother to his children than Tania had been. Guilt nipped on the heels of that admission. It wasn't something he'd ever needed to acknowledge—not when his mother had always been there to fill in the gaps that his nannies couldn't.

Or did he still wear the ring because he wanted to punish himself? To keep a permanent reminder of his failure as a husband in clear view?

It was, after all, *his* fault that his children were growing up without their mother, wasn't it? Had he been too absorbed in his work or too besotted with his babies to give Tania what she needed?

The ring had served its purpose even if he'd never articulated what that was. There had been times when the truth had been like acid, eating away at him, and he'd been desperate to tell someone. His mother or his sister perhaps. And then he'd touch the back of the ring with his thumb and would know that he couldn't.

Even the remote possibility that his children could learn the truth about their mother and be hurt by it was enough. This was a burden he had to carry alone. For ever.

He might have been wrong about there being no ghost in the attic but he'd been right when he'd worried about the ripple effect of things changing.

Unusually, he could actually *feel* that ring on his finger, without touching it with his thumb, late that night as he climbed the stairs to go to bed. They hadn't ended up decorating the tree after dinner because he'd spent the time before the children went to bed setting up the clockwork train set for Oliver, and Emma had been busy helping Poppy clean the cane pram. And when they'd looked into the box the children had been a little disappointed by the ornaments.

'They're all the same colour,' Poppy had pointed out. 'They're all *silver*.'

Of course they were. Everything Tania had done could have been photographed for a home and garden magazine, including the silver perfection of the family Christmas tree.

'I could get some special paint,' Emma had offered. 'And we could make them all sorts of colours...if that's all right with Daddy.'

Of course it was all right. How did she always seem to find an answer to everything that would make things better?

Would she have an answer to what he should do about the ring that seemed to be strangling his finger?

He could hear the soft sound of her singing again and, as had become a habit, he stopped before turning towards the other hallway and listened for a minute. The song was becoming hauntingly familiar, even though he was sure he'd never heard it before Emma had come into the house.

Was she sitting on her bed, with her guitar cradled on her lap and her head bent as she sang quietly? Did she have the fire going perhaps, with the light of the flames bringing out the flecks of red-gold he'd noticed in her hair sometimes?

The urge to find out was powerful. He could find an excuse to tap on her door, couldn't he? To reassure her that the blue dress meant nothing perhaps, and that she was more than welcome to cut it up to make Poppy's costume?

Any excuse would do, if it meant he could be close to her for an extra minute or two.

Because he was starting to feel lonely when he wasn't?

With a mental shake Adam stepped firmly towards his own room. She wasn't the first nanny his children had had and she probably wouldn't be the last. It was just as well this was a temporary position, though, because he'd never felt this way about any of the women who'd come to live here and look after his children before.

About any women he'd met in the last few years, come to that.

Maybe it was part of the ripple effect. The step forward. Something had been unlocked when he'd agreed that three years of grief was more than enough. Perhaps his body was following his heart and finally waking up again.

Three years of being celibate wasn't natural for anyone. It didn't mean that he had to fall for someone who happened to be in the near vicinity. It didn't mean he had to fall for anyone.

No. The last time that had happened had ended up almost ruining his life. He wasn't going to let it happen again.

Ever.

The solution, Adam decided over the next few days, was to focus on his work.

His priority in life was his children, of course, but

work came a close second. It had been his father, the first Dr McAllister, who'd built up this small general practice. Without it, the villagers would have to travel fifteen miles or so to the nearest town and a lot of them would find that difficult enough to make their health care precarious, especially in the middle of a harsh Scottish winter.

People like old Mrs Robertson, who needed dressings changed on her diabetic ulcers every couple of days and was on the list for this afternoon's house calls. And Joan McClintock, who had a phobia about getting into any vehicles smaller than a bus and was only happy when things were within walking distance. She was in the waiting room again this morning, as his somewhat disconcerting working week drew to a close.

At least here Adam could stop thinking about the Christmas tree in his living room sporting a rainbow of brightly painted balls that had only been the starting point for the hand-made decorations that Emma seemed to have unlimited inspiration about. Like the gingerbread stars she had baked last night and the children had helped to decorate with brightly coloured sweets.

It was probably just as well that the gingerbread was destined to be only decorative if Emma's baking skills were on a par with her cooking. The meals this week had been a fair step down from what his mother had left in the freezer. Not that the children had complained about the rather burnt sausages and that peculiar shepherd's pie. Everything Emma did was wonderful in Poppy's eyes and Oliver wasn't allowed to go and play with the clockwork train until he'd finished his dinner so even the carrots were disappearing in record time these days.

Adam found himself smiling as he walked through the waiting room. Miss McClintock looked surprised but nodded back at him. Old Jock, who was sitting in the corner, disappeared further under the brim of his cap. The smile faded. Old Jock—the farmer who owned the land behind his where the skating pond was located—was as tough as old boots. What was he doing in here, waiting to see the doctor?

And had he really thought that work was the solution to forgetting about the ripples disrupting his personal life?

It didn't help that Caitlin McMurray, the schoolteacher, came rushing in with a wailing small child even before he could call Joan McClintock into the consulting room.

'It's Ben,' she said. 'He jammed his finger in the art cupboard.'

'Come straight in,' Adam told her. 'Eileen, could you call Ben's mother, please, and get her to come in?'

'I can stay with him for a bit.' Caitlin had to raise her voice over the crying. 'Emma's practising carols with the children and the senior teacher's keeping an eye on everything.'

Adam eyed the handkerchief tied around Ben's finger. There was blood seeping through the makeshift dressing.

'Let's have a look at this finger, young man.'

'No-o-o... It's going to hurt.'

Distraction was needed. 'Did our Oliver tell you about the train he found in our attic?'

'Aye...but we didn't believe him.' Ben sniffed loudly. 'He said it's got a tunnel and a bridge even.'

'Well, it's true. It's a bonny wee train. I played with it when I was a wee boy, too.' Adam had the finger exposed now. A bit squashed but there were no bones broken. The pain was coming from the blood accumulating under the nail and that could be swiftly fixed with a heated needle.

'And he says he's bringing a donkey to the Christmas play.'

Adam raised his gaze to Caitlin's. 'Did the committee agree, then?'

'Aye. And that's not all. Have you heard about the recording?'

'What recording?'

'Moira Findlay heard about the children singing the carols and she came to listen. She says that Emma's got the voice of an angel and she's ne'er heard small children singing sae well. That's when we got the *idea.*'

'Oh?' Adam struck a match to get the end of a sterile needle hot enough. Ben was watching suspiciously.

'We're going to make a CD of the carols. To sell and raise funds to help fix the village hall. Or get a new piano for the school. Maybe both. She's amazing, isn't she, Dr McAllister?'

'It does sound like a grand idea. Moira's a clever woman.'

'Not Moira…' Caitlin laughed. 'I mean Emma. How lucky are we that she came to be the twins' nanny?'

'Look at that, Ben… Out the window… Was that a… *reindeer*?'

The split second it took for Ben to realise he'd been duped was enough to get near his nail with the needle and release the pressure. A single, outraged wail and then Ben stared at his finger and blinked in surprise.

'Not so sore now?' Adam swabbed it gently with some disinfectant. 'We'll put a nice big bandage on it and you can get back to singing your carols.'

With Emma.

'I hear she sings like an angel,' Joan McClintock informed him minutes later. 'Eileen says she might be joining the choir.'

'I don't know that she'll have time for that,' Adam

said. 'And she's only here until my mother gets back from Canada.'

'Och, well...we'll see about that, then, won't we?' The nod was knowing.

'Aye. We will.' Adam reached for the blood-pressure cuff. 'Now, let's see if that blood pressure's come down a wee bit. Are you still getting the giddy spells?'

Even Old Jock had something to say about Emma when it came to his turn.

'I'm losing my puff,' he told Adam. 'And it's no' helping with the pipes. Yon lassie o' yours saw me sittin' down after I was playin' in by the tree, like I always do at Christmastime. She tol' me to come and see you.'

'I'll have a listen to your chest,' Adam said. 'Your dad had problems with his heart, didn't he? We might do a test on that, too.'

'Aye.' Jock took his cap off. 'You do what you need to, lad. That lassie said you'd find out what was ailin' me.'

How could a complete stranger weave herself into the lives of other people so quickly? It seemed like the whole village was being touched by Emma's arrival in Braeburn. Maybe she didn't have a gypsy streak after all, because the sort of magic she was creating was more like that of a fairy.

A Christmas fairy.

And magic wasn't the only thing she was weaving. On Saturday afternoon, when it had stopped raining, they had taken Jemima down into the orchard so that Oliver could practise leading her, with Poppy riding. Not only had their little donkey proved herself very co-operative, Emma had spotted the greenery amongst the bare branches of an old apple tree.

'Is that mistletoe? *Real* mistletoe?'

'Aye. Looks like it.'

'Can we pick it?' Emma had asked. 'For Christmas?'

'It's poisonous,' Adam had told her. 'Causes gastrointestinal and cardiovascular problems.'

'We won't *eat* it, silly.' Emma had laughed. 'I'm going to make a wreath.'

So here she was, sitting at the kitchen table under all the paper chains, after the children were in bed, cutting sprigs of the mistletoe and weaving them around a circle she'd made with some wire she'd unearthed out in the barn. Adam had poured himself a wee dram to finish the day with and he paused to watch what she was doing.

'Where did it come from?' she asked. 'Do you know? The tradition of kissing under the mistletoe, that is.'

Kissing…

Adam stared down at Emma's deft hands weaving the sprigs into place. And at the back of her head, where the light was creating those copper glints in her curls. He took a mouthful of his whisky.

'It's very old,' he said. 'I've heard that it got hung somewhere and the young men had the privilege of kissing the girls underneath it, but every time they did they had to pick one of the berries, and when the berries had all been picked, the privilege ceased.'

Emma held up the half-finished wreath with its clusters of waxy white berries. 'It's got a lot of them,' she said, tilting her head to smile up at Adam.

That did it. The magic was too strong to resist. Adam put his glass down and then reached out and plucked one of the tiny berries from the wreath.

Emma's eyes widened. 'You can't do that,' she objected. 'You haven't kissed a girl.'

Adam didn't say anything. He just leaned down until there was no mistaking his intention.

And Emma didn't turn her face away. If anything, she tilted her chin so that her lips parted, and for a heartbeat—and then two—she held his gaze.

There was surprise in those blue eyes. She hadn't expected this but, then, neither had Adam. And she could feel the magic, too—he was sure of that, because there was a kind of wonder in her eyes as well.

Joy was always lurking there, he suspected, but this was an invitation to share it. An invitation no man could resist.

The moment his lips touched Emma's, the tiny white berry fell from his fingers and rolled somewhere under the table. Adam wasn't aware of dropping it. He was aware of nothing but the softness of Emma's lips and the silky feel of her curls as he cupped her head in his hand. And then he was aware of a desire for more than this kiss. A fierce shaft of desire that came from nowhere and with more force than he'd ever felt in his life.

He had to break the contact. Step back. Wonder how on earth he was going to deal with what had just happened when his senses were still reeling.

Emma's eyes were closed. He liked it that she'd closed her eyes. And then she sighed happily and smiled. There was no embarrassment in her eyes when she opened them. No expectation that any explanation or apology was needed.

'There you go,' she said softly. 'That's where it came from, I guess. Mistletoe is magical. I'd better finish this and hang it somewhere safe.'

'Aye.' Adam drained the rest of his whisky and took the glass to the sink.

What did she mean by 'safe'? Somewhere he couldn't find it or somewhere he *could*?

He hoped she wanted to put it somewhere he could find it.

There were a lot of berries left on those twigs.

CHAPTER SEVEN

FOR THE FIRST time in her life Emma Sinclair understood why they called it 'falling' in love.

Because she could feel that her balance was teetering. That there was a chasm very nearby that she couldn't afford to fall into. She could get hurt.

Or hurt someone else.

Poppy and Oliver perhaps?

Or Adam?

Her hands stilled in their task of hemming, sinking to end up in the folds of the silky blue dress puddled in her lap, as she stared through the window. It was snowing, she realised with a childish bubble of excitement.

And then she remembered the kiss yet again and the bubble exploded into something decidedly more adult and compelling.

Desire—pure and simple.

Except it wasn't that simple, was it? Oh, she'd noticed how good looking Adam McAllister was in the first moments of meeting him but she'd been a little afraid of him, too, if she was honest. The fierceness of him. The gruffness that came across as anger. The hidden depths that she'd glimpsed on that awful night when he'd ripped down the paper chains and caused the fire. And now she could add the capacity for passion into what this man was keeping hidden because she'd felt it in the touch of his lips.

She'd glimpsed the softer side to him as well, in the love he had for his children and the bond he had with his dogs. Pulling her gaze away from the softly drifting snowflakes, Emma glanced towards the fire. Benji lay on his back like a puppy, his speckled belly exposed, but Bob had his nose on his paws and he was watching Emma. She could swear that the old dog knew exactly what she was thinking and that the liquid gaze was encouraging.

He's worth loving, it seemed to say. *You won't be sorry.*

'But I can't, Bob.' Emma actually spoke aloud. 'I'm only here for a little bit longer.'

Time didn't matter to dogs, though, did it? They took their joy as it appeared, with no questions asked. Even if they were old or sick, they could still be in the moment and experience that joy a hundred per cent.

People could learn a lot from dogs. Especially people who could be facing a terminal illness?

What if she let herself fall for Adam—even if it was only for a blink in time? It wasn't just for the small McAllister family that she'd resolved to make this the best-ever Christmas for, was it?

If it was going to be *her* last Christmas, shouldn't she make it the best ever one for herself, too?

'It's been *such* a long time, Bob,' she whispered.

Such a long time since she had been loved…

Dear Lord, but it was tempting.

Bob's ears were pricked now. He looked like he was asking her a question and Emma found herself smiling at the dog. No—she didn't *have* to disappear right after Christmas, when Catherine McAllister returned, did she? Adam was still going to need a nanny and it wasn't as if she had another job prospect lined up. She didn't need to work at all, in actual fact, because the small inheritance from her mother would be enough for quite some time.

But she couldn't offer Adam anything real. She didn't do that kind of commitment. How could she, when she couldn't offer any guarantee of permanence? When, instead, she could be sentencing someone to share things no one would choose to share.

And he wouldn't want it anyway, would he? The blue of the fabric in her lap seemed to glow more brightly. How could anyone compete with the ghost of the perfect wife and mother? The love of his life that had been tragically ripped away from him and their beloved children?

The recently changed ring tone on her phone was for Christmas and Bob got to his feet as 'Jingle Bells' began. It was getting louder by the time Emma found the phone beneath the shimmery blue fabric.

'It'll be Sharon, I expect,' she said, as Bob gave her hand a helpful nudge.

Except it wasn't.

'*Jack…*' It was such a surprise to hear from him. A shock even, because it pulled her back instantly to somewhere she'd managed to distract herself from completely in the last couple of weeks.

'Hey, Emma. How's it going up there in the wilds of Scotland?'

'It's snowing,' she told him happily. 'And it's just gorgeous. What's it like in London?'

'Cold and grey. No snow. That's why I thought I'd pop up for a visit next week.'

'What?' Emma blinked. The relationship was a complicated mix sometimes and she wasn't sure if he was wearing his 'close friend' or 'oncologist' hat right now. '*Why*?'

'I'm meeting with an oncology guru who happens to

be over from the States, tracing his family tree. I must have told you about that international research project we're both involved in. Jenny says I bore everyone with it.' He chuckled, unrepentant. 'Anyway, I said I'd fly up for the day and then I had this idea and got hold of a mate who works in the infirmary in Edinburgh. I pulled a few strings but...how would you feel about having your BMT and maybe getting the results by Christmas?'

'Oh...' Emma had to swallow hard. The unpleasant prospect of having a bone-marrow aspiration done for testing had been off her agenda until she got back to London. 'I'm...not sure how I feel about that, Jack. I...' Oh, help. She could hear the wobble in her voice that threatened tears. 'I was trying to forget about it, you know? To make this Christmas really special, in case...in case...'

'I know.' There was a short silence and then Jack's voice was gentle. 'Things are going to shut down for a while down here, what with Christmas and then New Year. And the baby's not far off making an appearance, which could complicate things a bit for me, but it's entirely your call. It was just an idea.'

Another silence as Emma's mind raced. She would be thinking about it again now, wouldn't she? Distraction would get harder. It could spoil things.

She heard Jack clear his throat. 'How 'bout this for another idea? Get the test done and, if the result comes through in time and it's what we hope it's going to be, I can give it to you as your Christmas present. And we can all really celebrate.'

He was including Sharon in that 'we'. They'd got on famously from the moment they'd first met and had worked closely together to get Emma through the toughest of times.

'And if it isn't?' Emma's voice was so soft she didn't think Jack would hear her but he did.

'Then we'll deal with it. After Christmas.'

Emma closed her eyes. That errant thought that she could perhaps stay in Braeburn longer than originally intended was still lurking in the back of her head and it would be much more convenient to pop over to Edinburgh for the test than go all the way back to London. And the result of that test couldn't possibly be devastating, could it, given that she was feeling so good at the moment? The physical exhaustion that used to ambush her all the time had virtually disappeared so she knew she was getting stronger every day. How amazing would it be to get confirmation of something so wonderful as a Christmas gift?

'Okay...Let me find a pen and paper and I'll take down the details.'

It was proving to be a long day for Adam. Another one where it was difficult to separate his professional and personal lives.

He couldn't blame his patients for making Emma's presence felt in his consulting room or when he was making his house calls, though. No...it was his own disobedient mind.

Or maybe he should blame his body.

He hadn't touched a woman in that way since his wife had died. Hadn't even thought of touching like that, let alone *kissing* someone.

And it wouldn't go away. The memory of how soft her lips had been. How sweet the taste of her had been. The shaft of desire for more that had been sharp enough to be both a physical and emotional pain.

Maybe that was what was making his mouth go a little dry at intervals today and increasing his heart rate until he could feel it thumping against his ribs. Too much adrenaline being produced. And why?

He knew if he looked a little more closely, he would know exactly why.

Fear.

Fear of being inadequate.

What man wouldn't have lost confidence? Especially when avoidance had been the defence method of choice and it was now ingrained as a way of life? His children, his work and his community. Those were the things he could do and do well. Being a husband or even a lover?

That was what he wasn't so sure of any more.

He'd always been good at avoidance, too. Even way back he'd made allowances for Tania's dissatisfaction. She was a city girl, born and bred, so of course she found a small village like Braeburn boring to the point of suffocation.

Emma was a city girl, too, wasn't she? She seemed to love village life but it was just a change for her. A very temporary change. Maybe the novelty would wear off.

Adam drove back to the medical centre that afternoon after visiting a sick baby on a farm that lay on the very outskirts of his practice area. It was starting to snow lightly and the stone walls and hedgerows looked like they were being dusted with icing sugar. The fairy-lights on the village shops were twinkling merrily and the tree in the square couldn't have looked any more perfect.

He could see Old Jock over by the pub with his bagpipes under his arm. Hopefully, he'd go in by the fire and have a wee dram instead of getting too cold, serenading the village. He'd have to chase up those test results when he got back to his office. Something was going on with Jock and while nothing obvious had been noticeable when he'd examined the older man the other day, Adam wasn't happy about it.

He cared deeply about the people of Braeburn. *His* people. It wasn't just the physical beauty of this place that made it paradise for those who could see it. It was the embrace of a community tight enough to seem like an extended family with both its positive—supportive—side and the more negative—intrusive—one.

Eileen was in position, as always, guarding the reception desk, when he got back to the medical centre.

'Any calls while I've been out?'

'No' yet.' Eileen clicked her tongue. 'There will be, mind… It's snowing.'

'Aye.'

'Someone will fall over and break something, you mark my words.'

Adam smiled and Eileen looked shocked.

'It's no laughin' matter, Dr McAllister.'

'No.'

But the smile still lingered as he went into his office to make some calls. He needed to chase up Old Jock's results and ring to see how the Jessops' premature baby was doing. Still touch and go as far as he knew, but at least the little scrap was hanging in there.

And then he would be able to go home to be with his children and his dogs. And Emma… His home. His family.

It felt like the first time in his adult life that Adam wanted to be at home as much as he wanted to be at work.

Or was that unfair?

The twins had only been babies and then toddlers while Tania had been alive. Even with the help of a nanny it had been exhausting. It was no wonder that she'd demanded to be spoilt in the times he wasn't at work. To be taken out for a candlelit dinner or away to Edinburgh or London for a shopping spree. Away from home. Away from Braeburn. Away from their children…

But he couldn't deny that it had felt so much more *like* a family since Emma had come into their lives. There was music in the house. A Christmas tree in the living room. Secrets being planned and the excitement of the upcoming Christmas production that was making life crazily busy all of a sudden.

The idea came to him from somewhere out of left field.

Did Emma really love being here as much as she seemed to?

Could she be persuaded to stay *longer*?

It wasn't fear that made his heart rate pick up this time. It was something far more positive but still enough to make him feel oddly nervous. Hope, perhaps?

Amazingly, the snow hadn't been enough to stop the playing of the pipes that Emma was coming to rely on as being a highlight of her new daily routine. It had stopped falling for the moment and the roads were still clear but it was breathtakingly cold and she couldn't sit on the bench because it would be damp even if she swept off the thin white covering.

The village centre was busy. There was a delicious smell coming from the bakery and a cluster of people outside the general store. The women saw her walk past and, instead of pretending not to, one of them nodded in her direction. The acknowledgement came without a smile but it was enough to make Emma grin and wave back. Maybe if she stopped wearing her silly Tibetan hat, she would get a smile next time.

The pipes sounded a little strange today. Had it been

harder to warm them up because it was so cold? Sharon would say that some of those notes sounded like a cat being skinned alive and she wouldn't be far wrong.

No wonder the man in the kilt stopped and lowered his instrument to stare at it in dismay.

But…to drop it?

Emma was just registering how wrong the scene in front of her was when she saw the man crumple and fall. Dropping her guitar case, she ran towards him. She'd done a first-aid course before she'd got sick herself. She knew to turn him over and check to see if he was breathing and try to see if he had a pulse.

To start CPR and shout for help.

'Get Dr McAllister,' she heard someone shout. 'Tell him it's Old Jock who needs him.'

'Call an ambulance,' someone else said. 'He looks right poorly…'

It didn't seem like any time at all until the gathering crowd of onlookers parted for Adam's arrival. He was out of breath and carrying his bag in one hand and a large piece of equipment in the other. His ferocious-looking receptionist wasn't far behind either, cradling an oxygen cylinder in her arms.

'You're doing a good job, Emma. Can you keep it up while I get organised?'

'Sure.' Emma ignored the pain from the icy cobbles beneath her knees. She bit her lip and concentrated on where she had her hands—in the middle of the chest—and how hard and fast to push.

Had it been only a matter of weeks ago that expending this much energy would have been impossible? She just had to keep it up. The last thing Adam needed right now was to have someone else collapsing.

'Okay—stop for a moment.' The buttons on the man's

waistcoat popped as Adam ripped it open. The buttons on a shirt went the same way but the singlet beneath needed a cut with shears before it would tear. And then Adam attached sticky pads to the bony chest and turned to look at the screen on the equipment he'd brought.

'Move right back, Emma. Make sure you're not touching him. I'm going to give him a shock.'

Emma—and all those watching—got a shock as well, seeing the body jerk in front of them, but she didn't have time to wallow in feeling horrified.

'Start compressions again,' Adam ordered.

'I can help the lassie.' A big man was kneeling beside her. 'I've learned how to do this.'

'Good man, Bryan. Emma—can you hold this, please? And come up by his head. I need a hand to get a tube in so we can breathe for him.'

The next few minutes were a blur. How could Adam stay so calm? He slipped a tube down the man's throat and attached it to a bag that he showed Emma how to squeeze. He put an IV line into an arm and drew up and administered drugs without any discernible shake to his hands.

Emma was shaking like a leaf now from a combination of the horror and the cold.

'Can someone ring and find out how far away the ambulance is?'

'They're sending a helicopter,' someone said moments later. 'It's going to land on the school field. They need people to check that there are no loose objects the snow might be hiding.'

Several people peeled away from the anxious group. 'We'll do that,' a man called. 'And warn the bairns what's going to happen.'

Emma fought off a wave of dizziness. She focused on

holding the bag and squeezing it. Counting to ten slowly and then squeezing it again.

'You're doing really well.'

The words were quiet. Only Emma and the big man doing the compressions would have heard it. Bryan didn't look up from his task but Emma did. She met Adam's dark gaze and found encouragement there. Pride even?

She had to swallow an unexpected lump in her throat.

'Do...do we need to send someone to find blankets? It's s-so cold...'

'It's a good thing for Old Jock,' Adam said. 'Sometimes we make patients cold deliberately to protect them from the effects of a cardiac arrest.' He looked away. 'I'll take over in a sec, Bryan. Stand clear, both of you, now. I'm going to try another shock.'

Everyone had to be holding their breath to account for the silence that followed after the warning alarm and then the clunk of the machine delivering its charge. They could hear the beat of the approaching helicopter. And then another sound, much closer. A steady blip, blip, blip that was coming from the machine.

'Is that...?'

'Aye.' Adam caught her gaze again. 'We still need to help him with his breathing but we've got a heartbeat.'

There was triumph in those eyes now. Joy even. A ripple ran through the onlookers that suggested pride in their local doctor. Confirmation that their trust in him was not misplaced.

And then the helicopter crew was there, in their bright overalls and with even more equipment. Old Jock was put onto a stretcher.

'Can you come with us, Doc?'

'Of course.' But Adam turned back to Emma. 'I have

no idea when I'll get home. It could be tricky finding transport back from Edinburgh.'

'I could come and get you.'

'What about the children? It'll be too late to be dragging them out.'

'I can take the bairns,' a woman said. 'It's no problem.' She smiled at Emma. 'I'm Jeannie's mother. Jeannie's Poppy's friend. She'd love to have a sleepover.'

Emma saw the look on Adam's face. He never asked these people for help, did he? She could understand that he might want to protect his fierce independence but these were *his* people. They cared about him just as much as he obviously cared about them.

'Leave it with me,' she told him. 'I'll call you.'

How ironic was it that she was practising the run to the big hospital in Edinburgh, having only made her arrangements with Jack hours before?

Fate seemed to be stepping in again. It had been so easy to arrange care for the children. A very excited Poppy had gone home with Jeannie for the night and Oliver was having his first-ever sleepover at his friend Ben's house.

It made it easy to ask Adam what she needed to ask, after the initial conversation and reassurance that Jock was getting the best treatment possible had faded into silence.

Thank goodness Adam was driving. Emma had used up every ounce of energy she had and she knew she would fall asleep very soon. Maybe it was sheer exhaustion that stopped her feeling hesitant in making her request.

'Would it be all right if I had a day off next week?

I've…got a kind of appointment in Edinburgh that I need to go to.'

'Of course you can have a day off. You haven't had one since you came. I keep telling you I can cope at the weekends.'

'The thing is…it's a weekday, not the weekend, and I'd need to stay the night. The…ah…appointment's late so I'd need to wait until the next day to get the train back. It would be fine for the children to stay with their friends again. I…um…checked.'

The sideways look she received was disconcerting. It reminded her of that first time she'd met Adam, when he'd looked at her as if she was the last person he'd want to be looking after his children. The atmosphere in the car suddenly felt like it had on that first day, too, when he'd driven her home and she'd been imagining his wife buried somewhere under the driveway.

It did sound dodgy, didn't it? A late-night appointment? And it was on a day that would make child care a challenge for him and she'd taken a huge liberty in tentatively making arrangements herself. But she couldn't tell him the truth or he might realise he *had* made a mistake in trusting her with his children. That she was sick and…and unreliable.

'It's a…job interview…' she heard herself saying. Unconvincingly? She tried again. 'Music's my first love. That's why I don't take on full-time or permanent jobs. I'm seeing someone about the possibility of a future gig.'

That wasn't so far from the truth, was it? It was just about her whole future and not just a gig.

The silence kept growing. Becoming more and more loaded with every passing second, but Adam was being assaulted by unpleasant emotions.

Had he really thought Emma was incapable of lying? It was *obvious* she was not telling the truth right now. He could hear echoes of Tania.

There's a sale on... It's my favourite designer, darling... It's only for a day...maybe two...

But it wasn't fair not to trust Emma because of the skill with which Tania had manipulated him.

He wanted to trust her. So much.

And it wasn't her fault that it was so hard.

Finally—too late—he managed a grunt in response. But he couldn't meet her eyes. He had to keep staring at the road ahead of them.

'Do what you need to,' he growled. 'I'll cope.'

Emma woke up as the car jolted over the tree roots on the driveway and, almost instantly, found herself shivering.

It wasn't just the physical cold, although there was enough snow now for her feet to crunch through it as she followed Adam up the steps to the front door.

This was an emotional chill, too.

Adam McAllister had gone back into his shell, hadn't he? Back to being the man who never really smiled and who couldn't bear the celebration of something as joyous as Christmas.

And all because she'd asked for a day off?

No. Emma knew there was more to it than that. Maybe it was the way Adam was avoiding both eye contact and any conversation as they went into the house. Or it could have been the way Bob shot her an almost accusing look before going quietly to his master's side. Most likely, it was catching sight of the mistletoe wreath that Emma had hung in the corner near the coat stand that made it crystal clear.

This was about the kiss.

About *her.*

The desire wasn't one-sided, was it? But Adam didn't know what to do about it because he was still caught in his grief and she'd just made it clear that she couldn't wait to move on—to another *gig.*

For once Adam wasn't rushing into the kitchen where he'd drop his coat over the back of the nearest chair or on the arm of the sofa. He was taking it off slowly and deliberately and clearly intended hanging it on the rack.

Slowly enough for Emma to have another blinding moment of clarity.

She'd thought she had nothing to offer Adam but she had been wrong.

Catherine would applaud the fact that she'd pushed him into allowing Christmas into his house for the sake of the children but…what if she could give him—give *all* of them—more than that?

This man deserved to be loved again.

The children desperately needed a mother, not just a series of nannies.

How perfect would it be if it could be her?

But, if it couldn't, she could still help. She could help him take that first step. They had the house to themselves. Nobody but she and Adam need know.

Maybe the real gift she could give Adam was the permission to be really happy again? To show him what it *could* be like.

She could offer Adam hope. A belief that it was possible. He was an outstanding doctor and father but she could help him get over that huge barrier he'd put around himself as a man.

'Adam?' Slipping out of her own coat, Emma stood beside him at the coat rack. 'I'm sorry… I don't have to go to that appointment in Edinburgh. It's not that I don't want to be here with you and children. It's just that—'

'It doesn't matter. I told you that.'

'But it does,' Emma said softly. 'I don't want to make things difficult. I know I'm not here for very long but I want this to be a special time—one that will make special memories—for all of us…'

Herself included. The whisper in the back of her mind reminded her that this could turn out to be her last Christmas. She had nothing to lose. Adam had everything to gain.

Oh, help…he was standing so very still. His eyes were closed.

When his eyes slowly opened, he wasn't looking down at Emma. He was looking up—at the mistletoe wreath. And then he reached up and picked a whole bunch of those little, waxy white berries.

Finally, he made eye contact and the smouldering depths in those dark eyes stole Emma's breath.

And her heart.

He might be fighting it but he *wanted* her.

Needed her.

Emma had to close her eyes because her own wanting and needing was overwhelming and this had to be Adam's decision. His choice.

She heard his deep groan. And then she felt him move. One arm went around her waist and the other caught the back of her legs. She was scooped up as if she weighed almost nothing and she held on tightly and buried her face against his neck, allowing herself to sink into total trust as Adam carried her upstairs.

To his bed.

* * *

She felt so light in his arms. Thin enough to seem fragile as he set her down gently onto her feet when he'd reached his room and pushed the door shut with his foot to keep the dogs out.

To keep the whole world out.

Emma's arms were still around his neck as her feet touched the floor and she must have stayed on tiptoe to reach his lips with her own so easily.

There was nothing fragile about that kiss. He could feel only the strength of her desire and a need that was as great as his own for the comfort of intimate, human touch.

It had been *so* long. Adam's hands slipped beneath the woollen jumper to feel skin that was like silk. Small, firm breasts that seemed to push themselves into his hands and nipples that were as hard as tiny pebbles.

Touching them with his hands wasn't enough. Not nearly enough. As blissful as it was, kissing Emma, he needed his mouth and his lips to savour other parts of her perfect body.

A tug on her clothing seemed to be enough. Emma dropped her arms and stepped back. Just far enough to grasp her jumper herself and peel it off over her head. And then she began to unbutton her shirt but Adam stilled her hands.

'Let me.'

His fingers fumbled with the tiny buttons and Adam realised, to his horror, that they were shaking. She wasn't watching his hands, though. As he looked up he found she was watching his face. Waiting for a contact that went so much deeper than physical touch. And when he gave it to her, he couldn't look away.

Could he do this? Could he love Emma in the way she deserved to be loved? Without disappointing her?

Emma could feel the tears in her eyes as she felt the way Adam's hands were trembling.

This big, strong man who could save a life and do such intricate manoeuvres with those hands without the slightest tremor couldn't hide his emotions in this moment.

This was huge. So huge that Adam was nervous. It wouldn't last. She knew that as soon as they got over this awkward moment of shedding their clothing and they could touch each other properly, any doubts or nerves on either side would cease to exist.

But in this brief moment of such vulnerability she realised just how much she loved Adam. She wouldn't only be giving him her body tonight. She would be giving him her heart—for as long as he wanted it.

Or as long as fate would allow.

And maybe something of what she was feeling was communicated as they held each other's gaze for such a long, long moment, because she felt that trembling stop. She saw the doubt vanish from Adam's eyes and could see something that seemed to mirror what she was feeling herself. A reflection—or was Adam gifting her *his* heart?

And then she could see—or maybe sense—the moment that desire ignited and there was nothing but the need to be as close as physically possible. There was no further awkwardness. Anything that was going to stop them being skin to skin seemed to be discarded as easily as ice melting in hot sunshine.

Adam flicked back the bed covers and then drew Emma against his body. In a heartbeat they would be lying on that bed together but she loved it that he stopped to gaze at her for a moment longer. To bend his head and give her such a tender kiss that promised he would look after her.

That he intended to make this night unforgettable.

Not that Emma had the slightest doubt that this would be the case but she loved being given the promise. Along with her body and her heart, Adam McAllister had just won her lifelong trust.

CHAPTER EIGHT

THE MAGIC WAS getting stronger.

Emma's gift to Adam had been received so well it seemed that he wanted to unwrap it all over again the following night, and Emma was only too happy to participate, tiptoeing into Adam's room when the children were fast asleep.

How amazing that the same gift could be given in both directions.

And that parts of it could be given to others without them knowing how or why it was happening?

They were being very careful to make sure the children didn't realise what had changed between them but the magic was still happening.

The new connection between Adam and Emma was sending out tendrils that were touching the children. Making them all feel like a family.

Like when naughty Benji had mistaken the old teddy Poppy carried everywhere now, for a dog toy and had grabbed its leg. Poppy had tried to keep hold of it but ended up pulling off the damaged arm and she had been distraught.

'Emma can fix it,' Adam consoled her.

'Daddy can fix it,' Emma said at the same time.

They looked at each other and smiled.

'You're good at sewing,' Adam said. 'I've seen that pretty dress you made Poppy for the play.'

'You're the doctor,' she said solemnly. 'An amputated arm is much more in your line of work.'

'Aye…' Adam nodded thoughtfully but his eyes held a mischievous glint. 'I'll need a scrub nurse, though.'

'I love new jobs.' It was hard not to grin but Poppy was still sobbing.

'We need a clean sheet,' Adam told her, 'so we've got an operating table. Ollie? Can you go and bring my doctor bag, please?'

It was a treat, turning the small disaster into a game that the children were fascinated by. With a clean sheet on the table, Adam pretended to give teddy an anaesthetic with a nebuliser. He'd found masks and gloves for both he and Emma to wear and he seemed more than happy to use up other medical supplies, like the suture kit.

It might have been a game but watching Adam draw the teddy's furry fabric together and make the complicated-looking knots of real sutures impressed Emma as much as it did the children. Their father was doing his important, *real* work at home. For teddy.

'Pay attention, scrub nurse,' Adam growled at one point. 'You have to cut the thread now.'

Emma giggled and, after a startled moment, so did both the children.

Teddy's arm got bandaged when the operation was finished and then he got sent off to Intensive Care in Poppy's bedroom because it was bedtime. Ollie got to carry him because he'd been promoted to orderly.

'I'll bet they'll remember that for the rest of their lives,' Emma told Adam later that night as she lay in his arms yet again. 'The night Daddy operated on teddy.'

'I think I'll remember it,' Adam replied quietly. 'It was special.'

'Magic,' Emma agreed happily.

'Aye…' Adam bent his head to kiss her again. 'Like you…'

The newest member of the Braeburn McAllister clan was born in the new light of the day after teddy's surgery.

Everyone in the village assumed that was why Dr McAllister was looking so happy. He had a bonny new niece and everybody was fine and his mother would head home in a couple of weeks and life would carry on just the same but better.

'They've called the wee lassie Holly—did you hear? Because she's been born sae close to Christmas.'

If anyone wondered why that Miss Sinclair seemed to be just as happy as the rest of the family, even though she was no relation to the new bairn, they just gave each other knowing looks. She was always a happy wee thing, wasn't she? A bit different, mind, with strange clothes and carrying her guitar with her everywhere, but you couldn't say a word against how she looked after those twins and the way she was getting involved with the school's Christmas production and even with the fund-raising for the hall committee.

And, oh, my…she *could* sing like a wee angel, couldn't she?

Phone calls and texts and photographs pinged between Scotland and Canada but it was a couple of days before everything came together well enough for a family gathering, courtesy of an online video chat.

Marion and Holly were back home already with Ian—the proud husband and new father—and Catherine was using her tablet. Adam had set up his desktop computer in the living room. With a fire burning merrily in the grate and the lights on the Christmas tree twinkling, it seemed the perfect background for a digital reunion, but Catherine McAllister seemed overwhelmed by the initial visual contact.

'Oh…is that a…a…*Christmas* tree?'

'It's *our* Christmas tree, Gran…' Poppy leaned in close to the computer screen to make sure her grandmother could see her properly. 'Emma helped us paint the balls and we sticked the sweets on the stars and we made paper chains and…and *everything*.'

Catherine probably couldn't see anything except Poppy's nose, Emma thought, but there was no mistaking the pride and joy the small girl was radiating. She could see the screen but she was staying out of range of the camera, sitting on the floor near the fire, flanked by Bob and Benji.

There was no mistaking the voice thickened by tears from the other end of the connection either.

'That's wonderful, darling. It's the most beautiful Christmas tree I've ever seen. Emma's clever, isn't she?'

'Aye.' Adam gently pulled Poppy's head back to allow a wider camera view. 'She's made a dress for Poppy, too. For the school play. I told you that Jemima's going to be in the production, didn't I?'

Laughter came from behind Catherine and the picture on the screen changed angles sharply. They got a view of polished wooden floorboards and then feet and then the picture settled on a young woman sitting in an armchair with a small bundle in her arms. She could be Adam's twin, not just his sister, Emma thought. With that same dark hair and eyes and a smile that was so like Adam's when he was really happy.

She'd seen that smile so often in the last few days. Everyone had and it was contagious. There was so much laughter in this house now and even people in the village seemed to be smiling more.

'Are you trying to upstage me, Adam? Creating havoc in the village so nobody's got time to talk about my wee Holly? Whose crazy idea was it to take our donkey into the hall?'

'*Emma's*,' the twins chorused.

Oliver pushed past Poppy to take centre stage. 'Aunty Marion—can you come and see our play? I'm going to be Joseph and I get to lead Jemima until we get to the stage and I've got a…a rib that Emma made out of a sheet—'

'Robe,' Adam supplied.

'And I wear a stripy tea towel on my head and Emma's made a special rope thing to hold it on and…'

And Marion was laughing again. 'I can't come this time, pet. I have to be here to look after wee Holly. But *next* year we'll all be back in Braeburn and we'll all come and see the play.'

'But Jemima won't be in it next year.'

And I won't be here, Emma thought. She had to dip her head and swallow hard.

'I think I need to meet this Emma,' Marion declared. 'Where is she?'

'She's here.' Adam turned away from the computer and held out his hand. 'Come over, Emma. Come and meet my sister and our new niece.'

She couldn't not respond to that outstretched hand. To the invitation in those eyes and the smile she was coming to love more and more. With the children standing in front of them, nobody would notice that Adam caught her hand when she got close enough, would they? Or that he laced his fingers through hers and kept holding it as Emma smiled at the screen.

'Hi, Marion. Congratulations. I've seen the pictures of Holly and she's just gorgeous.'

Adam squeezed her hand and it was automatic to look up and return his smile. Hard to look away quickly enough to avoid making it obvious that her relationship with her employer had undergone a radical change recently.

Marion looked away from the screen for a moment, her face a question mark. Was she exchanging a significant look with her mother? But then she was smiling again, possibly even more widely than before.

'I hear you can sing,' she said. 'That you—and the children of Braeburn school—are about to become rich and famous.'

Emma laughed. 'I don't think so. But a local radio station got hold of the story about us making a CD of Christmas carols as a fundraiser. They've organised a bus to take us all into a recording studio and they're going to make it available as a download so lots of people can buy it. With a bit of luck, we'll be able to fix up the hall *and* get a new piano for the school.'

The twins were feeling left out.

'I've got a train, Aunty Marion. It's on the floor by the tree, see?'

'No, I can't see it, pet.'

'I'll get the engine and *show* you.' Oliver wriggled between Adam and Emma and they had to break their handhold.

'And I've got a bear.' Poppy held it up and pressed it against the computer screen. 'Benji pulled him and the arm felled off but Daddy and Emma poperated it and it's all better now.'

'Good heavens...that's *my* old bear,' came Catherine's voice.

'We found it in the attic when we went up to hunt out the Christmas decorations,' Adam explained. 'You don't mind, do you? Ollie's train was the one I had when I was his age. I'd forgotten it was even there.'

'Of course I don't mind.' Catherine's eyes were suspiciously bright. 'It's wonderful that you found things to use again. Oh...I wish I was there with you. You all look *so* happy.'

If they hadn't noticed anything significant in the glance Adam and Emma had exchanged before, they would surely pick up on something this time as Adam turned to Emma and smiled.

'We are,' he said.

'But what on earth did you do to the bear to fix it?'

'A poperation,' Poppy shouted. 'I *told* you.'

'An *operation*.' Emma was laughing. 'Daddy got a special needle and thread from his doctor's bag and sewed teddy's arm back on.'

'I growled at Benji,' Poppy added. 'And he looked sad.'

'Is Benji going to be in the play, too?' Marion asked.

''Course not.' Oliver was back with the train engine. 'He's a *dog*.'

'Maybe he could pretend to be a sheep?'

'No.' Adam shook his head. 'Don't go putting ideas in their heads, Miri. You're as bad as Emma. We've got more than enough going on right now. I'm helping to shift hay bales into the hall tomorrow. Bryan from the pub is making a manger.'

The connection crackled and the picture pixelated for a moment. By the time it cleared, baby Holly was crying and it was hard to hear conversation.

'We'd better go,' Adam said. 'It's very late for you.

We'll try again on Christmas Day, aye? Children—come and blow a kiss to your wee cousin.'

With a chorus of 'Miss you' and 'Love you lots' the call ended. For a moment the blankness of the screen seemed to dampen the atmosphere in the room.

Emma groaned. 'Oh, no…we forgot to sing the carol for the baby.'

The twins were good at speaking in unison. 'Deck the halls with boughs of *holly…*'

They were also good at looking equally disappointed.

'Never mind. We needed to practise a bit more anyway. We'll be extra-good at it for Christmas Day.'

But Poppy's lip wobbled and Oliver hugged the train engine more tightly.

'It's almost bedtime but why don't we have a quick practice now? Maybe Daddy could record it on his phone and we could *send* it to Gran and Aunty Marion.'

'I'll get your kit-ar,' Poppy offered.

'No.' Oliver glared at her. 'That's *my* job.'

Happiness had been restored yet again, thanks to Emma's way of dealing with problems.

No. Maybe it was being created rather than restored.

That was certainly the case for Adam, he realised much later that night as he held Emma in his arms yet again.

She was asleep but he pressed a gentle kiss to the top of her head and the pressure seemed to bounce back in a shaft that went straight to his chest, where it encased his heart and squeezed it tightly.

Was this what happiness felt like?

But this was something he'd never felt before and he knew there had been times he'd been happy. His childhood had been a happy one. He'd been secure and loved and he'd had friends and he'd loved school and his music lessons. It had been Old Jock who'd taught him to play the bagpipes and he'd been so proud that Christmastime when his pupil had been chosen to be the lone piper for the school production. He'd never said anything to Adam in the years since he'd stopped playing but he knew how happy the old man would be if he confessed that he was ready to pick up his pipes again.

Thank goodness Emma had been there and had known what to do the other day. Jock had been very lucky. He might have still survived his cardiac arrest but it had to be thanks to good-quality CPR that he'd come through without any neurological damage.

Gratitude added another layer to Adam's sense of well-being and his breath came out in a soft sigh.

It wasn't just Jock who was lucky that Emma had come to Braeburn.

His children were as happy as he'd ever seen them. Maybe it was partly due to the festive decorations that seemed to be creeping into every corner of the house. Today's addition had been big tartan bows at intervals all the way up the bannisters on the stairs. Or maybe it wasn't the decorations so much as his giving permission to *have* them?

Had he shut happiness out of the house without intending to? Had it just become a habit because he'd lived with his grief and his guilt for so long?

That he was letting go was thanks to Emma, too. She'd come here with her music and songs and…and her sheer *joie de vivre* and she'd given them all something that could never have been wrapped and put under a Christmas tree.

What was it that was creating this feeling that was almost euphoria?

Part of it was the kind of excitement he remembered from when he'd been a child. On Christmas morning when he would tiptoe downstairs before anyone else was awake to see if the magic had happened and there were mysterious, brightly wrapped parcels under the tree.

Part of it was hope. The kind of hope he'd felt when he'd persuaded Tania to marry him and come to live in his own little patch of the world? He'd thought that he'd never feel that kind of hope again. The one that suggested that he'd found all that he needed to keep him happy for the rest of his life. He'd been wrong that time but the hope had never been this strong, had it? It was time to put it all behind him. Time to take off the wedding ring that symbolised his entrapment in the past?

And Adam knew that part of it was also love. Maybe the biggest part. The kind of love he'd felt when he'd held his newborn babies for the first time. That almost desperate urge to protect them. To hold them and cherish them. For ever. He felt that urge about Emma now and it made him stroke her skin very lightly. Over her shoulder and along her collar bone. She had a tiny scar that interrupted the perfection of her smooth skin. Funny place for a scar—almost exactly where someone would have a central line inserted for a major medical procedure. He'd have to ask her some time how it came to be.

Emma shifted in his arms and made a tiny sound. She would wake soon. Maybe they would make love again. Even the thought of it stirred desire but Adam didn't want her to wake just yet because he knew she wouldn't sleep in his arms again tonight. She would creep back to her own room so that the children wouldn't know she hadn't been there all night.

To protect him—in case they said something at school

and then the whole village would know what was going on in the McAllister house?

Maybe it was to protect them—so that they wouldn't get ideas that Emma might be in their lives for ever?

If they asked, he might tell them that he hoped she might be but hope wasn't something to give lightly. He'd seen it in his mother's face tonight. And his sister's.

In the way they'd looked at each other as if they knew what was going on between him and Emma.

He would have seen it in his own face in the mirror all those years ago, when he'd been getting dressed for his wedding.

Hope was fragile. Like a glass bubble that could shatter all too easily. He hadn't intended ever trying to hold one himself again but it had formed without him really noticing.

And now it was here.

And it was huge.

The days were passing in a blur.

There was so much to do. Emma had never been so busy in her life but she was loving every minute of it. Final rehearsals for the school's Christmas production that would happen on Christmas Eve were in full swing. The junior-school trip to the recording studio had happened yesterday on the last day of school and the CDs were due to arrive today. There had been a picture of them all in the newspaper and already there were apparently orders coming in and people waiting to download the amateur production. Women in the village were not only smiling at Emma, they were *talking* to her. This was the most exciting thing that had happened in Braeburn since…

They never said what else had happened that was so

exciting but Emma had to wonder if it had been when their beloved doctor had brought his beautiful young wife home to his village.

Funny how a ghost could cast such a shadow but it wasn't the only shadow Emma was aware of today.

The arrangements were all in place. Poppy was spending the day with Jeannie and Oliver was with Ben. Their mothers would take them to the play practice later and Caitlin had offered to take Poppy to her dance class, where they were also doing a final rehearsal for their upcoming appearance, and Adam would collect her. He would also take Oliver to his music lesson tomorrow morning to prepare for the junior pipers' display. The Christmas Eve school production wasn't just a nativity play from the youngest pupils. It was more like a talent show. A celebration of everything the village children had accomplished for their year.

Nobody seemed to mind that Emma was skipping town for a day and a night. She would be back in time. The knowing looks and veiled comments she'd received had let her know that they thought she was really going to Edinburgh to do some Christmas shopping. The way Mrs McAllister used to. And didn't the bairns deserve something special? Their poor father never had the time to go far afield to create Christmas surprises but Emma was good at surprises, wasn't she?

Oh, yes…the shadows were gathering and, as she sat alone in the train on the way to Edinburgh, they formed a black cloud that threatened a storm.

Had she made a terrible mistake in trying to create a perfect Christmas for the McAllister family? For herself?

She hadn't intended falling in love with Adam but it had happened. And, if this was going to be her last Christmas, how magical was it to feel this happy?

This *loved*.

She hadn't intended to give Adam any more than the reminder of what it was like to let a woman close. To help him step forward from his grief. She hadn't expected him to fall in love with *her*. Not that he'd said anything but she could feel it in every touch. Every kiss. She could see it in his eyes when she turned unexpectedly and found him looking at her.

What if she'd set him up to suffer loss all over again?

And at *Christmas*time?

No. She couldn't afford to let a single bolt of lightning detach itself from that storm cloud. Jack was waiting for her to arrive at the infirmary. She would have the horrible test this afternoon, sleep off the effects of the drugs and then go back to Braeburn and enjoy every moment of this Christmas.

She had to remember to post the CD she had burned last night, too. Not that it would reach Sharon by Christmas Day, of course, but that was okay. The collection of photographs and the song she had written for her best friend would arrive electronically on the right day. The CD was just a back-up. She'd made one for herself as well.

It was snowing again by the time Emma carried her small bag into the brightly lit entrance to the huge hospital. There was a massive Christmas tree in the foyer, covered in silver decorations—like theirs would have been if she and the children hadn't painted all those balls. The girl at the reception desk was wearing a bright badge that had Rudolf the reindeer with a flashing red nose. Even the telephone she picked up to page Jack with was wrapped in tinsel.

And Jack's smile when he saw her looked like Christmas. So warm. Full of hope? His hug was comforting.

'Let's get this over with, Emma. Are you ready?'

Emma could only nod. Her throat felt tight and tears stung the back of her eyes. Hope was like a bubble, wasn't it?

A freshly blown one that caught all the colours of the rainbow and was so pretty that you wanted to catch it and keep it.

But it would only break if you tried.

CHAPTER NINE

THE HUM OF conversation stopped. Even the small girls stopped skipping about and giggling.

'Dr McAllister… What's happened?'

'Nothing's happened. I'm just here to collect Poppy.'

'Where's Emma?'

'She had to go to Edinburgh. She'll be back tomorrow afternoon.'

'Oh…thank goodness for that.' The young mothers shared relieved glances. 'She's not going to miss the performance, then. It wouldn't be the same, would it, without her singing with the children?'

'No.'

The mothers turned their attention to getting their daughters to change their shoes and put coats and hats on before going out into the snow. Having got over the surprise of seeing him at the dance class, nobody seemed to expect Adam to say anything else. People drifted away, leaving him alone with Poppy as he helped her with the laces on her dancing shoes. Because they were so used to giving him the space he'd always demanded by keeping people at a distance? Odd that it felt a little…disappointing?

At least the teacher came to talk to him.

'Did ye get the note, Dr McAllister? About the kilt?'

'Aye…' There had been a note, hadn't there? Weeks ago. Kylie had said something about needing to order a kilt for Poppy for her first dance performance but that had been about the time that his previous nanny had announced her pregnancy and intention of emigrating to Australia and life had suddenly become chaotic. He'd totally forgotten about it.

The teacher gave him a sympathetic smile. 'It's no' essential,' she said. 'I'm sure Poppy's got a skirt she could wear. We can give her a tartan sash.'

'But I want a kilt,' Poppy said. She tugged on her father's sleeve. 'I *love* kilts, Daddy.'

'We'll find you a kilt, pet, I promise.'

How he was going to manage to keep that promise within the next forty-eight hours was beyond Adam at the moment but there were other things to deal with first. Like getting the children home and fed. Looking after the dogs and collecting the eggs from the hens and making sure Jemima had plenty of fresh hay. Poppy took the little donkey a carrot.

'You're going to be in our play,' she said happily. 'You have to be very good and then you'll get more carrots.'

'She *will* have to be very good,' Adam agreed. He couldn't help shaking his head as a wave of bemusement caught him off guard. Were they really going to transport Jemima into the village hall to star in the nativity play?

Extraordinary.

As astonishing as the person who'd made it happen, in fact.

Emma's absence in the house that evening was far more noticeable than Adam had expected. It wasn't just that he had so much more that he needed to do. Everywhere he turned, he could see things that made him think of Emma. The paper chains hanging from the beams in the kitchen. The Christmas tree in the living room. The children asking for songs instead of a bedtime story.

He did his best but it wasn't the same.

'It's okay,' Oliver said kindly. 'Emma will be back tomorrow.'

It wasn't just the lack of music in the house that made it feel oddly quiet. The atmosphere was different. Emma didn't have to be singing, did she? She only had to be present for there to be a unique energy in the house.

A promise of something good.

Joy, perhaps.

Or love…

To distract himself from what was missing, Adam went online to check out the availability of kilts for small girls. But even that reminded him of Emma. Of the conversation in the kitchen that first weekend she'd been here. When she'd asked him if there was a McAllister tartan and whether he ever wore a kilt.

He'd been terse, hadn't he? Pushed her away, the way he always did when people got too close. It worked so well because they understood why he needed his space. Or they thought they did.

Emma hadn't respected those boundaries, though. She'd pushed until he could see them for what they were. Prison bars keeping him in the past. Hurting his children.

He found a specialist shop and clicked on the Clan Donald tartan. There was a children's section and he found a clan kilt in a new tartan that had been designed in recent years. With a purple background and small gold, red and green stripes, it was far more feminine than the dark colours of the kilt he had hanging in his own wardrobe. It would be perfect for Poppy. It seemed to be in stock in the right size but could they deliver it in time? Adam took note of the phone number. He'd give them a call tomorrow morning after he'd dropped Ollie at his music lesson.

With his hands still hovering over the keyboard, Adam caught the glint that the screen light coaxed from the dull gold band on his finger. It wasn't just the personal barriers he'd erected that were prison bars keeping him in the past, was it?

With a movement familiar enough to be automatic he used his thumb to touch the metal. Did he rub it as a reassuring link to a past he wasn't permitted to forget or was he actually trying to hide it?

On impulse, he closed the fingers of his right hand over the ring and gave it a tug. It didn't budge. He tried twisting it and it moved a little. Enough to make him get up abruptly and startle the dogs, who followed him curiously into the bathroom where he lathered his hands with soap until he could move the ring more freely. It took some effort to get it over his knuckle but—suddenly—it was off.

He was holding the symbol of his past and his failed marriage and the tragedy of losing his wife and… And he had no idea what to do with it now. The thought of taking it up the back of Old Jock's farm and hurling it into the pond was appealing. Just as well it was so late and the pond was frozen over anyway. Back in the library to shut down the computer, Adam dropped the ring into a drawer of his desk.

Walking up the stairs to bed, he was again aware of Emma's absence and this time it came with a yearning ache because he was going to his bed alone. He paused for a moment, in the spot where he'd first heard the haunting notes of that song coming from her room late at night, catching his breath as he realised how much he was missing her.

His left hand was curled, his thumb rubbing the empty place where the ring had been. There was nothing there to touch. Nothing to hide.

Or should that be no*where* to hide?

It wouldn't be long before someone noticed that he'd taken his ring off. Eileen's sharp eyes didn't miss a thing. There would be talk, of course, but he suspected that the consensus of the village women would be that three years' mourning was more than enough. He had done his duty and upheld the myth that the marriage had been too perfect to move on from and he'd done it for long enough to ensure that the children were protected. They would always have their 'angel' mother but they deserved more than that in their lives. Someone real, who made their lives more joyful.

Would the villagers go further and speculate how much influence Emma's presence had had on his decision?

Probably.

Did he mind?

If he did, he'd get used to it—the way he had got used to carrying the burden of the truth alone. Maybe—hopefully—he'd have to, because he had made more than one decision tonight. He was going to ask Emma to stay in Braeburn longer and he was pretty confident that she would agree. He'd had the strong impression today that she didn't really want to go. She'd seemed reluctant to even go to that job interview in the end. And it was good that she had gone because it gave her options. And if she chose to stay, it would be because she really wanted to.

If she did want to stay, he could start hoping for something more permanent. Not just for the children—he wanted that for himself as well.

* * *

The hotel in Edinburgh was a lovely old sandstone building that had been close enough to the hospital to make it the ideal place for Emma to spend the night and sleep off the effects of the drugs she'd been given for her procedure.

Not that she'd slept particularly well. Despite being only two days before Christmas, the hotel was very quiet, which should have been a bonus but it made Emma feel lonely. She missed the sound of children nearby. Even more, she missed being near Adam. So much that it was a physical ache that had nothing to do with the holes that had been bored into her hip bone. She longed for the sound of his voice. The way his presence filled a room. Just a shared look would have been enough—to see the warmth in those gorgeous, dark eyes and the promise that always seemed to be there now.

Oh…help. It was going to be very hard to leave, wasn't it?

At least she could distract herself with some Christmas shopping this morning. She wanted to find something special for Poppy and Oliver. And for Adam. Something that they'd keep for ever and it would remind them of her?

She needed something for Jack as well. He'd gone to a lot of effort to ensure she didn't have the results of this test as a dark cloud hanging over her future for any longer than was absolutely necessary and, as usual, he'd done his best to make the procedure as painless as possible. A bottle of really nice Scotch, perhaps? She could give it to him later because they'd arranged to meet in the hospital café for a coffee before she drove back to Braeburn. Just a quick check, Jack had said—to see that there were no complications from the test. And the results of the blood tests would be back by then, although the examination of her bone marrow would take up to seven days. From past experience, however, Emma knew that the preliminary results could arrive within forty eight hours and, so far, they'd always been an accurate prediction of what lay ahead.

It was a bit painful to walk this morning but a couple of painkillers along with her breakfast and she'd be fine to wander through the lovely boutique shops on the Royal Mile and Grassmarket. A quick coffee with Jack and then she could be on her way, heading back to Braeburn. She wished she could just get on the train and start travelling now. Not that she'd make it back in time for the big dress rehearsal of the play but at least she'd be going in the right direction.

On the way back to the people she had already come to love so deeply.

Caitlin McMurray was coping with at least fifteen over-excited children by the time Adam dropped Poppy and Oliver at the school.

'Och…here's our wee Mary and Joseph.' Caitlin looked relieved. 'Where are our shepherds? Over *here*, Jamie, thank you. No—we're not getting the paints out.' She grinned at Adam. 'Don't you love the silly season?'

Adam smiled back. 'I'm sorry I can't stay to help. I need to get to the clinic and see if anyone needs me.'

Except that he found someone who needed him even before he got as far as the clinic. Joan McClintock, almost buried in her cold-weather clothes, was standing outside the church.

'How are you, Joan?'

'Och…you know, Doctor. I've been better.'

'Still feeling peaky?'

'Aye…'

'You're sounding a bit short o' puff.' Automatically, Adam reached for Joan's hand, negotiating the heavy coat cuff and a woollen glove to find her pulse.

'Aye...I am at that. Must be the cold.'

'Come into the clinic with me. I'd like to check your blood pressure.'

'Och, I didn't want to be a bother, Dr McAllister.'

'It's no bother, Joan.' She was looking pale, Adam thought, and there was something about her that was ringing alarm bells. Made him think of Old Jock, who'd also been a bit 'short o' puff' shortly before he'd collapsed and nearly died.

There were two people in the waiting room but Eileen took one look at her friend's face and made no comment about a disruption to the morning's timetable.

'Och, Joan...you're no' looking right. It's a good thing you're here to see the doctor.'

His elderly patient's blood pressure wasn't concerning and her pulse seemed steady enough but Adam still wasn't happy.

'Is there anything else happening, Joan? You've no' got any chest pain or nausea or anything?'

'Noo... I've just... I don' *feel* right, you know?'

'Aye. I'm going to do a twelve-lead ECG.' He knew it would be a mission to get down to skin and attach all the electrodes but he wasn't going to let that deter him. It was quite possible for someone to be having a heart attack with almost no symptoms—especially a stoic, elderly woman.

Sure enough, the ECG trace showed unmistakeable evidence that Joan was, indeed, in the early stages of a heart attack. She needed to get to a hospital with catheter lab facilities as soon as possible.

'I'm going to send you into hospital,' Adam told her,

after carefully explaining what he'd found. 'The sooner you get treatment, the less damage there will be to your heart. I'll get Eileen to call an ambulance.'

'I'm no' going in any ambulance.' Joan was already pulling her clothes back on. 'I'm fine, Doctor.'

'You're not fine, Joan. Here—I want you to chew up these aspirin tablets and wash them down with some water.'

But Joan was too upset to co-operate. Her shortness of breath was increasing and Adam knew that a panic attack was not only imminent but would be the worst thing for her, given that the blood supply to her heart was already compromised.

'All right. No ambulance. I'll talk to Eileen and we'll find someone who can drive you.'

'No…' Joan's face crumpled. 'It's been snowing… it's dangerous… I don't trust *anyone*…to drive me *anywhere…*'

Her breath was coming in short gasps now and she had a hand pressed to the centre of her chest. He had to break this cycle before a catastrophe happened—but how?

Adam took hold of Joan's hand with both of his. 'Do you trust *me*, Joan?'

'Oh…aye, Doctor. Of course I do.'

'Would you let *me* drive you to the hospital?'

'But—'

'Wait here. I've going to have a wee word with Eileen and we'll get everything sorted. And then I'm going to pop a wee needle in your hand and give you something to help you relax.' He squeezed her hand. 'It's all going to be all right, Joan. You just need to let me look after you.'

Amazingly, Eileen didn't look remotely outraged at the prospect of having to reschedule the waiting patients and neither of them seemed bothered about the inconvenience. Perhaps the drama of Old Jock's narrow escape was fresh enough to have everyone watching out for each other.

'You just take care of Joan, Doctor.'

'And say hello to Jock while you're in there.'

That was a thought. He could not only check up on Jock but he could see how Aimee Jessop's baby was doing. He might even be able to pop into the specialty shop and see if he could pick up that kilt for Poppy.

'Oh…' About to head back to get Joan ready for the journey, Adam stopped in his tracks.

'Don't worry,' Eileen said. 'I'll take care of things here. If anyone's looking right poorly, I'll call an ambulance.'

'It's the children,' Adam said. 'They'll be finished their play practice by lunchtime. I'll no' be back in time to collect them.'

'I'll do that,' Eileen said. 'We'll get some lunch and they can come and play here until you get back.'

The suggestion that the children were welcome to come and play in Eileen's closely guarded domain was astonishing but Adam didn't have time to reflect on the fact that it wasn't only in his own home that things seemed to be changing. He needed to look after Joan.

Two hours later, his elderly patient was on her way to the catheter laboratory at the Royal. Adam visited Paediatrics to hear the good news that the Jessop baby was putting on weight and that her mother had been able to hold her, and then he got a surprise in the cardiology ward when he was told that Jock was well enough to go home. They were about to arrange transport.

'He can come back with me,' Adam said. 'I just need a quick coffee and a sandwich and I'll be back to collect him.'

The café at the infirmary was renowned for its good food and great coffee but Adam didn't even get as far as the queue at the counter.

At first, he simply didn't believe what he was seeing. It had to be a symptom of how much space Emma Sinclair was taking up in his head these days that made him see things in other women that reminded him of her.

The petite frame or a tumble of curly hair. Blue eyes or even a song on the radio…

But no. This time it wasn't just a glimpse of something that made him realise how special Emma was and how much he wanted to be with her.

It *was* her.

And she wasn't alone.

She was sitting at a table with a man who was roughly his own age. The way they were leaning towards each other suggested more than simply familiarity and if he'd been prepared to bestow the benefit of doubt, the inclination would have evaporated the instant he noted that they were holding hands. Staring at each other so intently there was no danger of him being noticed.

Not that the inclination to question the evidence had been there in the first place.

Emma had said she was coming to Edinburgh for a job interview and he'd believed her. Trusted her.

Had he really thought she was so completely different from his wife?

Tania had always said she came to Edinburgh to do her Christmas shopping.

He'd trusted her, too.

Were all women like this? No…he knew that wasn't true. So it had to be something to do with *him*. And whatever failing he had, it was accompanied by a blindness he'd never imagined he'd have to face again.

Maybe it was a good thing that he'd had so much practice in turning devastation inwards. Shutting it behind barriers that were impregnable. At least, they had been until Emma had come into his life.

Well… Adam turned on his heel and walked away. He'd just have to do a better job of building them this time, wouldn't he?

CHAPTER TEN

SOMETHING WAS WRONG.

Emma walked into the reception area of the Braeburn medical centre with a smile on her face because she'd been thinking about the first time she'd come through these doors and how different it felt now. Back then, she'd faced the snappy little terrier of a woman whom she'd thought was the children's grandmother and she'd been nervous of the fiercely uncompromising—almost angry—first impression of her potential employer.

Now she knew that Eileen was a loyal receptionist and that, behind the shield, Adam was a passionate and caring man. The most wonderful man she would ever meet in her life.

But her smile vanished as soon as she stepped through the door.

Caitlin had texted her to say that the children would be waiting at the clinic to be collected when she got back and Emma had assumed that Adam was too busy to take them home. Sure enough, the waiting room was packed and Oliver and Poppy were sitting in the corner, but Emma still knew that something was wrong.

There was a basket of toys in the corner but the twins were simply sitting there very quietly, looking as though they were in some kind of trouble.

Nobody else was talking either. Three women, one of whom she recognised as Moira, the Braeburn choir mistress, were intent on their knitting. Another rocked a pram that clearly contained a sleeping infant. Two men were invisible behind open newspapers.

Emma swallowed hard. She smiled at Eileen. 'I've just come to collect the children,' she said.

'Och, aye…' Eileen sniffed. 'We've been expecting you.'

Was that the problem? Was she later than she'd said she'd be? The coffee with Jack had turned into lunch but he'd been so kind and she'd needed someone to talk to. Somehow it made the new joy in her life more real to talk about it but it had the downside of making her fears a lot bigger as well. She'd ended up crying but Jack had held her hand and listened. He'd focused on the good results of the first blood tests that had come through and reminded her of how well they'd predicted results of the bone-marrow tests in the past.

But she'd said she'd be back by three p.m. and it was only a little later than that because it had started snowing again and the train journey had been slow. She'd gone to where the car was parked, too, to hide all her parcels so that the children wouldn't guess she'd been shopping for them.

'How was the rehearsal?' Emma pasted another smile onto her face. 'I'm so sorry I missed it. You'll have to tell me all about it on the way home.'

Oliver was staring at his hands. Poppy's bottom lip wobbled as she looked up at Emma.

'Daddy's cross,' she whispered.

'Is he? Well…he's awfully busy.' Emma glanced around the waiting room. Of course Adam would be annoyed that she hadn't been here to look after his children so he could do his job. That was what she'd been employed for, wasn't it? Except she was more than an employee now, wasn't she?

A prickle ran down Emma's spine. There was more to this than inconvenience. There was something heavy in the air. Something dark. Had somebody died maybe?

The door to the consulting room flew open and someone wrapped in a heavy coat bustled out. There was a short silence and then Adam appeared in their wake.

'*Next*,' he barked.

'That's you, Moira,' Eileen said in a stage whisper.

The choir mistress got hurriedly to her feet, clutching her knitting, but the ball of wool escaped and rolled an impressively long way across the floor. She bent to pick it up but the wool caught on the buckle of her shoe.

'Sorry, Doctor.' She tugged at the wool. A knitting needle came loose and clattered to the floor but Adam wasn't watching the progress of his next patient. His gaze had found Emma standing beside the children.

Suddenly it wasn't amusing to remember the first time she'd been here. Before Adam had known anything about her and had looked at her with a level of suspicion that had suggested she was the last person who might be suitable for looking after his precious children.

That kind of look paled in comparison to the chilly determination with which he was regarding her now. There was no suspicion in this glare. No doubt. No hint of warmth either.

'Take your time, Moira,' he snapped. 'Emma—could I have a word, please? It'll only take a minute.'

The last words were directed at the waiting room in general as Adam turned back to his consulting room. Or perhaps they had been intended to mollify Eileen. If so, it hadn't worked. Moira clicked her tongue and shook her head, the wool snapping as she gave it a harder tug. Eileen's eyes narrowed as she appeared to put two and two together and realise that Emma was somehow responsible for the doctor's bad mood.

This wasn't fair. Okay, she'd been absent for a little over twenty-four hours but it was hardly the crime of the century, was it? It certainly wasn't fair to make the children suffer and she'd never seen the twins look so miserable.

And her painkillers had worn off. A deep ache in her hip made it almost impossible to walk without a limp but somehow she managed it, knowing how many sets of eyes were watching every move she made.

'Shut the door, please,' Adam said, as she went in. 'Have a seat.'

'I'm...okay.' It was better to remain standing. Getting up from a chair might be painful enough to be difficult to hide.

'As you wish.'

He could have been speaking to a total stranger.

No. It was worse than that. He sounded as though he hated her and you couldn't hate someone you didn't know, could you? Emma couldn't stand this a moment longer.

'What's wrong, Adam? What have I done to upset you?'

A soft snort of unamused laughter came from Adam, accompanied by a head shake that emphasised his incredulity.

'I'm sorry if it's been difficult. Was there a problem with the children while I wasn't here or something?'

He was staring at her and, just for a heartbeat, Emma saw the barrier slip. If she'd thought the children looked miserable, it was nothing compared to the pain she saw in that instant in Adam's eyes. He looked...*betrayed.*

'I *know* why you had to go to Edinburgh,' he said.

'What?' Emma could actually feel the blood draining from her face.

'I took a patient through to the infirmary this morning.' Adam's eyes didn't leave hers. His tone was deceptively calm.

Dangerous.

'I *saw* you.'

Oh...dear Lord... He *did* know why she'd been there. He was a doctor who was well known at that hospital. How hard would it have been to get someone to check records and find out what she'd been even so briefly admitted for?

'I...I'm sorry, Adam. I should have told you the truth.'

'Just what the hell did you think you were playing at, Emma? Did you give any thought at all to how this was going to play out down the track? How it might affect the children? *Me*?'

When she *died*? Oh...help. She was going to cry. All she had wanted to do was offer her love.

To be loved in return, for just a blink of time. To make her last Christmas the best one ever.

How selfish had she been?

But the stunning effect of Adam's discovery was wearing off and guilt was getting overtaken by something else. Hurt. How cruel was this to be reminding her that she might not have much time left? To suggest that the effect on the McAllister family was worse than what she might have to face herself?

And why were the children looking so upset?

Emma's inward breath was almost a gasp. 'Have you told Ollie and Poppy?'

'No.' The word was a snap. 'And I don't want to.'

Thank goodness for that. The children must have simply picked up on the atmosphere and then assumed—as children were so good at doing—that it was somehow *their* fault. That was cruel, too, if it wasn't fixed. Emma would fix it as soon as she could.

'What I *do* want,' Adam continued, 'is for you to leave Braeburn. As soon as possible. I realise that it may be too late today but there should be trains running tomorrow. I've booked a room at The Inn for you. That's nice and close to the station.'

'But tomorrow's Christmas Eve.'

'I'm aware of the date.'

'I'm supposed to be helping with the school concert. The…the children's nativity play.'

'You can make some excuse. A family emergency perhaps.'

'And just…leave? Walk out and leave everybody to fill in the gap?'

'We managed before you came, Emma.' Adam was shuffling some papers on his desk now. 'We'll manage after you go.'

He expected her to go now, didn't he? To leave his office and then go home to pack and leave his house. She was being dismissed from her position as a nanny. From her position as his lover. Did he really have no intention of even *talking* about that?

Okay. She could understand why the barriers had gone back up. He knew she had made an offer of something she might not be able to follow through on and he'd seen history repeating itself with a loss in the near future that would have a dreadful effect on the children. And on himself? That was bitter-sweet. He was telling her how much she meant to him even as he pushed her away.

Maybe if it wasn't Christmastime, this wouldn't be happening like this. She'd been the one to force the celebration back into Adam's life and now it must seem like she was about to break his heart in exactly the same way it had been broken three years ago, when he'd lost the love of his life and his children had lost their beloved mother.

This was the first Christmas the children would be really celebrating at home and they were so excited about the play. About being the key characters of Joseph and Mary and—even more—about Jemima being part of the production. It had been her idea to include Jemima. Would that even happen if she wasn't here?

That did it. This might be all her fault but she wasn't going to let everything be ruined.

'No,' she said.

Adam looked up from his papers. 'I beg your pardon?'

'No,' Emma repeated. 'I understand why you want me to go…' Her voice wobbled. She couldn't say anything about how upset she was at him ending what they'd had between them like this because if she went down that track, she'd lose all the courage she knew she needed. 'But I'm not going to leave while I'm needed here. I can find somewhere else to stay but I promised Caitlin I'd be there to help with the singing and the play and…and I promised the children I'd be there.' She lifted her chin and took a steadying breath so that she could sound totally in control. 'I never break my promises.'

Caitlin would put her up for a night or two. Or she could stay at The Inn if that wasn't possible. She'd just have to dream up some reason for her absence to keep Poppy and Oliver as happy as possible.

Adam was looking at his papers again. 'Do what you need to,' he growled. 'I'll cope.'

Where had she heard those words before? Emma wondered, as she managed to find a smile for Oliver and Poppy as she led them out of the clinic.

Oh, yes… That had been exactly what Adam had said when she'd asked for the time off to go to Edinburgh. When she'd lied to him about the job interview.

'Is Daddy still cross?' Poppy asked as Emma clipped the belt over her car seat.

'No, sweetheart. And he was never cross with you.'

'Who was he cross with, then?' Oliver asked.

Me, Emma thought. And she had brought it on herself with her deception. She took another one of those steadying breaths.

'Sometimes grown-ups get cross because there's too much to do and people need things that are hard to give them. Daddy has to help lots of people and sometimes it's hard. Like when Mrs Jessop's baby was so sick.'

'But you help lots of people, too, and *you* don't get cross.'

Emma leaned in to kiss Poppy before she closed the door. In the time it took her to get to the driver's seat, inspiration had struck.

'Miss McMurray has an awful lot to do at the moment to get ready for your concert tomorrow. I know she doesn't get cross very often but I'm going to go and help her to make sure she doesn't. It might get very late so I'll probably stay at her house.'

'But you'll come back, won't you?' Poppy sounded anxious. 'It's only *two* sleeps till Christmas.'

'It *is*.' Emma turned on the car's lights and the windscreen wipers. 'Oh…look at how hard it's snowing. Isn't that pretty?'

Adam's parting words replayed themselves like an echo in Emma's head as she went through what had become such a joyous routine of caring for children and pets and trying to cook. She was getting better at it but it was a bonus to find one of Catherine's casseroles hiding in the freezer when she went to find some frozen peas. It had been wedged behind the turkey.

What had Catherine said about that? Didn't it need to come out of the freezer two days before Christmas so that it had time to thaw? Emma lifted the heavy bird and put it in the scullery tub. Not that she'd be here to cook it and maybe that was for the best. There was no way Adam could avoid celebrating Christmas now, what with all the decorations all over the house and the tree there waiting for the gifts to appear. At least she'd given this little family that much. And Adam probably knew how to cook a turkey.

As he'd said, he'd cope.

The first time he'd said those words had been the turning point, hadn't it? When Emma had decided that the real gift she could give Adam was hope. To show him what it could be like to let someone close. To be really happy again.

Well, it had worked, hadn't it?

Too well.

He'd accepted that gift and given his own in return. He'd shown her what it was like to be truly loved.

And now he knew that it had been false hope that she had offered.

But how could he be so sure? Did he know something that she didn't know? Emma stood there in the scullery, staring at the frozen turkey without seeing it. Had accessing her medical records somehow given him information that Jack had been unwilling to give her so close to Christmas?

A lightning bolt unleashed itself from the dark cloud that was pressing ever closer. If only she hadn't agreed to have the test so soon she could have kept it at bay for just a little longer.

There was no way to push it back now. All she could do was honour the promises she had made and then find somewhere she could gather strength to deal with the storm when it finally broke.

California maybe?

She was gone.

This time, the silence of the house had an almost ominous edge. It wasn't just an overnight absence. Emma was gone from his house and after tomorrow she would be gone from his life as well.

Adam had been late home after going to check that Jock was coping back on the farm and the children were already tucked up in bed and asleep. Emma's bag had been sitting beside her guitar case near the clock and within minutes of his arrival Caitlin McMurray had driven up to collect her. His dinner was keeping warm in the stove, she'd told him. The turkey was thawing in the scullery tub and she'd left some gifts under the Christmas tree and hoped that would be okay. And she'd said that she was sorry…so very sorry…

Too weary to feel hungry, Adam sat on a chair at the kitchen table beneath all those rainbow-coloured paper chains and downed the last shot his whisky bottle had to offer. The emotional roller-coaster of his day had left him drained enough to feel numb.

Or maybe not completely numb. There was pain to be found that had to be coming from the broken shards of that glass bubble of hope. And pain was a close neighbour to anger. Easy to step over the boundary and preferable to direct the anger towards someone else. He'd used this method of defence before but he knew it came with some fine print. It was only a matter of time before the anger turned inwards and became a sense of failure. He hadn't been enough as a husband.

He hadn't even been enough as a lover this time around.

Was he enough as a doctor? Joan McClintock probably thought so by now, as she lay in the cardiology ward of the infirmary, recovering from her angioplasty. And Old Jock definitely did. He'd said as much when Adam had taken the groceries that Eileen had put together and gone up the hill to visit him. He could swear there had been tears in the old man's eyes when Jock had gripped his arm in farewell.

'You and that wee lassie saved my life, son. I might not be up to playing my pipes tomorrow but I'll be back on deck next year, you wait and see.'

The Jessops would be spending a quiet Christmas in the neonatal intensive care unit but it would be a celebration because they'd be able to hold their precious new baby and talk about the day in the not-too-distant future when they'd be able to take her home. She'd need careful monitoring for her first years of life but it would be a joy to be responsible for that.

Yes. Adam could take comfort in knowing that he *was* enough of a doctor for this village. That he was deeply woven into the community fabric and he was needed here.

Was he enough as a father?

With a heavy tread and two unusually subdued dogs, Adam climbed the staircase of his old family home and went to check on his sleeping children. Oliver lay sprawled on his back at an angle that had his head almost touching the wheels of the train engine tucked in the corner beside his pillow. Adam gently moved the toy as he bent to kiss his son.

Poppy was rolled into a ball and her eyes were squeezed tightly shut. She had her Gran's old teddy clutched in her arms.

'Are you awake, sweetheart?' Adam whispered.

She must be dreaming, he decided when he got no response. He pulled the duvet up to cover her back and kissed the top of her head.

'Sleep tight,' he murmured. 'Love you.'

The hallway outside the children's rooms was quiet and still. The half-open door of the empty guest room further down was eloquent enough to be an accusation. There would be no music coming from that room again. No small, fairy-like woman would emerge with joy in her eyes and laughter just waiting to bubble free. With hands and lips and a body that could make a man feel like…like he was, well, more than enough.

Maybe it would help to shut the door.

Adam wasn't sure why he flicked the light on. Perhaps because it seemed suddenly beyond belief that Emma *had* really gone?

The room was empty, of course. The bed neatly made. A vase that his mother must have put in here before she'd left had a sprig of holly in it—a fragment of the festive bowl that was on the kitchen table downstairs. A tiny bit of the Christmas Emma had been so determined to spread throughout this house.

And there was something else. A glint under the bed that the light was catching. Stooping, Adam found it was a disk. A copy of the recording made with Braeburn school's junior choir? He'd heard all about it but he hadn't actually heard the singing, had he? And it wasn't good enough. With the disk in his hand Adam went back downstairs and into the library to turn on the computer. The fire was only a glow in the grate but the dogs curled up as close as they could on the rug.

He had expected to only hear sound when he pushed play on the menu. The image that filled the screen was a shock. It was Emma and another young woman. The photo must have been taken with a mobile phone. Two happy girls at a party somewhere. Emma looked so much younger. Her hair was a thick mass of curls and her face was different. Plumper. Carefree.

He should have stopped right there—the moment he knew that this was something personal and nothing to do with his children or their carol singing—but the photo was dissolving into the next image in the slide show and the exquisite plucked notes of the guitar were being accompanied by words.

It was the song he'd come to know from the snatches he'd heard late at night as he'd paused at the top of the stairs. A song about memories and friendship. About love. He knew he was seeing something never intended for his eyes when he recognised the man that he'd seen Emma with at the hospital today and he would have stopped it except that the next image was so shocking.

Emma in a hospital bed, completely bald and with her face unnaturally puffy. An IV line snaked beneath the hem of her gown.

Of course. He'd been right in thinking what that tiny scar was about. She'd had a central line inserted as a portal for major drug therapy.

Chemotherapy. That was the only thing that could make someone look like this. And you only got chemotherapy for cancer treatment.

And yet Emma was smiling. Laughing, even? It was so easy to recognise her despite the drastically altered appearance because the image captured that joy that was what Emma was all about.

The stunning effect was still there even as the image dissolved into a new one and it was only then that Adam could register the words of the song's chorus.

We've shared the sunshine and we've shared the rain...
Just by being there, you eased the pain...

He couldn't see the next image. Or the next, because his vision had blurred. He barely heard the rest of the song as he bent his head and covered his eyes with his hands.

The longing was too much.

He wanted to be the one to share the good times with Emma. To be there to hold her in the bad times.

Was she still sick? Was *that* why she'd been at the infirmary?

The longing morphed into a fierce protectiveness. A need to care for her for as long as possible—even if they both knew it might not be very long.

Maybe there was another man who was special to her and there was no future for *him* with Emma, but she might know that she didn't have much time left and she'd chosen to be *here*. Not with anyone else but with him and his children. To give herself in every way possible to make this Christmas special. It was only now that it was dawning on him how incredibly lucky they'd been.

The children were going to be heartbroken to wake up on Christmas morning to a house that contained the gifts but not the person who'd chosen them. The magic she'd created would be spoilt.

And he'd been the one to send her away. She would

be leaving Braeburn as soon as tomorrow's concert was over. He'd never have the chance to tell her what she'd given his children in making Christmas happen. What she'd given him in that he now knew he was capable of letting go of the past and that he could find real joy in his life again.

That he could feel hope.

A nudge under his elbow made Adam uncover his eyes. He hadn't noticed the dogs coming to flank his chair and the steady gaze from Bob offered limitless sympathy and something more. Wisdom? He scratched his old dog's ears.

'You're right,' he murmured. 'I can't let that happen, can I?'

CHAPTER ELEVEN

'JANET CALLED WHILE you were in the shower.'

'Oh?' Emma sipped the mug of coffee Caitlin had put in front of her. 'Who's Janet?'

'My brother's girlfriend's aunt. The one who runs the donkey sanctuary.'

'Oh…is there a problem? I thought she was delighted to help with getting Jemima to the concert. Is it the snow?' Emma took a worried glance out of the window. 'It is getting awfully heavy, isn't it?'

Caitlin laughed. 'Don't stress. I'm doing that enough for both of us. No. Aunty Janet's still as keen as mustard. In fact, she's bringing an extra donkey. He's called Dougal.'

'But we don't need *two* donkeys.'

'He's back-up—just in case Jemima doesn't want to co-operate. Apparently Dougal's done this sort of thing before. He's a darling, Janet says, and if Jemima's not used to getting into a float then having another donkey can help. Plus…'

Emma had to smile at Caitlin's expression and the raised forefinger that advertised how important this was. The connection she'd found with this new friend was partly due to how their imaginations were caught by the same things. She had to try and squash the sadness of how much she was going to miss this friendship. Caitlin hadn't asked about how soon she would be leaving Braeburn. She only knew that she was no longer needed as the McAllister nanny.

'Plus what?'

'Well… Dougal's looking for a new home. Janet was a bit worried when she heard that Jemima is an only donkey. She says they get very lonely by themselves and they can get very noisy.'

'Jemima's certainly noisy.' Poppy had said the same thing, hadn't she? That Jemima needed a friend. Another wave of sadness hit as she remembered the time with the children that day. When they'd picked the bunch of holly and made the paper chains. She was so going to miss their laughter and cuddles and the sheer joy of singing together.

'So what I'm saying is that Dougal doesn't necessarily have to go back to the sanctuary. He could be a Christmas gift for the McAllister family.'

'Oh…that's a lovely idea…but…' Emma bit her lip. It wasn't her place to accept, was it? She'd already given things to the McAllisters that were going to have long-term consequences. The thought of the damage she might have done had already formed a horrible knot in her stomach. 'You'll have to ask Adam about that.'

'I'll get Janet to talk to him. She's very persuasive.' With a nod and another smile Caitlin moved on to the next item on the agenda for her busy day. 'I need to talk to Moira about finding another piper to open the concert. Old Jock's always done it but he's not well enough this time. I don't want to offend him by asking someone whose playing he doesn't respect, though.'

Emma grinned. 'Village politics, huh?'

'You're not wrong there.' But Caitlin looked up from

her list, shaking her head. 'You know, it usually takes a generation or more before someone becomes part of the heart of a village like this. You've managed to do it in the space of a few weeks.'

'Hardly. I'm still a stranger.' But Emma had to swallow a big lump in her throat. She *felt* like a part of the heart of Braeburn, which was something that could only have happened so fast because it felt like the place she was supposed to be. With the people she was supposed to be with.

'You saved Jock,' Caitlin reminded her. 'You've saved the village hall with the funds that CD's going to raise. Plus...' She held up her finger again. 'You've saved my reputation as the teacher who can pull the end-of-the-year concert together.' She heaved a huge sigh. 'There are still a million things to do, though. There's the backdrop to paint and the hall to decorate and hay to get delivered and I don't know if Bryan's finished making the cradle yet. And I've got to ring Jeannie's mum to make sure they don't forget to bring the baby doll and...'

Emma finished her coffee. This was good. She would be too busy to dwell on what would happen after the concert. 'What can I do to help?'

'Ye canna say no.'

'But, Jock...I haven't touched the pipes in years.' The Velcro of the blood-pressure cuff made a decisive ripping sound as Adam removed it from Old Jock's arm. 'I'd be as rusty as your coronary arteries were before the stents went in.'

'Nonsense, lad.' The old man fixed Adam with a steely glance. 'No laddie I taught ever forgets and you were the best. There's no one else I'd choose to take my place and

I told that McMurray lassie from the school that I'd find my own replacement.'

He didn't have time to stand here arguing with Jock. It had taken time to organise the children this morning and get them to their friends' houses for the day so that he could check on his patients and be available for any emergencies. They'd been so slow, too. Uncooperative. Oliver had kicked his chair more than once and refused to even look for his songbook and Poppy had been in tears and refused to eat any breakfast.

'I want Emma to make my breakfast,' she'd sobbed. 'I *love* Emma.'

He had to try and be home at four p.m. as well for the woman who was coming to collect Jemima in a float. Emma should be there for that, shouldn't she? It had been her crazy idea in the first place. But it was his fault that she wouldn't be there and he had to start fixing his mistake somewhere.

But to wear his kilt… To pick up his beloved pipes that had been gathering dust for three years or more…

Emma would be there.

He wouldn't just be playing for the village and showing them that he was ready to embrace life fully again.

He would be playing for Emma. Showing her the man he really was—the man he wanted to be again. He'd heard so much of her music but she'd never heard his.

Could it be a way to connect again? A chance to talk?

Maybe even a way to persuade her to come back to where she was needed so much?

To come back home?

'All right, then.' The words were the kind of growl everyone was used to from Dr Adam McAllister. 'I'll do it. What song did you have in mind?'

'The usual.' Jock's nod was satisfied. There was even a hint of a smile on the craggy face. '"O Come All Ye Faithful".'

The stars didn't align well enough for him to make it home by four p.m. and see Jemima loaded into the float, but the donkey was missing so presumably they'd managed without him. At least now he had the time to go and let the dogs out and to collect his bagpipes.

He wasn't the only person who'd been out and about, doing his job, today. A courier had been to the farmhouse and left a special-delivery letter. Unfortunately, he hadn't chosen a good place to leave it and enough snow or sleet had landed to make it very soggy. Soggy enough for the envelope to disintegrate as he picked it up.

It was addressed to Emma, not him, so he had no right to look at its contents.

And he wouldn't have, except that he could see that the stationery was stamped with the logo of the infirmary and he thought that there had to be some mistake and that the letter *should* have been addressed to him.

They were blood-test results. A whole raft of them. With a sticky note stuck to the top one.

Proof. Couldn't be better so far, Em.
Happy Christmas, love, Jack.

Jack. The man in the photograph. The man at the hospital. The 'almost' brother who had become a specialist oncologist and had looked after Emma's mother.

Who was clearly looking after Emma now. His signature was on the test results. This *was* why she'd been at the hospital.

His head was spinning.

He'd known, at some level, how wrong it was to assume that Emma was deceiving him in the same way Tania had so often.

But why had she looked so stricken when he'd told her he knew why she was there? So *guilty*?

Because she'd been less than forthcoming about the nature of her 'appointment'?

Oh…dear Lord…did she think he was rejecting her because she was sick?

He *had* to talk to her as soon as possible. Never mind thanking her for what she'd done for the children or for him. He had the biggest apology in his life to make.

But he had a duty to do as well. He couldn't break his promise to Jock.

He had to find those pipes. And he had to get dressed for the part. A small part, thank goodness. He'd find a way to talk to Emma as soon as it was over.

Thc snow had stopped falling over Braeburn village on the night before Christmas. The cobbles of the narrow streets were sleek and dark where they'd been swept clear hours before but the perfect, white snow lay in a soft blanket on rooftops and gardens. It covered the bench where Emma had sat so many times to listen to Jock play his bagpipes and it coated the branches of the huge Christmas tree in the square, which only made the lights seem to twinkle even more brightly.

Not that there was anybody to appreciate the pretty picture. Most of Braeburn's inhabitants seemed to have squeezed themselves somehow into the village hall so that there wasn't even standing room any more.

Peeping through the curtains that were keeping several dozen excited children and just as many adult support crew hidden, Emma still couldn't see Adam anywhere.

Surely he wasn't going to miss seeing his children perform? Her frown deepened as she noticed the size of the gap visible in the crowded space that led in a straight line from the entrance to the stage. Would Jemima really cope with carrying Poppy down that narrow aisle?

Aunty Janet didn't seem to think they'd have any problem.

'She's a darling,' she'd informed Emma that afternoon. 'Went onto the float without any trouble at all and then she fell in love with Dougal on the spot. She'll be perfectly happy until it's her turn to perform.'

Which wouldn't be for a little while, although the concert was about to start. The main lights had been dimmed so that only the fairy-lights they'd hung on the walls were twinkling now, lighting up the spruce boughs and holly branches. An expectant silence grew until it felt like the audience was holding its breath, and then Emma heard a familiar sound—somewhere between a honk and a screech—that would have had Sharon putting her fingers in her ears, no doubt. Someone, out in the foyer, was warming up a set of bagpipes. Caitlin hadn't told her who she'd found that could replace Jock without causing offence, but as the first true notes sounded it was obvious that a good choice had been made.

Who knew that bagpipes could play a Christmas carol with such haunting beauty? Coming down the aisle, it was too dark to see the face of the man holding the pipes but he was pure Scot, with the folds of a kilt brushing bare knees and long socks as white as the snow outside. The sight and sound would have been stirring no matter what was being played but the Christmas carol gave it an extra depth that brought tears to Emma's eyes.

This was about Scotland—the place she'd fallen in

love with—and about such a special time of year that was all about celebration and family.

And there was a family she'd fallen even more in love with here.

As the lone piper came closer, Emma was sure it was her imagination—or the tears misting her vision—that made her think it was Adam playing the bagpipes. But right in front of the stage he stopped and lowered the pipes before turning to exit from the side door, and there was no mistaking his identity.

He was her gorgeous, gentle Scotsman. The lonely man whose heart she had touched—and then broken again.

She could feel a piece of her own heart being torn off in that moment.

Never again would she love someone as much as she loved this man.

Would it make any difference if she told him about thc conversation she'd had with Jack this morning? That the initial results of all her blood tests were so good that he was confident she'd beaten her disease and could look forward to a normal life? He'd known how hard it was for her to believe. He'd said he was sending a copy of the results for her by courier.

It was the Christmas gift she'd wanted above anything else. It should have made her feel ecstatic and yet here she was, watching Adam exit the crowded hall to loud applause, and she was having to fight back tears.

The fear that she had lost something that would have made every moment of the battle she'd had to keep her life more than worthwhile.

Not that there was any time for that dark thought to last more than a heartbeat. The curtains were being drawn back now. Poppy needed a kiss and words of encouragement as she joined the other tiny dancers to start the evening's proceedings.

'You look gorgeous, hon,' Emma whispered. 'I just love that new kilt that Daddy got for you. He's going to be *so* proud of you.'

She had expected Poppy to be bouncing up and down with excitement and that she would have to say how much she *loved* kilts. Or dancing. Or Christmas. But the little girl seemed uncharacteristically solemn and she clung so tightly to Emma's neck that she had to prise the little arms free as the dance teacher clapped her hands to shoo the troupe of girls into position.

It was Oliver's turn to perform with the other boys on the chanters next but Emma couldn't stop to watch. She had to get Poppy changed into her blue dress and shawl to be Mary amidst the chaos of mothers putting the final touches of moustaches and beards onto the wise men and shepherds and Caitlin trying to be in five places at once as last-minute adjustments were made to the nativity set behind the second curtain. The mothers would take care of Oliver's costume during the next item, which was an older girl reciting a Christmas poem. Emma's job was to go outside and help Janet get Jemima into position and primed for the grand entry.

The icy night air found the gap between Adam's socks and the hem of his kilt and made him shiver as he slipped outside during the applause for his son's performance. Behind him, he could hear Maggie MacEwen being introduced and then the girl's clear voice as she began her recital.

'"'Twas the night before Christmas, when all through the house…not a creature was stirring, not even a mouse…"'

Rounding the side of the village hall, Adam could see where the float was parked. He knew that Emma would have to bring the children and Jemima down this path so that they could make their entrance to the hall.

It still seemed unbelievable that his family's pet donkey was about to star in the traditional nativity play for the village. As extraordinary as the person who'd made it happen?

Yes.

Once she had Oliver and Poppy and Jemima into position at the front entrance of the hall, Adam knew she would take her position on the stage as the curtains were drawn back. With the music from her guitar and her lovely voice, she would lead the junior choir in singing the 'Little Donkey' carol for what would be a breathtaking opening for the traditional play that was the finale of the Christmas concert. Adam couldn't wait to see it.

But he didn't want it to start just yet. Not until he'd had a chance to talk to Emma.

Seeing her slight figure beside the float, holding the lead rope attached to Jemima's halter, made Adam's heart squeeze so tightly it felt like it might burst. She'd won the hearts of so many of those people tucked into the warmth of the old hall beside them, including his own children.

Especially including him.

He hadn't known it was possible to fall in love so fast—and so completely—with someone. Emma had not only won his heart, she would have it for ever, whether she wanted it or not.

She probably didn't want it. Not after the way he'd treated her. But he had to at least tell her how he felt. To explain why he'd reacted the way he had. To take the risk of making himself completely vulnerable in order to fight for the woman he loved so much.

'Emma…'

'Adam…' Emma looked startled but then relieved. 'Can you persuade Jemima to move? Ollie's still getting changed and she won't budge for me.'

Adam took hold of the donkey's halter and made encouraging noises but it was like trying to move a very large rock.

'She's no' going anywhere,' Janet—the woman who'd collected Jemima that afternoon—said. 'No' without Dougal. She's fallen in love.'

'What?' Adam peered inside the float to where he could see the fluffy back end of another donkey. 'There's another donkey?'

'Aye…' Janet's stare seemed intense in the soft light from the hall windows. 'I brought him in case she didn't like the idea of going in the float. But it seems that she's a very lonely donkey. She needs love in her life.'

'Don't we all?' Adam turned to Emma, who was also staring at him with a curious expression. One of hope? Janet had disappeared into the float. 'Emma, I need to talk to you. I—'

'Dougal needs a home.' The donkey had followed her down the ramp. 'Jemima doesn't need to be lonely any more.'

As if to add her opinion, Jemima made a soft, whickering sound and pulled away from Emma to touch her nose to Dougal's. The two donkeys stood there, side by side, their bodies pressed together.

'Do you think you could?' Yes. It was definitely hope in Emma's eyes. 'Adopt Dougal?'

Adam wanted to see her smile. To see the joy he knew would appear, even if it had nothing to do with him.

'Aye… If Jemima's in love then it wouldn't be right to separate them, would it?'

'No...' Emma was smiling. 'And it would make Poppy so happy if Jemima had a friend.' There was more than joy in her eyes. They were soft and full of love. Was it too much to hope that some of that love might include him?

Adam took a deep breath but just as he opened his mouth a figure came swiftly towards them from the street.

'Dr McAllister—thank goodness I've found you. You have to come—quickly. Bryan's fallen off his ladder. He was trying to fix the lights outside The Inn and he's come a cropper. I think he might have killed himself...'

For just a heartbeat longer Adam held Emma's gaze but there was nothing he could say. Not yet. All he could do was to try and communicate that this conversation wasn't finished.

It hadn't even begun, in fact.

He turned away. 'I'm coming,' he said. 'Let me grab my bag.'

It took only a few minutes to get to the scene of the accident. Bryan had, indeed, come a cropper and had probably knocked himself out for a short time. He had a good-sized lump on his head and had a mild concussion, but there didn't seem to be anything seriously amiss. But by the time they'd got him inside to the warmth and Adam had given him a thorough check, repeating his neurological checks at five-minute intervals, and finally decided it wasn't necessary to call an ambulance, at least half an hour had passed.

By the time he got back to the village hall, he knew he had probably missed everything. The entrance of the children, with Poppy riding Jemima, the singing of the children, the whole play perhaps. At least it was being videoed but the twins would be so disappointed that he hadn't been there. He searched for them on the stage where every performer had gathered for a final carol but he couldn't see them.

Emma wasn't there with her guitar either.

And where was Caitlin? Was there a problem backstage?

The children gathered on the stage were getting restless. A hum of conversation began in the audience, too. It was getting later and a new snowfall could start at any moment. Everybody was ready to go home.

Adam ducked back out the front door and raced around to the side entrance near the stage. He almost knocked someone over who was rushing in the opposite direction.

'Adam… *Oh…*' Emma sounded distraught. 'Have you seen the twins?'

'No. They're not on the stage with the other children.'

'They're not anywhere…' Emma's breath came out in a sob. 'They've *disappeared…*'

Janet and Caitlin weren't far behind Emma. 'The donkeys are gone too. I had them in the float. I was just looking for someone to help me lift the back door.'

'Jemima must have undone the knots.' Emma's voice was shaking. Oliver had told her how clever she was at doing that, hadn't he? 'The children must have gone looking for them…'

Caitlin put her arm around Emma's shoulders but she was looking at Adam. 'They can't have gone far, surely?'

'But it's so dark…' Emma whispered. 'And cold…'

Adam had had plenty of practice in his career of not allowing panic to gain a foothold but this was the hardest test ever.

'It's been snowing,' he said, struggling to keep his tone calm. 'The tracks will be easy to follow. We'll get a group to follow where the donkeys have gone and others to look for what direction the children have gone, just in case they're not together.'

The snow was falling more thickly now. Silent, fluffy, fat flakes that would quickly obliterate any tracks.

They were already running out of time.

'Caitlin—go inside and round up as many people as you can to help us look. Make sure they've got at least one person with a mobile phone in each group. Janet—go with someone who'll help you follow the donkeys' tracks. You'll be the best person to manage them. Emma?'

Her gaze locked with his instantly.

'Come with me.' Her hand joined his outstretched one just as quickly. He held her gaze for a heartbeat longer but he didn't need to say anything.

They both knew they had to find the children. Nothing else mattered.

CHAPTER TWELVE

THE CALL TO action was taken up by every able-bodied adult present in the village hall on that Christmas Eve.

The children were kept in the warmth, guarded by Caitlin and a group of mothers. Braeburn's policeman, Angus, organised everybody else into groups that fanned out from the hall to cover every possible direction the children might have taken.

By the time the groups began moving, Adam and Emma were already in the village square. The lights on the big tree and in the shop windows twinkled as merrily as ever but the square was deserted and Adam's groan of frustration a loud sound in the kind of silence that only came in a snow-covered landscape.

'I thought they'd be here. They could never get enough of coming to see the tree in the last couple of years.'

Having her own hope snatched away had left too much room for fear to fill. Emma's gaze raked the area she knew so well now but there was no sign of any small people and the snow was a smooth carpet. The only footprints to be seen were the ones they were making themselves.

'But it hasn't been like that this year.' Adam seemed to be thinking aloud. 'Because they've got a Christmas tree at home, haven't they?' He raised his voice. '*Ollie*? *Poppy*? Can you hear me? Where *are* you?'

In the distance, they could hear others calling the children's names. Much closer came another shout as a square of light appeared between the windows of the local pub.

'What's going on? Is that you, Doc?'

'Aye, Bryan.' Adam walked towards the inn keeper. 'The twins have wandered off from the hall. We don't know where they are.'

'On a night like this? I'll get my coat and help you look.'

'No. You're supposed to be resting that head of yours. But if you see anything, call Angus. He's in charge of the search parties.'

'I will but I canna understand why the bairns would have done that.' Bryan shook his head as he stepped forward to grip Adam's arm. 'But they'll be all right. They've got an angel looking out for them, haven't they?'

'Aye…' But Adam had already turned away.

Why *had* the children run away? Emma's hand was on Adam's arm the moment Bryan let go.

'They must be looking for you,' she said. 'Maybe they realised you weren't there to see the play.'

'I *wanted* to be there.' The growl reminded Emma of when she'd first met Adam. 'I had no choice…'

'I know that. I'm not blaming you.' Emma squeezed his arm more tightly. 'But where would they go if they wanted to find you? The medical centre?'

'Aye… That's a thought.'

Adam started to move so swiftly that Emma slipped on the cobbles as she tried to keep up. This time it was Adam who caught her arm and then he took hold of her hand again and slowed his pace a little.

Please, be there, Emma prayed silently. *Be sitting on the steps of the clinic, waiting for your daddy.*

But they weren't. The steps were covered by inches of perfect white snow.

'Oh…*no*…' Emma whispered. 'I'm sorry, Adam. We've come the wrong way.'

'It's not your fault. It was a good idea.'

'It *is* my fault. I should have been watching them. It was my job and I didn't do it well enough.' The tear that trickled down felt hot against her frozen skin.

'If it's anybody's fault, it's mine,' Adam said. 'I sent you away. It was my responsibility to look after my children.' He hit his forehead with the palm of his hand. 'I didn't *think*…'

'You're the only doctor this village has. Of course you had to go when you were called to an accident. The children were safely in the hall with dozens of people.'

'I'm no' a good father. Just like I wasn't a good husband.'

'How can you *say* that?' Emma was shocked. 'You're a wonderful father. You love those children to bits, even if you've found it hard to show it sometimes. But everyone understands why. You had a perfect marriage. Everybody knows that your heart was broken when you lost the love of your life.'

'Nobody *knows*…' Adam was looking away from her. Poised to walk in the direction he was looking. To continue their urgent search.

'They do,' Emma insisted. '*I* know, too. And I'm sorry. I've only made things worse but I didn't mean to. I—'

'She wasn't alone.' The words were torn out of Adam. He still hadn't turned to meet Emma's gaze. 'When she died in that bed. Tania wasn't alone. She was with her lover. I wasn't enough of a husband for her.'

'No...' Shock was laced with anger this time as understanding sank in. As she realised that Adam had been living a lie for so long. To keep such an awful truth to himself to protect his children. Even his own mother didn't know because she'd never have spoken of Tania the way she had that first night if she did.

There was a complete lack of understanding mixed in as well. How could any woman have won the love of this beautiful man and then trampled on it with such devastating effect?

No wonder it was so hard for him to trust again. Or that he'd reacted to her own deception the way he had.

She had to get him to look at her so that he could see the truth. Reaching up, Emma touched his cheek, turning his head so that she could meet his eyes.

'*No*,' she repeated fiercely. '*She* wasn't a good enough wife for *you*.'

She could have come up with any number of reasons why Adam deserved to be truly loved but this wasn't the time and the interruption of Adam's phone ringing made Emma catch her breath. Good news? Had the children been found?

Adam's voice was loud a few moments later. 'What—no sign at all? What about the donkeys?'

He listened again. 'We'll have to go further than the village, then. It's stopped snowing now. If they're moving, they'll start leaving tracks again.'

If they were moving?

Emma couldn't bear to think of why they might not be moving.

Having snapped his phone shut, Adam stood very still and Emma knew he wasn't seeing the street. Or the square at the end where they could still see the flashes of the Christmas tree's lights.

'We need help,' he said slowly. 'A search and rescue team. Dogs.'

'Dogs…' The word was too quiet for Adam to hear. Maybe she hadn't even spoken it aloud but it was enough to trigger a powerful image. An old stone farmhouse at the end of a long drive, with a big kitchen and a fascinating attic. Fireplaces with dancing flames and snoozing dogs on the rugs.

Home.

The image morphed into something that felt like an absolute conviction.

'Adam? I know where they are.'

'Where?'

'They've gone home.'

'Why would they do that? It's miles away. They wouldn't make it. They're just wee bairns…'

'I just know it's the direction they will have taken. Let's get your car and check.'

'But how can you be so sure?'

'It's where I'd want to be,' Emma said softly. 'To be with you.'

For a long, long moment Adam held her gaze. Asking for something. Reassurance that the children would be found safe? Or maybe he was asking if *she* wanted to be with him?

All she could offer was hope.

And a hand to hold.

The house wasn't locked but as soon as they got out of the vehicle Adam knew there was no point in going inside, despite the urgent barking they could hear.

The driveway had been sheltered from a heavy cover of snow by the trees but the tracks were obvious in the headlights as soon as they got close to the house. Messy tracks that were more than just footprints that were marking a path that led towards the orchard and stables.

There was no time to find a torch so Adam used the light from his phone. He offered Emma his hand to guide her through the half-open gate and was still holding it when they got to the door of the stable.

It was a picture he would never forget as long as he lived.

Two donkeys curled up in the thick layer of straw, their noses touching. Between them, protected by the warmth of the fluffy bodies, were the two children. Oliver had one arm around Jemima's neck, his face pillowed on her neck. His other arm was around his sister. Poppy, in her blue dress, still had the baby doll clutched under her arm. Both the children had a healthy, rosy glow to their cheeks and were clearly deeply asleep. An exhausted Joseph and Mary with the baby. It was a nativity scene like no other.

The donkeys were awake. Four huge, dark eyes met the light but neither Jemima nor Dougal disturbed the children by even a twitch.

Adam's first instinct was to gather both children into his arms as if he would never let them go, and he would do that. But first there was something else he had to do. Quietly, he stepped back and made the call to Angus to relay the news that the children were safe and the search could be called off. The inhabitants of Braeburn village could go to their own homes and prepare to celebrate Christmas with their own families.

Emma was still close by and he turned to her as he ended the call. It was time to take the children in to their own beds but catching Emma's gaze stopped Adam again.

'I've been alone for a long time.' His voice caught. 'In a place that I never thought I could share with anyone.'

'I know.' She held his gaze. 'Thank you.'

'What for?'

'Trusting me.' She moved a little closer. 'I understand why you've kept the truth to yourself and that's something that will never go any further. The children—and the people of Braeburn—can always think that the mother of your children is an angel.'

'But you'll know…' Adam could hear the note of wonder in his own voice. 'And that means I'm not alone any more.' He had to swallow hard. 'It's me who should be thanking *you*.'

'There's no need.' It looked like Emma was trying to smile but he could see the way her lips trembled. He suddenly felt a little fragile himself.

'I found your song,' he told her. 'With the photographs. You left it behind yesterday. I'm sorry…I had no idea you were sick.'

'But you saw me at the hospital…'

'I got things wrong…' Adam closed his eyes. 'I saw you with Jack. Holding hands. I didn't know who he was and I thought…I'm sorry. It's no' been easy for me to learn to trust again.'

'But you trusted me tonight. You told me your terrible secret.'

'Aye…I already knew how wrong I'd been. Even before I knew who Jack was.' It was Adam's turn to move closer. Close enough to touch. To cup Emma's face and make sure she knew how much every word meant. 'I've been wrong about a lot of things but there's one thing I can never be wrong about. I love you. I want you to stay. With me. With the children. For as long as we've got.'

He saw a whole range of expressions flicker over the face of this woman he loved. Shock as she probably guessed what he'd thought when he'd seen her with another man. Forgiveness as he admitted his error. The birth of joy as he confessed his love.

And then she smiled.

'It might be a very long time. I haven't got the final results of my bone-marrow test but so far everything's looking as good as it possibly could.'

'It could never be long enough.' Adam put his arms around Emma and drew her close. His kiss was slow and tender. A promise of what he intended to show her properly, very soon.

'Let's get these bairns safely into their own beds.'

'Aye…' Emma's smile was one of pure joy. 'And then we can get to ours?'

'Aye…'

With their arms still around each other, they went back into the stable.

Poppy stirred as her father lifted her into his arms. 'Daddy…' Her eyes opened and she turned her head. '*Emma*…you're back. You've come home.'

'I have, sweetheart.'

Oliver had woken up, too. 'I told you she wasn't going away for ever,' he told his sister.

'But I saw you leave,' Poppy said. 'I saw you talking to Daddy and you took your kit-ar and…and I was sad.'

'You don't need to be sad any more,' Adam said. 'Emma's not going anywhere.'

'You didn't see our play,' Oliver said. 'We went outside to find you and saw Jemima going home. We tried to catch her and then we got lost.'

'She's got a friend now.' Poppy smiled at Emma. 'She's got Dougal.'

'Dougal likes me,' Oliver said. 'He let me ride him and Poppy rode Jemima and she took us home.'

'I was scared, Daddy.'

'So was I, poppet. So was I.'

'But everything's all right now.' Emma's eyes were bright with tears as she held out her hand to Oliver. 'Let's go inside and get you two into your nice warm beds.'

Poppy was almost asleep again in her father's arms.

'Emma came back,' she murmured. 'I *love* Emma.'

'So do I, pet.' Adam's whisper was loud enough for them all to hear. 'So do I.'

Emma, with Oliver's hand in hers, came close enough to lean against Adam's arm as she returned his tender smile. He could feel the connection of her body against his and he could see a far deeper connection in her eyes. Here they were—the four of them—all connected.

His family. And they were together. And safe. And very, very soon they would celebrate their first Christmas together. A new and wonderful joy misted his vision.

He knew that it would be the first of many, many Christmases.

EPILOGUE

A year later...

No Christmas could ever be as wonderful as this one.

Even the joy of being present for Holly's birth in Canada last year was completely outshone by this day, as far as Catherine McAllister was concerned.

They should have used the table in the big dining room to host a Christmas feast for so many people but the inhabitants of this house had been adamant that they wanted to eat in the kitchen. Like they always did.

Adam was at one end and his gorgeous wife of six months at the other. Darling Emma. Catherine had known as soon as she'd set eyes on the lass that magic was going to happen but she'd never have guessed at quite how much.

At the sides of the table it had been a fair squeeze to fit everybody in. Marion and Ian on one side, with baby Holly in her highchair beside her gran. On the other side was Emma's best friend Sharon, whom they'd all come to love when she'd come over from America to be the bridesmaid for a summer wedding in the Braeburn village church. This time she'd brought her husband Andy as well, and they were flanked by Poppy and Ollie.

There was so much laughter. Like when Adam had

been telling the story of how disastrous last year's Christmas dinner had been.

'Neither of us had any idea what to do with that turkey. It wasn't till after we took it out of the stove that we realised there was a plastic bag inside it.'

Sharon needed a pat on the back so that her amusement didn't choke her. 'I could have told you Emma didn't know how to cook,' she said finally.

'I'm learning,' Emma protested. 'I have the best mother-in-law in the world.'

The real truth was that Catherine was lucky enough to have the most amazing daughter-in-law in the world but she didn't say anything aloud. She just shared a fond glance with Emma and then smiled at how quickly Adam defended her.

'My wife has talents that are far more important than cooking.'

'What's a talent?' Oliver asked.

'It means you're really good at something. Like Emma is with playing her guitar and singing.'

Oliver's nod was solemn. 'Mummy's going to be famous, isn't she?'

'You bet she is, buddy.' Marion had come back from Canada with new expressions. 'I'm not surprised a record company's signed you. That song you wrote for Sharon is just beautiful. No, Holly, don't blow raspberries. Oh… I've got custard all over my new dress.'

Poppy giggled. 'That's really *icky*.'

The delicious sound of the child's laughter and that odd word took Catherine straight back to the day she'd met Emma. To that interview for a position that Adam had clearly intended not to give her. He'd been so closed away back then.

Had he had any idea of how unhappy he'd been?

Things couldn't be more different now. Her son was not only happy again, he was happier than he'd ever been. And Emma looked better than she ever had. It had been such a shock to learn she'd been so sick but she'd just had her twelve-month check a couple of weeks ago and the news had been brilliant. Her doctor had told her she had beaten that dreadful disease and he didn't even want to see her again for at least two years.

No wonder Adam was fair glowing with happiness now. She was loving the grin on Adam's face as he listened to Ian's incredulous query.

'Is it really true that Jemima's pregnant? You're going to have *three* donkeys?'

Adam smiled at Emma as he responded. 'The more the merrier.'

Catherine remembered that smile later as she shooed everyone out of the kitchen to deal with the final clearing up. She put some turkey scraps into the dog bowls, wiped the last crumbs of plum pudding from the table and bent to pick up a scrap of paper left over from the crackers that had been pulled.

Had there been something significant in that shared look and smile? Maybe they were waiting for her to join them before making an announcement? Ducking her head beneath a paper chain that was drooping lower than the others and trying not to get her hopes up, Catherine headed for the door.

In the hallway, she had to smile at the wreath of mistletoe crowning the grandfather clock and the big tartan bows on the banister rails. She could hear a guitar being strummed but obviously not by Emma. The enthusiastic but inexpert performance had to be from Ollie, who would probably be taking his treasured Christmas gift to bed with him. Sure enough, as Catherine entered the living room she saw her grandson sitting at Emma's feet as she showed him where to put his fingers to make a chord.

Adam was right beside her on the couch, with his arm around his beloved wife. Poppy was tucked under his other arm and she was holding her favourite gift as well—fluffy drumsticks that she intended to learn to twirl so that one day she could join a real pipe band. The kind her daddy was playing in once again. The dogs weren't far away either as they lay on the rug in front of the fire.

The other sofa and chairs were taken up with the rest of her family and the special friends who'd been invited to celebrate with them. With the backdrop of the enormous Christmas tree and the screwed-up wrapping paper that Holly seemed to think was her special gift, it all added up to being the picture of a perfect Christmas.

How could life get any better than this?

And then Adam spoke and Catherine realised that life could get even better.

'We have something to tell you all,' he said. 'This summer we're going to have a baby.'

'I *know*,' Poppy squeaked. 'Jemima's baby.'

Adam and Emma exchanged a look that brought a lump to Catherine's throat. Had two people ever been so much in love?

'No, pet.' Adam smiled. 'A real baby. Emma's going to be a mummy.'

The shriek of excitement from Marion and Sharon faded as they all noticed Oliver's frown.

'Emma's already a mummy,' he growled. 'She's *our* mummy.'

Emma leaned down to kiss the small boy. 'I am,' she

agreed. 'But you won't mind having a little brother or sister, will you?'

'No-o-o…' But Oliver hugged his guitar more tightly.

'I won't,' Poppy said firmly. 'I *love* babies.'

* * * * *